The Fractured Veil

Book One

Nexara Academy Series

B.R. Vazquez

Edited by
Book Bunny Editing

Cover Design by
Artscandare Book Cover Design

To the one who has always felt like they didn't belong,

Welcome to Nexara.

The Shadow Brothers are waiting for you.

IMPORTANT NOTICE

Contents

Prologue

T he world remembers in hushed whispers, tales passed down through generations, of a time when darkness threatened to consume all.

The Great Cataclysm, they called it—a chasm torn between realms, an unraveling of existence that poured forth despair. It began as a subtle tremor, a quiet disturbance in the heart of the universe, but soon escalated into an all-consuming void. Shadows surged, coiling around the strong, shattering the gentle, leaving a wasteland of broken souls and extinguished dreams.

Like ink spilling into water, its influence spread, staining even the purest hearts, twisting the strongest wills. Realms trembled, their foundations groaning beneath its oppressive weight. Cities crumbled to dust, their cries fading into the emptiness, whispers carried on the wind. And all the while, they spoke of a being born of chaos, nurtured by fear, driven by an insatiable hunger. Its power choked the land, suffocating light, strangling hope, and silencing any thoughts of a brighter tomorrow.

The Great Cataclysm was not just a battle—it was the unraveling of hope itself. The ancient veils that separated the realms fractured under the strain, allowing its malevolent touch to reach further. One by one, realms fell, their lights extinguished, their cries becoming ghostly echoes devoured by the void.

Yet, amid the despair, one realm remained untouched—a world shielded, its protective veils holding strong. But even here, where light still lingered, there was something different. A power that could either amplify the darkness or destroy it entirely. This power lay within a young woman, unaware of the monumental destiny that awaited her, her heart beating with the pulse of both life and death. The prophecies, long dormant, began to stir.

"When the veil trembles and the shadows rise, one will emerge from the darkness—a child of life and death, her heart beating with the pulse of both."

The words echoed through the ages—a promise and a threat, a power that intrigued and terrified in equal measure. A power that could reshape the realms, its potential both a source of salvation and destruction. But prophecies are fickle, shaped by belief and fear, lost in translation overtime, and even now, the ancient veils groan beneath the weight of its approach.

In Nexara, the name spreads in whispers, rumors of an encroaching darkness like cold winds. Shadows move beneath the surface, signaling that the Phantom of Dark is not waiting—it is inevitable. Its arrival is not a matter of if, but when.

Aethrax.

Chapter 1

Thalia's POV

The café buzzed with life, but I felt like a ghost among the living. Mindlessly wiping down the table, I glanced through the smudged glass window. The city outside was a blur—a mess of lights and shadows, as chaotic as the thoughts swirling in my head. Another day, another routine. Another night of wondering why I felt so...empty.

I'd had dreams once, ambitions that felt just out of reach. I wanted more than this—a life that mattered, that had some kind of purpose beyond mere survival. But every day felt like a step further away from the person I wanted to be. I had no direction, no spark. I was drifting, trapped in a cycle of work and sleep, with nothing to show for it. I craved something to break the monotony, a reason to feel alive again, but all I had were fading hopes and the persistent fear that this was all there would ever be.

Maybe it was inevitable, given my past. Growing up without a family, aging out of the system, and being forced to fend for myself had left scars—ones that never truly healed. I was alone, and the weight of that loneliness pressed down on me, making it hard to believe that anything could ever change.

The bell above the door chimed, the familiar sound signaling another customer. I turned automatically, cloth still in hand, and froze.

A figure stepped inside, cloaked in shadow despite the café's warm glow. A hood obscured their face, but I felt the weight of their gaze—as if they saw straight through me. For a moment, the bustling café seemed to fade into silence, the sounds of laughter and clinking mugs muffled, as though I'd been pulled into a bubble outside of time.

"Can I help you?" I managed to ask, though my voice sounded distant, even to my own ears.

"Just a black coffee, please," the figure said, his voice smooth and low, carrying a subtle undertone that sent a shiver down my spine.

I blinked, realizing I was still gripping the cloth, my knuckles white. The weight of his presence lingered—unnerving and...familiar. I knew that feeling. I'd felt it before, fleetingly, on rare occasions when they ventured into this part of Nexara.

Gifted. That's what they were called—beings with abilities far beyond anything ordinary. They weren't like the rest of us, though they walked among us when it suited them. Some claimed the Gifted were descendants of ancient beings; others said they were a mistake of nature. Either way, they were powerful, dangerous... and rare.

We were taught to fear them—tales of their strength, their magic, and the devastation they could bring. They looked just like us, but with subtle differences. Some could shift into creatures that haunted human nightmares. Others were demons, their magic thrumming in the air like a heartbeat—witches and Fae who could summon fire or call storms with a flick of their wrist. Each kind had carved out its own territory in the world, leaving us with only a small portion to fend for ourselves—and, for the most part, they left us alone.

Chapter 1

"Of course," I replied, trying to steady my voice. My hands moved on autopilot as I stepped behind the counter, reaching for a coffee cup and the pot of coffee. My thoughts scattered like leaves in the wind, each one trying to piece together why he was here—in this café, of all places.

I slid the cup across the counter, keeping my eyes on him as he reached out.

"Thanks," he said simply, his tone calm, but the corner of his lips twitched, as if he'd noticed my nervousness.

"Do you... need anything else?" I asked, inwardly cursing how shaky I sounded.

He didn't answer right away. Instead, he glanced around the café, his gaze lingering on the table I'd just cleaned before returning to me.

"No. That's all—for now," he said, a faint smirk playing at the edge of his mouth.

And then, just like that, he turned and walked away, his movements smooth and purposeful. The bell chimed again as he exited, leaving me standing there, gripping the counter for support as my heart pounded against my ribs.

"They've been coming around more," Vicki called, her voice raspy but warm. I glanced up to see the familiar gray-haired woman, a regular Tuesday visitor, engrossed in her latest mystery novel. The laugh lines around her tired eyes deepened as she looked at me from her table by the window, a knowing glint in her gaze.

"Yeah, thankfully I've been able to avoid them for the most part," I responded, forcing a casual tone as I refilled her coffee, the aroma of dark roast filling the air.

"You'd think with all the stories, people would be used to them by now." Vicki chuckled as she took a sip of her coffee. "But no, everyone still gets their knickers in a twist whenever one of them shows their face. You'd think they were seeing a ghost."

"Well, it's not like they're exactly friendly," I pointed out, the image of the hooded figure flashing in my mind. "Most of them barely acknowledge our existence, let alone make an effort to be sociable. And the ones that *do*... well, let's just say I've heard enough stories to last a lifetime," I added.

"True enough," Vicki conceded, a thoughtful frown creasing her brow. "Still, I can't help but be curious as to why they're in Nyvorthia. What brings them to our little corner of the world?"

"It *would* explain all the disappearances," I murmured, the thought sending a fresh wave of anxiety through me. Our city held its dangers even without the presence of the Gifted in our small, isolated territory. Rumors and whispers of shadowy figures haunting the city streets and tales of people vanishing without a trace kept us on edge—a constant hum of fear beneath the surface of everyday life.

"Maybe, but I don't think so. The Gifted have come and gone over the years, and this is a recent issue. Something darker is at play," Vicki sighed, tucking her book away in her worn leather bag. "Anyhoo, be careful getting home, sweetheart. These streets can be treacherous after dark." She smiled, a genuine warmth in her eyes, as she grabbed her cane, making her way slowly towards the door.

"You too, Vicki," I said, smiling back. The bell above it jingling softly as she exited. I watched her go, a familiar pang of loneliness settling in my chest. I didn't have a lot of good things going on in my life, but Vicki, with her kind eyes and gentle spirit, was a reminder that the world wasn't as horrible as it seemed. I cleared her table, my thoughts drifting back to the hooded figure. A knot of unease tightened in my stomach.

Chapter 1

As I finished another grueling twelve-hour shift at the café, my feet ached, and my eyelids felt heavy. I locked the door, the click echoing quietly, and started my walk home. The familiar route offered little comfort.

The city felt different at this hour—alive yet strangely still, as though the city itself were watching me. I'd lived here my entire life, but I'd always felt as though I was never meant for this place—an intruder walking amongst my own people.

The streets shimmered under a silvery glow, the streetlamps flickering like distant stars in the dark night. My footsteps echoed softly against the sidewalk, the cool air intertwined with the fading aroma of coffee and pastries clinging to my clothes.

Taking a deep breath, I watched as my breath formed a delicate mist. *What now?* The question echoed in my mind, a constant reminder of the instability and uncertainty that had taken root in my life.

The café's routine had offered a sense of normalcy for a while, but even now, that comfort was wearing thin. There had to be more than this—some kind of purpose meant for my life, right?

As I turned the corner, the warmth of the café slipped away, replaced by the chilly late-September air. Tugging my jacket tighter, I wrapped my arms around myself, attempting to shield against the biting cold and the shadows playing at the edges of my vision.

I stood at the crosswalk, bathed in the soft red glow of the pedestrian light. A couple passed by, their laughter echoing in my ears—a fleeting echo of the connections I craved but could never seem to grasp. I swear the gods, for whatever twisted reason, took pleasure in my misery. As the light changed to green, I stepped off the curb, trying to ignore the tingling at the nape of my neck, as if something whispered from the shadows. Glancing over my shoulder, I quickened my steps but saw nothing.

"It's just your imagination," I muttered, thinking back to the caretakers at the orphanage who would dismiss my cries of shadowy figures as nothing more than a lonely child's delusion.

Heading into the narrow, dimly lit alley, I studied the rusted fire escapes lining the walls like veins, rising up towards the sky. The air was thick—a mix of damp concrete and faint smoke—while the bridge above added to the boxed-in feeling.

A shiver ran down my spine as I continued to ignore the shadows that danced in my peripheral vision. I'd seen them for as long as I could remember—the darkness constantly playing at the edges of my vision, swirling and shifting like restless spirits. It was unsettling, this feeling of being watched, of something lurking just beyond the veil of reality. I'd learned to mostly ignore it, to chalk it up to an overactive imagination, but the unease never truly faded.

As I made the final turn onto my street, I glanced up at my apartment building—its brown bricks dull and battered, washed out by years of grime. The front door was worn, chipped at the edges —a testament to countless uses, with the lock still broken from the most recent break-in.

My footsteps echoed in the stairwell as I trudged up to the fourth floor, the scent of stale cigarette smoke clinging to the peeling wallpaper. I stopped in my tracks when I saw a small box sitting on my doorstep. Intricately carved from dark wood and painted a deep navy, it was tied with a delicate silver ribbon. The ornate box looked strangely out of place against the chipped paint and worn carpeting of the narrow hallway.

Chapter 1

I surveyed the deserted corridor, glancing over my shoulder before cautiously approaching my door. The silence was broken only by the faint hum of the flickering fluorescent lights overhead.

A small gasp fell from my lips as I picked up the mysterious gift. I'd never received anything like this before. The ornate wooden box felt heavy in my hands. I strained my eyes, noticing the elegant script written in small lettering across the top: *To Thalia Cross, destined for greater things.*

I scanned the hallway once again before carefully unknotting the ribbon and lifting the lid. Inside was a stack of neatly arranged papers. At the top, bold letters read: **Nexara Academy**—an institution whispered about in hushed tones in Nyvorthia, a place where the powerful and Gifted were trained, hidden away in the western mountains.

The invitation seemed to glow in the fluorescent lights. *"You are invited to join Nexara Academy. This is your chance to explore the depths of your abilities and find your path in the Nexara."*

I froze, the crisp paper crinkling between my fingers before I started flipping through the documents. Yep, it definitely said *Thalia* on all of them.

Was this some kind of joke? This couldn't be real—me, *Gifted*? No way. Sure, sometimes I saw shadows darting at the edge of my vision or felt a strange tingling on the back of my neck, but those weren't gifts. They couldn't be. Just paranoia and an overactive imagination, courtesy of my childhood.

I ran my fingers over the words again: *Explore the depths of your abilities.*

A spark within me began to simmer, a long-suppressed desire struggling to resurface from beneath the weight of self-doubt and anxiety. I forced down the lump in my throat. I carefully tucked the papers back into the box, the lid clicking shut.

Sliding the key into the old, worn door of my studio apartment, I took a deep breath and muttered to the empty room, "Might as well take the opportunity to get away." A bitter laugh escaped my lips. "It's not like anyone would miss me here anyway."

I placed the box on the small coffee table, its presence an uncanny beacon in the dim light. Nexara Academy. Just the name sent a shiver down my spine, a tangled knot of fear and anticipation tightening in my gut.

"How do you even *get* there?" I mumbled, tracing the box one more time. I know it's somewhere out west, past the Witches' domain, but humans don't venture out of our lands often, let alone into *that* territory. Grabbing the paperwork again, I started reading for more details, desperate for some clue, some hint of an explanation. There had to be something in here about why I'd received an invitation—why *me* of all people—and, more importantly, *how* to get there if I accepted. The ornate script offered no practical information, just flowery pronouncements about my "unique potential" and the "honor" of attending. It was maddeningly vague. I flipped through heavy paper over again, hoping for a map, a hidden inscription—*anything*.

Just as I was about to give up, a small, folded piece of parchment slipped from between the pages. It was almost the same color as the invitation, easily missed if you weren't looking for it. Unfolding it carefully, I scanned the brief message, my heart pounding in my chest. *Instructions*.

"To reach Nexara Academy, present yourself at the northwest docks at midnight tomorrow. A vessel bearing the academy's crest will await you there."

That was it. No explanation, no further details. Just a time and a place. The northwest docks—that was practically on the other side of Nyvorthia, a rough part of the city and dangerous at night.

Chapter 1

Who in their right mind would arrange a rendezvous in such a place? And why *midnight*? It all felt so...illicit.

"This has to be some kind of mistake," I muttered, pacing the small confines of my apartment. Me? At Nexara Academy? The thought was absurd. I was just Thalia, a nobody. I didn't belong in a place like that—a place for the gifted, the powerful.

I glanced at the invitation again, the elegant script mocking me with its promises of "greater things." Could this be real? Could I actually possess some hidden ability, some dormant power waiting to be awakened?

I thought back to the shadows, the whispers, the strange feelings that had plagued me for years. I'd always dismissed them, convinced they were nothing more than figments of my imagination. But what if...what if they weren't? What if there was something more to me than I realized?

"It's crazy," I said aloud, my voice echoing in the quiet apartment. "Absolutely crazy."

The northwest docks. Midnight tomorrow. It was a risky proposition, a step into the unknown. But something—some inexplicable force—was drawing me towards it, urging me to take the leap.

I glanced around my small apartment. The peeling paint on the walls and the mismatched furniture had been my sanctuary for the past few years, my first real home after fleeing the orphanage. It wasn't much, but it was mine. A haven built out of scraps and solitude, a testament to my resilience and independence. A world away from the sterile, suffocating atmosphere of the orphanage and the lonely streets I'd roamed before finding this place. It represented the life I'd painstakingly built for myself—a life of quiet anonymity, where I could finally let my guard down and just *be*.

Thalia's POV

Was this my chance? My chance to finally belong somewhere, to be something *more*? Tomorrow, I'd walk straight into whatever this was. Maybe it was a trap, maybe it was a joke, maybe it was the beginning of the rest of my life. I couldn't afford to keep second-guessing myself.

I'd pack the few possessions I truly valued—the worn leather-bound journal filled with half-formed poems and sketches, the smooth river stone I'd found as a child—along with my meager collection of clothes, and I'd decide to embrace this opportunity. Maybe Nexara Academy held the key to discovering who I truly was, unlocking the secrets of my past. Maybe I'd finally find the answers to the questions that haunted me—the questions about my background, my parents, my very existence.

THE TAXI PARKED AT THE ENTRANCE OF THE northwest docks. As I shut the door, the car immediately sped off, leaving me alone beneath the oppressive, stormy sky. I looked out at an endless stretch of wooden planks leading into the darkness, illuminated by sparse, flickering lampposts that cast long, dancing shadows.

The soft hum of distant waves crashing against the shore was drowned out by the eerie cries of seagulls circling overhead. Pools of sickly yellow light reflected on the choppy water below, but there were no signs of life—no dockworkers, no ships. Just the endless expanse of the docks and the dark, churning sea. It was as though the place had been forgotten by time itself, left to decay in the embrace of the restless sea. A shiver ran down my spine, a prickly sensation that had nothing to do with the cold and everything to do with the unsettling atmosphere.

Chapter 1

I started my way down the dock, the shadows in my peripheral vision shooting forward like grasping claws, as if directing me further into the abyss. Each step I took echoed in the stillness, the sound amplified by the emptiness surrounding me.

"I knew this was a fucking joke," I muttered, reaching the splintered end of the dock. The wood groaned beneath my boots, a mournful sound that seemed to echo the churning sea below. A jagged fork of lightning split the inky sky, the sudden flash illuminating the rolling storm clouds gathering on the horizon. For a moment, I felt a small sense of peace in the face of the brewing chaos—a perverse comfort in the untamed power of the elements. It mirrored the turmoil within my own soul.

"Thalia Cross?" a deep voice boomed, startling me so violently I stumbled, my arms flailing wildly as I fought to regain my balance. My heart hammered against my ribs. Whipping my head to the right, I saw the dark silhouette of a large boat emerge from the gloom, its form momentarily illuminated by another flash of lightning. A large, bearded man leaned against the railing, his features obscured by the shadows. My eyes scanned the vessel, finally landing on a large crest emblazoned on the side, the words "Nexara Academy" etched in elegant script of navy blue and silver.

"What are you standing there for? We need to go," the man said gruffly, extending a calloused hand towards me. Hesitantly, I approached, the scent of salt and brine clinging to him, and handed him my suitcase and backpack before climbing onto the deck.

"Thanks," I mumbled, trying to steady myself as the boat rocked gently beneath me. I clutched the railing, my knuckles white, as I tried to ignore the dizzying sway.

The man grunted in response, his eyes, dark and piercing, scanning the horizon. "Go sit over there," he instructed, jerking his thumb towards a cluster of benches near the stern. "I'm assuming you haven't been on a Gifted vessel, eh? Well, brace yourself. It's not like your little human ones." He let out a rough chuckle that held no humor. "You can call me Captain," he added, turning back to the helm. "Just yell if you need me. Stay in your seat, and we'll get there soon." His words held a finality that said the conversation was over. I made my way to the indicated benches, my legs feeling unsteady beneath me, and sat down heavily, clutching my backpack in my lap.

The boat lurched forward, heading straight into the heart of the approaching storm. A knot of anxiety tightened in my stomach as the rocking intensified. I gripped the railing, the rough wood digging into my palms. The vessel sliced through the waves, sending water misting over the deck, the salty droplets stinging my face. Our speed increased dramatically, the world outside becoming a blur of gray and black. I squeezed my eyes shut, my stomach churning, fighting the rising nausea. The roar of the wind and the crashing of waves filled my ears—a deafening symphony of chaos. I focused on my breathing, trying desperately to keep my dinner down. Just when I thought I couldn't take it anymore, everything went still.

I cautiously opened my eyes, expecting to see the raging storm, the churning sea. Instead, I was met with an otherworldly spectacle. Streaks of vibrant color, like ribbons of light, danced around the boat, swirling and pulsing in the air. It was as though we were moving at impossible speeds—so fast that reality itself seemed to distort and bend around us. But despite the visual chaos, there was no movement, no wind, no sound of crashing waves—just an unnerving stillness.

"Told ya, eh?" the Captain chuckled, his voice raspy with amusement at my reaction. I glared at him, trying desperately to swallow the bile that was still rising in my throat.

"What in the hell is happening?" I asked, my gaze fixed on the mesmerizing spectacle of colors swirling around us. They pulsed and shifted like a living aurora, painting the air with impossible hues.

"Sailing," he said simply, laughing again. Well, not going to get much out of this guy. I could practically see the amusement dancing in his eyes, the way they crinkled at the corners as he watched my bewildered expression. He was clearly enjoying this bizarre show a little too much, while I was still trying to figure out if I was dreaming or hallucinating. Maybe both.

My eyelids started to feel heavy, like the colors were putting me in a trance. A pleasant, warm drowsiness spread through my limbs, making me want to just lean back and let the swirling hues consume me. I fought to keep my eyes open, my mind screaming at me to stay alert, but the tiredness won. My lashes fluttered, then closed completely, and the world dissolved into a kaleidoscope of vibrant nothingness.

"Time to get up!" the Captain yelled over the roar of crashing waves and the shriek of wind whipping through the sails. My eyes shot open, instantly alert. Land loomed ahead—stark and imposing. Jagged, sky-high mountains clawed at the horizon, their peaks shrouded in mist. We were approaching a shore unlike any I'd ever seen, a place that felt both ancient and forbidding.

After we docked, the Captain approached, his weathered face etched with a mixture of concern and something akin to pity. He offered a calloused hand to help me deboard, his grip surprisingly gentle as I navigated the swaying gangplank.

"Just follow the path," he said, his voice rough but not unkind, gesturing towards a narrow, overgrown track that snaked inland. "The entrance isn't far from here. Good luck to ya, lass." He gave my shoulder a reassuring pat before turning back, leaving me standing alone on the strange, unsettling shore.

My suitcase, stuffed with the few belongings I possessed, felt suddenly heavy. I hesitated for a moment, listening to the mournful cry of a distant seabird. Taking a deep breath, I started up the path—each step a reluctant farewell to the familiar and a hesitant embrace of the uncertain future that awaited me at Nexara Academy.

Chapter 2

Thalia's POV

The twilight sky casted an menacing glow over the academy, the shadowed landscape both beautiful and daunting. The gothic towers with sprawling arches... It looked carved from the very essence of the mountains, as though it had always been there, existing beyond time. Its towers reached skyward, intricate and jagged, blending seamlessly into the peaks behind it, defying gravity with impossible elegance.

The stone bridge arched across a canyon beneath, connecting to the structure before me that rose with terrifying grace, its exterior covered in moss and carvings that seemed to move with the setting sun. It looked less like an academy and more like a place where forgotten magic had made its home.

I hesitated at the base of the bridge, my heart racing as I gazed at the academy's monstrous beauty. The silence was suffocating, broken only by the soft whispers of wind. It felt as if the academy itself was alive, watching me, judging me—deciding if I was worthy to enter.

My fingers tightened around the handle of my suitcase, the worn leather creaking in protest as my knuckles turned white. Forcing my feet to move, I crossed the threshold of the bridge. The wrought-iron gates glistened with symbols that seemed to pulse with power. A shiver ran down my spine as the gates opened with a low, ominous creak.

This was it.

No turning back now.

With each step, the gates creaked shut behind me, the sound growing fainter until all I could hear was the pounding of my heart and the whispers of the academy itself, drawing me deeper into its darkness.

Nearing the towering doors, their pointed arch at the top giving them an imposing appearance, I felt a strange hum vibrate through the stone. The iron handles were cold and slick beneath my fingertips as I pushed them open, causing a light creak reverberating through the grand foyer.

The foyer unfolded before me like an overwhelming dream. Towering marble columns, decorated with elaborate carvings, stretched towards the vaulted ceiling, where three chandeliers hung like stars in the sky. A lavish staircase, its steps worn smooth by generations of Gifted, swept upwards, where students walked.

"Welcome to Nexara Academy," a voice called, bringing me back to reality. I turned to find a tall man with silver hair and light brown eyes approaching. "I'm Professor Lorian, and I'll be guiding you through orientation."

"Thalia," I managed, offering him a small, nervous smile.

"Ah, yes, Thalia," he said, his smile tightening slightly. "The one destined for *great* things." He paused, his eyes seeming to bore into me, as if trying to discern something.

"Yeah, guess that's me." I laughed, the sound a little too high-pitched, shifting my weight from one foot to the other, suddenly feeling very small beneath the towering marble columns and the weight of his expectation. "Do you know why I received the invitation? I don't think I have any gifts to be here, and I—" I stammered, but was cut off.

"In time, Thalia, you'll get your answers. In time. For now," he gestured towards a dimly lit corridor branching off from the foyer, shadows clinging to its edges, "let's get you settled in. Right this way."

Trailing behind, the echo of our footsteps mingling with the distant murmur of the students above us. We continued through what felt like endless corridors, each one decorated with portraits of past graduating classes and complex tapestries that spoke of ancient tales. As we walked, Professor Lorian filled me in on the events and lessons I had missed so far this semester.

Stepping out into the courtyard, the cool evening air washed over me, carrying the scent of pine needles and damp earth. The sky had deepened to a velvety indigo, and the vast reach of the courtyard seemed to stretch endlessly before us. Buildings of different shapes and sizes were scattered across the emerald lawn, connected by winding cobblestone paths.

"The campus is small but spread out. We just left Evermore Hall, which houses most of the faculty offices, the library, and the auditorium. The north side of the campus contains the men's dorms, cafeteria, and women's dorms. The south side will have the training grounds, locker rooms, and Eldrin Hall. Eldrin Hall is where a few classes take place, as well as our academy events. Directly west of us will be Leyndell Hall, which is where most of your classes will take place." Professor Lorian explained as we passed the men's dorms, their dark windows giving nothing away of the life within.

Ahead, I noticed a large lake shimmering through the trees, its surface reflecting the dusky hues of the sky like a mirror to another world. Beyond, the towering silhouettes of mountains encircled us, their peaks piercing the heavens as if standing watch over the grounds—silent guardians of this hidden world.

"Do you know who I would talk to about why I was invited here?" I asked as I followed him deeper into the heart of the academy grounds. I still couldn't quite believe I was here—that this was real.

"Dean Astor, but he is terribly busy and is away right now," he responded, his tone short, almost dismissive.

"I'm just trying to wrap my head around why this is happening." I sighed, running a hand through my hair, feeling the weight of the being here pressing down on me. I studied the statues that stood guard near each building—majestic griffins, fierce dragons, and creatures I couldn't even name, their stone eyes gleaming with an eerie life as if they were watching my every move, judging my presence here.

Finally, we reached the women's dorms, nestled within a grove of towering trees at almost the end of the grounds, their branches intertwining to create a natural awning. Lanterns hung from wrought-iron hooks flickered like captive fireflies, casting playful shadows that danced along the path. With every step, the academy seemed to come alive.

"This is where you'll be staying," Professor Lorian said, gesturing towards the dormitory. He gave me a quick nod and practically vanished into thin air, like he couldn't wait to escape.

Charming.

I took a moment to admire the building, its walls a deep, brooding gray, like storm clouds gathering. A small stone path, lined with overgrown shrubs and flower beds bursting with untamed blooms, snaked its way towards a wooden door, its surface weathered and worn.

I stepped inside, the heavy door closing behind me with a soft thud that echoed through the entryway. The dim lighting gave the space an almost brooding elegance, with deep green walls that seemed to swallow the light, leaving only the glimmer from the chandelier hanging above. I paused, taking in the polished woodwork, the molding framing the walls, and the ornate railing that ran along the stairs. Everything felt old, regal—imposing in a way that screamed I didn't belong here.

My eyes studied the chandelier. It gave the room a strange warmth, contrasting the cold, dark tones. A plush rug lay before me, rich with detailed designs, its deep green color complementing the somber decor, leading my eyes to the staircase.

When I reached the top floor, I found another hallway lined with doors, each one uniquely decorated, reflecting a different personality. I stopped at the door marked with a simple plaque: 313, just as it said in my paperwork. Taking a deep breath, I pushed it open and stepped into my new sanctuary.

Inside, the room had deep green hues that matched the foyer downstairs. A large window with diamond-patterned panes overlooked the courtyard, allowing the moonlight to spill in, casting a silvery glow across the room. Heavy, dark curtains framed the window, their thick fabric lending an air of privacy.

To the left, an inviting small bed was tucked against the wall, dressed in deep green and dark gray linens, with a few throw pillows in muted crimson. A small black dresser sat beside it, which was more than enough room for what little I had. Against the opposite wall, a sturdy desk sat bathed in the warm glow of a brass lamp. Placing my suitcase on the bed, I glanced out the window, letting the weight of my new reality settle in.

This was it. My new room. This wasn't a joke, though a nagging voice whispered the possibility of a trap. But why? What did I have that anyone would want? Like Vicki would say, I needed to start looking at life as a glass half full instead of perpetually empty. Shaking my head slightly, I pushed away the lingering unease. Maybe this was my time—maybe this was the start of the exciting new life I'd always dreamed of. A small smile touched my lips as I started to settle in.

THE NEXT MORNING, I FOUND MYSELF STARING INTO the mirror of the tiny ensuite bathroom, the unfamiliar weight of my new uniform settling heavily on my shoulders. There were six uniforms hanging in the small closet in the bathroom, crisp and identical—a stark contrast to the worn, mismatched clothes I was used to. Folded neatly on the shelf above were several thick white towels and a basket filled with basic hygiene products—soap, shampoo, even a new toothbrush. The deep blue blazer, trimmed with silver accents, felt more like a costume than a uniform, and the crisp white blouse beneath it did little to stop the rising tide of imposter syndrome.

What am I doing here? I thought, the question echoing the nervous flutter in my chest.

Following the map I found in my welcome packet, I followed the cobblestone path towards Leyndell Hall. Rushing into my first class of the day, I slipped into the middle row, hoping to blend into the background. The room buzzed with the energy of students already engaged in lively conversations, their easy confidence only intensifying my anxiety.

The classroom itself was grand, with the branded high-arched windows lined the far wall, letting in soft, diffused light across the wooden floor. The room was arranged in a semicircle, with tiered

rows that rose up like a theater, giving every student an unobstructed view of the professor.

The dark wood of the desks was polished to a gleaming finish.
Paintings of distinguished-looking individuals hung between the
windows—I assumed to be past professors or scholars.

As I settled into my seat, a prickling sensation danced across my
skin. I turned my head to find a massive, broad-shouldered figure
slouched in the back row. His posture exuded an aura of quiet
authority, his broad shoulders tense, hinting at a disciplined
strength. Intense emerald eyes, framed by thick, dark lashes, were
fixed intently on mine—his gaze unwavering and almost predatory.

He was undeniably striking. His sharp, angular features were
perfectly proportioned, and his dark hair, styled in loose curls,
framed his face with effortless grace. His expression was unreadable, but something flickered in the depths of those emerald eyes,
sending a jolt of electricity through my veins.

A shiver ran down my spine as I tore my gaze away, my cheeks
flushing with a heat that had nothing to do with the stuffy classroom. Sure, he was ridiculously handsome, but was I seriously
blushing? Over a guy who looked like he'd murder someone for
breathing wrong in his direction?

Get it together, Thalia.

Before I could dwell on the hot stranger, the loud thud of the
door shutting took my attention toward the professor—an older
man with a permanent frown etched into his face. The hum of
conversation faded into silence as he made his way to the front of
the room.

"Good morning," he rasped, his voice a low, gravelly baritone that
commanded instant attention. "Today, we delve into the fasci-
nating world of ancient runes."

I attempted to focus as the lecture began, scribbling notes on the origins of different runes and their mystical properties—which, honestly, sounded like a completely foreign language. *Sigils for protection, symbols of power, gateways to other realms...* My hand cramped as I tried to keep up, the symbols blurring together in a dizzying swirl of lines and curves. Was it even possible to memorize all of this? I glanced around the room, wondering if anyone else felt as lost as I did. But the feeling of eyes boring into my back persisted, and I couldn't resist stealing another glance towards the back row. Mr. Tall, Dark, and Brooding had gone from an unreadable expression to full-on scowling. Before I could even begin to understand the reason for his sudden mood shift, he abruptly stood up, his chair scraping against the polished floor with the screech of a banshee. Without a word, he stormed out of the classroom, slamming the door behind him with enough force to rattle the very foundations of the academy.

A wave of whispers rippled through the room. The professor cleared his throat, momentarily silencing them. He gave a weary shake of his head, a gesture that spoke volumes about the temperamental stranger, before launching back into his lecture.

With a few minutes to spare, the professor's eyes narrowed as he scanned the room, his gaze landing on me. "You. The newcomer."

I held my breath for a second, feeling the weight of all everyone's eyes on me.

"Would you care to share your gift with the class?" His tone was sharp, almost accusatory, as if he were daring me to admit I didn't belong here.

"I—I don't... I'm not sure..." I stammered, my throat constricting with a mixture of fear and embarrassment. Was he really calling me out in front of everyone? On my first day?

The professor's eyebrow arched. "Not sure?" he echoed, a hint of amusement lacing his gravelly voice. "Then perhaps you should think about that. Quickly. This sacred institution is reserved for the most gifted and powerful in Nexera, not for those who wander in blindly." His smile was tight as his eyes studied me.

Heat flooded my cheeks as the whispers erupted once more:

"What is she doing here, if she doesn't even know what she can do? Do you think she's even Gifted?"

"That's so pathetic. How did she think coming here was okay?"

"How did she get an invite? There are so many Gifted who'd kill for her spot."

I felt like a deer caught in headlights, paralyzed by the scrutiny and judgment. The weight of their eyes was suffocating, each snicker cutting deeper than the last. My throat tightened, and I desperately searched for words—anything to defend myself—but nothing came. I grabbed my things and fled the room, my heart pounding as the whispers got louder, their laughter following me out into the hallway.

Entering the cafeteria that looked more like a cathedral, the design echoed the Evermore Hall with soaring arches and expansive floor-to-ceiling windows. The room filled with students gathered in groups, their laughter and chatter filling the grand hall. Tall columns twisted upward to meet at the carved ceiling, covered with symbols and glowing accents that gave an otherworldly effect. Grand chandeliers hung above, casting flickering patterns across the stone floor and rows of long wooden tables. It was more a banquet hall than a cafeteria, with its grandeur and enchanting atmosphere.

As I moved through the crowded space, I couldn't ignore the lingering glances cast my way, the whispers that followed me like a shadow. The energy of the room felt heavy, almost suffocating, and every chuckle seemed like it was at my expense.

I kept my head down, focusing on the seemingly endless food line, but the weight of their scrutiny bore down on me, making my stomach churn. I tried to distract myself with the impressive array of dishes—platters piled high with exotic fruits, steaming cauldrons of fragrant stews, and glistening trays of pastries. But my heart hammered against my ribs, a frantic drumbeat against the backdrop of the cafeteria's din.

And then I saw *him*.

The mysterious stranger from this morning, seated at a table slightly apart from the others, flanked by two equally striking figures. Those green eyes locked onto mine with an unwavering intensity that sent a shiver down my spine. His posture relaxed yet exuding an unmistakable air of command. He sat with an almost royal confidence, the black curls on his forehead just as unruly as before. His gaze was sharp and unrelenting, pinning me in place.

The first figure beside him glared at me with dark blue eyes, a mix of challenge and suspicion swirling in their depths. I felt like an unwelcome intruder, an irritant disrupting their carefully constructed world. His hair was perfectly styled—deep brown with the sides cut shorter while the top was textured and brushed back, a single rebellious strand falling across his forehead, doing nothing to soften the harshness of his gaze. His features were striking, rugged, and intense. He carried himself with an undeniable aura of power and authority, every movement deliberate, as if he were always in control, assessing and judging.

And the last one, with amber eyes met mine with open curiosity —their warmth a welcome break from the icy glares of his friends. His dark hair cascaded in soft waves, partially obscuring his face, and elaborate black tattoos snaked around his arms and hands, their patterns shifting and shimmering as he idly toyed with the rings on his fingers. There was an airy quality about him, a delicate, otherworldly beauty that drew my gaze like a moth to a flame.

He must be a fae, I thought, mesmerized by his presence. I had never seen one in person before, but the pull I felt was undeniable—almost intoxicating. His lips curled into a subtle smirk as he watched me, clearly enjoying the attention.

I was frozen, like a rabbit caught in a predator's spotlight. There was something about them that held me captive. I couldn't tear my eyes away, my gaze darting between them, taking in every detail.

"Ah, you must be the famous human I've been hearing about," a melodic voice snapped me out of my trance. I turned to see a girl with long chestnut hair and eyes with the faintest red tint, like glowing embers.

"I'm Elara, but you can call me El," she added with a playful wink, as if we were already old friends. "You can sit here."

"Thalia," I replied, offering a small, hesitant smile as I took the seat across from her. "And yeah, it's... been interesting."

El laughed. "I bet. Heard you've made quite an impression already." She leaned in, her eyes glinting with amusement, but there was a kindness there too—like she understood more than she was letting on.

"I didn't realize how quickly news travels around here," I muttered, glancing down at my tray. I could see them clearly in my peripheral vision and could feel the weight of three intense stares bore into me from across the room.

El shrugged, flicking a lock of hair over her shoulder. "Welcome to Nexara Academy, where rumors spread faster than fire in dry grass. When you're surrounded by powerful Gifted, they love a good story—especially one about the mysterious new girl." She rolled her eyes, though there was no malice in her voice. "But don't worry, I've got your back. They may be talking now, but soon enough, they'll get bored and find someone else to gossip about."

Her words were a lifeline, and I felt a surprising warmth in my chest. "Thanks."

El grinned. "No problem. Besides, I've already decided we're going to be best friends. You've got that whole 'mysterious outsider' vibe going on, and I'm the fiery witch who's going to show you all the ropes. It's fate."

I blinked at her, a laugh escaping before I could stop it. "Is that so?"

"Absolutely," she said with a mock-serious nod, as if sealing the deal. "Now, let's eat. You're going to need your strength to survive the rest of the day. What class do you have next?"

"Combat Training," I groaned, picturing myself being tossed around like a rag doll. "It'll be the cherry on top of the worst first day ever."

"Oh, me too!" she exclaimed, her eyes widening with surprise. "Don't worry, we can be partners. Trust me, it'll be fun. Or at least less miserable with me around."

I blinked at her, startled by how easily she'd decided we were in this together. It was strange, this sudden camaraderie—yet it felt... right. A wave of relief washed over me. Thank the gods for El. For the first time all day, I didn't feel completely out of place. Maybe this whole academy thing wasn't going to be so bad after all.

Chapter 2

WHEN WE REACHED THE WOMEN'S LOCKER ROOMS, I slipped into the academy-issued gym clothes—a simple but comfortable set of dark sweatpants and a long-sleeve top with Nexara's emblem on the chest.

My anxiety started again, my chest tightening... Combat training? No way I would do well in this class. El, on the other hand, looked completely unfazed, her fiery red eyes glinting with excitement.

"Ready?" she asked, grinning as she tied her long hair into a high ponytail.

I gave her a smile. "As ready as I'll ever be."

The training field stretched before us, vast and intimidating. Its borders blurred into the dense forest that encircled the academy, its towering trees casting long shadows across the manicured grass. The air thrummed with an electric energy—an unmistakable anticipation that sent a chill coursing through me.

Scattered across the field lay a seemingly endless array of training equipment: wooden dummies, weathered punching bags, and intricate obstacle courses that resembled jungle gyms designed by a sadistic genius. Groups of students sparred against each other, their movements a blur of flashing limbs and crackling energy. The air filled with the rhythmic thud of punches, the sharp snap of kicks, and the occasional roar of laughter or victorious yells. A nervous flutter erupted in my stomach. I shoved my hands into my pockets, trying to appear nonchalant, but the sheer display of raw power and honed skill was more than a little intimidating.

As I stepped onto the field, the immensity of it all threatened to overwhelm me. It was a world unto itself—a crucible where warriors were forged, and here I was. *What am I doing here?*

El let out a small laugh at my expression. "Yeah, it's pretty impressive. You'll be okay, but—oh no," she said, lowering her voice with a teasing lilt, "looks like you've caught the attention of the Shadow Brothers."

I followed her gaze, and sure enough, there they were—the trio of impossibly handsome men I had noticed earlier, lounging against the stone wall with an air of effortless cool. Heat crept up my neck, and I quickly turned back to El, lowering my voice. "Why do they keep staring like they want to murder me? It's terrifying."

El laughed, shaking her head. "They're the Shadow Brothers— Nox, Zarek, and Damon. The most powerful guys at the academy, maybe even all of Nexara. And by the looks of it, they're intrigued by you. I'm not surprised. Word about the mysterious new girl is already flying around campus." She smirked. "And before you ask, no, they're not actual brothers. They're closer than most real siblings, though. No one really knows what their deal is. They're powerful and secretive, and frankly, a little intimidating. Although," she added with a thoughtful hum, "Zarek does have a certain charm."

"Charm isn't enough to offset the whole 'murderous vibe' they've got going on," I muttered, groaning inwardly. "Great. Just what I needed—attention from the three most powerful Gifted here. I'd rather face a horde of snarling dogs." I cast another glance over my shoulder at them, only to see them still watching me, their gazes intense and unwavering.

El patted my shoulder with a sympathetic smile. "Don't worry, they'll get bored eventually. Hopefully." But the playful glint in her eyes told me she didn't believe it for a second.

Professor Lorian strode into the field with the confidence of someone who had seen more battles than he cared to admit. His presence was commanding, and as soon as he stepped into view, the murmurs among students stopped. He walked to the center of the field, taking in the class with a steely gaze.

"Today, we'll be focusing on sparring," his deep voice carried across the expansive field. "Find a partner. The rules are simple: no drawing blood, no magic, no abilities. First one to tap, loses."

I glanced around, noticing the students started to pair up. Turning my attention back to Professor Lorian, I realized his eyes had locked onto me. They lingered for a moment—too long. Then he smiled, clapping his hands together with finality.

"Let's begin."

El flashed me a playful grin, her red-tinted eyes gleaming with excitement as she sized me up. "I'll take it easy on you," she teased, winking before getting into position. She looked confident—like this wasn't her first time sparring. Meanwhile, I awkwardly mimicked her stance, feeling the unfamiliar tension in my muscles as I got ready to defend myself.

"I'm not sure I'm cut out for this," I muttered, trying to loosen the nerves tightening in my chest.

El laughed softly. "You'll be fine. It's just for practice."

But as I stood there, preparing for whatever El was about to throw at me, my mind wandered to darker memories. I'd never had any real training in fighting—only the kind of experience that came from desperation. I hadn't thought about that night in a long time—the night after I got kicked out of the orphanage for being "too old." I had been walking home from a late shift at the diner, my feet aching and my body exhausted, when a man approached me.

I still remembered the stench of alcohol rolling off of him in waves and the way his eyes tracked me like prey as I tried to slip past him. My heart felt like it was going to explode from the frantic beating, but I kept walking. His wicked smile still haunts me. Before I knew it, his hand had clamped down on my arm with a bruising force, yanking me into a dark alley.

Terror choked my scream, a silent cry trapped in my throat. Even if I could have screamed, it wouldn't have mattered in that part of town—nobody was coming to save me. I fought, kicking and scratching like a wild animal, my movements frantic and uncoordinated. My nails raked across his face, my feet connected with whatever flesh they could find, but he only laughed. That guttural sound—a chilling symphony of amusement and cruelty—still echoed in the darkest parts of my mind. My body shuddered involuntarily at the resurfaced memory. I clenched my fists until my nails bit into my palms, the sharp pain a lifeline dragging me back to the present.

"Thalia?" El's voice was soft, laced with concern, her head tilted as she studied my face. "You okay?"

I shoved the memory back into the shadows, forcing a casual tone. "Yeah," I lied, my voice catching slightly, "just... let's do this."

El didn't push, sensing my unease. She offered a small, reassuring smile and stood up straight. "Okay. Let's start slow."

I nodded, grateful she didn't question me further. My past wasn't something I wanted to dwell on, but it had a way of creeping up when I least expected it.

After a few rounds of El taking me down effortlessly, I started to find a rhythm. My body—still a little hesitant—slowly caught on to her moves. Each time she lunged at me, I learned to anticipate her, blocking her strikes more and more successfully. Though I still couldn't quite manage to take her down, I was at least able to defend myself, and that felt like a victory in itself.

We laughed as we went back and forth, testing each other's reflexes. El was quick—quicker than I'd ever be—but after a while, the fear of failure melted away, replaced by the thrill of the sparring. Time flew as we traded jabs and dodges.

The sharp sound of the whistle rang out across the field, cutting through the noise of our laughter. I glanced around, seeing other students gasping for breath, their faces red and sweaty as they stood with ease. Professor Lorian's booming voice echoed from the center of the field, instructing everyone to head to the showers.

I wiped the sweat from my forehead, still catching my breath as I turned towards the locker rooms. Across the field, those mesmerizing amber eyes locked onto mine, the same curious expression dancing in their depths—making my heart skip a beat.

He had draped his shirt carelessly over his shoulders, giving me an unobstructed view of his sculpted chest. Sweat glistened against his sun-kissed skin, catching the light and emphasizing every chiseled muscle—from the curve of his shoulders to the sharp definition of his abs.

Black, mesmerizing tattoos sprawled across his chest and down his arms. They were like living art—vines entwined with symbols so ancient they seemed alive, shifting subtly as his muscles flexed. My eyes, betraying me completely, trailed downward, lingering far too long on his torso, down to where his sweatpants hung low on his hips—the sharp lines of his V-cut disappearing beneath the waistband.

Heat crept up my neck as I forced my gaze back to his face, catching him watching me with an amused smirk playing on his lips. He clearly enjoyed the blatant appreciation in my eyes. With a teasing wink that sent my pulse racing, he turned and disappeared into the men's locker room

"Which one was that?" I asked, still watching the door he had just gone through, my curiosity getting the better of me.

El glanced in the direction I was staring, her lips curling into a smile. "That," she said, drawing out the word, "was Zarek. Dangerous, powerful, and way too good-looking for his own good." She sighed, shaking her head. "He's beautiful, but pure trouble."

El laughed as she continued, shaking her head. "Those brothers are dangerous in their own way. Most of the guys around here fear them, and the girls? They're all fighting for their attention."

As we walked toward the women's locker rooms, I couldn't help but wonder what it meant to catch the attention of someone like Zarek—someone who, by El's account, was far more dangerous than he appeared. His amber eyes, the way they seemed to pierce through me, the subtle smirk that played on his lips—it was all so intoxicating, yet troubling. Was it genuine interest, or was I just another conquest for him?

Chapter 3

Thalia's POV

A few weeks into the academy, the rhythm of my days settled into a familiar pattern. Mornings were a blur of lectures in the Leyndell Hall, where dust motes danced in the sunbeams slicing through the arched windows. Lunch with El, her easy grin chasing away the shadows that always seemed to linger at the edges of my mind. Combat training was a grueling dance of sweat and aching muscles. Evenings were spent hunched over books in the flickering lamplight of the library. For the first time, the gnawing loneliness that had been my constant companion for so long began to recede. El wasn't obligated to be my friend—she *chose* to be.

The Shadow Brothers, with their intense gazes and apparent annoyance towards me, hadn't been seen in days. Their presence, though brief, still lingered in my mind. According to El, this was normal. While the academy's attendance rules were strict for everyone else, the brothers seemed to be above them. I found it... irritating. Maybe it was the fact they could ignore the rules, or maybe it was because I hadn't seen them at all.

I pushed the thought away. *No, Thalia,* I told myself firmly, you don't need to worry about them. They clearly don't think you belong here anyway—just like everyone else. Why waste any more energy on them? They already get enough attention elsewhere.

My thoughts were interrupted as El burst into my room, a whirlwind of energy that filled the space. It was my own fault for not locking the door, but I barely had time to register that before she launched into her announcement.

"Listen," she declared, hands on her hips, "there's a party tonight, and we are going. I'm not sure what you did in the human territory, but you've been cooped up studying since you got here, and as much as I love you, it's time to live a little!"

Her eyes sparkled with determination as she nodded to herself, marching toward my closet and rifling through my clothes as if she owned the place. "I won't take no for an answer," she declared from the bathroom, pulling out a few outfits and holding them up with a critical eye.

"I really don't think—" I began, but she waved me off, her vibrant energy drowning out my protests.

"Girl!" she exclaimed, tossing the clothes onto my bed. "You don't have anything that screams 'fun' or 'party' in here!"

I opened my mouth to argue, but she was already shaking her head, cutting me off with a playful grin. "You need to borrow something of mine. I'll be back with a more appropriate outfit!" With that, she dashed out of the room.

After a couple of hours, El finally pulled back, beaming at her handiwork. She had insisted on doing my makeup, claiming she knew just the trick to make my eyes pop. I turned to look in the mirror and was stunned by the transformation. The woman staring back at me was polished and confident—my hair styled in loose waves that cascaded just above my waist, eyeliner wings sharp enough to kill, and bold red lipstick that contrasted beautifully against my pale skin. I had to admit, I looked damn good.

My confidence surged as I admired the black sequined shirt that hung loosely around my torso, leaving my back open, paired perfectly with dark jeans that hugged my curves. El had agreed to the jeans as long as I wore the shirt—there was no way I was leaving this room in some of the other... *interesting* options she had brought over.

El herself looked incredible in a red dress that clung to her in all the right places, exuding the fierce energy she was known for. Her hair was straightened, and smoky eyeshadow emphasized her tinted red eyes, making them smolder. As I took in our reflection, I felt a surge of excitement for the night ahead. Maybe this party was just what I needed.

THE PARTY PULSED WITH LIFE DOWN BY THE LAKE—THE same one I'd spotted when I first arrived. Wooden stairs leading to the shore were strung with fairy lights that twinkled against the darkening sky, casting a soft glow over the gathering. As we descended, the crackle and pop of a bonfire filled the air, sending sparks dancing into the night. Familiar faces filled the space, their laughter and chatter mingling with the pulse of the music.

"The academy doesn't have a problem with this?" I asked El, scanning the crowd of students who looked a little more than tipsy.

"Nope, not when the hosts can do whatever they please," she replied with an eye roll. "But honestly, I'm thankful they can throw parties like this."

I hesitated, a wave of insecurity washing over me. Two of the three Shadow Brothers had made it abundantly clear that my presence was a nuisance, and the other probably just wanted to study me for some twisted scientific curiosity.

"Oh, come on!" El urged, a mischievous glint in her eyes. "I know you would've fought me harder if you knew whose party it was, but I promise you, basically half the campus is here. They won't even notice you." She tugged me playfully toward the drinks.

"Fine," I conceded. "But if I hate it or one of those psycho brothers tries to kill me, it'll be on you." I laughed, accepting the drink El offered with a dramatic flourish.

As we made our way to the bonfire, its warmth radiated through the cool night air, mingling with the gentle breeze from the lake. El introduced me to a few of her friends, their curious eyes studying me like I was some exotic creature. While they were cautious, their demeanor wasn't hostile—it felt more like they were unsure how to approach the human girl with no gifts. I could sense the unspoken questions hanging in the air, a silent weight I tried to ignore.

"Don't mind them," El said, her gaze softening as she read my expression. "They just need a little time to warm up, just like this fire." She gestured toward the crackling flames, their dance casting flickering shadows across our faces. The music pulsed around us, vibrating through my bones.

"Let's dance!" El cheered, pulling me toward the swaying crowd. The alcohol loosened my limbs, and I found myself moving to the rhythm, surrendering to the beat.

After a few songs—and maybe a few too many drinks—a sudden urge to explore overcame me. The liquid courage coursing through my veins made me feel fearless as I waved El off mid-story —something about accidentally setting a house on fire as a kid. "I'll be right back," I called over the music, ignoring her protests as I grabbed my jacket. My feet carried me forward, the sound of crunching leaves and snapping twigs underfoot growing louder as I approached the tree line.

Stepping across the invisible boundary where the manicured grounds gave way to untamed wilderness, I felt an irresistible pull deeper into the forest. Curiosity battled with a growing sense of unease. This part of the campus felt different—darker, wilder, almost forgotten. The shadows seemed to both beckon and repel, while the trees swayed around me with a life of their own, their branches reaching out like skeletal fingers. Moonlight struggled to penetrate the dense canopy, dappling the forest floor in an eerie, silvery glow. The music from the party faded to a distant hum, replaced by the rustle of unseen creatures in the undergrowth.

An outline of a strange structure began to emerge from the gloom, its silhouette taking shape against the moonlit sky like a jagged tooth. A mixture of fear and fascination washed over me, prickling my skin with goosebumps. What *was* this place, and why did it feel so... significant? So familiar, like a half-forgotten dream. Before I could get a better look, a deep, raspy voice sliced through the silence from right behind me, freezing me in my tracks. My breath hitched in my throat, and every instinct screamed at me to run.

"What are you doing here?" the voice asked, calm but laced with an underlying current of something darker, something that made the hair on the back of my neck prickle. "It can be very dangerous out here, especially for a human."

My heart hammered against my ribs as I slowly turned, my pulse a roar in my ears. Tilting my head back to meet his gaze, I found myself staring into piercing green eyes. Nox. He towered over me, easily six foot five, his hood pulled up but doing little to conceal those damned black curls that peeked out, tempting my fingers to reach out and touch them.

"I—I was just curious about that," I finally managed, my voice a shaky whisper as I gestured towards where the structure had been. For a fleeting moment, his gaze softened, but just as quickly, the icy mask was back in place. He glanced past me, following the direction of my pointed finger.

"There's nothing there," he stated flatly, his voice devoid of any warmth.

"Yes, there is," I insisted, my own irritation flaring as I turned to look—but the structure was gone. Vanished. Nothing but the endless stretch of trees stood before us.

"Don't come back here," he warned, his voice low and serious. "The protection ward only goes as far as the tree line. Beyond that, it's free game for the creatures that roam these woods." His lips curled into a faint smirk, a predator enjoying the fear in his prey's eyes.

"Well, thanks for your concern, but I can take care of myself," I snapped, rolling my eyes and attempting to brush past him.

In an instant, his hand shot out, encircling my arm in a grip that was firm but not painful. He drew me closer, the sudden warmth of his body a shock against the chill in the air. I could feel his breath on my skin, and the scent of cedar and rain—potent and intoxicating—filled my senses, making my head spin. The tingling sensation where his fingers touched me intensified, becoming a distracting heat that spread through my arm and settled in my chest. Yet it was the intensity in his eyes, a burning emerald fire, that truly stopped me in my tracks.

"Stay out of the forest, Thalia," he growled, his face inches from mine, his voice raw with barely contained anger.

I yanked my arm free, stumbling slightly as the alcohol hit me harder than I'd anticipated. He gave me one last piercing look, his eyes flashing with an emotion I couldn't quite decipher, before he turned and vanished into the shadows of the woods.

What the hell is his problem? I thought, my annoyance battling with a strange flutter in my stomach as I made my way back

Chapter 3

toward the party. But the scene that greeted me was a far cry from the lively celebration I'd left behind. The bonfire had dwindled to ashes, the once-vibrant crowd had thinned to a scattered few, and the cool night air—which had felt refreshing earlier—now seemed to bite with a lonely chill.

How long had I been gone?

Wrapping my arms around myself for warmth, I scanned the dwindling crowd for El or any familiar face, but it was as though the party had moved on without me. With a sigh, I started the trek back towards the dorms, the sound of gravel crunching underfoot a lonely counterpoint to the wind whistling through the trees. The shadows seemed to dance just beyond my vision, their whispers pulling at the corners of my mind, begging for attention.

I shook my head, trying to clear the strange thoughts. Shadows weren't some mystical gift—unless you were a demon. And I'd know if I was a demon... right?

No, I'm just exhausted and on edge. Nothing had changed since I came to this academy—no answers about my past or why I was invited here in the first place. The Dean was always unavailable, his office perpetually locked, and nobody could tell me anything. Just more questions swirling in my mind like restless spirits and unsettling encounters with shadows that seemed to know my name. It was enough to make anyone paranoid. Maybe a hot shower and a long sleep would help. Maybe.

A sharp snap of a branch to my right brought me to a halt. My eyes darted to the dark tree line, and there—just beyond the edge of the forest—I saw two large, round emerald eyes watching me intently. I squinted, trying to make out the rest of the creature, but only its glowing eyes pierced the inky blackness.

The creature remained motionless, its gaze unwavering. An inexplicable pull drew me closer, my body moving slowly forward

43

against my will while my mind screamed for me to stop. The beast emitted a low, deep growl, making the gravel tremble beneath me.

"Thalia! Wait up!" a voice called from behind me. My body tensed as I instinctively glanced back, hoping that whatever magical ward protected the academy grounds would keep the green-eyed creature at bay. My heart pounded against my ribs, but instead of a monstrous predator, I was met with the sight of a familiar figure jogging towards me.

I exhaled a breath I hadn't realized I'd been holding and turned back towards the tree line. The glowing eyes were gone, swallowed by the impenetrable darkness. I shook my head, trying to steady my nerves, before turning my attention to the approaching figure.

A blonde tall figure, slightly out of breath as he caught up to me. His sun-kissed hair was tousled in a way that looked effortlessly perfect, and his icy blue eyes sparkled with a friendly warmth.

"I thought that was you," he said, his grin both charming and reassuring as he shoved his hands into his pockets. "I'm James. I don't think we've officially met, but we have Combat Training with Professor Lorian."

His boyish charm was disarming, a stark contrast to the fear that had gripped me moments before. "Yeah, we do," I replied, still feeling rattled as I cast one last glance at the tree line, where those piercing green eyes had been just moments ago. "What's up?"

James gestured ahead, offering a small, casual smile as he fell into step beside me. "I thought I'd walk you back. You looked... like you might want some company." His voice was gentle.

I nodded, appreciating the gesture but still a little on edge. "Thanks," I replied, my voice a bit hesitant as I tried to shake off the lingering unease.

We walked in uncomfortable silence for a moment, the crunch of gravel beneath our feet the only sound as we headed toward the girls' dormitory. In a lighthearted attempt to break the ice, James started asking me questions about class, how I was settling in at the academy, and if I'd been to any of the previous parties. I answered politely, though my mind kept wandering back to the woods. *What was that creature I saw? And why did Nox seem so intent on warning me away from the forest?*

James' voice broke through my thoughts. "So, how are you liking the academy? It must be... different for you, right?"

His question was innocent enough, but I could hear the underlying curiosity in his voice—he wanted to know what it was like for the powerless human at an academy for the magically gifted. It was a question that seemed to linger in the minds of everyone I met.

"It's... an adjustment," I replied, offering a wry smile. "I didn't exactly plan on being here, but I'm managing."

"I hear that," he chuckled. "It's a lot for anyone to handle, even with abilities. But hey, you've got Elara on your side, so that's something." He flashed a grin, trying to put me at ease.

"Yeah, El's been great," I agreed, my tone softening as I thought of her. "I've been lucky to have her around."

We continued to walk, the silence between us growing more comfortable as the dormitory came into view, its soft lights a welcome beacon of safety and normalcy. Still, I couldn't shake the lingering unease from my encounter in the woods—the weight of Nox's warning and the memory of those glowing eyes watching me from the darkness.

As we neared the steps, James cleared his throat, his hands still buried in his pockets. "If you ever want to talk, or you know, need someone to walk with at night... I'm around," he offered, a genuine warmth in his eyes that softened the awkwardness of the moment.

I smiled back, a genuine smile this time. "Thanks, James. I'll keep that in mind."

He gave a quick nod before turning and heading back down the path. I watched him disappear into the distance before I glanced back at the tree line one last time. Whatever had been out there, lurking in the shadows, was gone now. Or at least, it was hidden from sight. I couldn't shake the feeling of being watched—the unsettling awareness of unseen eyes on me, even now, hundreds of miles away from the bustling streets of Nyvorthia. It was a prickling sensation, like phantom fingers brushing against the back of my neck, a constant reminder that I wasn't alone, even when I appeared to be.

Chapter 4

Thalia's POV

The next morning, my head was pounding, and my mouth felt like a desert. *What the hell was in those drinks?* I'd had my fair share of alcohol before—like any normal twenty-three-year-old—but this hangover was something else entirely. I dragged myself out of bed, cursing my internal clock for always waking me up at the crack of dawn, even on a Saturday. The room spun a little as I stumbled towards the bathroom— it's tiny, but I was grateful for the privacy.

After a long, hot shower, the steam worked its magic, and I felt almost human again. My head still throbbed with a dull ache, but at least the room had stopped swaying. Throwing on a pair of leggings and my trusty Nyvorthia High sweatshirt, I decided to head to the cafeteria for some much-needed food. It was Saturday morning, so I figured most students would either be sleeping off the effects of the party or off campus, enjoying their weekend freedom.

As I made my way down the cobblestone path, my eyes drifted towards the tree line. The image of those unsettling green eyes from the night before flashed through my mind. *What else is out there lurking in those shadows?* The weight of unanswered questions pressing against my already aching head.

Lost in thought, I collided with what felt like a solid wall. I stumbled backward, my heart skipping a beat, before a pair of strong hands reached out, encircling my waist and steadying me.

A low, amused sound reached my ears. I looked up, my breath catching as I met Zarek's eyes. This close, I could see the flecks of gold swimming in those amber irises. A lazy smirk played on his lips, radiating a confidence that bordered on arrogance. He knew exactly the effect he had on me, and he seemed to revel in it. His dark hair, slightly tousled, framed a face that was both handsome and intimidating. He was about the same height as Nox—*why were all the Shadow Brothers so damn tall?* Even at five foot nine, I still had to crane my neck to meet his gaze, which did little to help my already flustered composure.

"Careful there, Firefly," he drawled, his voice smooth like velvet, laced with a playful tease. "I didn't think you'd be this eager to run into me this morning." He looked down at me, a hint of challenge in their depths.

I blinked, still trying to fully register that I'd literally collided with him. His hands lingered on my waist for a heartbeat too long, sending a fresh wave of tingles through me. I quickly stepped back, heat creeping up my neck despite the cool morning air. *What is wrong with me?*

"Eager? More like distracted," I retorted, rolling my eyes, hoping he wouldn't notice the slight tremor in my voice.

Zarek's lips curled into a grin that made my stomach do a flip. "Distracted, huh?" His eyes gleamed with mischief. "And what could possibly have you so lost in thought?"

"Uh, nothing—just... stuff," I mumbled, cursing my inability to form a coherent sentence in his presence. *Great answer, Thalia, real smooth.* Why did he have to stand so close? And why did my brain suddenly feel like it was misfiring?

He tilted his head, watching me with that same curious, almost predatory intensity that seemed to be a trademark of the Shadow Brothers. I crossed my arms defensively, trying to regain some semblance of composure.

"You're the one who's built like a damn brick wall," I shot back, my cheeks burning.

He raised an eyebrow, amusement dancing in his eyes. "Ah, so it's my fault, is it?"

"I'm just saying, a warning sign wouldn't hurt," I replied, finally finding my footing.

Zarek chuckled, a low, rumbling sound that sent shivers down my spine. "Noted. Next time, I'll hang a sign around my neck just for you, Firefly." He winked, and I felt my heart skip a beat.

Rolling my eyes, I tried to ignore the way his teasing sent my pulse racing. "I'm late for breakfast," I muttered, attempting to step around him, but he shifted slightly, effectively blocking my path.

"Late for breakfast, huh?" His tone was casual, but the way his eyes locked onto mine sent a wave of heat through me. "Or are you just trying to avoid me?"

I swallowed, unsure how to answer that. The truth was, avoiding Zarek and his brothers had been my strategy since I arrived. But there was something about him standing here now—so close, so undeniably captivating.

He seemed to notice my hesitation, and his smirk softened—just a fraction. "Relax, Thalia. I'm not here to cause trouble." He stepped aside, giving me a clear path. "But maybe I'll see you later?"

His words hung in the air, heavy with unspoken possibilities. I quickly brushed past him, grateful to escape the intensity of his gaze. But as I hurried towards the cafeteria, I couldn't resist glancing back over my shoulder.

Zarek was still watching me, his smirk firmly in place, eyes glinting with that same unreadable expression that left me feeling more flustered than ever.

Sitting alone at my usual spot in the cafeteria, my stomach growled in anticipation of the feast before me. Just as I lifted a spoonful of fluffy eggs to my mouth, a voice shattered the peaceful quiet.

"Where did you go last night?" El's tone was sharp enough to cut through butter. I froze, spoon midway to my mouth, completely caught off guard by her sudden appearance.

She plopped down across from me, arms crossed, her usually vibrant eyes narrowed with suspicion. Her normally flowing hair was pulled back into a messy bun, and despite the casual look, her expression screamed anything but relaxed. If looks could kill, I'd be six feet under. She was definitely pissed.

"I—" I started, but the look on her face made it clear she wasn't in the mood for excuses. "I went for a walk," I said carefully, setting the spoon down and trying to appear nonchalant.

"A walk?" El repeated, her voice dripping with disbelief. "By yourself? In the woods? At night?" Each word was punctuated with a glare that could have melted steel.

"Well, yeah," I mumbled, trying not to sound defensive. "I just needed some air. You were in the middle of your epic saga about accidentally setting your neighbor's prize-winning petunias on fire, and I figured I wouldn't be gone long."

El's eyes narrowed further, her fingers tapping a staccato rhythm on the table. "You know how dangerous that is, right? The wards only go so far, and the woods... Well, let's just say things can get nasty out there. Not to mention you disappeared without telling anyone." Her voice softened slightly, but her frustration was still palpable.

I blinked, surprised by the genuine concern in her voice. "I didn't mean to worry you," I said sincerely, feeling a pang of guilt. "I honestly didn't think it would be a big deal."

She huffed, leaning back in her chair and crossing her arms tighter. "Well, it is a big deal. You can't just wander off like that, especially not here. This place is crawling with things you and I don't even fully understand."

I sighed, rubbing my forehead as the events of last night flashed through my mind. The strange structure that had vanished, Nox materializing out of thin air... "I wasn't alone for long," I admitted, hesitant to reveal too much.

El's eyes widened. "Wait, what do you mean? Who found you?"

I hesitated, biting my lip. "Nox," I finally confessed, watching her face carefully for her reaction.

Her expression shifted instantly, her jaw dropping slightly before snapping shut. "Nox?" she repeated, her voice a little too high-pitched. "What do you mean, *Nox?*"

I shrugged, trying to downplay the encounter. "He materialized out of nowhere and told me I shouldn't be in the woods. Gave me the usual icy glare and then stormed off. Nothing happened," I explained, rolling my eyes at the memory of his arrogant demeanor.

El stared at me, her eyes searching mine, before letting out a long, slow breath. "Thalia, you really have a knack for attracting the strangest situations," she muttered, shaking her head in disbelief. "First, you catch the attention of all three brothers, and now you're wandering into their territory at night."

"What do you mean, *their* territory?" I asked, my brow furrowing in confusion.

El pressed her lips into a thin line, her fingers drumming against the table as she carefully considered her words. "The Shadow Brothers... they have more control over certain parts of the academy grounds," she explained slowly, her voice laced with caution. "Especially places like the forest."

She leaned forward conspiratorially, lowering her voice. "It's not just the forest, Thalia. There are areas of Nexara that nobody messes with—places that fall under... their domain." Her red-tinted eyes darted around, making sure no one was eavesdropping. "I don't know all the details, but from what I've heard, the forest —particularly the deeper parts—is off-limits for a reason."

I frowned, recalling the eerie feeling I had last night—how the shadows seemed to both beckon and repel. "And Nox just... appears out of nowhere?" I asked, still unsettled by his sudden appearance.

"Exactly," El confirmed, her expression growing serious. "They have a connection to the dark, to the shadows. Some say it's part of their power, their gift—or curse, depending on who you ask. That's probably why Nox found you so quickly. You were trespassing in their space."

I swallowed hard, her words settling uneasily in my stomach. "So, you're saying they have some sort of... claim on the forest?"

El nodded grimly. "That, and a few other places. No one really talks about it openly, but everyone knows to stay clear of those areas unless they want trouble. And you, Thalia, just went waltzing right into one of them."

"Well, *fuck*," I muttered, a wave of frustration and anxiety washing over me. "So now they think I'm... what? Trespassing? Spying?"

El sighed, rubbing her temples. "No, but it's not the kind of attention you want, trust me. They don't care about the rules like the rest of us. They do what they want, and no one challenges them."

I bit my lip, the weight of her words sinking in. "But why didn't Nox just... do something about it then? He could have easily scared me off or worse."

El let out a small huff, leaning back in her chair. "That's the million-dollar question, isn't it?" she mused, staring off into the distance as if trying to decipher a complex puzzle. "Nox is unpredictable. Hell, all of them are. But the fact that he didn't do anything outright... that's what's strange."

I crossed my arms, a shiver running down my spine. "Strange how?"

Her fingers tapped rhythmically against the table, a nervous habit that suddenly became more pronounced. "Look, most people who wander into their territory don't leave without... consequences. The fact that Nox didn't make you regret it on the spot means there's something more going on. Maybe he's testing you, watching how you react. Or maybe—" El hesitated, her eyes locking onto mine with a seriousness I'd rarely seen. "Maybe he's *curious*."

A chill ran down my spine at the word. *Curious?* About *me*? The thought was both unsettling and strangely intriguing. Why would someone like Nox, shrouded in mystery and power, be interested in me at all?

"I don't want their curiosity," I muttered, my voice thick with apprehension. "I just want to get through this academy without being dragged into their mess."

"I get it, Thalia. I really do," El said sympathetically, her voice softer now. "But at this academy, avoiding their mess might be harder than you think. Especially with Damon." She hesitated, her tone growing more serious. "His bloodline makes the academy... nervous. Let's just say it's not exactly a comforting legacy. His father is basically the boogeyman of the Shadow Kingdom. Cruel, powerful, and completely without remorse."

I sighed, the weight of it all crashing down on me. Just when I thought I was starting to get a handle on this place, it turned out I'd been unknowingly stumbling into the lion's den. Worse yet, the lions had apparently taken an interest in me.

As if on cue, the psycho brothers made their entrance into the cafeteria, their presence an undeniable force that rippled through the room like a shockwave. Conversations stuttered to a halt, forks froze midair, and the once-bustling energy dimmed as every eye in the room snapped towards them. An invisible aura seemed to command the crowd to part, creating a path for the brothers as they moved with an almost predatory grace. No one dared to break the unspoken rule of deference that surrounded them.

Nox led the way, his signature black hoodie pulled low, casting his face in perpetual shadow. The effect was both mesmerizing and unnerving, as if he were a creature of the night, comfortable only in darkness. His hands were tucked casually into his pockets, his stride long and deliberate, radiating an unsettling calm that hinted at a dangerous power simmering beneath the surface.

Behind him strode Zarek, his posture relaxed, almost languid. He wore a fitted black shirt and jeans that molded to his athletic frame, his shoulders loose, but his eyes gleamed with a mischievous glint, scanning the room with a barely concealed smirk. He exuded an air of someone who thrived on the hushed whispers and stolen glances, reveling in the attention without needing to demand it.

Damon, however, was a stark contrast to his brothers. Dressed in black jeans and a crisp white button-up shirt that accentuated his broad shoulders and lean physique, he moved with an almost regal grace. Every step was deliberate, every glance measured. His storm-blue eyes—cold and sharp as shards of ice—seemed to dissect everything they landed on, unaffected by the nervous reactions of those around him. He exuded an air of authority and power, the kind that could command a room with a single look. His raven hair was styled impeccably, though that same single rebellious strand fell across his forehead, lending him a subtly unruly edge. A faint shadow of stubble framed his jawline, adding a rugged charm to his otherwise polished appearance—as if every detail, from his attire to his demeanor, had been meticulously crafted to project an image of absolute control.

They moved as one, a perfectly synchronized unit, their gazes fixed ahead, indifferent to the people parting before them. The trio claimed their usual table—the one no one dared to occupy, not even in their absence. It was theirs, a silent claim of ownership that resonated louder than any spoken word.

I shifted uncomfortably in my seat, trying to shrink into the background, to become invisible. But it was impossible to ignore the weight of their presence, the way the very air thrummed with their power.

Damon's eyes flicked in my direction, his sharp gaze piercing me like a laser. There was no warmth, no amusement in his stare—only cold calculation, as if he were dissecting me, assessing my every flaw and vulnerability. I quickly averted my gaze, hoping he wouldn't notice the tremor in my hands.

Zarek, on the other hand, seemed to relish the tension. His lips curled into a slow, knowing smirk as his eyes lingered on me, a silent challenge in their depths. It was as if he were privy to some inside joke, some elaborate game I was unknowingly playing. His smirk tightened the knot in my stomach—a blunt reminder that I was caught in a web I didn't understand.

Perfect, I thought, sinking lower in my seat, wishing I could disappear. El shot me a knowing glance, one eyebrow arched, as if she could practically see the waves of tension radiating off me.

Why did I have this uncanny knack for attracting the worst kind of attention? Damon's chilling stare still lingered in my mind, a silent promise of something I couldn't quite grasp. And Zarek's playful smirk was a clear indication that whatever their next move was, I wouldn't be ready for it.

But it was Nox who truly unsettled me. Even though he didn't look my way, I could feel his presence like a suffocating weight pressing down on me. It was as though the shadows themselves emanated from him, reaching out with icy fingers to brush against my skin. His aura was that of a gathering storm—a silent tempest of power held in check, waiting to be unleashed.

I risked a glance in his direction, but his hood remained stubbornly in place, obscuring his face in shadow. He sat with an almost casual detachment, yet I couldn't shake the feeling that he was acutely aware of my every move. It was as if he didn't need to acknowledge me directly for me to feel the intensity of his attention, the way his mere presence could bend the atmosphere to his will.

El shifted beside me, her gaze flitting between me and the brothers as if trying to decipher the silent communication passing between us. She didn't say a word, but her red-tinted eyes held a mixture of concern and curiosity.

It was absurd. I felt like a fly caught in a spiderweb, dangling precariously on the edge of some unseen danger. I clenched my fists beneath the table, my nails digging into my palms, trying to ground myself—to focus on anything but the three men who held the room captive.

Why did they have this effect on me? Why did their mere presence evoke so much within me—a swirling vortex of emotions I couldn't decipher? And why, of all the students in this academy, did they seem to fixate on *me*? What had I done—what was I— that made me such a threat in their eyes? Was it my lineage, something hidden within me that they could sense?

The questions churned within me, a constant nagging hum beneath the surface of my thoughts. I desperately wanted to understand the strange, almost magnetic pull they had on me— the way they could make me feel so utterly vulnerable and exposed with a single glance, as if they were peeling back layers I hadn't even known existed. I wanted to know why they watched me with such intensity, why they toyed with me, why they seemed to be everywhere I turned, their shadows lurking just beyond my peripheral vision. Were they testing me? Taunting me?

But most of all, I wanted to know what they wanted from me. What dark purpose did I serve in their intricate, unspoken game?

Chapter 5

Thalia's POV

The weekend vanished in the blink of an eye. I was stretching with El, preparing for Combat Training, when James approached. His boyish smile was charming —a welcome change from the intense stares I had grown used to. He settled beside me, casually joining in our stretches, his presence bringing a lighter energy to the morning.

James and El were exchanging playful banter about today's challenge, teasing each other about who would emerge victorious. His blond hair gleamed in the sunlight, and every so often, he'd flash that charming smile—the kind that could easily put anyone at ease. He casually mentioned being a wolf shifter and, almost as an afterthought, that he was next in line to become alpha of his pack. His confidence was subtle, yet I still couldn't decipher whether he was flirting or simply being friendly.

Lost in my own thoughts, I nearly missed El's sharp whisper. "Uh-oh, they look extra pissy today. Even Zarek looks like he wants to kill you," she warned, her gaze darting behind me.

Dread coiled in my gut, a serpent tightening its grip with every inch I turned my head. And sure enough, there they were—arms crossed, their gazes laser-focused, each glare a venomous strike that made my skin prickle. Zarek's, especially, hit me with the force of a physical blow.

"Fuck this," I mumbled, a wave of bitterness washing over me. Weeks of this silent intimidation—enough icy stares to freeze over hell itself. My patience had reached its breaking point. I was done being a character in their silent, psychological thriller.

Without a second thought, I raised my middle finger in their direction, a surge of reckless satisfaction coursing through me.

Their reaction was instantaneous. Their hardened masks shattered. For a fleeting second, shock registered in their eyes—a flicker of disbelief that vanished as quickly as it appeared. A laugh escaped me, sharp and unexpected, the satisfaction of catching them off guard exhilarating.

"Gods, I'm so fucking sick of them," I muttered, the words laced with a bitter frustration.

El snorted beside me, a lazy stretch rippling through her body. "Their problem, not yours," she drawled, amusement lacing her voice. "Besides," she added, a grin spreading across her face, "that was absolutely priceless."

Professor Lorian's booming voice echoed across the training field, his hands clapping together to command attention. "Today's task will take place in the forest." He paused, letting the words hang in the air as he surveyed the students. I couldn't help the ironic chuckle that escaped my lips.

The forest? I thought. *Isn't that their territory?*

Professor Lorian finished outlining the rules with another sharp clap, signaling the start of the exercise. The challenge was simple: pairs race to locate a hidden flag. Before I could even turn to survey my options, James appeared beside me, his grin bright and infectious. He took a step forward, hand outstretched in invitation. But the smile faltered, his eyes darting above me, his expression hardening. A frown creased my brow as I followed his gaze, curious what had caused such an abrupt shift.

A shadow fell over me as Nox stepped behind me, his presence suffocating, his hooded face obscuring any readable expression. "She's already got a partner," he stated flatly, his voice a chilling blade that cut through the air.

"Yeah, no, I don't," I retorted, not bothering to hide my frustration. Nox might have a penchant for lurking and a desire to see me dead, but that didn't give him the right to dictate my partnerships. I turned back to James, ready to solidify our alliance, when I felt a shift in the air.

El stepped in beside us, a tight smile plastered on her face. Before I could utter another word, she seized James's arm, her grip firm. "James," she chirped, "you can be my partner, right?" The forced sweetness of her tone and the tug on his arm betrayed her true intentions. As they walked away, El cast a knowing glance over her shoulder, her eyes pleading with me to let it go.

I sighed, turning to face Nox, who stood rooted in place, arms crossed, his gaze fixed on the departing pair. His expression was a mask of icy fury, the air around him thick with simmering rage.

So much for a fun training session.

I stormed towards the forest, my pace quickening, desperate to put some distance between Nox and myself. A futile effort, really —his strides were twice the length of mine—but the act of ignoring him, of *choosing* to ignore him, offered a sliver of control. I could feel Damon and Zarek trailing behind, their presence an ominous shadow looming over me as I crossed the threshold into the overgrown trees.

Anger simmered beneath my skin, intensifying with every step. I didn't care about their supposed danger, or the academy's insistence on appeasing them. Their minds had been made up the moment I arrived. I was an outsider, an anomaly, a blemish on their pristine landscape. They didn't need to voice their disdain— every frigid glare, every dismissive glance had already spoken volumes.

And I was done with it.

My thoughts drifted back to my childhood, to the memories of isolation, of being the unwanted, the discarded. Abandoned as a baby, left to navigate a world that seemed to have no place for me. But I survived. I had clawed my way through, and I wasn't about to let anyone, not even the so-called elite of Nexara, diminish my worth.

Powerful or not, they would know I was not the one to back down. I was done being treated like a mistake. I would carve my own place, forge my own path, and demand the respect I deserved.

"So, if this is *your* territory," I drawled, letting sarcasm lace my tone, "we should win this with no problem, right?" I turned to face Nox, meeting his impenetrable gaze. The air crackled with unspoken tension.

For a fleeting second, I thought I saw the hint of a smirk play at the corner of his lips, a flicker of amusement quickly extinguished. "Just stay close," he said, his voice a low, controlled rumble that revealed nothing.

I rolled my eyes at his non-answer, irritation prickling my skin. *Stay close?* As if that was the issue. If he expected obedience and blind compliance, he was in for a rude awakening.

Without another glance, I bolted. My feet pounding the forest floor before Zarek and Damon could even reach us. Direction was irrelevant; escape was the goal. The moment Nox assumed command, treating me like an obedient child, a defiant fire ignited within me. I would not be leashed, my pace dictated by their whims.

Branches snapped beneath my feet as I tore through the jungly undergrowth, my heart pounding a rhythm of rebellion. The weight of their stares bore down on me, their irritation a palpable force.

Good. Let them fume. I wasn't here to play their games.

Slowing my breath, I attuned myself to the stillness of the forest. A strange awareness settled over me—I could sense the presence of other students, their movements like ripples in a pond—though the forest remained eerily silent. The dense covering swallowed the sunlight, casting long, dancing shadows that played tricks on my eyes. The air hung heavy, thick with an unseen energy that set my nerves on edge.

Then, I felt it—a subtle tug, a whisper in the shadows, pulling me eastward. The darkness seemed to shift and sway, beckoning me forward. Instead of resisting, I surrendered. My feet moved instinctively, weaving through the heavy foliage with an unexplainable certainty.

The sensation of being led by the shadows was both unsettling and strangely comforting, as if I were fulfilling a hidden purpose.

I didn't look back. They were undoubtedly following, but their presence no longer mattered. I maintained my pace, gliding through the trees, each step purposeful and light. A surge of adrenaline coursed through me, invigorated by the cool breeze that kissed my skin and urged me onward. For the first time in what felt like an eternity, I felt truly alive, free from their suffocating presence, guided by an unseen force.

The forest became a blur of shadows and light, my senses sharpening with every stride. Defiance mingled with an exhilarating sense of freedom—a heady cocktail of breaking free and forging my own path.

After what felt like an eternity of running, I burst through a thicket of branches, their rough bark scraping my skin. I winced at the sting but pressed onward, adrenaline propelling me forward. Suddenly, the dense foliage gave way to a sun-drenched clearing, the brightness almost blinding after the shadowy depths of the forest. The air here was lighter, the vibrant green meadow a stark contrast to the oppressive woods.

And there, in the center of the clearing, stood the flag—a solitary beacon swaying gently in the breeze. My heart leaped.

This is it.

I had the flag in my sights, victory a mere heartbeat away, when a shift at the edge of the clearing drew my attention. A figure emerged, tall and imposing, bathed in the golden light of the afternoon sun. Her hair, the shade of shimmering dark violet, framed a face that was both strikingly beautiful and fiercely determined. She moved with a feline grace, her gaze fixed on the flag, her every step radiating an aura of unwavering confidence. This was someone accustomed to winning, someone who saw the flag not as a goal, but as an entitlement.

Her eyes, the color of glacial ice, met mine for a fleeting moment —a silent assessment passing between us. In that instant, I knew this was more than a race; it was a clash of wills. A battle for dominance. The air crackled with unspoken challenge, the sudden awareness of a formidable adversary.

A primal surge of adrenaline coursed through my veins, igniting a competitive fire within me. This was no longer just about proving myself to Nox and his brothers. It was about proving myself to *me*. Without hesitation, I launched myself forward, my muscles coiling and releasing with a newfound power. The forest floor blurred beneath my feet, the wind whipping through my hair as I poured every ounce of strength and determination into the pursuit.

Victory was within reach—my fingertips grazing the silken fabric of the flag. But in a cruel twist of fate, a force like a runaway train slammed into me, sending me hurtling backward. The world dissolved into a chaotic blur of colors and disorienting motion, the wind screaming a symphony of chaos past my ears.

With a bone-jarring crunch, I crashed to the earth, my body skidding across the unforgiving terrain. The air was ripped from my lungs, leaving me gasping as a searing pain exploded in my back. Dazed and disoriented, I lay sprawled in the dirt, the world tilting precariously around me. A wave of nausea washed over me, and I fought the urge to give in to the darkness encroaching on my vision.

"Better luck next time, human," the girl sneered, her laughter a grating melody that pierced through the haze of my pain. It wasn't just the words, but the condescending tone—the way her lip curled with disdain—that ignited a spark that fueled the inferno of rage burning in my soul. I forced my blurred vision to focus, finding her standing over the flag, her eyes gleaming with a smug satisfaction that sent a wave of heat coursing through my veins.

The clearing began to fill with students. I caught glimpses of wide eyes and smirking faces, but their reactions were a distant blur compared to the maelstrom of emotions raging within me.

Gritting my teeth against the throbbing in my head, I slowly pushed myself to my feet, the world swaying precariously around me. Each movement sent a fresh jolt of agony through my body, but I refused to give them the satisfaction of seeing me crumble. My gaze snapped to Nox, Damon, and Zarek, who stood at the edge of the clearing, their expressions a study in contrasts. Damon wore a mask of cruel amusement, his lips curled into a predatory smirk, clearly relishing my defeat. Nox, as always, remained an enigma, his face an impenetrable wall, betraying no emotion.

But it was Zarek who caught my attention, his reaction a stark contrast to his brothers' indifference or amusement. His eyes, usually a cool, detached gold, now burned with an intense, almost fiery hue—fixed on me with an expression of barely concealed frustration. His jaw was clenched, the muscles in his neck corded with tension, and his hands were fisted at his sides, as if he were restraining himself from some unseen force. It was a reaction I hadn't expected—a flicker of something akin to protectiveness in his usually cold gaze—and it sparked a flicker of confusion within me.

For a moment, our eyes locked, his frustration battling with an emotion I couldn't quite decipher. Was it concern? Annoyance? Or something else entirely? The intensity of his gaze sent a shiver down my spine, a strange mix of apprehension and an unfamiliar warmth. Then, as quickly as it appeared, the emotion vanished, replaced by his usual mask of indifference. He turned away, his shoulders rigid, leaving me to grapple with the bewildering encounter and the lingering question of what, exactly, had just transpired between us.

"Thanks for the fucking help, *partner*," I spat, venom lacing every syllable. My shoulder connected with Nox in a satisfying thud, a petty act that definitely hurt me more than him.

He barely shifted, a testament to his strength and unwavering composure. But beneath that stoic mask, I noticed a flicker of enjoyment, a hint of surprise that I dared to challenge him, even in such a childish manner. His head tilted slightly, those emerald eyes following my retreat.

"Told you to stay close," he observed, his voice a low rumble that resonated through the clearing. The words were simple, a mere statement of fact, yet they carried an undercurrent of something more. Was it a reprimand? A warning?

I didn't bother to reply, my anger and frustration propelling me forward. The clearing blurred around me, the cheers and jeers of the other students fading into a distant hum as I focused on putting as much distance between myself and Nox as possible. But even as I walked away, I could feel his gaze burning into my back.

I bypassed the training grounds and headed straight for the sanctuary of my room, ignoring any lingering obligations to Professor Lorian. He could get his explanations from Nox. I was done. The adrenaline that had fueled me earlier had long since evaporated, leaving behind a residue of exhaustion and simmering rage.

The sight that greeted me in the bathroom mirror was a jarring reflection of my inner turmoil. All I could see in the mirror was the wreckage—a reflection of failure staring back at me with hollow, stormy eyes. Dirt and dried blood clung to my skin and clothes. My once high ponytail had surrendered to the chaos, strands of hair escaping their confines, interwoven with twigs and leaves, a testament to my wild flight through the forest. My stomach churned at the reflection, a reminder of my physical and emotional exhaustion.

Anger flared—hot and consuming, tightening my chest and blurring my vision. It surged like wildfire, licking at the edges of my composure, threatening to reduce what little strength I had left to ash. This wasn't just a defeat—it was a public dismantling of every defense I had, leaving me bare, exposed, and vulnerable.

My hands gripped the edge of the sink, knuckles white, the cool porcelain biting into my skin. My reflection glared back at me, stormy and defiant, but beneath it, I saw the cracks forming. My jaw clenched so tightly it ached, teeth grinding as if sheer force alone could hold me together.

But it wasn't enough.

The tide of frustration roared in my ears, drowning out reason. Every step today had been a stumble. Every challenge, a sharp reminder of how far I still had to go—of how out of place I truly was here. The weight of it crushed me, threatening to collapse my chest and squeeze the air from my lungs.

A sharp, ragged breath escaped my lips. "Pathetic," I spat at my reflection, the word cutting through the thick silence like a blade.

Hot tears filled the corners of my eyes, a final insult to my resolve. But I refused to let them fall. They wouldn't win. Not the tears. Not the doubt. Not the crushing voice inside me screaming that I would never be enough.

Chapter 6

Zarek's POV

It had been days since I last saw her, and the deprivation was starting to get to me—a persistent itch beneath my skin that no amount of distraction could soothe. She had an unsettling effect on me, a perplexing dissonance I couldn't quite reconcile with my usual experiences. From the moment our eyes met across the crowded cafeteria, I was captivated—not just by her undeniable beauty, but by a depth, a fire that burned beneath the surface, hinting at a spirit as untamed as the wild forests of my homeland.

I had pursued her, naturally, with the effortless charm inherent to my fae nature, expecting the same effortless conquest I was accustomed to. But Thalia, unlike the countless others who threw themselves to my allure, resisted. And her resistance sparked a flame within me that I hadn't felt. Why? Women were drawn to me, enchanted by the power I exuded, the world I could offer. They never sought to delve deeper, content with the surface illusion—the seductive glamour that veiled my true nature.

But my Firefly... She was different. She saw through the glamour, resisted my magic with a strength of will that both intrigued and frustrated me. It was a game, a dance of wills, and I found myself inexplicably drawn to her—captivated by her refusal to conform. It was a novelty, yes—but more than that, it was a refreshing change from the predictable submission of others.

And beneath the frustration, a deeper emotion stirred within me —a grudging admiration. A burgeoning respect for the woman. She was a wildflower amidst a garden of cultivated roses, her untamed spirit a light in a world of darkness. I found myself craving her presence, wanting to understand the depths of her, to unravel the secrets hidden behind her guarded gaze.

The days without her stretched into an eternity, each breath a reminder of her absence. I found myself seeking her out in crowds, my senses hyper-alert. The scent of her—a unique blend of calming lavender and earthy sage—lingered in my memory. Even the faintest whisper of that intoxicating aroma, carried on the breeze or clinging to a stray lock of hair, was enough to send a jolt of electricity through my veins.

The echo of her laughter, a melody that haunted my thoughts. And the flash of her fiery hair, a vibrant flame amidst a sea of mundane hues, was like a beacon—drawing my gaze, igniting a spark of longing within me.

When I saw Mira casting against Thalia, something inside me snapped. My blood turned to fire, and a rage, a darkness I had long kept dormant, clawed at the surface, threatening to consume me. The intensity of the emotion was staggering, an unfamiliar fury that shook me to my core. *Why?* The question echoed through my mind, a desperate plea for understanding in the face of this overwhelming surge of protectiveness. Why did her pain resonate so deeply within me? Why did I feel such a profound need to protect this fragile human?

But even as the need to protect her overwhelmed me, a darker thought crept in. Why is she even *here*? The academy isn't for ordinary mortals—it's a haven for beings of immense power, a crucible where the supernatural hone their abilities. How did *she* receive an invitation if she's just a human?

Nexara Academy doesn't make mistakes; its wards, its very foundations, are designed to repel those who don't belong. And yet, her presence felt like a glaring anomaly, a disruptive crack in the constructed order of things. It was as if someone had placed a flickering candle into a hall of mirrors—captivating, but undeniably vulnerable. There had to be a reason, a hidden purpose behind her arrival. I just couldn't fathom what it could be. Whether it was the academy's oversight or something far more deliberate, her being here made her vulnerable.

The last time our paths crossed—after that humiliating defeat in the clearing—I had glimpsed a flicker of vulnerability in her eyes, a depth of pain that hinted at a breaking point. An unfamiliar urge to soothe those wounds, to lift the weight she carried, took root within me. And now, she had vanished, retreating behind the fortress of her own making, leaving me to grapple with this unfamiliar turmoil.

My fists clenched involuntarily, the familiar surge of power rippling through my veins, the darkness within me straining against its bonds. I fixed my gaze on the floor, the cool stone a stark contrast to the fire raging inside. I fought to keep my mind from drifting back to Thalia, but it was a losing battle. No matter how hard I tried to focus, her image kept intruding, her storm-grey eyes and that maddening strength of hers pulling at my thoughts like a siren's song.

Tension filled the air as Nox returned, his presence a noticeable weight that pressed down on the room. His usual calmness was laced with an underlying restlessness, a barely contained energy that spoke volumes. His shifts had become increasingly erratic, his control wavering that bordered on dangerous. We were forced to skirt the edges of the academy's wards, isolating ourselves from the other students to prevent any... *incidents*. He remained tight-lipped about the cause, the trigger for his beast—but a suspicion festered within me, a truth I was reluctant to confront.

It was the same woman who haunted my every waking thought. She was the reason for Nox's internal chaos, just as she was for mine.

The memory of Combat Training surfaced, a puzzle piece clicking into place. Nox, typically aloof and indifferent, had been swift to claim Thalia as his partner, intercepting that preening peacock, James, before he could open his mouth. It was an act so out of character that it sent a jolt of surprise through both Damon and me. And then there was the look on his face when he saw James attempting to flirt with her—a fleeting shadow that crossed his features, a flash of something dark and possessive.

A heavy silence had fallen between us brothers, an unspoken acknowledgment of the rabid emotions swirling beneath the surface. We haven't spoken a word about it, each of us grappling with this unfamiliar territory in our own way.

Damon on the other hand, retreated into a facade of indifference, acting as though Thalia were a phantom, a figment of our imaginations. He seemed to believe that if he ignored her, the unsettling pull we had to her would simply dissipate like morning mist. But his carefully constructed indifference was a brittle mask, cracking under the strain of his suppressed emotions. I saw the way his shadows—those living extensions of his own being. They reacted to her presence—reaching for her in an almost desperate way, as if drawn in by an irresistible force. He always reigned them back in, of course, his expression carefully blank. But the effort it took to maintain that facade was evident in the subtle clench of his jaw, the flicker of frustration in his usually placid eyes.

Damon, the eldest of us three, had always been the steady one— the anchor in our chaotic existence. His presence was a calming force, a reassuring constant in a world of disarray. It took a cataclysmic event to even ruffle his feathers, and he never allowed his actions to be dictated by fleeting emotions. But lately, even Damon's ironclad control seemed strained, his composure faltering whenever she was near.

It was a testament to Thalia's potent influence—her undeniable charm—that even Damon, the most disciplined of us all, struggled to maintain his composure in her presence.

"It's getting worse," Damon's voice, low and laced with a rare tension, sliced through the silence of the room. Nox and I turned towards him, a silent acknowledgment of the shared dread that hung heavy in the air. His words were merely confirmation of what we had all been sensing.

I scrubbed a hand over my face, frustration evident in my shoulders. Maintaining focus was like trying to grasp smoke—every time I thought I had a hold, it slipped through my fingers, leaving me with nothing but lingering thoughts of her.

Damn it, Zarek, I cursed inwardly. The self-reproach felt bitter on my tongue.

A destructive force was stirring, reaching out from the shadows—and it would demand our unwavering attention. The thought of my captivating Firefly caught in the crossfire sent a shiver of unease through me.

Nox remained silent, his face an impenetrable mask. But the tension emanating from him was undeniable. Even Damon showed signs of strain, his shadows writhed and flickered with a nervous energy. We were all tethered to this invisible thread of dread, the ominous pull of something ancient and lethal awakening.

And we had to be ready. Not just for ourselves, but for *her*.

Chapter 7

Thalia's POV

B anging on my door jolted me from my studies, the sound echoing through the stifling silence of my room. Dusty textbooks and crumpled papers littered my desk—a testament to the days I'd spent holed up here. My door was my only shield against the whispers and stares that followed me everywhere. Even the teachers seemed to pity me, their voices hushed, their eyes averted as they handed me assignments to complete in the solitude of my dorm.

"GIRL, I KNOW YOU'RE IN THERE!" Her sharp voice boomed through the door. "I will burn this door down if you don't open up in five... four... three—"

I scrambled from my desk, throwing the door open. Relief flooded through me. El stood there, arms crossed, a triumphant smirk on her face.

"You really think I wouldn't follow through?" she teased, pushing past me into the room, bringing with her a gust of fresh air and the faint scent of vanilla. She marched straight to my bed, scattering a pile of notebooks as she plopped down with an ease that suggested ownership.

I glared at her, my cheeks burning. "Couldn't you at least wait for an invitation?"

El just grinned, stretching out on the bed. A beat of silence hung in the air, thick with unspoken questions.

"Listen," she finally declared, "I know it seems bad, and it kind of is—but no need to worry. I'm here."

I couldn't help but roll my eyes. "Comforting," I muttered, leaning against the doorframe. Yet despite her lightheartedness, there was something about El's presence that made the suffocating weight on my chest feel a little lighter.

"Hey, no sarcasm!" She shot back, pointing at me with a mock scowl that couldn't hide her playful intent. "I'm serious, Thalia. You've been hiding here long enough. It's time to get back out there—I let you have a few days, but now it's over."

"I needed time to heal; I don't know what you're talking about," I mumbled, my gaze falling to the cluttered desk. I couldn't meet her eyes, not when they saw right through me. I wasn't ready to face it all. Every time I pictured myself stepping back into the hallway, I felt the sting of eyes on my back, and heard the snickers echoing in my ears. The memory of that day, of being shoved to the ground, of the laughter and the whispers, still burned like a fresh wound. I could almost taste the dirt in my mouth.

El propped herself up on her elbows, her expression softening as she studied me. "I get it. I really do. But hiding away isn't going to make it disappear."

Her words hit me like a punch to the gut. I winced, but kept my back to her, staring blankly at the stack of assignments as if they held the answers I needed. She wasn't wrong, I knew that. But knowing didn't make it any easier to confront the knot of fear twisting in my stomach. My hands clenched, nails digging into my palms. A wave of heat flushed through me, and I had to bite back the urge to scream, to tell El to leave, to let me wallow in my misery. But beneath the anger and the fear, a flicker of gratitude warmed me. I was glad she was here.

"And besides," El continued, her tone turning playful again, "someone's gotta knock Mira off her pedestal. She's been acting like you ran off and left the academy."

I stiffened at that. That bitch thinks I left? The thought of her parading around, that superior smirk plastered across her face, sent a surge of anger coursing through me. I could practically see her—nose held high, lips curled into that infuriatingly perfect smile that made her look like she owned the whole academy. El knew exactly what she was doing, and it was working. The urge to get back out there, to prove her—and everyone else—wrong, was building within me, a fire slowly melting the ice of my fear.

"Let's get off campus and go to town," El suggested, her excitement bubbling over. "We could use a change of scenery, and I know just the place for a coffee date."

"Fineee," I groaned, dragging the word out as I finally relented. "Let me shower, and then we can go."

El grinned, hopping off the bed like she'd just won a prize. "That's the spirit! I'll be waiting out here, so don't even think about backing out."

I rolled my eyes as I headed toward the bathroom, the cool tile a welcome relief against my bare feet. I couldn't suppress the small smile tugging at my lips. More than El's persistence, more than the distraction she offered, I was grateful for her unwavering belief in me. Even when I doubted myself, she never did.

"Don't take too long!" El called after me.

WE RODE THE BUS TO HAVENBROOK, A LITTLE TOWN nestled in the forests. As we stepped off the bus onto the cobblestone streets, the morning light painted the scene in a golden hue. It felt like we had stumbled into a forgotten corner of the world, where time moved at a slower, gentler pace. The market square bustled with activity—a vibrant mix of sights, sounds, and smells. A magnificent fountain, carved with figures of mythical creatures, held court at its center. The water cascading down its tiers with a soothing melody. All around it, a maze of narrow alleyways and winding lanes branched off into town.

We wandered past timber-framed buildings with gabled roofs, their walls decorated with colorful murals showing scenes of local legends and folklore. Window boxes overflowed with flowers in every shade imaginable, spilling onto the streets below. Market stalls, draped with brightly striped awnings, lined the square, offering a tempting selection of goods. Merchants, their faces weathered by the sun and wind, displayed their wares with pride —handcrafted jewelry, intricately woven tapestries, baskets overflowing with ripe fruits and vegetables. The air, crisp and clean, carried the enticing scents of freshly baked bread, roasted meats, and sweet pastries, mingling with the fragrant perfume of blooming flowers. Laughter and lively chatter echoed through the square, punctuated by the cheerful calls of vendors pushing their goods.

In the distance, a grand stone tower, its silhouette stark against the azure sky, stood watch over the town. A flock of birds circled its peak, their cries echoing through the crisp morning air. This was Havenbrook, a place where magic seemed to linger in every stone and whisper on every breeze. A world away from the pretentious walls and hushed corridors of the academy, it offered a sense of freedom and escape that I hadn't realized how desperately I craved.

We ducked into a winding alley, its path worn smooth by time, and emerged into a hidden courtyard bathed in dappled sunlight. Tucked away in the corner, we found a little café, the front draped with cascading ivy and vibrant geraniums. The rustic sign, swaying gently in the breeze, read "The Nook."

As we stepped inside, the aroma of freshly brewed coffee enveloped us. Soft jazz music played in the background, creating a soothing ambiance. We chose a table under a striped umbrella, nestled in a cozy corner of the courtyard. El's face lit up with a smile, her eyes crinkling at the corners as she took in the peaceful surroundings.

"You know, this place reminds me a bit of my home village," El began, her gaze drifting to the bustling street as a group of children raced by, their joyous shrieks echoing through the square. "It was just like this—full of life and laughter. The houses were painted in all sorts of bright colors, just like those ones over there," she said, gesturing towards a row of buildings with facades in shades of sapphire, emerald, and ruby. "And the people were always so friendly. Everyone knew each other, and there was always something going on—festivals, markets, music in the streets..."

A small smile played on her lips. "I can almost smell the baking bread from Mrs. Willowbrook's bakery," she murmured, closing her eyes for a moment as if savoring the memory. "And hear the blacksmith's hammer ringing out..."

But the smile faded, a shadow passing over her face. "It's funny," she said, her voice barely above a whisper, "how even the happiest places can hold painful memories." She opened her eyes, a flicker of pain in their depths. "When I was younger, I went through something... incredibly humiliating. Right there in the heart of my village. It was during the annual Summer Solstice festival, with the whole clan gathered in the square. I was just a young girl then, barely old enough to control my magic..."

She paused, her gaze distant, as if reliving the scene. "There was this competition for young witches," she continued, her voice catching slightly. "Everyone expected me to fail. They thought I didn't have the fire in me—literally and figuratively."

She chuckled, but the sound held a sharp edge. "So, I spent weeks holed up, much like you, doubting myself because of what everyone else believed." Her eyes hardened, her voice taking on a steely quality. "Until one day, I just snapped. I was done hiding, done with feeling sorry for myself."

El straightened her back, her chin lifting with newfound confidence. The air around her seemed to crackle with energy, the remnants of that fiery determination. "I walked right into the middle of the village during the next gathering," she declared, her voice ringing with conviction. "Called out the strongest witch— my own cousin—and challenged her to a duel." A slow smile spread across her face. "Everyone thought I had lost my mind."

"And?" I urged, leaning forward, completely captivated by her tale.

El held my stare for a beat, the silence hanging heavy with anticipation. Then, a proud grin broke across her face. "And I won," she said, her voice filled with quiet satisfaction. "It wasn't because I was stronger—far from it. It was because I was angrier, more desperate to prove, not just to them, but to myself, that I wasn't what they labeled me to be."

The waitress arrived with our coffee, and El took a sip, her eyes sparkling with mischief. "Sometimes," she said, her voice low and conspiratorial, "you need to step into the fire—feel the flames lick at your skin, see the embers glow—to see how you'll come out on the other side."

El set down her cup, her playful demeanor fading again as she leaned back in her chair. Her brow furrowed slightly as she recalled the next chapter of her story. "After that duel," she began, her voice taking on a newfound gravity, "I knew I had to train harder than ever. I was determined to prove I wasn't just a fluke, that I could hold my own against anyone."

"It wasn't easy," she admitted. "There were days when I wanted to give up, when the exhaustion and the self-doubt crept in. But then I would remember that feeling—that surge of power when I faced my cousin—and I would push myself harder."

"I threw myself into my training like a firestorm," she continued, her eyes gleaming with the memory, "practicing my spells until my body ached, honing my control until I could summon a spark with a mere flick of my wrist. I sought out the elders, pestering them with questions, absorbing their wisdom like a sponge."

"Eventually, all that effort paid off," El said, a hint of satisfaction in her voice. "I became the strongest witch in my clan. People started seeking my advice, even the elders. Young witches looked up to me, eager to learn my techniques. My name...well, it commanded a certain respect."

She paused, a soft smile gracing her lips. "And that's when the invitation to Nexara Academy came," she continued, her eyes sparkling with the memory. "They'd heard of my abilities, of how I'd defied expectations and risen to the top. It was an honor. A validation of all my hard work I'd poured into becoming more. They wanted me to join the most prestigious school for gifted individuals."

"You might not feel it yet, Thalia," she continued, "but there's a fire in you waiting to be unleashed. Remember those weeks *I* spent hiding, doubting myself? You're there now. But you won't stay there. I know it. You're going to rise from the ashes, stronger and more powerful than ever before. Just like I did."

Her words ignited a flicker of hope within me, but the fear still lingered. "But what if I'm not *Gifted*?" I asked, my gaze falling to my hands clasped tightly in my lap.

El leaned forward, her expression fierce. "Strength isn't just about power, Thalia; it's about resilience and the willingness to face your fears. You've already taken the first step by being here today. You faced your humiliation, and now you're ready to step back into the light. Just remember, I'll be right by your side, cheering you on."

A small smile touched my lips. "Thanks, El," I said, her unwavering support easing some of the tension knotting my stomach.

"I guess it was nice not having the psycho brothers around for a bit," I replied, chuckling as I recalled the moment I had flipped them off. Their stunned expressions—a mix of shock and disbelief—had been priceless. "But I guess I can't hide away forever."

El's laughter rang out, a melodic sound that filled the cozy café. "Honestly," she said, her voice softening as her laughter subsided, "I think they're more afraid of you than you realize."

A puzzled frown creased my forehead. "Scared of *me*?" I echoed, "El, that's a good one!"

"Thalia, I'm serious!" she insisted, though a playful smirk tugged at the corners of her mouth. "Yes, they're intimidating and dangerous, but they've never focused on someone as much as they have with you." She paused, her expression turning thoughtful. "There's something about you, Thalia—something that rattles them."

"What do you mean?" I asked, my curiosity piqued.

El leaned forward, the aroma of her hazelnut coffee wafting across the table. "They don't usually care about anyone," she explained, her voice low and serious. "People steer clear of them, and they like it that way. But with you..." She paused, turning her head slightly, as if trying to solve a puzzle. "It's different. They're watching you, paying attention in a way I've never seen before."

"Well, those assholes can shove it," I retorted, throwing my hands up in exasperation. "I'm so sick of their glares. And what the hell was up with Nox? One minute he looks at me like I'm a bug he wants to squash, and the next, he wants to be my partner? What kind of game is he playing?"

"That is weird, I'll admit," El replied, a nervous laugh escaping her lips. "I felt the shift, too—which is why I pulled James away when I did. It's strange; the brothers usually partner up with each other. Professor Lorian never fights them on it."

I scrunched up my nose, a mix of bewilderment and irritation swirling within me. It was infuriating to be treated like a pawn in their twisted game, especially when I had no clue what the rules were. "Exactly!" I exclaimed, my voice laced with frustration. "It's like they're toying with me, and I have no idea why."

El nodded slowly, "Nox and his brothers can be unpredictable, and their intentions might not be clear yet. But with how Nox— out of all of them—has been acting... there's definitely something about you that's caught his attention."

"Great," I muttered, burying my face in my hands. "Just what I need—another layer of crazy on top of everything else." I let out a long sigh. "Why can't anything be simple?"

As we walked along, browsing the charming boutiques that lined Havenbrook's streets, a familiar tingling sensation prickled the back of my neck. It was a feeling I'd grown accustomed to while living in Luminaria—and hell, even at the academy—a subtle warning, like a whisper in the shadows, that something wasn't right. I paused, scanning the bustling street, my gaze flitting from the vendors pushing their goods to the groups of people absorbed in their conversations. Nothing seemed out of place... yet the unsettling feeling persisted, coiling in my stomach like a know. I tried to shake it off, chalking it up to the lingering anxiety from my recent ordeal in the forest.

"Everything okay?" El asked, her brow furrowed with concern as she noticed my sudden hesitation.

"Yeah, fine," I replied, forcing a smile, hoping to reassure her—but mostly myself. "Just a little on edge, I guess."

We continued our walk, the vibrant atmosphere of Havenbrook momentarily distracting me from the nagging unease. We stopped to admire a display of handcrafted jewelry, the designs catching the light as they swayed gently in the breeze. El pointed out a pair of earrings, their delicate silver filigree shaped like tiny dragons, their eyes sparkling with miniature gemstones.

"Those would look amazing on you," she remarked, nudging me playfully.

I laughed, the tension easing slightly. "Maybe," I replied, my fingers tracing the intricate patterns of the earrings. "But I'm not sure I can pull off the whole dragon look."

As I turned away from the display, the tingling sensation returned— stronger this time. A wave of dread washed over me, cold and suffocating, like a dark cloud descending upon my soul. I scanned the street again, my heart pounding in my chest, a sense of foreboding gripping me. The laughter and chatter of the townsfolk seemed to fade into the background, replaced by a low, ominous hum that vibrated in my bones. The bright colors of the market stalls dulled, as if a veil had been drawn over the world, casting everything in a muted, sinister light. I felt a growing sense of dread, as if something unseen was watching us, its malevolent gaze fixed upon me.

I squeezed my eyes shut, taking a deep breath as I started counting down from five, focusing on the thump of my own heart, trying to drown out the ominous hum. When I opened them, the vibrant colors of Havenbrook had returned, the laughter and noise no longer muted but ringing in the air. But the feeling—that cold, suffocating dread—was still there, clinging to me. El, thankfully, didn't notice my momentary lapse. She was engrossed in conversation with the older woman who owned the jewelry display.

"Just your imagination," I whispered to myself, the words barely audible over the bustling market sounds. But deep down, a part of me knew better than that. Something was wrong.

AS THE SUN DIPPED BELOW THE HORIZON, PAINTING the sky in fiery hues of orange and purple, we made our way back to campus. The towering trees lining the road cast long, eerie shadows that danced and swayed in the twilight breeze. I couldn't shake the unsettling thoughts that swirled in my mind, my mind constantly replaying the encounter with the beast from the night of the party.

Those emerald eyes, sharp and piercing, haunted me. Their glint cutting through the darkness. They held an intensity I'd never encountered before, both terrifying and captivating. What was it about their eyes that drew me in, despite my fear?

The memory clung to me like a vivid dream, the chill down my spine as real now as it was then. Those eyes had seemed to pierce my soul, stripping away my carefully constructed facade. Even now, a wave of unease washes over me as I recall the sheer power radiating from that creature.

"Thalia?" El's voice broke through my thoughts, pulling me back to the present. "You okay?"

I managed a shaky nod, forcing a smile despite the anxiety churning within me. The gothic spires of the academy loomed into view as the bus shuddered to a halt, signaling our arrival. A wave of relief washed over me, the familiar sight of the academy offering a sense of security, a temporary haven from the darkness that lurked beyond its walls.

As we reached the edge of the bustling courtyard, El turned to me, her eyes sparkling with an infectious enthusiasm. "I've got plans tonight," she declared, a playful sternness in her voice, "but promise me you'll be in class tomorrow."

"Yeah, yeah, I promise," I replied, rolling my eyes playfully.

With a cheerful wave, she disappeared into the crowd of students, leaving me to navigate the path towards the dorms alone. The solitude was a welcome break, allowing me to dig into the whirlwind of thoughts that plagued me. The encounter with the beast, the unsettling whispers of the shadows, the lingering unease that had taken root since as long as I could remember – all swirled within me,

Lost in the maze of my anxieties, I collided with something solid, the impact jarring me back to the present with a jolt that sent a tremor through my very core. A startled gasp escaped my lips as I stumbled, my hands grasping at empty air before finding my balance on a sturdy arm. Warmth radiated through my fingertips, I looked up, ready to offer a flustered apology, but the words evaporated before they could reach my lips.

Zarek.

But it wasn't just his presence that stole my breath. An intoxicating scent enveloped me—an unexpected blend of ocean and cedar, a fragrance that spoke of untamed wilderness and hidden depths. It filled my senses: warm and inviting, grounding yet exhilarating, a captivating blend of strength and serenity. The earthy aroma wrapped around me like a comforting embrace. It was a scent that stirred something deep within me—a primal recognition, a kindred spirit, a connection that transcended words.

"Sorry about that," a deep voice rumbled, amusement lacing his tone. "Forgot my 'Caution: May Cause Unintentional Collisions' sign." His golden-amber eyes, alight with mischief, met mine, and a faint smirk played on his lips. Zarek stood before me, his presence radiating a blend of power and playful charm. The unexpected encounter sent a jolt of surprise through me, a flutter of something unfamiliar stirring within my chest.

"Right," I retorted, folding my arms across my chest—a defensive posture that belied the flutter of something parallel to excitement in my stomach.

He chuckled, a low, harmonic sound that danced in the air between us, sending a shiver down my spine. "You know," he said, his voice a silken purr, "I'm flattered you were so lost in thought that you didn't even notice the wall of charm blocking your path."

"Charm?" I countered, arching an eyebrow, letting my sass flow freely. "I think you mean the wall of arrogance. And trust me, it's not as impressive as you think."

Zarek leaned down slightly, his expression a mixture of playful amusement and enigmatic allure. The subtle shift in his demeanor sent a ripple of awareness through me, a tingling sensation that danced across my skin. "Oh, but you're intrigued, aren't you, Firefly?" he murmured, his voice a low thrum that resonated deep within me. "There's something about me that keeps you coming back."

"More like annoyed," I shot back, my voice sharper than intended, betraying the flicker of truth in his words. I couldn't deny the undeniable pull I felt towards him, the way his presence ignited a spark within me that I couldn't quite extinguish. "What do you want, Zarek?"

"Just checking in on my favorite distraction," he replied, his smirk widening, revealing a flash of those perfectly straight, white teeth. "I haven't seen you in a while." His eyes flickered, a fleeting shadow of something unreadable crossing his features before settling back into their familiar glimmer of mischief.

"Fantastic," I retorted, my patience wearing thin. "But I really don't have time for games. So, if you'll excuse me..." I attempted to sidestep him, but he moved closer, his scent enveloping me once again. It took every ounce of willpower to resist the inexplicable pull I felt towards him—the urge to lean into his warmth, to lose myself in the depths of his eyes. He had to be using magic, some fae trick to lure me in, to weaken my defenses.

"Games?" he repeated, his voice dipping low, each word rolling off his tongue with a teasing lilt that sent shivers down my spine. His golden eyes filled with an unreadable intensity, a mixture of curiosity and challenge that made my breath catch in my throat. "Oh, I'm just getting started, Firefly," he murmured, his voice a seductive whisper. "But I promise, it's more fun when you play along."

I clenched my jaw, forcing myself to meet his gaze without flinching. "You really have nothing better to do, do you?" I shot back, my voice dripping with sarcasm, hoping to mask the tremor of anticipation that ran through me.

His smirk grew, a dangerous glint sparking in his eyes. "Nope," he admitted, his voice a low rumble that resonated deep within me. "You're just too interesting to ignore."

I huffed, frustration bubbling to the surface, mingling with a strange sense of excitement that I couldn't quite suppress. "Well, get used to it, Zarek," I declared, my voice firm despite the erratic beating of my heart. "I'm not playing your little game."

He stepped aside with a mocking bow, his gaze never leaving mine, a silent challenge lingering in the air. "I'll see you later,

Thalia." The way my name rolled off his tongue, a sensual caress that sent a shiver down my spine, made my stomach do flips. I cursed under my breath, my cheeks flushing with a warmth that had nothing to do with the setting sun.

I shot him one last glare, a poor attempt to mask the undeniable attraction I felt, before brushing past him, my heart pounding in my chest like a war drum. There was something infuriatingly charming about Zarek, a mesmerizing mix of arrogance and vulnerability that drew me in. But I refused to let myself fall under his spell, to become another pawn in his games.

Chapter 8

Thalia's POV

S tepping into the Principles of Magical Theory classroom, my gaze instinctively sought out Nox, drawn to his familiar presence at the back. Our eyes met for a fleeting moment before he quickly turned his attention back to his book. A surprising pang of disappointment—a sting of rejection—echoed through me.

He's finally moving on, I told myself, attempting to push down the unexpected ache in my chest. *This is good. This is what I wanted.*

Mira's voice, sharp and laced with venom, cut through the low murmur of the classroom. "Oh, look who decided to crawl back," she sneered, her words dripping with disdain. "Was it not understood that a human shouldn't be here? Or are you just *stupid*?"

She rose from her seat in the first row, a picture of arrogant confidence, her cronies flanking her like loyal guard dogs. Their snickers echoed through the room, their eyes gleefully anticipating my reaction. A familiar anger began to simmer in my stomach—a fiery response to her blatant attempt to humiliate me.

"No, I'm fine—wasn't that bad," I responded nonchalantly, injecting a hint of dismissiveness into my tone as I turned back to my notes. My casual dismissal hung in the air. A beat of silence stretched. Mira's carefully constructed composure was starting to crack.

"Excuse me?" she sputtered, her voice laced with disbelief. "Did you just... try to *dismiss* me?"

I slowly lifted my gaze, meeting her eyes with a cool composure that hid the nerves within me. "I believe I did," I replied calmly, my voice carrying through the silent classroom. "Unless you have something relevant to say, I'm done talking."

"You insolent little—" she began, her voice rising with fury, but before she could unleash another torrent of insults, a calm, authoritative voice interrupted.

"Everyone, please be seated," Professor Walkins interrupted without missing a beat, setting his materials on the desk with a quiet authority that warranted attention.

A smirk tugged at my lips as I met Mira's eyes one last time. Her face was contorted with a mixture of fury and disbelief, her carefully crafted mask of superiority crumbling before my eyes. It was a small victory, but a satisfying one. This "giftless" human wasn't about to take it lying down. I held her gaze for a beat, a silent challenge simmering between us, before turning back to the front of the room, a newfound sense of confidence blooming within me.

Game on, Mira.

The lecture stretched on, each minute an eternity. My attention, however, was hopelessly ensnared by Nox's presence at the back of the classroom. It was as if an invisible thread connected us, a taut line of awareness that vibrated with unspoken tension. The professor's voice droned on, a monotonous backdrop to my own thoughts, but my focus remained stubbornly fixed on Nox.

I found myself stealing glances over my shoulder, each one a thrilling act of defiance against my own better judgment. My heart quickened with a mixture of anticipation and trepidation each time, but our eyes never met. He remained immersed in his studies, seemingly oblivious to my scrutiny. Yet, I could feel him— his presence carried a weight that was impossible to ignore, a magnetic pull that kept me anchored to my seat, preventing me from escaping the invisible web we had woven.

A wave of conflicting emotions washed over me every time I considered turning to face him fully, to acknowledge the undeniable connection that fizzled between us. What was he thinking? Did he feel this strange tension, this electric charge that thrummed in the air between us?

My fingers fidgeted with the edges of my notebook, the crisp pages a poor substitute for the touch I craved—the touch I knew I couldn't have. The professor's lecture faded into a distant hum, a mere echo in the chamber of my own swirling thoughts. Nox's image consumed me: the way his dark hair fell across his forehead, the intense focus in his eyes as he leaned over his desk, the subtle flex of his muscles beneath his shirt. Each detail was etched into my memory, a testament to the unwilling fascination that held me captive.

But still, no glance was exchanged, and the frustration grew— mingling with a gnawing sense of longing, a yearning for something I couldn't quite name. I was caught in limbo.

As the bell rang, I slowly gathered my things, my movements deliberate as I stole one last glance at Nox. Still nothing. He remained hunched over his book, pointedly ignoring me. I shook my head, trying to shrug off another sting of disappointment, the familiar ache of rejection settling in my chest. With a sigh, I turned and headed for the hallway, the noise and bustle of the students washing over me.

I made it about five steps out the door when my path was blocked. Mira and her entourage of hyenas materialized before me, their sneering faces and predatory grins forming an impenetrable barrier. Escape routes vanished, and I could feel the fuse to my temper shortening. Mira's lips twisted into a smug grin as she stepped forward, arms crossed over her chest, her posture radiating an air of arrogant superiority.

"Do you really think you can speak to a high-gifted like that and not suffer the consequences?" she sneered, her voice dripping with condescension, each word a bitter strike aimed at my already bruised ego.

Her words grated on me, her tone as irritating as nails on a chalkboard. I straightened, refusing to cower under her intimidation tactics. I tilted my head to the side, eyes widening in mock surprise. "Oh, I'm sorry," I shot back, my voice laced with biting sarcasm, "I didn't realize you were one." I paused, letting the insult hang in the air, before adding sweetly, "Perhaps you could enlighten me on the proper etiquette for addressing your esteemed high-giftedness?"

Mira's eyes narrowed, her nostrils flaring with barely suppressed rage. Her cronies shifted uneasily, their smirks faltering as they sensed the shift in power. I had caught her off guard—challenged her status with a simple twist of words and a healthy dose of sarcasm.

A flicker of uncertainty crossed her face, but it was quickly replaced by fury. Her voice rose, laced with renewed venom. "You think you can talk to me like that?" she hissed, taking a step closer, her hand reaching out as if to strike me. "You pathetic little—"

But before she could make contact, a voice, smooth as silk yet laced with steel, cut through the tension. "That's quite enough, Mira."

The voice, though calm, resonated with an undeniable control that silenced the hall. We all turned to see Zarek leaning against the doorframe, arms crossed, his expression a mixture of amusement and barely concealed disdain. His golden eyes, usually sparkling with playfulness, now held a chilling glint that sent a shiver down my spine.

Mira froze mid-gesture, her hand hovering in the air like a startled bird. Her face, normally a mask of haughty confidence, contorted with a mixture of shock and irritation. "Zarek," she sputtered, her voice losing its usual imperiousness, "I was just—"

"I really don't care," Zarek interrupted, his tone still smooth but edged with steel. He pushed himself off the doorframe, sauntering towards us with a predatory grace that made me hold my breath. The air crackled with his presence, a wave of power that pressed down on my chest.

Mira, despite her usual bravado, visibly recoiled under his intense stare. Her face flushed crimson, her anger battling with a flicker of fear. "This isn't over," she hissed, her voice barely a whisper, before turning on her heel and stalking off—her lackeys scurrying after her like frightened shadows.

"Can't wait," I muttered under my breath, feeling the adrenaline slowly drain from my body. I took a deep breath, forcing myself to relax as my shoulders slumped slightly as the tension eased.

"Always getting into trouble, Firefly," Zarek chuckled, his voice a low rumble that vibrated through the air. He stood beside me, close enough that I could feel the warmth radiating from him—a comforting presence that both soothed and unsettled me.

"You didn't need to intervene, Zarek," I snapped, turning to face him.

Zarek let the silence linger for a beat, his golden eyes studying me with an intensity that made my cheeks flush. "Couldn't let anything happen to that pretty little face, now could I?" he finally replied, his voice smooth and laced with a playful flirtation.

I rolled my eyes, a defensive mechanism against the warmth that spread through me. "Right," I muttered, unable to come up with a witty retort, my usual sharp tongue momentarily dulled by his disarming charm. I decided to cut my losses and walk away.

The courtyard called to me with its peaceful atmosphere. But instead of seeking comfort in the open space, I found myself drawn towards the gloomy edges of the 'forbidden' forest—a refuge for my racing thoughts.

Growing up in the orphanage had honed my survival instincts, teaching me to be quick on my feet and even quicker with my words. Each sarcastic retort, each sharp comeback, was a weapon forged in the fires of adversity—a shield against a world that often seemed intent on breaking me down. But Zarek... he was different. His presence disrupted my carefully constructed defenses, his words and actions chipping away at the walls I had so thoroughly built.

The stone paths snaked through the courtyard, weaving between ancient oaks and neatly kept flowerbeds. The air was rich with the scent of damp earth and foliage, enveloping me in a serenity that made the rest of the world feel distant. Yet, as I moved further from the main buildings, an uneasy feeling crept in—a sensation of being watched.

I paused, my senses on high alert, every nerve ending thrumming with awareness. The rustling of leaves in the wind seemed amplified, each shadow lengthening and contorting into menacing shapes that danced at the edge of my vision. I strained my ears, trying to discern any unnatural sounds, but the only thing I could hear was the frantic rhythm of my own heartbeat echoing in the sudden silence.

Scanning my surroundings, I noted the emptiness of the court-yard. At this hour, most students had either retreated to the sanctuary of their dorms or huddled in the dimly lit corners of the library, leaving me alone in this tranquil yet increasingly unsettling space. I was far from the bustling areas of the academy now, the lively noises muffled by the dense foliage that surrounded me. My eyes narrowed, searching for the source of my unease—a fleeting shadow, a flicker of movement, anything that might explain the prickling sensation on my skin.

But there was nothing. Just the rustle of leaves whispering secrets in the breeze, the distant caw of a crow echoing through the stillness, and the quiet crunch of gravel beneath my feet. I shook my head, trying to dispel the unsettling sensation. Maybe it was just the lingering adrenaline from my confrontation with Mira, my senses still heightened, my nerves frayed.

My eyes drifted towards the forest, its dark, impenetrable depths beckoning me with a siren's call. The pull I felt wasn't just curiosity; it was an intuitive feeling, a magnetic force that tugged at my very core, urging me to cross the boundary. I knew I shouldn't. Every rule, every whispered warning, forbade venturing into that territory – *their* territory. Yet, the silence, the sense of untamed wilderness that emanated from its depths, was calling me.

Just a few steps closer, I told myself, my curiosity outweighing my apprehension. *Just to see.* My steps grew bolder as I approached the edge, where the manicured lawns gave way to wilder, untamed terrain. With each breath, the scent of damp earth and ancient wood filled my lungs, grounding me, anchoring me to the present, while simultaneously urging me onward.

The shadows danced playfully around me as I ventured deeper into the forest's embrace, their sinuous movements casting an enchanting spell that eased the tension in my shoulders. The thick canopy overhead filtered the sunlight, creating a mosaic of warm, dappled light that danced across the forest floor, dappling the mossy undergrowth with an ethereal glow. Each step felt lighter, the soft earth cushioning my footsteps, muffling any sound and creating a serene cocoon of contentment.

For the first time in what felt like an eternity, I found solace in solitude. The quiet hummed with a gentle energy, a welcome relief from the constant noise and chaos of the academy. Here, away from prying eyes and whispered judgments, I could breathe freely, my lungs expanding with the fresh, earthy air. The weight of expectations—the burden of proving myself—seemed to lift, replaced by a sense of belonging, a connection to something ancient and profound.

As I moved deeper into the forest's embrace, the world outside faded away, replaced by a tapestry of vibrant greens, earthy browns, and the occasional splash of color from wildflowers blooming in hidden corners.

I paused, closing my eyes, and inhaled deeply, allowing the blend of scents to wash over me. It was a grounding experience—a connection to the earth, a reminder that I was a part of something larger than myself, something timeless and enduring. In that moment, I felt a sense of peace I had never known before, a tranquility that settled over me like a soft blanket, easing the anxieties that had harassed me for so long.

But the tranquility was shattered, replaced by a prickling sensation that skittered across my skin, raising goosebumps on my arms. That feeling of being watched—of being hunted—returned with a vengeance, sending a jolt of fear through my heart. My eyes flew open, scanning the shadows, searching for the source of my unease.

The playful dance of light and shadow now seemed ominous, the whispering leaves carrying warnings instead of secrets. My heart pounded against my ribs, a frantic drumbeat against the sudden silence, as a wave of vulnerability washed over me. I was alone, exposed, a trespasser in a world that didn't belong to me. The forest, once a sanctuary, now felt like a trap, its beauty masking a hidden danger that lurked just beyond my perception.

A sudden rustle in the undergrowth sent a jolt of fear through me. I spun around, my breath catching in my throat. But there was nothing there—only the shifting shadows and the whispering leaves, playing tricks on my overactive imagination.

"Get a grip, Thalia," I muttered to myself, my voice a shaky whisper in the oppressive stillness. I forced my breathing to steady, trying to alleviate the rising panic that threatened to consume me. But the shadows danced around me, teasing the edges of my vision, their movements mimicking the unseen creatures that I imagined hiding just beyond my sight.

Despite the growing unease, I pressed forward—my steps cautious, my senses hyper-alert. The deeper I ventured into the forest's embrace, the stronger the pull became.

Chapter 9

Damon's POV

Irritation coiled within me, a spiteful serpent tightening its grip with every step the human took deeper into our territory. *What was she doing here?* This forest, cloaked in shadow and steeped in ancient magic, was *our* domain—a place where even the most seasoned of the Gifted tread with caution. Yet here she was, a mere human, venturing into its depths with an audacity that bordered on reckless abandon.

The pull I felt towards her was maddening, an unwelcome distraction that threatened to shatter my carefully constructed walls. Worse yet, the shadows—my ever-loyal companions—mirrored my own unrest. They writhed and twisted, drawn to her like moths to a forbidden flame, their whispers echoing the questions that plagued my mind. I clenched my fists, forcing them back into submission, my control tenuous at best. Never before had I struggled to maintain such a basic command over my own abilities. The last thing I needed was a distraction, and she, with her daring spirit and cryptic aura, was precisely that.

Her auburn hair shined in the filtered sunlight, catching the flickering rays like embers glowing in the twilight. Her eyes, a captivating shade of dark grey, sparkled with an inner fire—a fierce intelligence that only fueled my shadows' restlessness. They longed to move closer, to envelop her in their protective embrace, and I fought against the urge with a grim determination. There was no logical reason for this connection, this strange draw towards a human, yet it persisted, gnawing at my resolve, chipping away at the walls—slowly.

Most Gifted knew better than to venture into our domain—but not her. She moved with an intriguing mix of confidence and caution, her footsteps silent and sure, as if she belonged here—a notion that ignited a spark of possessiveness within me. This forest was not meant for just anyone, especially not a human. Least of all one who didn't seem to grasp the risks she was taking.

The shadows quivered, their whispers growing louder, brushing against my skin like phantom touches. I forced myself to take a deep breath, the cool air calming the fire that burned within me. I couldn't afford to lose control now, not over a human whose presence both lured and repelled me. I watched her carefully, my jaw clenched, frustration boiling beneath the surface.

For a fleeting moment, our gazes met, and I felt a sharp pull—a dangerous desire to step forward and confront her, to demand answers, to unravel the mystery that surrounded her. But I held back, remaining cloaked in the shadows, my curiosity battling with a deep-seated caution.

She was a wild card, an unknown element in a carefully balanced equation, a potential threat to the delicate equilibrium. The way she moved, her confidence unwavering, her gaze drawn to the deepest shadows, set off alarms in my head. The shadows themselves seemed to respond to her, swirling with a sinister familiarity —almost as if they recognized her, welcomed her. I couldn't shake the gnawing suspicion that her presence here was far from coincidence.

Could she be connected to *it*? The entity that had been stirring in the depths of the realm—the malevolent force that threatened to disrupt the balance of Nexara? Everything about her felt too deliberate, as though she were part of something much bigger—something dangerous.

The way the shadows danced around her, caressing her form with an almost possessive intimacy, made my skin crawl. It was an unnatural alliance—a disturbing harmony between light and darkness that set my teeth on edge. She moved with a purpose that spoke of secrets buried deep, of a hidden agenda veiled in layers of shadow, and her very presence filled me with an instinctive dread —a premonition of impending chaos that chilled me to the bone.

I watched her closely, my suspicion hardening into resolve. Whatever she was searching for, I would find out. And if she was tied to that encroaching darkness, I would be ready. I would protect my brothers, even if it meant confronting this paradoxical human, this strange creature who had captured the attention of both Nox and Zarek.

Chapter 10

Thalia's POV

Hours of exploration had bled the sun from the sky, leaving only the moon's faint, silvery glimmer to pierce the deepening shadows. A chill, sharp and sudden, settled over the forest as dusk surrendered to night. Yet the bizarre pull I felt only intensified, urging me forward—deeper into the wooded maze.

Thorns tore at my clothes, and branches raked across my skin as I wrestled through a dense thicket. Emerging into a clearing, breathless and disoriented, my eyes fell upon it—that damn structure, half-consumed by creeping vines and shrouded in the oppressive gloom of the towering trees.

The very same structure I had noticed the night of the party, dismissed then as a figment of my imagination, a trick of the fading light. But here it stood, undeniably real. Its stone walls, weathered and scarred by time, stubbornly resisted the encroaching wilderness.

It was a house—a magnificent, sprawling manor adorned with intricate stonework and an air of haunting grandeur. Moonlight bathed the steps leading to its imposing entrance, an invitation to unravel the secrets hidden within.

"I knew I wasn't crazy," I murmured, taking a hesitant step forward. The shadows around me seemed to writhe and coil, wrapping me in their cool embrace.

Questions flooded my mind. Was anyone living here? Or had it been abandoned to the whims of the forest? It didn't look abandoned; it seemed almost... maintained. What magic—what force —was protecting it from the effects of time and decay?

A low growl—a sound both primal and terrifying—ripped through the stillness of the night, startling me from my thoughts. It was a guttural rumble that resonated deep within my bones, triggering an instinctive terror that froze me in my tracks. My blood ran cold, every nerve ending screaming at me to flee.

Slowly, agonizingly, I turned towards the source of the sound, my heart pounding against my ribs like a trapped bird. And then I saw them—those eyes. Piercing green eyes, glowing in the darkness, locked onto mine with an intensity that stole my breath.

The creature stepped fully into the moonlit clearing, its colossal form casting a long, ominous shadow. It was a behemoth of a panther, easily eight feet tall at the shoulder, its powerful muscles rippling beneath a coat of midnight-black fur that blended seamlessly with the surrounding darkness. With each deliberate step, its enormous paws slammed against the ground, sending tremors through the earth. Its claws, long and sharp, glinted menacingly in the moonlight, and its fangs, equally formidable, protruded from its powerful jaws. It was a predator in every sense of the word— and I, a trespasser in its domain, was its prey.

This wasn't like the creatures I had encountered before. This was ancient, primal, and utterly unstoppable. The horrifying realization that there was no protective ward—no magical barrier to shield me this time—sent a fresh surge of fear coursing through my veins.

Trapped between the beast and the towering house, despair washed over me. My legs felt like lead, my mind a whirlwind of panic. But survival instinct kicked in. I forced myself to take a step back, my eyes glued to the creature, every muscle in my body coiled and ready to spring. The beast tilted its head—a curious gesture that sent shivers down my spine. Was it toying with me? Savoring my fear?

My gaze darted to the house, its dark silhouette looming against the night sky. Maybe, just maybe, it was open. Maybe it offered sanctuary, a temporary reprieve from the terrifying reality before me. My thoughts raced, desperately seeking an escape route, a solution—anything to avoid the fate that seemed to await me in the clutches of this monstrous creature.

A cracking branch in the underbrush caught the beast's attention, momentarily distracting it. Now was my chance. Adrenaline surged through me as I turned and dashed toward the house, heart pounding in my chest. The cold night air rushed past me, and I pushed myself to run faster, hoping that the sanctuary I needed would be more than just an illusion in the darkness.

Hitting the door with a force born of sheer desperation, I barely managed to slow my momentum as I frantically pushed it open, silently thanking the gods it was unlocked. A bone-rattling growl echoed from behind—louder and fiercer than before.

I slammed the door shut and threw my weight against it, my back pressed to the cold, rough wood. I could hear the creature's heavy paws thudding against the ground as it lumbered closer, its growls growing louder and more menacing with each passing moment.

Panic clawed at my throat, but I forced myself to stay calm. I needed to think—to find a way to keep the beast at bay until I could figure out a way to escape.

The heavy silence of the house pressed in on me, broken only by my own ragged gasps. I took a moment to steady my breathing, my eyes darted around, drinking in the unexpected elegance of my surroundings.

This was no abandoned ruin. Someone lived here. Dark, rich decorations filled the space—timeless, tasteful, and utterly at odds with the wild creature guarding the door. Soft, ambient light bathed the foyer in a warm glow, highlighting the deep texture of the stone walls. Velvet curtains framed tall windows, and ornate furniture was arranged with meticulous care.

The foyer itself was enormous. To my right, a fire crackled invitingly in a grand hearth, plush furniture arranged around it, creating an air of intimacy. To my left, another spacious room, its walls lined with bookshelves overflowing with ancient-looking books—a reading room, with its comfortable chairs and a small table nestled near the shelves.

Beyond, the hallway stretched into shadows, leading to a stunning staircase at the far end. Its banister was a masterpiece of carvings, each swirl and curve seeming to whisper forgotten secrets. I swallowed hard, my heart still hammering against my ribs.

Okay, Thalia, think. If I could just glimpse that beast through a window, I might be able to slip out while the owners were occupied... elsewhere. But a chilling thought crept in: if they coexisted with that creature, were they any less dangerous? Panic tightened its icy grip around my throat. I had to get out—now.

With a deep breath, I ventured down the hallway, my footsteps muffled by the plush rug beneath my feet. The silence was unnerving, a heavy blanket pressing down on me. My eyes flickered towards the staircase—high ground meant a better vantage point, a chance to assess my situation and maybe even see an escape route.

Slowly, I ascended the stairs. The air grew thick with a strange stillness. My senses were on high alert, every nerve straining for the slightest sound, the faintest hint of movement. But there was nothing—only the hollow quiet of a place that felt suspended in time, as if holding its breath.

Reaching the top, I found myself on a spacious landing bathed in the pale glow of moonlight streaming through a large window at the far end. Four doors, arranged symmetrically in two pairs, lined the hallway.

I approached the window, peering out into the inky blackness of the forest beyond. Perhaps I could catch a glimpse of the creature that had driven me here, its glowing eyes a beacon in the darkness.

But there was no sign of the beast. A heavy sigh escaped my lips, a mixture of relief and lingering fear. Had it grown bored and wandered off? Or had it found some other unfortunate prey to stalk? I rubbed my hands over my face, a wave of self-recrimination washing over me. What had I been thinking, venturing out here alone? This whole night was a testament to my own reckless curiosity—a dangerous habit that seemed determined to be my undoing.

My self-recrimination was abruptly cut short by a familiar voice— deep and laced with a playful charm that sent an unwelcome shiver down my spine. "And to what do I owe this pleasure, Firefly?"

Zarek.

I froze, panic surging through me as I turned to face him. He stood in the doorway, a silhouette against the dim light emanating from the room behind him. His features obscured by shadow, yet I could still see that glint of amusement in his eyes—the curve of that infuriating smirk that always sent a flutter through my stomach. Damn him. Why did he have this effect on me? The shadows around him seemed to writhe and twist, mirroring the turmoil he always seemed to stir within me.

"What are you doing here?" I stammered, my pulse quickening. The last thing I needed was another complication, especially not this one.

He stepped forward, his presence both magnetic and unsettling. "I could ask you the same thing," he countered, his voice a low purr. "Wandering around a place like this... it's not exactly safe for a human, is it?" His eyes held a mix of mischief and curiosity, and I couldn't shake the feeling that he knew far more than he let on.

I narrowed my eyes, unwilling to let him see how much his presence affected me. "Well, I'm not exactly here for a party," I retorted, trying to sound braver than I felt. "I was just trying to find a way out."

"Out?" He stepped closer, the playful lilt in his voice belying the gravity of my situation. "But you got in." He tilted his head, his gaze sliding down my body with an amused glow in his eyes. "How did you manage to get in here?"

His blatantly checking me out sent a wave of heat creeping up my neck. Why did he always have to look at me like that?

"How did I get in here?" I snapped, my voice thick with irritation. "Breaking and entering, if you must know. And speaking of getting in..." I gestured vaguely downstairs. "Is that oversized panther beast your pet? Perhaps you could charm it into letting me leave? I'd really rather not be stuck here with you."

He chuckled softly, the sound both captivating and infuriating. "My pet? I assure you, Firefly, that beast belongs to no one." His eyes shone, clearly enjoying my frustration. "And as for charming it... well, I suppose it would depend on what I get in return."

My eyes narrowed, and I crossed my arms aggressively. "Stop calling me that," I demanded. "And how about I don't report you for harboring a monstrous man-eater in the forest? Sounds like a fair trade to me."

He threw back his head and laughed, the sound echoing through the hallway like music, drawing me in despite my better judgment. His eyes met mine again, flickering with mischief—and something deeper, something that made my stomach do a slow flip.

"A tempting offer," he conceded, his voice dropping to a husky murmur. "But let's focus on why you're really here." He stepped closer, invading my space, and his scent washed over me, making my head spin. "This house isn't a place someone stumbles upon by accident, *Thalia*. Not by any Gifted I've met—and certainly not by a human. So, what truly brings you here?"

The way he said my name sent a shiver down my spine, and I fought the urge to step back. "I—well—"

Before I could answer, a loud slam echoed from downstairs, followed by the heavy thud of footsteps. I flinched involuntarily, my heart leaping into my throat. Zarek's smirk widened at my reaction, amusement dancing in his eyes.

"Looks like we're not alone anymore," he purred, turning on his heel and heading towards the staircase.

I hesitated for a moment, my mind a whirlwind of questions and unease. The fragile sense of security I had felt in his presence evaporated, replaced by a fresh wave of anxiety. With a deep breath, I followed him reluctantly, my heart pounding as I descended the stairs, unsure of what awaited me below.

The sound of raised voices drifted from one of the rooms off the foyer. My steps slowed, apprehension gripping me as I approached. Peeking through the doorway, I saw Zarek lounging casually on the sofa—a picture of relaxed amusement, as if he were thoroughly enjoying the chaos I had inadvertently stumbled into.

Damon sat with his back to me, his posture rigid, muscles tense beneath his shirt. I hesitated at the threshold, unsure whether to intrude. But my presence was quickly noticed. As I took a few cautious steps forward, Nox emerged from a door at the back of the room.

He sauntered in, wearing only low-slung sweatpants. The waistband resting just above the deep V of his pelvis, emphasizing his athletic build. The hoodie he typically wore was absent, allowing his bare chest to glisten with water droplets that cascaded down his perfectly sculpted stomach. Every inch of his sun-kissed skin seemed to radiate power and grace, drawing the eye to the black tattoos decorating his arms. The dark ink seemed to come alive as he moved, emphasizing every ripple and bulge. His damp curls clung to his forehead, giving him a devil-may-care look as he nonchalantly tousled them with a towel. But it was the way he carried himself that truly drew me in—confident yet effortless, exuding control and dominance with every step. Nox was undeniably sexy, and I couldn't tear my eyes away from him.

The moment he noticed me, his movements stilled. His head snapped up, those intense green eyes narrowing as they locked onto mine with a predatory glint. I felt pinned in place, like a butterfly impaled beneath his gaze.

"Who brought her here?" His voice was low, edged with a growl that made the room temperature drop a few degrees. Every word dripped with irritation, and I instinctively took a step back.

The air crackled with tension, each of them reacting to my intrusion in their own way. Zarek's amusement seemed to grow—a stark contrast to Nox's evident displeasure and Damon's silent intensity.

"No one," Zarek chimed in, his voice light and teasing, clearly relishing the tension. He leaned back on the sofa, one arm draped casually over the backrest, his eyes glinting with mischief as they flicked to Nox. "It seems our guest here is quite the explorer. She found her way into our lovely little home all on her own. Quite impressive, wouldn't you say?"

Damon finally turned to look at me, his expression unreadable—a mask that hid any emotion he might be feeling. But Nox's gaze remained fixed on me, intense and unwavering, making me squirm under his scrutiny. The dynamics in the room shifted subtly, the undercurrents of their relationships rippling beneath the surface like a disturbed pond. My presence had clearly stirred something deeper—something that went beyond mere annoyance at an unexpected guest.

"You shouldn't be here," Nox growled, his voice low and controlled, yet laced with an underlying threat that made my breath catch in my throat. "This isn't a place for you, *human.*"

"Well, she's here now," Zarek interjected, breaking the tension with a casual shrug. He had a knack for that—defusing a situation with a light touch even as his eyes danced with trouble. "Might as well make her feel at home, don't you think, brothers?"

Nox's eyes burned into me for a moment longer—a silent warning that sent shivers down my spine—before he looked away with a shake of his head. Clearly, he wasn't happy about my presence.

"Well, if someone could control that beast outside," I retorted, my voice a bit shaky despite my attempt to sound confident, "I'd gladly leave right now and never come back to your... little oasis."

Just my luck to end up here, I thought, crossing my arms defensively as I stepped further into the room. Out of the frying pan and into the fire, as they say.

Zarek raised an eyebrow, a smirk playing at the corners of his lips. "Oh, but you're just getting to know us, Thalia," he purred, his voice laced with amusement. "Surely you can't be so quick to judge."

"Quick to judge? Are you fucking kidding me?" I exploded, my frustration finally reaching its breaking point. "Ever since I arrived, you three have treated me like I personally offended your ancestors or murdered you in a past life! I've done absolutely nothing to any of you! But oh no, the 'powerless little human' is such a threat to the 'almighty, infallible gods of Nexara Academy'," I snarled, throwing in even more dramatics than I intended, my arms flailing as I emphasized each word.

My voice dripped with sarcasm as I continued, "And here I am, standing in a house filled with Gifted who apparently despise my very existence, while a giant, man-eating beast is waiting outside for me. Forgive me, 'oh mighty ones'," I practically spat, rolling my eyes before meeting each of their stares. Nox was now seated on the couch beside Damon, both of their gazes unwavering—watching my every move like hawks circling a field mouse.

I felt a flush creep up my neck under their intense scrutiny, but I held my ground, glaring back at them with defiance. "You know what?" I said, my voice shaking with a mixture of anger and fear. "I'm done. I'm done with the glares, the snide comments, the constant judgment. I'm just trying to survive here. I didn't ask to be here—I didn't ask to be dragged into your little supernatural drama. So if you'll excuse me, I'd really like to get back to my own life, where I don't have to worry about being eaten by a monster or judged by a bunch of arrogant, pretentious little as—"

I cut myself off, taking a deep breath to calm my racing heart. "Just... tell me how to get out of here," I finished, my voice barely above a whisper.

Silence descended upon the room, thick and heavy. The brothers simply stared at me, their expressions unreadable. Finally, Damon spoke, his tone flat, his face an impassive mask. "The beast won't come in here. This place is protected. But you shouldn't be here, and you should never come back."

I took a steadying breath, trying to hold onto my rapidly dwindling composure. "Then maybe you should put a sign on the door," I snapped back, my voice dripping with sarcasm, "'Beware of the Beast and the Psycho Brothers'."

Zarek's laughter shattered the tension, warm and infectious. His amusement was undeniable, and even Nox's lips twitched in a ghost of a smile, though he quickly schooled his features back into neutrality. Damon, however, seemed to grow even more somber, his brow furrowed.

Zarek looked at me, his smile widening. "You've got fire, I'll give you that." He leaned back on the couch, his eyes shining with mischief. "Maybe you'll survive after all, Firefly."

I caught myself almost smiling in return, my frustration momentarily softened by the hint of humor in Zarek's voice. But Nox's gaze pulled me back to reality—still intense and assessing—and Damon's stony stare was a harsh reminder that I was far from welcome.

"Okay, you know what? I'll take my chances with the beast," I replied, my voice lighter but still edged with annoyance.

Zarek gave me a cheeky grin. "I like her," he declared, looking over at his brothers as if daring them to disagree. Nox's eyes narrowed slightly, but he said nothing, while Damon's gaze remained cold and distant.

"I don't care if you like me, Zarek," I shot back, irritation flaring once more. The smirk on his face didn't waver, but there was a glint in his eyes that suggested he found my attitude rather entertaining.

"Look, I didn't come here to play games or earn anyone's approval," I continued, my voice steadying as I tried to regain control of the situation. "I just stumbled into your weird, isolated home while trying to find my way out of the forest. I don't need any of this," I gestured between us, frustration lacing my words.

"I told you to stay out of the forest, didn't I?" Nox interjected, his arms crossed tightly across his chest, his tone brooking no argument.

"Yeah, well, I didn't see any 'No Trespassing' signs," I shot back, raising an eyebrow at him. "Besides, it's not like I was expecting to run into you three while I was lost out here."

Zarek, clearly enjoying the back-and-forth, grinned. "Maybe she just can't keep away from us."

I rolled my eyes, scoffing at his words. "Please, don't flatter yourself," I replied, my voice dripping with sarcasm. "If anything, I'd rather not be anywhere near any of you. But since your pet decided to chase me here, I guess I didn't have much of a choice."

Zarek's grin widened, clearly unfazed by my retort. "Oh, come on, Firefly—admit it. You're intrigued."

Before I could snap back, Nox's glare deepened, and his voice cut through the moment. "This isn't a joke, Z. She doesn't belong here."

The smile faded slightly from Zarek's face, but his eyes still glinted with mischief. "Maybe not, but she's here now. And considering she managed to find her way into our home, that has to count for something, doesn't it?"

I glanced between them, the tension in the air thick enough to cut with a knife. Damon's silence spoke volumes, his gaze moving from Nox to Zarek before finally settling on me. He let out a sigh, his tone flat and controlled. "She shouldn't be here, but she's here now. We'll figure out what to do with her."

I frowned, crossing my arms again. "I'm not some stray animal you found on the side of the road. I just want to find my way out of here without becoming a beast's dinner."

"Then stay out of the fucking forest, Thalia." Nox said, his voice like a warning, eyes narrowing.

I held his gaze, unwilling to back down. "Noted," I said, my voice unwavering. "But maybe you should focus on keeping your 'pet' on a leash."

Chapter 11

Thalia's POV

The next morning, I was groggy and confused, the images of the last night flickering behind my eyelids. Zarek had insisted on escorting me back to the dorms, his fake version of chivalry stubbornly overriding my protests. We'd bickered most of the way until my resistance dwindled away out of pure exhaustion. The silent walk back had been strangely peaceful, though; Zarek's voice had eventually faded into the night, leaving us in a shared quiet that was surprisingly comforting.

The brothers hadn't seemed remotely concerned about the beast lurking outside—which I assumed was some kind of bizarre, oversized guard panther—and that left a gnawing unease in my stomach.

"She doesn't belong here"

Nox's words echoed through my mind as I got ready for the day. Another reminder of my outcast status here at Nexara Academy clung to me like a shadow. But shadows or not, I was determined to make something of my time here. After pulling on my uniform, I decided to find El and James later, maybe they'd be willing to help me train.

Classes were an endless loop of information that felt irrelevant to my existence. While other students discussed their gifts and control techniques, I could only sit and absorb theories and histories that seemed more fantasy than reality for someone like me. I was learning plenty about the world I'd been thrust into, but nothing that explained why I was here.

With each lecture, the sense of isolation grew sharper—like a thorn lodged beneath my skin. These were lessons for witches, shifters, fae—beings with power flowing through their veins. And there I was, just Thalia. The powerless human. An anomaly among prodigies.

I masked my frustration with attentive scribbling in my notebook —notes that might never be useful but kept me anchored in each moment. Despite feeling like an outsider peering into a world where I didn't quite fit, I wasn't ready to give up. Not yet. Not when there was still so much left unexplained.

By lunch, I had lost all interest in being around people. I opted to skip the crowded cafeteria, instead grabbing some snacks before heading to Combat Training. The leaves were turning, painting the campus in shades of orange and gold as fall settled in. My academy sweatshirt did little to shield me from the cool breeze as I made my way to the training field, but the brisk air felt good. It was refreshing—a reminder that I was alive, still standing.

I started running laps around the track, trying to clear my head, the rhythm of my footsteps grounding me. Each step seemed to push away the lingering unease, the doubts, the feeling of being watched. After a couple laps, I began to notice other students making their way to the field, their voices mixing with the rustle of leaves in the wind.

Grabbing my water, I took a deep breath, the crisp air filling my lungs as I scanned the growing crowd. I needed to find El and James—if anyone could help me right now, it was them.

I spotted El first, her chestnut hair catching the light as she laughed with a group of students near the mats. Relief washed over me as I made my way toward her. James appeared moments later, his smile as bright as always.

"Well, there's the sunshine," he beamed, throwing an arm over my shoulder and pulling me in close. A blush crept up my cheeks, and I glanced away, trying to hide it as El gave me an amused smile.

"Where were you at lunch?" she asked, her tone casual but with a hint of curiosity.

"I wanted to get a head start on training," I replied, shrugging. "Speaking of training—" I was cut off mid-sentence by an unmistakable feeling—shadows looming over me, making my skin prickle. James's arm slipped away, and he took a step back, his expression shifting slightly. I let out a small scoff, already knowing who it was without having to look.

Wonder who that could be.

I turned to see none other than the psycho trio. Their presence was as imposing as ever, each of them radiating that strange combination of power and intensity that seemed to fill the entire space around them.

"Can I help you?" I asked, raising an eyebrow, my voice dripping with sarcasm.

Zarek's grin spread across his face—that lazy, annoying smile that always seemed to say he knew something I didn't. "Just wanted to see if our favorite troublemaker was planning on causing any more scenes today," he said, his eyes bright with playfulness.

Nox's gaze was as sharp as ever, those violent eyes locking onto mine. He didn't say anything, but the intensity in his expression spoke volumes. Damon, standing beside him, looked as stoic as always, his eyes narrowed slightly as if assessing my every move.

"Scenes?" I repeated, crossing my arms over my chest. "Are we really doing this?"

El cleared her throat beside me, stepping forward with a bright smile. "Oh, are we starting drama already? I thought we'd wait at least until the warm-up," she joked, her eyes darting between the brothers and me, her tone light but not without an edge.

James chuckled, his boyish smile returning as he took his place beside me again, his presence warm and steady. "Yeah, fellas, give the girl a break."

Nox's expression darkened at James's comment, but Zarek only seemed more entertained. "You wound us, sunshine," he purred, his voice smooth as silk, a hint of laughter in his eyes as he emphasized the nickname.

I rolled my eyes, refusing to give them the satisfaction of a response. Zarek simply winked at me before turning away with his brothers. Damon looked relieved to escape my presence, but Nox lingered for a moment, his eyes still locked on mine, something unreadable flickering in their depths. Then, without a word, he turned and followed after Damon and Zarek.

I let out a breath, turning back to El and James. "They are going to drive me crazy," I muttered under my breath. "I don't know why they have to make my life so complicated."

El laughed, her amber eyes sparkling with mirth. "Because they enjoy it, obviously. And I have to say, you're handling it pretty well. Most people would've cracked by now."

I snorted, feeling a hysterical edge creeping into my laughter. "I'm pretty damn close, El."

Professor Lorian's normally rigid structure seemed to crumble today, allowing us some freedom. We were expected to use the time to hone our skills, but beyond that, the field was ours. Still, even as I moved through the motions, practicing the techniques

El and James were teaching me, I could feel the brothers' eyes on me—tracking my movements, their gazes as evident as the chill in the autumn air.

El demonstrated a defensive stance, her body fluid and graceful as she explained the nuances of balance and leverage. "Remember, it's not just about strength," she said, her voice steady and reassuring. "It's about using what you have to your advantage."

James took his turn, his approach more hands-on as he guided me through the steps of a takedown. His presence was calming, a relief against the relentless attention from the Shadow Brothers. With each successful move, my confidence grew. I was getting better, and for the first time since arriving here, I allowed myself to feel a flicker of hope.

"Alright, now try it on me," James challenged, his blue eyes alight with excitement. I squared my shoulders, mirroring the stance he had just demonstrated, my focus narrowing to the space between us.

With a burst of energy, I lunged forward, wrapping my arm around James and throwing my weight into his. The next thing I knew, he was on the ground, looking up at me with a surprised yet impressed grin.

"See? You're a natural," he said, his words igniting a spark of pride within me.

El clapped her hands enthusiastically. "Nice one, Thalia!" she exclaimed, crossing the distance between us to give me a high-five.

As I caught my breath, my gaze inadvertently drifted to where the brothers were sparring amongst themselves. Nox moved with a predatory grace, his strikes precise and lethal. Damon's shadows swirled around him, adding an extra layer of danger to his already formidable skill. Zarek, ever the show-off, was a blur of speed and agility. They were a sight to behold, a trio of power and controlled chaos. Despite everything, I couldn't deny the pull I felt. They were like magnets for my attention, an enigma I couldn't quite solve.

And that fact irritated me to no end. What was it about them that made them so impossible to ignore?

I hated that I wanted to figure it out—that I couldn't seem to stop myself from analyzing their every move, trying to piece together the puzzle they represented. Nox's quiet intensity. Damon's simmering hostility. Zarek's playful arrogance. Each so different, yet somehow connected. My jaw tightened as frustration bubbled beneath the surface. Why did it matter? Why did *they* matter? They were just distractions—obstacles in my path.

I need to focus on myself, not get caught up in the enigmatic aura of the psycho brothers. But no matter how much I tried to push it aside, the pull remained—a quiet, infuriating hum in the back of my mind.

Taking some of frustration out on James, I brushed the grass off my pants, trying to regain some semblance of composure. He didn't deserve my misplaced annoyance, but he was the closest target. I glanced at him, offering a small, apologetic smile.

"Not bad for a human," Zarek called out, his voice carrying across the training field. I couldn't tell if it was a compliment or another one of his teasing remarks, but I decided to ignore him as I turned my attention back to James, offering him a hand to help him up.

"Oh, he's just doing it to get in her pants. I'm sure it's not that hard, James!" Mira yelled, her pack of hyenas erupting in laughter around her.

"I've heard it's easy! Just be careful not to catch anything!" one of her hyenas shouted.

I stiffened at the sound of their voices. The laughter that followed felt like a swarm of wasps, stinging and relentless. I clenched my fists at my sides, fighting the urge to let the hurt show on my face. My cheeks burned with a mixture of embarrassment and anger. James' body tensed beside me, his earlier amusement gone as he stood up.

"Ignore them," El muttered, shooting Mira a glare that could've set the grass on fire. "They're just looking for a reaction."

I nodded, but could feel my temper was wearing thin. James' hand found my shoulder, squeezing gently in a silent show of support. "They're not worth it," he said quietly, his eyes meeting mine with understanding.

My gaze snagged on Mira, who stood by Zarek's side with that ever-present smirk playing on her lips. Her eyes locked onto mine, a challenge simmering in their depths. She leaned closer to Zarek, whispering something in his ear, her hand covering her mouth as if they were sharing a private joke at my expense. Her other arm snaked around his bicep, fingers playfully tracing the lines of his sweatshirt. She had to stand on her toes to press her body against his, and the possessive way she clung to him made my blood boil. I could feel my heart pounding, each beat a drum against my ribs.

There she was—all smiles and flirty gestures, flaunting her closeness to Zarek—while he just watched me, his eyes never leaving my face, a knowing smirk playing on his lips. It was like a silent taunt, a game they were playing.

"Fucking playboy," I mumbled under my breath as the whistle blew, signaling the end of our training session. My gaze drifted to Professor Lorian, who was already looking at me. His eyes, sharp and discerning. It seemed like he was evaluating more than just my performance on the field.

I broke eye contact first, turning away to gather my things. Zarek's laughter echoed in my ears, a reminder of his little display with Mira. It was a performance. I knew that much. But it didn't make the sting of rejection any less painful.

El approached me, her expression a mix of concern and irritation. "Don't let them get to you, Thalia," she said, her voice low so only I could hear. "They're just trying to throw you off your game."

I forced a smile, appreciating her attempt to lift my spirits. "I know, El. It's just... frustrating."

James joined us, his arm brushing against mine in a comforting gesture. "You did great today," he reassured me, his blue eyes sincere. "Don't let Mira and her cronies distract you from that."

I nodded, taking their words to heart.

As I slung my bag over my shoulder, preparing to leave, I felt a familiar presence behind me. I didn't need to turn around to know who it was. The scent of fresh rain—earthy and clean, filled the air. I closed my eyes for a moment, savoring it, before turning to face the source

"You're improving," Nox's voice was gruff, almost reluctant. I turned to face him, surprised by the unexpected compliment. His emerald eyes met mine, a flicker of respect—or was it reluctant admiration?—hidden beneath his usual hostility.

"Thanks," I replied, my tone guarded. "I have good teachers."

A muscle in Nox's jaw twitched, and for a moment, I thought I saw the ghost of a smile tug at the corner of his mouth. But it was gone as quickly as it appeared. He didn't say anything else, just turned on his heel and walked away, heading back towards his brothers, his shoulders radiating a silent dismissal.

I watched him go, a strange sense of satisfaction settling over me as I made my way across the field, El and James at my side. The sun was beginning to set, casting long shadows across the campus. The day was ending on a high note, and despite the rollercoaster of emotions I'd experienced, I felt a spark of hope today.

As we neared the edge of the training field, I couldn't help but glance back at the brothers. They were locked in their own world, their movements synchronized as they sparred with each other. There was a beauty in their unity, a silent understanding that only came from years of shared experiences.

EXHAUSTION CLUNG TO ME LIKE A SECOND SKIN, THE kind that burrowed deep into your bones after pushing yourself too hard. Yet there I sat at my desk, surrounded by ancient texts and scribbled notes, the clock's hands inching toward midnight. A yawn threatened to split my face, but a strange sensation crawled up my spine—a tug, insistent and nagging. It drew my gaze to the window, where the night cloaked the campus.

Outside, Professor Lorian's silhouette emerged from the shadows, draped in a black cloak that fluttered against the breeze. His hood obscured his face, but his sly glances revealed enough under the silver moonlight. Something about his posture spoke of secrets and silent urgency.

What could a professor be up to at this ungodly hour? My curiosity overpowered exhaustion, beckoning me to follow. I grabbed my black hoodie, slid it over my head, and slipped out into the cool night air. The back door closed with a hush behind me as I caught sight of his receding figure.

Treading softly, I kept a safe distance. The shadows seemed to reach out to me, whispering paths through the trees as if guiding me, until we reached a small river glimmering under the moon's watchful eye.

I melted into the embrace of forest shadows, eyes fixed on Lorian's pacing form. He halted abruptly and dropped to his knees with an air of desperation—or devotion—I couldn't tell which. He raised his face skyward, and I leaned forward, straining to catch his murmured words.

"My lord, you have returned to me," he whispered with reverence that sent shivers down my spine.

He paused as if listening for an answer only he could hear.

"She is here," he continued after a beat of silence. "But are you sure she is the one you need?"

Interest sparked within me like flint against steel—dangerous and compelling.

"I-I'm sorry, my lord. I will make sure she's ready for you. But my Lord," he hesitated as doubt laced his voice, "the human hasn't shown any signs of power. I don't think she—"

A gasp almost escaped me—was he talking about me? Panic laced with adrenaline surged through my veins. In an instant of shock-induced clumsiness, my foot slid against the slick mud by the riverbank.

Lorian's head snapped toward me like a compass finding north.

I didn't wait for him to confirm what I already knew—he'd heard me. Instinct took over; I bolted like a startled deer back toward the safety of my dorm room. My mind was a whirlwind of questions: Was he talking about me? Ready for what? Why would this 'lord' need someone powerless like me?

Reaching my dorm room, I fumbled with the knob, my trembling hands betraying my fear. I slammed the door shut, leaning against it as if to hold back the shadows that seemed to press against the wood.

A wave of dizziness washed over me, and I stumbled toward my bed, collapsing onto the mattress. The springs groaned beneath my weight. I curled up, pulling the blankets tight around me, as if they could shield me from the questions clawing at the edges of my mind.

Was I in danger? The thought whispered through me like a chill wind, freezing me in place. The walls seemed to close in, suffocating me with the weight of everything I didn't understand.

My gaze fell upon the carved wooden box on the desk—the one that held the invitation, the one that had lured me to this place. Its polished surface gleamed faintly in the dim light, mocking me with its silence. Had it been a mistake?

A bitter laugh bubbled in my throat, but it never escaped. Maybe I should have stayed in the familiar misery of my old life. At least there, the dangers were known, the loneliness predictable. Here, even my own shadow seemed to carry secrets.

There's no way I could be in danger... right?

I let out a shaky breath, willing my heart to slow down. This was *Nexara Academy*—one of the most secure places in existence. They wouldn't have brought me here just to let something happen to me. Would they?

I shook my head, trying to dispel the thought. The professors— hell, even the students—were all powerful. The wards around the academy were unbreakable. If there was one place in the world where I was supposed to be safe, it was here.

And yet, my mind didn't let go of the possibility. What about the strange glances? The cryptic warnings? The feeling that I didn't belong here?

No. I was overthinking it. I always did this—spiraled into worst-case scenarios when I didn't have all the answers. Maybe that's all it was: fear of the unknown. It wasn't like I'd been chased by shadows or attacked in my dorm.

Thalia's POV

The logical part of my brain fought to take control. *This place is safe, Thalia,* I told myself firmly. *You're just letting your imagination get the best of you.*

Still, I couldn't shake the feeling that my presence here had started a domino effect I didn't understand.

Chapter 12

Thalia's POV

We all filed into the auditorium in the Evermore Hall, the air buzzing with conversation as students gathered in response to the Dean's summons. It was unusual for everyone to be called together like this, and a wave of curiosity rippled through the crowd.

James's laughter was infectious, and as he retold the tale of his siblings' encounter with the garden squatter. El's high-pitched giggle was the perfect counterpoint to James's deep laughs. I watched her, her hazel hair cascading over her shoulders as she threw her head back, her amber eyes filled with joy.

The three of us were huddled in the plush seats of the auditorium, the rest of the academy fading into a distant hum. James's imitation of his siblings' shock at finding the gnome, and the way he mimicked the gnome's gruff voice, had us all in stitches.

James leaned back in his seat, his blue eyes shining with nostalgia. "Oh, they were beside themselves. Mother was not pleased about the state of the garden shed, but Father thought it was the funniest thing he'd ever seen."

The lights in the auditorium dimmed, signaling the start of the assembly. The Dean's assistant, a stern-faced fae, took to the stage. Her voice echoed through the hall, commanding silence. "Please rise for Dean Astor."

We stood, the moment of lightness fading as we turned our attention to the front. Dean Astor exuded an air of authority, his presence electrifying the room as he moved confidently across the stage. He reached the polished wooden podium at the center, his expensive navy suit impeccably tailored, his glasses perched perfectly on the bridge of his nose. He surveyed the room, the gleam of his bald spot catching the harsh stage lights, and a hush fell over the eager audience.

"Thank you for coming," he began, his voice resonant and commanding. "You may be seated." The room obeyed, falling into a respectful silence. His smile was practiced, honed from years of addressing student bodies, yet there was an underlying sense of gravity in his demeanor that held everyone's attention.

"We are here today to discuss the upcoming Wonders of Nexara," Dean Astor continued, pausing for dramatic effect. "It's fast approaching, and with winter break following close behind, we wanted to take a moment to go over a few reminders and preparations."

Excited squeals and murmurs of enthusiasm erupted throughout the auditorium, spreading like wildfire. I exchanged a glance with El, who raised her eyebrows at me, a wide grin spreading across her face. The excitement was contagious, and despite my initial apprehension, I couldn't help but feel a flutter of anticipation.

James leaned over, his eyes alight with excitement. "Wonders of Nexara is a huge event here. It's like a mix of a tournament and a celebration—a showcase for the gifted," he explained, his voice hushed with reverence.

I nodded slowly, trying to process the information. "Sounds intense," I murmured, my gaze drifting back to the stage, where Dean Astor stood, waiting for the excited chatter to subside before continuing.

"As you know, the Wonders of Nexara is an opportunity for all of you to demonstrate your skills, your dedication, and your ability to rise to a challenge. It's a long-standing tradition at Nexara Academy, one that showcases the very best of our students. I expect everyone here to participate and take their preparation seriously."

El shot me a sideways look, a glimmer of excitement mixed with mischief in her eyes. "You should totally do this," she whispered, her voice barely audible above the murmurs around us.

James nodded enthusiastically, nudging my shoulder with a playful grin. "Yeah, Thalia, imagine how awesome it'd be. Besides, it's a chance to show everyone what you've got."

I swallowed, suddenly feeling the weight of their expectations. What did I *really* have to show? The thought of participating in such a public showcase—where every eye would be on me, judging my every move—was overwhelming. I had been here for weeks, and while I had grown stronger and more confident, I still had no discernible gifts.

The Dean's voice pulled my attention back to the stage. "This year's event will feature a series of challenges designed to push you beyond your limits," he announced, his tone growing serious. "The competition will be fierce, but remember—this is about growth, camaraderie, and testing your potential. I urge each of you to think carefully about what it means to participate." His words hung in the air—a challenge and an invitation.

Whispers rippled through the crowd, an electric buzz of excitement charging the atmosphere. I could feel the anticipation, the curiosity, and the undercurrent of anxiety hanging in the air. The phrase "beyond your limits" echoed in my mind, a stark reminder of how out of place I still felt at times.

El nudged me again, her grin widening, her eyes practically daring me to accept the challenge. "Come on, Thalia," she whispered, her voice a conspiratorial mix of excitement and encouragement. "I can see those wheels turning. You know you want to do it."

I glanced at her, then at James, who was already nodding with an enthusiastic gleam in his eyes. A smile tugged at my lips despite the nervous flutter in my stomach. "Maybe," I conceded, the possibility taking root in my mind. "We'll see."

The Dean's gaze swept across the crowd, a final appraisal before he wrapped up his speech. "For those of you who choose to participate," he announced, his voice ringing with authority, "we will have additional training sessions and guidance available starting next week. I look forward to seeing what each of you will bring to the Wonders of Nexara."

He stepped away from the podium, and the room erupted in a cacophony of excited chatter. The energy in the auditorium was palpable, a wave of anticipation washing over the students. The Wonders of Nexara is clearly more than just a competition—it was a celebration, a rite of passage.

Walking through the hallways, I was engulfed by the buzz of excitement and anxious chatter about the Wonders of Nexara. The higher-year students were practically vibrating with enthusiasm, their voices animated as they speculated about the upcoming challenges. Theories flew back and forth, whispers of past trials and legendary victories echoing through the corridors. The younger students, on the other hand, spoke with a mix of nervous anticipation and steely determination, their words hinting at both the thrill and the fear of the unknown.

El and James, having participated in last year's event, couldn't stop reminiscing about their experiences. According to them, the

Wonders were never the same twice—the element of surprise adding to the excitement. The event was designed to push students beyond their comfort zones, forcing them to either sink or swim, to discover hidden strengths and overcome perceived limitations. It was about survival. Pure, brutal survival. If you survived to the end, it was like wearing a badge of honor—not just around campus, but throughout all of Nexara.

El, a creature of chaos herself, thrived in the unpredictable environment. She described her experience with such enthusiasm, her eyes lighting up as she recounted dodging enchanted obstacles and narrowly avoiding well-aimed hexes. It was easy to picture her —quick and agile—navigating the challenges with a mischievous grin. James, on the other hand, focused on the camaraderie—the bonds formed in the heat of competition. He spoke of the deep connections made when facing the unknown with nothing but your instincts and your allies by your side.

As I walked, my thoughts inevitably drifted towards Damon, Nox, and Zarek. Had they participated in previous years? Of course they had. They were practically Nexara's own personal demigods, worshipped and feared in equal measure. I could already picture them effortlessly gliding through every challenge, barely breaking a sweat while the rest of us mere mortals struggled to keep up. They probably even managed to strike dramatic poses while doing it, with the wind conveniently whipping their hair just right. I rolled my eyes at the mental image – why did they always have to be so... *them*? So effortlessly cool, so impossibly perfect, so utterly infuriating.

I scoffed under my breath, annoyed at myself for letting my thoughts drift towards *them* yet again. Why did those three always seem to occupy prime real estate in my brain, rent-free? It was utterly ridiculous. I had far more important things to focus on— like, oh, I don't know, trying to survive this year at Nexara without making a complete and utter fool of myself. But no, apparently, my brain preferred to fixate on the brooding, annoyingly handsome trio instead. Absolutely absurd.

Maybe it was their coldness, their air of mystery, or the way they seemed to effortlessly order attention wherever they went. Or maybe it was just the sheer frustration of not being able to figure them out. Whatever the reason, they were a constant presence in my thoughts—a puzzle I couldn't seem to solve. And the more I tried to ignore them, the more persistent they became. It was like my mind had developed a mind of its own, and it had a *serious* crush on the Shadow Brothers.

"Will your little pathetic human be participating?" Mira sneered, her voice dripping with malice. "I would *love* to run into her during the challenges." The giggles from her entourage, like a chorus of vultures, sent an instant headache pounding behind my eyes. She leaned in closer, her eyes glowing with malicious glee. "You know, once the challenge starts, the academy isn't liable for injuries... or casualties."

A wave of nausea washed over me. It wasn't just the thinly veiled threat; it was the way her words seemed to hang in the air, infecting the atmosphere with a toxic dread. Before I could respond, El's voice cut through the tension like a whip.

"Oh my god, Mira," she drawled, her smile as sharp as a shard of ice. "Let's hope *I* don't see *you* out there. I'd hate for that pretty little face of yours to get scarred forever." Her eyes glinted with a dangerous light, a promise of fiery retribution. "You know, I can cast fire that not even your precious healing abilities could fully mend."

Mira's smirk faltered for a split second, her hand instinctively flying up to touch her cheek—a flicker of fear betraying her usual arrogance. I couldn't help but laugh, the sound escaping before I could stop it.

"I really appreciate your concern, Mira, I really do," I said, my voice dripping with fake sincerity. "But maybe you should be more focused on yourself and less on the 'pathetic human.' I'm sure Zarek wouldn't want you hanging around if your face wasn't so... *intact.*" I let the last word hang in the air, a pointed reminder of El's earlier threat.

Her smirk wavered, and I could tell I'd struck a nerve. Whether it was the mention of Zarek or the sheer audacity of a human talking back to her—again—it clearly got under her skin. For a delicious moment, she was speechless. But Mira's eyes quickly narrowed, the icy blue hardening with a venomous glare. She regained her composure quickly, but the crack in her facade remained—a testament to the sting of my words.

"Are you just upset because they don't want you?" she sneered, her voice a whisper that slithered into my ear. "Because they actually *despise* you." Her cruel smile widened, as she twisted the knife. "God, you should hear the way they talk about you. You wouldn't be enough for them. They need someone strong, someone powerful by their side. And, well..." Her gaze raked over me, dripping with condescension, daring me to rise to the bait. I leaned in just slightly, my eyes locking onto hers.

"Honestly," I murmured, my voice low and laced with a playful challenge, "if they despise me so much, they sure spend a lot of time around me, wouldn't you say?" I tilted my head, feigning innocence. "Maybe you could do me a favor, Mira, and tell them to leave me the fuck alone. I'm sure they'd listen to you." I let the last sentence hang in the air, a subtle dig at her desperate attempts to gain their attention.

Her eyes widened, the smirk momentarily slipping as a flash of anger. I let the silence hang between us, savoring her stunned expression before I straightened up, turning away with deliberate calmness. I wouldn't give her the satisfaction of a response, not while she was still reeling from what I said.

El was grinning beside me, her eyes practically dancing with glee. "Come on," I said, my voice light and casual, though my heart still pounded with the lingering rush of adrenaline. As we walked away, I could feel Mira's seething gaze burning into my back, but I didn't give her the satisfaction of looking back. I had won this round, and the knowledge of that small victory was enough to fuel me for the rest of the day.

El laughed, nudging me playfully. "You really know how to get under her skin," she said, her grin a mix of pride and amusement. "That was amazing!"

El and I parted ways after the Dean's unexpected announcement that classes were canceled for the rest of the day. With the gift of an unscheduled afternoon, I decided to head back to my dorm, hoping for a bit of peace and quiet to process everything—Mira's threats, El's fiery defense, the Dean's surprising declaration about the Wonders of Nexara, and the lingering curiosity about those cryptic words Professor Lorian had uttered in the dead of night.

But as I approached the Women's Dorms, I screeched to a halt. Leaning against the stone archway—as if he were a part of the building itself—stood Zarek. He was a figure of contradictions: relaxed yet alert, casual yet intense. His usual laid-back, teasing demeanor was nowhere to be found; instead, he stood with arms crossed, staring at the entrance with an unreadable expression.

My first instinct was to avoid him entirely. To pretend I hadn't seen him and slip past, unnoticed, into the relative safety of the dorm. I had no idea what he was doing there, and frankly, I wasn't in the mood for any of his usual cryptic pronouncements or flirtatious games. But as I attempted to execute my avoidance maneuver, he turned his head, his gaze zeroing in on me with an intensity that made my stomach flip.

"There you are," he said, his voice low and husky.

"Stalking is taking things a bit too far, don't you think?" My usual sharpness was there—the instinctive defense mechanism kicking in—but the bite lacked its usual force. Something about his presence felt different today, and it threw me off balance.

What is wrong with me? I inwardly groaned, frustrated by my own involuntary reaction to him.

Zarek's eyes narrowed slightly, his gaze sweeping over my face as if he were trying to decipher my thoughts. "I'm not stalking you," he said, his voice carrying a sharp edge I hadn't heard from him before. It was a tone I associated with Nox, with Damon—one that held an underlying current of something dangerous. "We need to talk."

His words stopped me in my tracks. Talk? This wasn't the Zarek I knew, the one who delighted in playful banter and veiled innuendos. A flicker of apprehension, mixed with a strange, unwelcome curiosity, sparked within me. I crossed my arms defensively, my usual shield against their confusing world.

"About what?" I asked, my voice cautious, wary. The intensity in his eyes was unsettling, and the air thrummed with an unspoken tension that made me want to bolt. But something held me rooted to the spot—a strange compulsion to hear what he had to say.

Zarek stepped closer, his expression more serious than I'd ever seen it. "The Wonders of Nexara," he said, his voice low and resonant.

I blinked, momentarily taken aback. He wasn't smiling. He wasn't teasing. There was an urgency in his eyes, a sense of purpose that made me hesitate despite my reservations.

"Why do you care?" I shot back, though my voice wavered slightly. His seriousness was unnerving, throwing me off balance.

"Are you going to participate?" His tone was low, serious—demanding an answer.

I swallowed, a strange tension coiling in the space between us. This was unlike any of our previous encounters. I found myself answering without even thinking.

"Yes." The word left my lips before I could stop it, and I held his gaze, my own eyes locked on his deep golden amber ones. Shadows seemed to dance at the edges of my vision, shifting and swirling as he took a deep breath, running his fingers through his hair before looking down at the ground. Was he... concerned?

"If you're going to join," he said, his voice firm, brooking no argument, "you're training with us." He looked back up at me, his eyes devoid of emotion, a mask firmly back in place.

"I'm good, thanks." I scoffed, turning to leave, eager to escape the intensity of him and the confusing emotions swirling within me. But his hand shot out, catching my bicep. His touch was warm—almost burning—setting my skin on fire even through the fabric of my sleeve. His grip was firm, insistent, but it didn't hurt. It was more like a brand, searing his presence onto me.

"You will, Thalia," he said, his voice steady and commanding, leaving no room for argument. I looked down at his hand on my arm, the warmth of his touch still lingering on my skin, then back up at him, my gaze hardened into a *get the hell off me* glare.

He held my gaze for a beat, a silent battle of wills playing out between us. His hand lingered a moment longer before he finally let go. The warmth quickly dissipated, replaced by an almost uncomfortable chill—as if his touch had left an imprint on my skin.

"I'll be here in a few hours to pick you up for training," he said, the sharp edge in his voice softening as his usual playful smirk returned, a hint of challenge dancing in his eyes. "Be ready, or I'll drag you out there myself."

The threat, though delivered with a playfully, held an undercurrent of seriousness that made me shiver. "Don't threaten me, Zarek," I warned, my voice low but firm. "I'm not one of your fangirls to be bossed around."

"No, you're not," a light laugh escaped his lips, his eyes twinkling with amusement. "But you *are* going to train with us. Whether you like it or not." He turned to leave, then paused, glancing back at me over his shoulder. "And Thalia?"

"What?" I asked, my voice laced with annoyance.

"Don't be late," he said, a wide grin spreading across his face. "I wouldn't want to have to resort to drastic measures."

As I walked away, I heard his voice call after me, laced with that signature teasing warmth. "I'll see you later, Firefly." I didn't turn around, but I could hear the smile in his words.

I made a beeline for my dorm. The audacity of him, thinking he could just decide I was training with them. As if I needed their help. As if I was just going to fall in line because he commanded it. The nerve.

I pushed open the heavy wooden door, stepping into the relative peace of the dormitory. I could feel the tension of the day slowly starting to melt away as I made my way down the dimly lit hallway to my room. Or at least, it would have—had my mind not been occupied with Zarek's proposition—or more accurately, his demand.

Train with them? Yeah, right. I scoffed to myself, the thought alone was laughable. Sure, they were powerful—and annoyingly attractive—but that didn't mean I needed them. I had managed just fine on my own so far, hadn't I? I didn't need their help, their pity, or their presence messing with my head any more than it already was.

As I reached my door, I paused, my hand resting on the cool metal of the doorknob. I closed my eyes, taking a deep breath, trying to clear my mind. But Zarek's words still lingered, echoing through my thoughts with an unsettling persistence.

I'll be here in a few hours to pick you up for training. Be ready, or I'll drag you out there myself.

The memory of his hand on my arm sent an unexpected warm down my body. His warmth, his closeness—it had taken me by surprise, catching me off guard. It wasn't just his touch, though. It was the look in his eyes, the urgency in his voice. It was... different.

I shook my head, trying to dispel the thoughts. *What am I even thinking?* This was Zarek we were talking about. The same Zarek who teased me relentlessly. Who flirted with every girl in sight. Who always seemed to be playing some kind of game. I couldn't let myself get swept up in... whatever this was. I needed to stay focused.

I pushed open the door to my room, stepping inside to the soft click of it closing behind me. The room was just as I'd left it—a small haven amidst the chaos of the academy. My gaze fell on the scattered notes and books strewn across my desk, remnants of my attempts to catch up on what I'd missed.

I moved towards the desk, gathering up the notes and trying to organize them into some semblance of order. I was supposed to be studying, to be preparing for the challenges ahead. That was what mattered—not Zarek, not his ridiculous proposition, and certainly not the confusing mess of emotions he seemed to stir within me.

I sat down at my desk, pulling out my textbook and flipping it open to the bookmarked page. I stared at the words, my mind refusing to focus. Frustrated, I let out a sigh, running my fingers through my hair as I leaned back in my chair.

Why can't I just stop thinking about them?

My focus should have been on my studies, on desperately trying to unlock whatever dormant abilities I supposedly had. The Wonders of Nexara was a daunting reminder of the expectations of being gifted. I needed to be ready. To prove to myself—and to everyone else—that I was more than just a human amongst gods.

I glanced at the clock, the hands ticking away with relentless precision. Time was slipping through my fingers, and I felt powerless to stop it. I had a decision to make, and I knew I couldn't put it off forever.

Train with them, or face the challenges alone?

The thought of training with Zarek—and by extension, Damon and Nox—was both thrilling and terrifying. They were the best of the best, the epitome of power and grace. If I trained with them, I would be stepping into their world—a world I wasn't entirely sure I was ready for. But if I didn't... would I be passing up an opportunity to grow stronger? To become the person I was meant to be?

I stood up, pacing the small confines of my room as I weighed my options. The walls seemed to close in around me, the pressure building with each passing second. I needed to clear my head, to escape the suffocating silence of my room.

Without allowing myself to second-guess, I grabbed my jacket and slipped out the door, heading towards the one place where I could find some semblance of peace: the forest.

As I walked, the sounds of the academy faded into the background. The midday sun beat down mercilessly, casting a harsh light over the path ahead. I breathed in the cool, crisp air, letting it fill my lungs as I ventured deeper into the forest.

Chapter 13

Thalia's POV

I wandered deeper into the trees, seeking a moment of solitude away from the prying eyes and whispers. But that damn unsettling sensation of being watched crept over me, a prickling at the back of my neck that I couldn't shake off. I tried to dismiss it, to convince myself it was just paranoia, the result of too much stress and too little sleep. The usual.

But the feeling persisted, growing stronger with each step I took. It was like a prickling at the back of my neck, an itch I couldn't scratch. I stopped in my tracks, my senses on high alert as I scanned the surrounding forest. Then I saw him, leaning casually against a tree with a mischievous glint in his amber eyes—Zarek.

"For someone who says they don't want to play games, you sure do," he drawled, his voice laced with amusement. "Enjoying a little game of cat and mouse, are we?"

I rolled my eyes, crossing my arms over my chest. "So you *are* stalking me," I accused, my voice sharp with annoyance. "What the hell, Z—"

Before I could finish my sentence, Zarek closed the distance between us in the blink of an eye—his movements a blur of speed that left me reeling. With a swift, effortless motion, he hoisted me over his shoulder as if I weighed nothing, his strong arms securing me in place.

"I swear to the gods, Zarek, put me down!" I snapped, my voice echoing through the trees. I squirmed against his shoulder, but the movement only seemed to tighten his grip—his fingers pressing into my side just enough to send a shiver down my spine.

"Nope, I'm good," he replied, the laughter in his voice infuriatingly clear.

I huffed in frustration, my heart pounding in my chest. The world spun around me as Zarek moved with inhuman speed, his footsteps silent against the forest floor. I could feel the muscles in his shoulder shift and flex beneath my body—a blunt reminder of the raw power he possessed.

"This isn't funny, Zarek!" I protested, pounding my fists against his back in a futile attempt to break free. "Put me down right now!"

"Relax" he said, his tone light and teasing. "We're just taking a shortcut."

"You know, you could have just asked nicely," I grumbled, my annoyance giving way to a grudging amusement.

"Oh, but I did ask nicely," he countered, a playful lilt in his voice. "But you... you just have to make it difficult." He chuckled, the sound vibrating through his chest and into mine, and I hated that it made me smile. There was something undeniably charming about him, the way he seemed to know exactly how to push my buttons, how to make my heart race when I least wanted it to.

I sighed dramatically, letting my body go limp in an attempt to make it more difficult for him to carry me.

"Really, Firefly?" he asked, his voice low and amused. He didn't miss a beat, continuing on as if I weighed nothing at all.

"Yes, really," I insisted. "And stop calling me that. It's bad enough your little girlfriend wants to murder me. Word's going to spread about this little kidnapping situation, and hopefully, she'll kick your ass."

He tensed for a moment. "She's not my girlfriend, Thalia," he corrected, his voice firm. Then, with a teasing lilt, he added, "But is that jealousy I hear in your voice?"

I rolled my eyes, even though he couldn't see it. "Jealous? Me? Please," I scoffed, trying to sound nonchalant. But I could feel the heat rising to my cheeks, and it was taking everything I had not to let it show in my voice.

"Uh-huh, sure. Keep telling yourself that," he teased, his voice laced with a knowing edge. "But I can definitely hear it. You're blushing, aren't you?"

"Oh, please. You're not that charming," I retorted, my tone light but playful. "I mean, you are—but I'm not affected by it."

His laughter echoed through the trees, and I felt the warmth of his body against mine. "Is that so? Because you seem pretty affected right now."

"Hardly," I replied, trying to maintain my composure. "You're just another pretty face in a sea of chaos."

"Pretty face, huh? I'll take that as a compliment," he said, his voice a low purr. "Face it, Firefly, I'm growing on you."

"You're delusional," I retorted, but my voice lacked conviction.

He finally set me down once we reached the clearing, the silhouette of that familiar house sitting before us. His hands lingered on my waist for a heartbeat longer than necessary. His eyes met mine, a hint of a smirk playing on his lips, as if he knew the effect he had on me.

"Is your pet beast under control this time?" I asked, raising an eyebrow as I glanced into the forest, attempting to diffuse the tension that crackled between us. I studied the very house I had practically crashed into—the place where I had come face-to-face with their enormous guard panther, who had decided that my presence in the woods was an affront to its very existence.

The shadows danced at the edge of my vision, their movements mimicking the unease swirling within me.

"Yes, our pet beast is under control," he said with a chuckle, shaking his head at my attempt to deflect.

We stood in comfortable silence for a moment, the only sounds the rustling leaves and the distant calls of birds. But eventually, Zarek broke the quiet, his voice gentle yet curious.

"What do you see when you're out here?" he asked, his gaze fixed on the dappled sunlight filtering through the trees. "In the forest?"

I hesitated, unsure how much I wanted to reveal. My connection to the shadows felt deeply personal—something that belonged only to me. "Shadows," I replied, glancing back at him with a slight shrug.

He hummed thoughtfully, studying me with an intensity that made my heart skip a beat. "Shadows, huh? They seem to like you," he observed, his voice laced with intrigue. "I've never seen anything quite like it."

I arched an eyebrow, a teasing smile playing on my lips. "And how exactly would you know that?" I asked, my voice light. "Are you admitting to following me?"

Zarek smirked, his eyes a darker shade of amber, meeting mine with a heat that made my cheeks burn. "Maybe I have," he admitted, his voice a low purr. "Or maybe I'm just good at noticing things that others miss."

I rolled my eyes, but couldn't suppress the smile tugging at the corners of my lips. "Well, congratulations on your excellent observation... or stalking skills," I conceded.

"Do they speak to you?" Zarek's question was softer this time, almost hesitant, as if he were worried he might break some invisible barrier by asking.

I considered his words. I couldn't hear them, not in the traditional sense. But they weren't just darkness; they were alive, a presence that seemed to understand me in a way nothing else did.

"They don't speak," I answered, my voice barely above a whisper. "But they guide me. It's like they know where I need to go before I even realize it."

Zarek fell silent, and when I glanced at him, I saw an expression of wonder on his face. He looked almost... fascinated.

"Well, the shadows seem to always lead you back to this house," he said with a smirk, a glint of mischief returning to his eyes. "Seems like they want you here."

"Yeah, I'm not quite sure why they always lead me here," I admitted, tilting my head in contemplation. Then, with a playful glint in my eyes, I added, "Or why I seem to be so drawn to your... territory." I paused, letting the implication hang in the air. "Plus, let's not forget that they were basically responsible for my death at the paws of a glorified house cat."

Zarek threw his head back and roared with laughter, the sound echoing through the clearing like a melody. My heart tightened at the sound—a strange mix of joy and something deeper, something akin to warmth, swirling within me.

"So, are we going to train, or did you just want to kidnap me and bring me to my potential doom?" I asked, quirking an eyebrow at him, my voice dripping with mock seriousness.

"Kidnapping was definitely on the agenda," Zarek replied with a smirk, his eyes twinkling. "But alright, let's focus. I want you to concentrate on what you feel when you're out here. Focus on those shadows."

I took a deep breath, the levity of our earlier banter fading as I tried to center myself. The clearing thrummed with energy, and as I closed my eyes, I attempted to tune out everything except the whispers of the shadows that surrounded me. But instead of feeling empowered, a wave of uncertainty washed over me.

"What do I do?" I murmured, glancing back at Zarek, who was watching me intently.

"Imagine the shadows as an extension of yourself," he instructed, his voice calm yet firm. "They're not just darkness; they're your allies. Let them guide you, but remember, you're the one in control."

I nodded, but more doubt crept in as I concentrated. The shadows seemed to shift and swirl around me, but I struggled to connect with them. Instead of flowing, they felt chaotic and disjointed, like a wild river refusing to be tamed.

"What do you see?" Zarek's voice was so gentle that I almost felt guilty for the frustration bubbling inside me.

I furrowed my brow, my voice snapping with irritation. "I don't know! It's like they're dancing away from me. I just can't catch them."

"Can't catch them?" Nox's voice, cool and detached, cut through the air. "Maybe they sense your hesitation."

I opened my eyes to find Nox standing beside Zarek, his expression unreadable, as if he were a statue carved from stone. Zarek shot him a warning glance, but Nox remained unfazed, his gaze fixed on me. "Fear can be a powerful deterrent, Thalia. If you're not confident, the shadows will only mock you."

"Thanks for the pep talk, Nox," I retorted, sarcasm dripping from my voice, though inside, anxiety gnawed at me. "I didn't realize this was a motivational seminar."

Zarek stepped forward, placing a reassuring hand on my shoulder. "You're doing fine. It takes time to build that connection. You just have to keep focusing."

Nox's lips curled into a slight smirk, but his expression remained impassive. "Focus, huh? You can't just wish them to obey you. The shadows will test you, like any other opponent. They need to know you're serious."

My frustration mounted, my confidence crumbling. "I'm trying!" I shot back, my voice rising in exasperation. "I don't know what I'm doing!"

"Where's Damon? Maybe he can help," Zarek suggested, tightening his grip on my shoulder reassuringly.

Nox raised an eyebrow, his smirk fading slightly. "Damon? He's not exactly the hand-holding type, you know that."

Zarek didn't back down, his gaze steady. "Maybe not, but she needs to understand her connection with the shadows—and he knows more about them than anyone. If she's struggling, he might be able to help."

Nox sighed, clearly unenthusiastic about the idea. "I'll talk to him, but don't expect any miracles." With that, he turned and started towards the house, his movements swift and silent, like a shadow melting into the night.

The moment he was gone, I let out a long breath. Zarek's hand remained on my shoulder, anchoring me in the midst of my rising anxiety.

"Damon?" I asked, my laugh bordering on hysterical. "I'm definitely screwed."

Zarek's lips curved into a gentle smile, his eyes warm with understanding. "He can be intense, sure. But he understands these shadows better than anyone. If anyone can help you push through, it's him."

I swallowed, a wave of dread washing over me. The thought of Damon watching me struggle—judging my every move—twisted my stomach into knots. I closed my eyes and tried to focus again, honing in on the shadows that seemed intent on taunting me. Now that I was finally acknowledging them, they chose to play coy, swirling just out of reach. It was infuriating.

My entire life, they had been my silent companions, dancing around me, weaving in and out of my periphery, wrapping me in their embrace like a protective blanket. As a child, I had lived in their presence, finding comfort in their dark, gentle caress. They had always been there during my moments of isolation, flickering playfully in the corners of my vision, but I had never understood their significance until now. Now, they felt both familiar and elusive, their movements almost mocking, as if they were aware of my struggle to connect.

This could be my chance to discover what they are—what *I* am—how I'm connected to this gifted world. I needed this more than anyone realized. To finally not be an outsider, perpetually on the fringes, looking in. I wasn't welcome in Nyvorthia, cast out like a stray. And I wasn't entirely welcome here at the academy either, not yet. Maybe this strange, swirling darkness held the key to finally belonging—to finding a place where I wouldn't have to constantly hide the strange whispers that echoed within me.

I could feel their energy pulsing, a living entity just beyond my grasp. The way they danced around me reminded me of fireflies on a warm summer night—beautiful, mesmerizing, but frustratingly unattainable. Every time I reached for them, they would shift away, refusing to reveal their secrets.

I breathed in the stillness of the forest, letting go of the fear and frustration that had been building within me. I focused on the memories of comfort the shadows had always offered, the sense of belonging they gave me in the quiet moments. I reached out to them, not as a master seeking control, but as a friend seeking connection.

Chapter 14

Thalia's POV

Flashback: 15 years ago

I watched the children play from the window, their laughter a distant melody that only sharpened the pang of loneliness in my chest. They looked so happy, so carefree—their world a vibrant tapestry of games and shared joy. I never meant to hurt anyone; I never meant to scare them. But the whispers followed me like a shadow, and the fear in their eyes felt like daggers piercing my heart. Each outburst, every flicker of anger or frustration, pushed them further away, leaving me isolated—trapped behind the cold glass of the window.

"Thalia!" The sharp voice of Glenna, the caretaker, startled me, slicing through my thoughts. "Get away from the window."

I flinched, my eyes widening with fear as I turned to face her. The familiar look of disgust twisted her features, as if my very presence offended her. The disappointment in her gaze cut deeper than any words could. Glenna, with her stern face and perpetually pursed lips, had always been quick to reprimand—her sharp voice echoing through the halls like a harbinger of doom.

"What did I tell you about staring?" she snapped, her eyes narrowing. "You need to stop lurking around like that. It frightens the others."

I shrank back, the sting of her words wrapping around me like a vise. "I don't want to scare them," I whispered, my voice barely audible. "I just want to play."

"Why do you always have to be like this?" she retorted, her hands planted firmly on her hips. "You know the other children don't want to play with you. They're scared of what you can do."

I swallowed hard, my gaze falling to the worn floorboards as I mumbled, "I wasn't doing anything wrong. I was just watching."

Glenna scoffed, her expression hardening. "Watching, yes. Until another 'incident' happens. You know what happens when you lose control, don't you, Thalia?" She stepped closer, her imposing figure looming over me, and I instinctively recoiled.

I nodded quickly, tears stinging my eyes. "I—I know. I promise I won't... I won't let it happen again."

"Promises," Glenna sneered, her voice dripping with disgust. "You've promised before, haven't you? And still, trouble follows you."

Her expression remained cold, unforgiving. "You need to control yourself. You're a danger to them, and to yourself."

The weight of her words settled heavily upon me, deepening the familiar ache of rejection. I wanted to scream, to let my emotions spill over in a way that wouldn't hurt anyone, but instead, I stood frozen in silence.

I looked up briefly, a desperate plea for understanding in my eyes. I wanted to defend myself. To explain that it wasn't my fault, that I didn't ask for this strange power that seemed to surge within me— uncontrollable and terrifying. But the words caught in my throat. All I saw in Glenna's eyes was a chilling mix of fear and disap-

pointment. Defeated, I lowered my gaze once more, letting the silence speak for me.

"Good. Now, get back to your room," she ordered coldly. "Stay there until I say otherwise."

Without another word, I turned and fled, my small feet carrying me quickly down the narrow, dimly lit hallway. The carefree laughter of the other children echoed behind me, a painful reminder of everything I was excluded from. I reached my room, a small, sterile space with bare walls and a single window overlooking the desolate backyard, and pushed the door shut. Leaning my forehead against the cool wood, I finally let the tears flow freely.

The shadows were already there, waiting for me, dancing along the walls, curling into the corners of my tiny sanctuary. They were my only companions, my silent confidantes. I watched them, letting their presence fill the emptiness inside me, wrapping me in their dark embrace like a comforting blanket. They never judged me, never turned away; they simply stayed, soothing me when no one else would.

"Maybe I am the problem," I whispered to the shadows, my voice cracking with despair. "Maybe this is where I belong—hidden away, alone."

TEARS WELLED IN MY EYES, BLURRING THE PRESENT AS the memory, sharp and vivid, resurfaced from the depths of my subconscious. A memory I had apparently suppressed, buried beneath layers of forced resilience and false indifference. But now, the feeling of rejection and isolation came flooding back, raw and overwhelming, a tidal wave that threatened to drown me in its intensity.

Chapter 14

"Maybe I am the problem," the echo of my younger self whispered in my ear. *"Maybe this is where I belong—hidden away, alone."*

The words replayed in my mind, a haunting refrain that refused to be silenced. What had really changed? *Nothing*, I thought bitterly. I'm still the outcast, the anomaly, the one who doesn't belong. I'm *still* the problem.

The shadow swarmed around me, their cool touch a comforting presence amidst the storm of emotions. They were silent reassurances, their darkness a shield against the pain that threatened to consume me.

But this time, I wouldn't just let them comfort me. I would embrace them, become one with them. I grabbed hold of them, twisting them into myself, pulling them closer, deeper. I let them seep into me, embracing the familiar darkness, letting it weave through my veins until I felt it within every fiber of my being. This time, I wouldn't let it just be a blanket, a shield; I would let it become a part of me, my strength, my power, not my burden.

Opening my eyes, I felt a jolt of energy—a surge of power that resonated through my entire being. It was as if a part of me had reconnected, a piece of myself that had been shattered long ago finally clicking back into place. A wave of warmth spread through me. A sense of wholeness I had never experienced.

Tears threatened to spill again, but these weren't tears of sadness or loneliness. They were tears of awe, of recognition—of finally *understanding*. I looked down at my hands, mesmerized. Delicate black swirls, like tendrils of smoke given life, danced around my fingertips. They moved with a mesmerizing grace, shimmering faintly before settling into intricate patterns that wrapped around my fingers and spiraled up my hands, disappearing beneath the fabric of my sweatshirt. A gasp escaped my lips—not a breath, but a release of years of pent-up longing. These weren't merely tattoos; they were living extensions of the shadows I had

151

embraced, pulsing with a subtle energy that mirrored the rhythm of my own heartbeat. It felt like coming home after a lifetime of wandering lost in the wilderness.

My fingers trembled as I traced the path of the markings, a sense of awe and disbelief washing over me. This wasn't just a manifestation of the shadows; it was a part of *me*—etched into my skin, woven into my very being. A symbol of belonging, a mark of acceptance in a world that had always rejected me. It was a physical manifestation of the connection I had forged. A symbol of the power I had finally claimed as my own. A choked sob escaped my throat, a mixture of relief and pure, unadulterated joy. For the first time in my life, I felt truly *seen*—not by others, but by myself.

"Beautiful," I whispered, my voice thick with emotion. My eyes traced the swirling patterns once more, marveling at the intricate designs that now decorated my skin. The shadows seemed to flicker in response—a silent affirmation of my wonder, a promise of the strength I now possessed. It wasn't just beautiful; it was *me*.

"Looks like she didn't need me," a cool, detached voice cut through the quiet, snapping me out of my reverie.

I turned, my gaze colliding with the familiar depths of Damon's dark-blue eyes. He stood between his brothers, his presence radiating an oppressive weight that seemed to steal the air from my lungs. His expression was as impassive as ever, hiding any hint of emotion, just as it had been every other time I'd been unfortunate enough to cross his path. His eyes flicked down to my hands, lingering on the black swirls that still shimmered faintly against my skin, before returning to my face, his gaze piercing and intense.

The shadows that had been so comforting moments before now felt like a spotlight, highlighting my every flaw under his scrutiny. I straightened my spine, refusing to cower beneath his judgmental stare. There was something unnerving about the way Damon looked at me, as though he were dissecting every piece of me, searching for weakness, assessing me as a potential threat.

"Didn't need you?" Zarek chimed in, a playful grin tugging at his lips, attempting to lighten the tension that had descended upon the clearing. "Come on, Damon, don't be so dramatic."

Nox remained silent, his gaze flickering between me and Damon, his lips pressed into a thin line. But Damon's eyes never left mine, and I could feel the intensity radiating off him like a storm cloud, cold and charged with an energy I couldn't quite understand.

I clenched my fists, feeling the shadows swirl and respond beneath my skin, a flicker of newfound power thrumming through my veins. "I'm managing," I said, my voice steadier than I felt, meeting his gaze with a confidence I didn't know I possessed. "I've got this under control."

Damon's expression remained emotionless, but a faint spark of something – anger? surprise? – flickered in his eyes. "We'll see about that," he murmured, his voice low, almost a whisper, yet it carried through the clearing, hanging heavy in the air.

I held his gaze, refusing to back down, even as the weight of his judgment pressed down on me. The shadows pulsed within me, a tangible reminder of what I had just achieved—a testament to my own strength and potential. They danced beneath my skin, a dark ballet that was as much a part of me as my own heartbeat. This power was mine, claimed without *his* help, without *his* approval.

"Let's not call out your attack house-cat just yet; I still don't know what I'm doing," I snapped, meeting Damon's gaze head-on, refusing to be intimidated by his piercing eyes. The tension crackled between us, his presence like a storm on the verge of breaking.

"House cat? What cat?" Nox interjected, his eyebrows shooting up in surprise as he turned to his brothers. "What is she talking about?"

It was the most genuine, unguarded expression I had ever seen on Nox—a mix of pure confusion and vulnerability that he made no attempt to conceal. It was utterly disarming. And before I could fully take in the rare sight, Zarek's laughter erupted, filling the clearing with its rich, unrestrained sound.

I bit the inside of my cheek, trying to suppress my own smile, but it was nearly impossible with Zarek's infectious laughter echoing around us. His eyes sparkled with amusement, and the corners of his lips quirked up as if my antics were the highlight of his day. Damon, meanwhile, rolled his eyes, shaking his head slightly—a ghost of a smile playing on his lips, but never quite materializing.

"She's talking about the beast from the night she broke into our home," Damon deadpanned, his expression a perfect blend of irritation and suspicion that always seemed reserved just for me.

"You're calling it a *house-cat*?" Nox exclaimed, his voice rising in disbelief. His eyes widened, and he gave me a slow once-over, as if re-evaluating my sanity. He seemed utterly confused, his gaze lingering on my face, searching for any hint of a joke. The perplexed frown creasing his brow and the tilt of his head made it clear: he thought I had completely lost my mind.

"Yes, the big kitty is beautiful," I declared with a dramatic sigh, waving a hand dismissively as if it were the most obvious thing in the world. "But you guys seem to have trained it to devour anyone who dares enter your precious territory, so if you could keep it on a leash, or maybe invest in a scratching post, I would appreciate it." I finished with a shrug, giving Nox a pointed look before glancing back at Damon.

Zarek's laughter erupted again, and I couldn't help but steal a glance at him. His eyes met mine, his expression softening as he shook his head slightly, that trademark smirk still firmly in place.

"Beautiful and insane," he mused, his voice laced with a teasing lilt that sent a familiar flutter through my stomach. "I knew there was something different about you, Firefly."

"I think she's serious," Nox scoffed, his voice a blend of amusement and annoyance. He turned back to me, one eyebrow arched incredulously. "Really? You think it's *beautiful*?"

I met his gaze head-on, a playful challenge sparking in my eyes. "Well, sure," I replied, my voice laced with a touch of sarcasm. "If you ignore the whole 'wants to eat me' part, it's got this majestic, untamed vibe. Besides," I added with a small grin, "it's probably just misunderstood. Honestly, I'd want to kill everything too if I had to be around the three of you all the time."

For a split second, I could have sworn Nox's lips twitched upward, a hint of a smile threatening to break through his usual stoicism.

Zarek clapped Nox on the back, leaning into the moment with a mischievous glint in his amber eyes. "See, Nox?" he teased, his voice brimming with amusement. "She gets it. Maybe we should let her *handle* the beast next time."

Damon shot Zarek a warning look, his dark blue eyes narrowed into slits. "That's enough," he said, his voice laced with a chilling authority. "These shadows are different," he mumbled, more to himself than anyone else, his gaze fixed on the swirling darkness that clung to me like a second skin. "Let's see if she can actually do something *useful* with them."

He began circling me, his movements predatory, his gaze sharp and unyielding, like a hawk assessing its prey. I could feel the pressure mounting with each deliberate step he took. My heart hammered against my ribs, a frantic drumbeat against the silence of the clearing. I fought to maintain my composure, refusing to cower, even as a wave of fear threatened to consume me.

Without a word of warning, a shadow detached itself from the ground beneath Damon's feet. It shot towards me with terrifying speed, morphing into the shape of a dagger—its edges sharp and menacing. I barely had time to register the threat before instinct took over. My hand flew up to shield my face, my eyes squeezing shut in a reflexive act of survival.

Then—silence. A heavy, expectant silence that hung in the air like a shroud.

Slowly, cautiously, I opened my eyes. The clearing shimmered with an eerie stillness, the air thick with tension. But something was different. A dark mist enveloped me, swirling and coiling, forming a protective barrier that pulsed with an almost sentient energy. The shadows—once playful and elusive—now moved with a determined fluidity, wrapping around me like a living shield, their touch strangely comforting.

I stared at the shadowy barrier, my heart still racing, my mind struggling to comprehend what had just happened. I had instinctively summoned the shadows, bending them to my will, creating a defense against Damon's unexpected attack. A wave of exhilaration, mixed with disbelief, washed over me. I had done it. I had actually *done* something.

Zarek let out a low whistle, his eyes widening with genuine surprise. "Well, would you look at that," he murmured, his voice softer now, laced with a hint of awe.

Nox's gaze met mine, his expression no longer one of annoyance but something more like curiosity. "Guess there's more to her than we thought," he admitted, his tone a blend of disbelief and respect.

Damon stopped circling, his eyes locked onto mine. There was something new in his gaze—an emotion I couldn't quite decipher. His eyes narrowed slightly, as if he were trying to peer inside my mind, to uncover the secrets within my soul.

I let out a long, shaky breath, my fingers hesitantly reaching out to brush the dark mist that still lingered around me. The shadows responded instantly, dissolving back into nothingness as if they had never been there, leaving me feeling strangely exposed.

THE NEXT MORNING, AFTER MY INTENSE TRAINING session with the brothers, I found myself alone on the training field. My muscles screamed in protest, a mixture of aches and twinges, a testament of the demanding exercises they'd put me through. But I was determined to use the early morning stillness to explore my shadows more. So far, though? Spoiler alert: *Nothing. Zip. Zilch. Nada.*

I settled on the edge of the field, the cool, dew-kissed grass a welcome contrast against my palms. My gaze drifted towards the shadowy woods encircling the academy grounds. The air was crisp and refreshing, a welcome change from the sterile atmosphere of the academy buildings. The first rays of sunlight, like golden fingers, started to shine, painting the landscape with a soft, delicate light.

My shadows seemed eager to explore, to merge with the long silhouettes cast by the trees, as if yearning to claim the entire forest as their domain. I swallowed hard, a knot of apprehension forming in my stomach. There was a raw, untamed power in those shadows, an energy that both fascinated and intimidated me.

Despite my efforts, controlling them was more difficult than I'd thought. I could summon them, yes, and they seemed to respond to my emotions, swirling and shifting with my every mood. But true mastery eluded me. I couldn't quite grasp the reins, couldn't direct their movements with the precision I craved. Frustration chipped away at me, a constant reminder of my limitations.

Closing my eyes, I inhaled deeply, attempting to clear my mind and reconnect with the power I had felt the day before. I recalled the sensation of the shadows enveloping me, their cool embrace a protective shield against Damon's attack. But now, as I reached out with my senses, they remained elusive, their movements erratic and unpredictable. It was like trying to capture smoke. Like trying to hold water in my hands.

"They're a part of me," I whispered to myself, the realization settling deep within my bones. It wasn't a sudden epiphany; it was a truth I had known for a while. A truth I had tried to ignore, to bury beneath layers of denial and self-doubt. But yesterday's training session had forced me to confront it, to acknowledge the undeniable connection between myself and the shadows.

Damon, with his piercing blue eyes and hostile demeanor, had watched my every move—his gaze intensifying each time my control faltered, my shadows slipping from my grasp. Was he waiting for a mistake? A sign of weakness? I wasn't sure, but the weight of his presence had been almost unbearable. There were no smiles, no jokes, no attempts to soften the edges of his demanding presence. His shadows, when they flared to life, were a force of nature—dark and powerful, dwarfing my own fledgling abilities

Nox, though less hostile than his brother, had exuded a different kind of tension—an energy that hinted at something hidden, something restrained. He had been more casual in his approach, his instructions less demanding, but there was an underlying wariness in his eyes, as if he were holding something back.

Zarek had tried to lighten the mood with his playful banter and teasing smiles. But even beneath his lighthearted facade, I could sense a deeper intent, a mix of curiosity and something else, something that felt almost protective.

I heard footsteps approaching, and my eyes snapped open, the peace of the morning gone. He stood a few feet away, his tall frame casting a long shadow across the grass. His expression was unreadable, as usual.

Nox.

"You're up early," he observed, his voice carrying less of its usual sharp edge.

I shrugged, "Couldn't sleep. Shadows don't really take a break, you know."

Nox's gaze dropped to my hands, where the shadows flickered and danced, their movements mirroring how I felt. For a brief moment, I thought I saw something soften in his eyes—a flicker of curiosity, or even... concern? My heart skipped a beat, and I looked away, focusing on the horizon, where the sky was beginning to lighten with the promise of dawn.

"What are you doing out here?" I asked, trying to keep my tone casual.

Nox didn't respond immediately. He took a step closer, his presence surprisingly comforting despite his usual aloofness. He knelt beside me, his eyes searching my face as if trying to decipher a hidden message written there. The silence stretched between us, but it wasn't uncomfortable; it was filled with an unspoken understanding—a shared connection that transcended words.

He hummed softly, his gaze lingering on me before he finally spoke, his voice barely above a whisper, as if he didn't want to break the spell that had woven itself around us. "You really don't know."

I turned my head, meeting his gaze. His eyes—usually so guarded—seemed different now—softer, more vulnerable. As if he were letting me see a part of him he rarely showed to anyone. My breath hitched in my throat, and a warmth spread through my chest, a mixture of surprise and something else. Something that felt dangerously close to longing. What was this pull I felt towards him? Why did his presence make my heart pound as if it were trying to escape my chest?

Nox reached out, his fingers brushing against mine, a feather-light touch that sent a jolt of electricity through my body. The shadows beneath my hands stilled, as if responding to his touch. His touch was careful, almost hesitant, as if he feared he might shatter me with a single careless movement.

"Know what?" I asked, my voice barely a whisper, my senses heightened, every nerve ending attuned to his presence.

Nox's eyes searched mine, a flicker of something pained—something yearning—flashing in their depths. He sighed, a sound laden with unspoken emotion, and stood up, putting distance between us. His expression hardened once more, the brief vulnerability vanishing behind his usual stoic mask. "You should get back," he said, his voice regaining its familiar coolness. "Classes will be starting soon."

He turned and walked away, the shadows seeming to cling to him as he disappeared into the trees. He didn't offer a second glance, no lingering farewell—leaving me with a whirlwind of unanswered questions and a heart that ached with a longing I couldn't explain.

Chapter 14

THE DAYS WERE LONG, STRETCHING INTO AN ETERNITY of lectures and endless training sessions. Every morning began with the Wonders of Nexara training, Professor Lorian's booming voice echoing across the grounds, pushing us to the brink of exhaustion and demanding we surpass our limits from the day before. For everyone else—the naturally gifted ones—it was an exhilarating opportunity to showcase their gifts. For me, it served as a constant, agonizing reminder of just how far behind I seemed to be, struggling to keep up with the rigorous pace and the power radiating from everyone around me. After Lorian's intensive training, I was forced into yet another grueling session with the Shadow Brothers. Each day felt like hell.

Still, it wasn't the endless physical strain—or even the humiliation of falling short—that kept me up at night. It was the memory of Professor Lorian in the woods. His voice, low and reverent, addressing some unseen *lord*. I hadn't seen anyone else there— just Lorian, speaking as though he was reporting on my progress.

At least, that's what it had felt like at the time. But now, days later, nothing unusual has happened. No cryptic comments from him, no strange encounters. Maybe I'd imagined it. My mind playing tricks on me, warping his words into something sinister—something more than a simple conversation with himself.

And yet, I couldn't shake the feeling that there was more to Lorian than he let on. Was it paranoia, fueled by my own insecurities and the pressure of being here? Or was he watching me for a reason, his gaze lingering a moment too long when he thought I wasn't looking?

Whatever it was, I had no proof. Just a nagging suspicion that made the hairs on the back of my neck stand on end whenever I was around him—whenever his voice boomed across the training grounds. Until something concrete happened, some solid evidence to support my fears, I had no choice but to push it aside and focus on surviving each relentless day.

All I could summon was a flickering, translucent shield—a fragile barrier shimmering around me. I supposed that was my unique ability, though it hardly felt impressive compared to the raw powers others wielded. A shield—a simple, defensive construct designed to protect me from harm. Not a dazzling display of offensive power, not a weapon to vanquish my enemies, just a simple shield. It was fine, I told myself, trying to ignore the rising tide of insecurities, especially considering I didn't have any magical gift at all just a few weeks ago. Still, the frustration persisted—a constant feeling of self-doubt.

Damon, the ever-critical and perpetually scowling Shadow Brother, had observed my clumsy attempts at shield conjuring for barely a minute before dismissing me entirely. His disapproving gaze—sharp as shards of ice—making my skin prickle with unease. He still treated me like I was the enemy—or worse, a bothersome inconvenience. A fragile human disrupting the carefully constructed world he shared with his brothers. The way his eyes narrowed, his jaw tightening almost instantly whenever I stepped into the training circle.

Zarek, on the other hand, was still his flirtatious self. His teasing smile—a flash of white against his tanned skin—and his sly comments, often whispered in my ear as he leaned in close, were becoming a staple of my day. The banter between us flowed effortlessly, a comfortable rhythm developing amidst the chaos of Nexara. And despite my better judgement, I found myself looking forward to it. He made me laugh—even when I didn't want to. A genuine, carefree sound that surprised even me, and his charm, a potent mix of playful arrogance and genuine warmth, was beginning to wear me down. My usual sharp retorts—honed over years of solitude—were softening, losing their edge. And I hated that part of me almost liked the attention, the way his amber eyes lingered on me, the brush of his hand against mine.

But Nox—Nox had avoided me since the morning after training with them. I would catch glimpses of him across the grounds, his hood pulled low over his dark curls, his eyes never meeting mine —always averted, as if I was a stranger, someone he didn't know. It was like he had vanished into the shadows, blending seamlessly with the darkness that seemed to cling to the edges of the world. His presence felt like a ghost haunting my life at the academy. I couldn't stop replaying that moment—the way his emerald eyes had softened, the gentle, hesitant touch of his hand against mine. A spark igniting between us. A connection that felt both familiar and frightening. There was something there, but now it felt like he regretted it. Like he regretted *me*.

The gnawing uncertainty clung to me as I sat on the training mats, watching the others spar. El was off in the distance, her fire blazing as she practiced with another student, her laughter carrying on the wind, bright and carefree. She was thriving here, her power evident in every flick of her wrist, every burst of flame. A vibrant contrast to the shadows that clung to me. I envied her —not her power, but her confidence. The way she embraced who she was, without hesitation or doubt. She seemed to fit in, while I felt like a misplaced piece of a puzzle, unsure where I belonged, or if I even belonged at all.

I sighed, running a hand through my hair. The shadows beneath my fingers flickered, restless, responding to my frustration, swirling around me like curious spirits. I needed to figure this out —whatever I was meant to be here for. What purpose did I serve in this world of magic and power? The Wonders of Nexara is tomorrow, and here I was... already regretting signing up. The thought of displaying my... whatever *this* was, in front of the entire academy filled me with a sense of dread.

"Let's hope your shield can withstand the challenges—and the *threats*," Mira sneered, her voice dripping with condescension, each word a venomous barb aimed at my vulnerabilities. She stood over me, her entourage flanking her like a pack of wolves, their predatory gazes adding to the intimidation. Her icy blue eyes held a glint of amusement, a cruel satisfaction in my apparent discomfort. Her blonde hair, catching the sunlight like a halo, only amplified the irony—her presence was anything but angelic.

I looked up, forcing myself to meet her gaze, refusing to cower. "I guess we'll find out, won't we?" I retorted, injecting a note of defiance into my voice, though my insides churned with a mixture of anger and apprehension. Mira had made it her personal mission to remind me of my shortcomings, her words cutting deeper than any blade, leaving invisible scars that ached with every encounter.

Her smile widened—a predator savoring the fear in its prey. "Oh, I'm sure we will," she purred, her voice laced with a faux sweetness that made my skin crawl. "Try not to embarrass yourself too much, Thalia." She paused, her eyes glittering with malice. "Wouldn't want to tarnish the academy's reputation with someone as... *pathetic* as you."

Her cronies erupted in a chorus of snickers, their laughter echoing in my ears like a pack of hyenas reveling in a kill. They turned and walked away, their heads held high, their arrogance a suffocating presence that lingered in their wake.

I clenched my jaw, the shadows beneath my skin flickering with a restless energy, urging me to lash out—to unleash the power that simmered within me. But I forced myself to remain still, taking deep breaths, channeling the anger into a cold, sharp resolve. I would not give them the satisfaction of seeing me break.

El's voice called out from across the field, breaking through my thoughts. "Thalia! Are you coming?" She waved, her smile warm and encouraging. I pushed myself to my feet, brushing off the dirt and the lingering sting of Mira's words. I had to keep moving forward, no matter what Mira or anyone else thought. I wasn't here to impress them; I was here to find my place, to uncover the truth of who I was.

"See you tomorrow, Firefly," Zarek's voice carried across the training grounds, a soothing balm to my raw nerves. I turned to see his cheeky smile as he stood with his brothers, a familiar sight that brought a sense of comfort amidst the chaos.

Zarek leaned casually against a tree, his amber eyes shining as he watched me, a silent message of support passing between us. Damon and Nox stood beside him—Damon with his arms crossed, his usual brooding expression firmly in place, while Nox kept his gaze averted, his hood casting a shadow over his face, concealing the emotions that simmered beneath the surface.

Mira's eyes narrowed as she looked between him and me, her lips curling in distaste. Her hands clenched at her sides, her knuckles white against her skin, and I could practically see the smoke fuming from her nostrils. The tension in the air was palpable, her jealousy like a storm brewing on the horizon, threatening to unleash its fury. Despite myself, I couldn't help but smile—a wide grin that I directed straight at Mira.

Zarek's smile widened at my reaction, and he gave me a playful wink, a spark of connection igniting between us. I felt a warmth spread through my chest, a flicker of reassurance that I desperately needed in that moment.

As Mira turned on her heel, her friends trailing behind her like obedient shadows, I caught sight of Nox. For a split second, his emerald-green eyes met mine, something flashing in his gaze—a flicker of vulnerability, of understanding—before he looked away, the hood of his sweatshirt falling back into place, shielding him once more. It was enough to send my heart pounding, a mix of emotions swirling within me—curiosity, confusion, and a strange, burgeoning sense of hope.

Chapter 15

Thalia's POV

T he morning the Wonders of Nexara arrived, the air was so thick with tension, I could taste it. We had gathered in a large, empty hall, the walls lined with sleek, polished stone that seemed to absorb and amplify the nervous energy buzzing around us. Sunbeams, fractured by high, arched windows, cast long, geometric patterns across the floor, but they did little to dispel the gloom that clung to the edges of the room. Everyone was dressed in their Academy training gear, a uniform of black and deep navy. The tight clothes clung to my body like a second skin, making it hard to breathe. The long sleeves, fitted pants, and heavy, leather boots felt restrictive—each piece a reminder of what lay ahead. I tugged at the collar of my tunic, trying to loosen the fabric's grip around my throat.

I could feel the anticipation vibrating in the room—a collective mix of fear and excitement that settled deep in my bones, a tremor that resonated with my own apprehension. My palms were slick with sweat, despite the cool air of the hall. I glanced around, trying to gauge the expressions of my fellow classmates, searching for a flicker of reassurance, but found only mirrored reflections of my own unease.

"Ladies and Gentlemen, welcome to the Wonders of Nexara!" a voice boomed, echoing off the cold stone walls of the hall. We couldn't see the announcer or the audience, hidden behind some magical barrier, but the roar of the crowd filtered in through unseen speakers, making my pulse quicken with a nervous thrum. This was real—no more training mats or practice rounds against illusionary opponents. We were about to be dropped into the unknown: a simulated wilderness filled with magical creatures and perilous traps, with no weapons but our own nascent abilities. My stomach churned with a mixture of fear and a strange thrill.

A chill ran down my spine as I glanced around at the others, trying to discern some sense of camaraderie—a shared sense of impending doom. Elara stood beside me, a pillar of fiery resolve, her eyes narrowed in fierce determination, a faint shimmer of flame flickering at her fingertips like a warning. Zarek caught my eye from across the room, and he gave me one of his signature cocky smiles—a flash of white teeth, his amber eyes glinting with a reckless excitement that did little to ease my apprehension. Damon, predictably, was emotionless as always—a statue carved from shadow and indifference, his gaze focused straight ahead, as though he could already see through the veil separating us from the simulated world. Nox stood beside him, his hood down for once, revealing the dark curls of his hair and the sharp angles of his face. His expression was unreadable, his emerald-green eyes carefully avoiding mine, making me wonder what thoughts he had beneath that calm exterior. He seemed more withdrawn than usual, and the subtle shift in his demeanor only amplified my unease.

The ground beneath us shifted, and I stumbled, barely managing to regain my balance before falling flat on my face. The floor began to split apart, each section separating as if to send us in different directions—like some twisted game of chance. The uncertainty tightened around my throat, choking off my breath. We were being taken somewhere—somewhere we couldn't see, somewhere unfamiliar and undoubtedly dangerous. A shiver traced its way down my spine, a primal fear gripping me.

The disembodied voice returned, booming through the strange space. "Contestants, prepare yourselves. You will be dropped into the wilderness. Survive, overcome, and prove yourselves worthy." The words hung in the air, heavy with an unspoken threat. "You have only your skills, your instincts, and each other—if you dare to trust." *Trust*. A hollow laugh threatened to escape me. Trusting anyone—especially in this situation—felt like a fool's errand.

The ground beneath me gave way without warning, and I felt myself plummeting into the abyss. My stomach lurched, a sickening twist that sent bile rising in my throat. I clenched my teeth, squeezing my eyes shut, my hands scrabbling for something—anything—to hold on to. The wind roared in my ears, a deafening rush that drowned out all other sounds. Everything was a blur of color and noise, a chaotic kaleidoscope of sensations. I barely had time to register the rush of air before I hit the ground with a jarring thud, landing hard on my feet. My legs buckled slightly beneath the impact, but somehow, miraculously, I managed to stay upright.

Towering trees rose around me like ancient sentinels, their branches intertwining to create a dense canopy that blocked out most of the light, casting long, eerie shadows across the uneven forest floor. The air was cool and damp, heavy with the scent of earth and moss. And the silence, broken only by the rustle of unseen creatures, was almost deafening. I pushed myself up, my heart still pounding a frantic rhythm against my ribs, and tried to get my bearings. Disoriented and alone, I scanned the shadowy depths of the woods, searching for any sign of El, James, Zarek, Nox, hell even Damon. But, there was nothing. Just me, surrounded by the looming trees and the oppressive silence, alone in this unfamiliar wilderness.

I took a deep breath, trying to steady my nerves, and surveyed the area around me. The trees stretched endlessly in every direction, their trunks gnarled and covered in strange, iridescent fungi that seemed to glow faintly in the dim light, casting an otherworldly glow on the scene. Thick underbrush, tangled with thorny vines, made it difficult to see far, and every rustle of leaves, every snap of a twig, made me jump. The forest floor was uneven, littered with fallen branches and thick patches of ferns that made each step treacherous. I stumbled over a gnarled root, barely catching myself before I fell, my hand instinctively reaching out to grasp the rough bark of a nearby tree. I could hear the distant sound of rushing water—a stream or a river—the rustle of leaves in the breeze, and the occasional call of an unrecognizable creature echoing in the distance, each sound amplifying the sense of isolation.

This was it—the Wonders of Nexara, a place of both breathtaking beauty and hidden dangers. I had no idea what lay ahead, what trials or dangers I would face. But I wasn't going to back down.

Somewhere out there, everyone else was facing their own challenges, their own personal demons in this strange, magical forest. I had to trust myself—trust this growing ability of mine—even if it felt like the weakest weapon out here. I reached out, feeling the shadows respond to my touch, flickering and curling around my fingers like curious, sentient tendrils. Maybe they were all I had, but they were *mine*. A small, hesitant smile touched my lips.

"Okay, okay," I whispered to myself, squaring my shoulders and trying to project an air of confidence I didn't feel. "Time to prove you belong, Thalia."

I started moving, my steps cautious as I navigated the unfamiliar terrain. The forest was dense—claustrophobic, even—and the shadows seemed to shift and sway around me as if they were alive, responding to my presence, my emotions. I kept my senses sharp, listening for any signs of movement, any indication that I wasn't alone in this wilderness.

The distant sound of running water became my guide. If I could find a source, it would be easier to figure out where I was in this unfamiliar territory. Plus, water meant a better chance of finding others, maybe even some sign of direction. I didn't want to be completely alone out here, not with whatever dangers lurked out there, waiting to pounce on someone like me.

As I moved through the trees, the dense foliage brushing against my skin, I caught a glimpse of something out of the corner of my eye—a flash of movement, too quick to be a trick of the light. I froze, my heart pounding against my ribs, and slowly turned my head, my eyes scanning the surrounding trees. *Nothing.*

The forest was still, eerily still. I shook my head, trying to push down the rising paranoia that was creeping into my mind like a poisonous vine. I had to stay focused, stay alert. Giving in to fear would only make me more vulnerable.

After what felt like hours of walking, my legs aching and my stomach growling, I finally reached a small clearing. A narrow stream cut through the center, the water glistening like a silver ribbon in the dappled sunlight that managed to break through the thick trees. I knelt down, grateful for the break, and cupped my hands to take a long, refreshing sip of the cool water. It was a welcome relief, calming the dryness in my throat and easing the tension that had knotted in my chest.

As I sat there, catching my breath, my shadows flickered, drawing my attention to my hands. One darted out—a playful wisp of darkness—twirling around me before suddenly shooting off towards the north, as if beckoning me to follow. I frowned, watching the shadow move with an unnerving intent, as if it knew exactly where it was going, as if it had a purpose I couldn't yet understand. The sun was still low in the sky, casting long, dancing shadows across the forest floor. Hesitantly, I rose to my feet and moved quietly toward the tree line, hiding in the shadows as I followed my silent companion.

A tumultuous mix of fear and curiosity is what kept driving me forward. Each step felt heavy, weighted with unease, my breath shallow as I pushed my body to its limits. The forest seemed to grow darker with each step I took, the thickening covering that made it hard to see, blurring the line between reality and illusion. The eerie calls of unseen creatures echoed through the air, each sound setting my nerves on edge, making me flinch at every rustle and snap. It felt like the forest itself was alive, a sentient being watching me, testing me, waiting to see if I was worthy of being here.

I had no idea where my shadow was leading me. The uncertainty gnawed at me, tightening around my chest like a vice, but I couldn't afford to stop. The thought of giving up made my throat tighten with panic; "Just keep moving," I whispered, my voice barely audible above the rustling leaves. "You can do this." One foot in front of the other, that's all I needed to do. Focus on the small victories. Don't think about what could be lurking just beyond the veil of trees, waiting to snatch me up and drag me into the darkness.

The wind started to pick up, causing some hair to fall loose from my braid as I continued down the uneven path, tugging at the strands that now tickled my cheeks. The trees groaned as they swayed, branches scraping against each other in a dissonant symphony. It was a melody of unease, a soundtrack to my growing fear. The feeling of being watched grew stronger, a prickling sensation at the back of my neck put me on high alert. It felt like invisible eyes were boring into me, assessing my every move. Every instinct told me to be careful, to stay hidden, to turn back and run as fast as my legs would carry me. But the shadow continued to guide me, unwavering in its direction, a silent, insistent pull. And I, trapped between terror and an unknown compulsion, had no choice but to trust it. Or rather, I had no choice but to trust the strange magic that held me captive.

Suddenly, the underbrush rustled, and I froze, my eyes darting around, searching for the source of the noise. The shadows curled protectively around my fingers, a comforting weight in the growing darkness, ready to respond if I needed them. I held my breath, my ears straining to catch any hint of movement.

A few tense moments passed, each one stretching into an eternity, before a small creature—something that looked like a cross between a rabbit and a squirrel, its fur a patchwork of vibrant colors—darted out of the bushes and disappeared into another as quickly as it had appeared. I let out a shaky laugh, my shoulders sagging in relief as the tension in my muscles slowly eased.

I pressed on, my steps careful as I navigated around thick roots and patches of thorny brush, the forest floor a treacherous maze beneath my feet. The terrain was unforgiving, and every step seemed to bring a new challenge—an unexpected dip in the earth, a jagged rock hidden beneath the ferns, a low-hanging branch that snagged at my hair.

My shadow, my silent guide, led me to a break in the trees where the forest opened up slightly, revealing a rocky incline bathed in the soft glow of the sun. I found myself squinting against the sudden brightness after the brutal darkness of the woods. I could see a narrow path winding up the incline, disappearing into the thick trees above, and the shadow seemed intent on taking me that way.

"Great, thanks," I muttered, my voice barely a whisper. Taking a deep breath of the crisp, pine-scented air, I began the climb.

The incline was steeper than it looked from below—a cruel deception of the forest—and my muscles screamed in protest with every upward lunge, my boots slipping slightly on loose stones that threatened to send me tumbling back down. The higher I climbed, the more rewarding the view became. The forest stretched out below like an endless sea of green, dark and wild, the treetops swaying gently in the breeze like waves on a dark green ocean. For a moment, I paused, clinging to a gnarled root, and simply stared, a sense of awe washing over me at the sheer vastness of it all, the raw, untamed beauty and the ever-present danger so intricately intertwined. It was a breathtaking, terrifying sight, and a strange sense of belonging settled in my chest.

Reaching the top of the incline, I paused to catch my breath, my chest heaving. The world stretched out before me—a painful reminder of just how alone I was here. The silence up here felt heavy, as if the world was holding its breath, waiting for something to happen. But there, in the distance, nestled between the peaks of towering pines, I spotted something—a structure, partially hidden by the leaves. It looked like a tower, old and weathered, its stone surface covered in a thick layer of ivy that clung to it like a second skin. A flicker of movement caught my eye, and I realized it was my own shadow, stretching long and distorted on the ground before me. It seemed to dart ahead, as if urging me forward with a sense of urgency that made my heart skip a beat.

A surge of hope welled up inside me—a fragile butterfly fluttering against the cage of my ribs, mingling with the fear that still lingered, a cold serpent coiled in the pit of my stomach. Maybe there was something—or someone—there that could help, could shed some light on what the fuck to do. Or at the very least, maybe the tower offered some semblance of safety. I wiped the sweat from my brow with the back of my hand, straightened up, and continued onward, my legs trembling with exhaustion.

The forest seemed to grow louder as I approached the tower, the eerie calls of unseen creatures getting closer as the soft rustle of leaves beneath my boots grew more pronounced. The air itself felt different here, heavier, thicker, charged with an energy I couldn't quite name. My pulse echoing in my ears like a frantic whisper as I drew closer to the tower, each step a hesitant echo in the expectant hush.

"Only a hundred or so more yards," I mumbled, forcing my aching limbs to move. The tower offered some semblance of safety, though what kind of safety could it really offer here? Before I could finish the thought, the ground began to shake. It started as a low rumble, almost imperceptible beneath the leaves and the frantic thump of my own heart, but quickly grew stronger, more insistent. The trees around me trembled, their leaves rustling violently as if in a sudden windstorm. My heart leapt into my throat, a cold knot of fear tightening in my chest, and I instinctively crouched, trying to find cover. I moved quickly, adrenaline taking over the exhaustion in my legs, ducking behind a large, moss-covered boulder, hoping it would shield me from whatever was coming.

A roar tore through the air—a deep, guttural sound that made my entire body tremble. It echoed through the trees, a sound of pure, unadulterated rage. I peeked out from behind the boulder, my eyes widening in horror as I saw the creature emerge from the forest. It was enormous, its shoulders easily over six feet, its muscular body covered in dark red fur, as if embers burned beneath its skin. Its head was a terrifying mix of feline and demonic features, with glowing red eyes that seemed to pierce through the shadows, pinning me in place with their malevolent gaze. Long, twisted horns, the color of polished obsidian, jutted out from its head, curving menacingly towards the sky, and its powerful legs ended in sharp, clawed paws that dug into the earth with each step, leaving deep gouges in the soft soil. Large, bat-like wings unfurled from its back, leathery and scarred, casting a dark shadow over the ground as it moved.

The creature's eyes scanned the area, and I held my breath, pressing myself tighter against the cold, rough surface of the boulder. It sniffed the air, its nostrils flaring, and I could feel the ground vibrate beneath me as it took a step closer, the tremors sending shivers down my spine. My heart pounded so hard it felt like it might burst from my chest. The fear felt like a physical presence clawing at me, urging me to run, to flee from the monstrous being before me. But I knew that I couldn't outrun something like that, not with the speed and power it had. I had to stay hidden, had to blend into the shadows and hope—pray—that it wouldn't notice me, wouldn't catch my scent on the wind.

The creature let out another ear splitting roar, its wings flaring as it reared back, its massive body blocking out what little light filtered through the canopy above. I could see the raw, untamed power in its movements, the muscles rippling beneath its thick, dark fur—and I knew, with a chilling certainty, that this was something I could not fight. My shadows twitched and writhed around my fingers, eager to lash out, to protect me, but I forced myself to stay still, to remain hidden, praying the creature would move on.

I clenched my jaw, my body trembling uncontrollably as I watched the creature sniff the air again, its glowing red eyes narrowing as it slowly, deliberately turned its head in my direction. I tried to press myself even closer to the ground, becoming one with the earth, every muscle in my body tensed, coiled like a spring, ready to react, to defend myself if absolutely necessary. The seconds stretched into what felt like hours.

The only thing between me and the beast—the massive boulder I'd desperately hoped would offer some protection—was gone in the blink of an eye, sent flying as if it weighed nothing. It crashed into the surrounding trees with a sickening thud, and the creature's roar—that deep, jarring sound—rattled my bones. There was no time to think, no time to react in any way other than pure instinct. My shadows, my only defense, burst from my hands, swirling and coalescing into a protective shield just as the creature lunged. Its claws, sharp as razors, slammed into the barrier with enough force to send a shockwave through my entire body, the impact reverberating through me, leaving me momentarily stunned. I gritted my teeth, digging my heels into the soft earth, trying to hold my ground against the relentless pressure, but the sheer strength of the creature was overwhelming.

My shadows wavered, flickering under the immense strain, the darkness thinning, threatening to break. I felt my knees buckle, my body trembling with the effort of maintaining the shield. The creature roared again, the sound echoing through the forest, its massive jaws opening to reveal rows of sharp, yellowed teeth. Its hot, glowing eyes locked onto mine with deadly intent as it pushed relentlessly against the shield, its claws digging into the swirling darkness. I screamed—a raw, primal sound born of pain and terror—the agony lancing through me as I desperately tried to maintain the barrier, every muscle in my body straining, screaming in protest. My shadows were not strong enough—not against something like this, something so ancient, so powerful.

With a final, brutal shove, the creature shattered my shield. The force of the blow sent me flying backward through the air like a rag doll. I hit the ground hard, the air driven from my lungs in a painful whoosh, my head snapping back against the unforgiving earth. Pain exploded across my back and shoulders—a searing, white-hot agony that stole my breath. I gasped, struggling to breathe, my vision blurring around the edges as I tried to push myself up, my hands scrabbling at the ground, finding only loose dirt and leaves. It was too late. The massive form loomed over me, casting a long, ominous shadow, its glowing eyes filled with malevolent intent, promising a swift and brutal end.

Desperation surged through me, a wave of adrenaline momentarily clearing my head. I reached for my shadows again, willing them to respond, to protect me—but they were weak, scattered, barely responding to my call. My body ached, every part of me screaming in protest as I forced myself to my feet, my legs trembling beneath me, threatening to give way at any moment. The creature snarled—a low, rumbling sound that vibrated in my chest —its massive wings flaring out to their full, terrifying span as it prepared to strike again, to finish what it had started.

I stumbled backward, fear felt a cold hand squeezing the air from my lungs. I had nothing left—no strength to fight, no shield to protect me. The creature lunged, a monstrous shadow against the fading light, and I braced myself, the bitter taste of despair coating my tongue. I knew I couldn't avoid it this time, couldn't summon even a flicker of the power that had saved me before.

Its claws sliced through the air, razor-sharp and imbued with a dark energy I could feel even before they touched me. I tried to move, to twist away from the inevitable blow, but the pain came before I could react, a searing agony that shot through my arm like a bolt of lightning. Its claws cut deep, straight to the bone, tearing through muscle and tendons with sickening ease.

I cried out, the sound raw and filled with terror, as blood poured down my arm, hot and sticky, staining the ground beneath me in a spreading pool of dark red. My vision swam, the world tilting and blurring around me, and I lost my footing, falling backward onto the cold, hard ground. My head hit the stone with an awful thump, and the world went black for a moment, then returned in a dizzying rush of pain and fear. My heart pounded in my ears like a drum, each beat a frantic countdown, as I squeezed my eyes shut, waiting for the final blow—preparing for death to claim me in its icy embrace.

But instead of a fatal blow, I heard another roar—this one different, filled with pain and fury. I opened my eyes in time to see the creature staggering backward, its massive form crashing into it. A panther. The panther from the Shadows Brothers' territory was here. It was even larger than I remembered, its muscular frame towering over the beast that had attacked me. Its sleek, midnight-black fur glistened, and its green eyes blazed with fierce intensity. A low growl rumbled in its chest, a promise of bloodthirsty violence. Without hesitation, it lunged at the creature, its powerful paws colliding with the beast's side, knocking it off balance. The impact echoed through the trees, a loud crash that made me wince.

The two creatures clashed again, the ground trembling beneath their combined weight. The panther moved with a fluid grace I'd never witnessed, every muscle in its body rippling as it dodged and attacked with lethal precision. Its claws—like honed raven blades —slashed through the air, tearing at the creature's leathery wings and thick shoulders, leaving deep gashes that oozed dark, viscous blood. The demonic beast roared in pain—a sound that sent shivers down my spine—its twisted horns thrashing wildly as it tried to fight back. But the panther was relentless, its powerful jaws snapping at its opponent, fangs sinking into the coarse red fur. A coppery tang filled the air, thick and metallic.

I watched, stunned, as the battle unfolded before me like a gruesome ballet. The panther's growls were low and feral, a stark contrast to the guttural roars of the creature. It was as if the panther had been waiting for this moment—its every move filled with a primal purpose and raw power that radiated outwards like a physical force. It dodged the creature's desperate strikes with an almost supernatural agility, lunged forward with explosive speed, and sank its teeth deep into the beast's neck, drawing a howl of pain that reverberated through the silent forest, echoing back from the towering trees.

The creature tried to spread its massive, bat-like wings, desperately attempting to lift its heavy body off the ground, but the panther pounced with a ferocity that left no room for escape. It slammed at the creature's neck, pushing it back down, its claws digging deep, pinning it to the forest floor like a pinned rabbit. Dirt and leaves erupted into the air like a miniature explosion as the ground cracked beneath the force of the impact, and the creature's wings flapped wildly, a futile attempt to break free from the panther's iron grip.

The panther's claws held fast, unyielding, and with a final, savage bite, it tore into the creature's throat, severing the thick artery. A burst of dark blood sprayed into the air, coating both the panther and the forest floor in a horrific painting. The demonic beast let out one last gurgling roar—a sound that echoed with the finality of pain and desperation—before its body went limp, collapsing beneath the panther's weight. The once-glowing red eyes faded to dull embers, the life draining from them as an eerie silence fell over the forest, broken only by the panting breaths of the victorious panther.

The tension that had gripped the air dissipated, leaving an eerie stillness in its wake. The panther stood, its chest heaving with exertion, blood staining its dark fur. It turned its gaze to me, those piercing green eyes locking onto mine. My entire body trembled, and I couldn't breathe, fear and disbelief warring within me.

Here we go, I thought, a strange calm settling over me. Finally, we'd finish what we had started weeks ago. This deadly game of cat and mouse was coming to an end. A small, humorless laugh escaped my lips. If this was how it ended, then so be it. I kept my eyes on the panther's, bracing myself for the inevitable, the vivid image of its fangs sinking into my flesh, the searing pain, flashing through my mind.

The panther took a step back, its fierce expression softening ever so slightly. Its eyes seemed to study me, searching for something in the depths of my own, and I saw something flicker there—an understanding, or maybe a curiosity, a spark of something I couldn't quite place. It approached slowly, almost cautiously, each step deliberate and measured, as if it didn't want to scare me. The raw power emanating from the creature was there, yet there was a hesitant grace in its movements that didn't add up to its predatory nature.

The panther stopped in front of me, lowering its massive head to sniff my injured arm. The scent of blood, *my* blood, filled the air. Was my blood attracting it? If it wanted to kill me, it could have done so already, back in the forest, and yet here it was, standing before me, its warm breath ghosting over my skin. Slowly, its eyes lifted to meet mine, and it leveled its head with mine, staring deep into my eyes—as if peering into my very soul, searching for answers to questions I didn't even know how to ask.

My instincts screamed at me to move, to run, to fight, but something else—a small flicker of an unexplainable feeling, a fragile tendril of trust—told me to stay, to trust it. With my hand trembling, I slowly reached out, my fingers brushing against the panther's soft, blood-splattered snout. Its eyes fluttered shut in a long, slow blink, and it leaned into my touch, the tension in its powerful body easing as it pushed gently against my hand—almost like a cat seeking affection.

A low rumble arose from its chest—not a growl, but something almost similar to a purr—a deep, resonant vibration that seemed to hum through the very ground beneath us. It was strangely comforting, and despite the pain radiating from my body and the exhaustion that weighed me down, a sense of calm washed over me—a fragile peace in the aftermath of the chaos.

I sank to the ground, my body fully giving way. My breaths came in ragged gasps as the adrenaline faded, replaced by an overwhelming fatigue. Pain throbbed through my injured arm and chest—an ache that intensified with each heartbeat, sending a fresh wave of agony through my body. My vision blurred, the edges softening, darkness closing in on me like a heavy fog, threatening to swallow me whole. I didn't know why the panther had saved me. I didn't know what any of it meant. The snarling, the fighting, the echoing roars of rage—it was all a blur now. My mind was slipping, the darkness calling to me with a seductive whisper. I let my eyes drift shut, surrendering to it, the last sounds I heard being a low growl and the distant echo of my own weak, faltering heartbeat.

Chapter 16

Nox's POV

The world around me was quiet, the forest filled with the usual sounds of falling leaves and the chirping of unseen crickets. The distant calls of creatures echoed through the trees—a familiar tune that usually soothed me. But today, everything seemed to blur together in my head, overshadowed by something else, something urgent, that gripped my senses with an icy dread.

A scream—loud, piercing, and filled with unadulterated terror—cut through the silence, and my entire body froze, every muscle locking into place. It was *her*. I could feel it—her fear a tangible wave reverberating through me, echoing in the depths of my mind like a shattered mirror. My heart pounded violently against my ribs, my vision narrowing as that primal instinct—the one I fought so hard to suppress—surged within me, hotter than any fire I'd ever known. It was a feeling I rarely allowed myself to give in to, a dangerous, uncontrollable force that would consume me.

Without warning, my vision darkened, the vibrant greens and browns of the forest bleeding into a swirling vortex of black. The world around me began to blur, the trees becoming indistinct shadows, the sounds of the forest fading into a dull roar. I felt my control slipping, the rigid grip I held over my emotions loosening, breaking apart like dry twigs underfoot. The beast inside me—the one I kept chained and hidden in the darkest recesses of my mind —began to claw its way to the surface, its enraged roar echoing in my ears, drowning out everything else. The pressure in my skull intensified, a searing pain that threatened to split me in two.

I had no choice. I couldn't fight it, I had to let go.

A rush of raw, untamed power coursed through me—an electric current that made my nerves stand on end. My senses sharpened to an almost painful clarity, the smells of the forest intensifying a thousandfold, the sounds becoming crystal clear. My bones twisted and cracked, my muscles shifting and expanding as the forest floor rushed up to meet my changing hands—now massive paws slamming against the earth. The change came faster than I could even comprehend—a whirlwind of fur and bones. My thoughts scattered like leaves in the wind, replaced by the panther's singular, burning drive—*find her.*

I was the panther, yet I was also Nox, watching the beast take over. I was both observer and participant, a prisoner in my own body. Each muscle, each sharpened sense, was mine, yet driven by an alien will. The scent of blood, sharp and metallic, mingled with the delicate notes of lavender and sage— *her* scent—ignited a white-hot rage.

My massive frame gliding through the trees, the wind whipping past me. When the beast took over, I would have no memory of what happened. It was a blackout—a terrifying gap in my mind that left me with only the fragmented images of the aftermath, the chilling echo of the beast's rage. But this time was different. This time, I was fully conscious, fully aware—watching as my beast took the reins. A terrifying yet exhilarating experience. I could feel every muscle coil and release, every rush of raw, feral power and fury that drove me forward, a primal instinct that both terrified and thrilled me.

My heart pounded in terrifying sync with hers, each beat pushing me faster and faster, my heightened senses guiding me towards her —an invisible thread pulling me through the dense forest. No one would touch her. No one would dare harm her.

I moved with a swiftness and agility I'd never known in my human form, my powerful legs propelling me forward, the forest a blur of green and brown shadows around me. Every instinct, every fiber of my being, screamed at me that I had to reach her— that she needed me. I could feel her presence, her fear—a palpable beacon in the swirling chaos of my mind—and I followed it without hesitation, my entire being, human and beast, focused on one purpose: saving *her*.

The creature—massive, grotesque, with an aura of dark energy far greater than any creature native to these woods—stood over her. Thalia lay crumpled beneath it, a broken doll amidst the carnage. The moment I saw her, something inside me snapped. A roar tore from my throat, pure rage and desperation flooding through me. The world narrowed, tunneling down to a single point of focus— the beast that threatened her.

My leap propelled me through the air, a missile of black fur and fury, colliding with the creature's side with bone-jarring force. The impact sent the creature reeling, disoriented, giving me the opening I needed. My panther took over—fangs bared, claws extended—every movement driven by a primal need to protect.

Each strike, each bite, was fueled by the overwhelming, instinctive need to protect, to keep her safe. And as the fight raged on, a disturbing realization began to dawn—I was enjoying it. I was okay with it. The raw, wild power surging through me was intoxicating. I wanted my beast to unleash hell on whoever dared messed with what is *mine*.

The creature snarled and fought back, its claws slashing at my flanks, tearing through muscle and fur, but I barely registered the pain. The rage inside me, inside the panther—the burning need to defend her—numbed everything else. Each time we tore into its flesh, each time our teeth sank into its throat, a thrill, dark and exhilarating, ran through me. It had hurt what's *mine*, dared to kill what's *mine*. It would pay. I wanted it to suffer, to feel every ounce of my fury, the full force of my wrath.

I could see the fear in the creature's eyes—the dawning understanding of its impending fate—as I overpowered it, our claws raking across its body, leaving deep, bleeding wounds in their wake. It tried to fight back, its wings flaring in a desperate, pathetic attempt to escape. Biting down on its shoulder, the metallic tang of blood filling my mouth, hot and coppery, as the creature let out a pained howl that was quickly choked off. It was exhilarating, a dark, savage satisfaction I had never experienced before. In that moment, lost in the bloodlust, it felt right. Terribly, terrifyingly right.

For the first time, the panther and I were working as one. Not fighting for control, not a desperate struggle for dominance, but a unity. It was as if the beast within finally understood, finally accepted, this shared purpose.

The beast within me reveled in the power, the raw, untamed dominance. I could feel its heart hammering against my ribs, a frantic, desperate beat as it struggled in vain to escape, to survive. But I wouldn't let it. I couldn't. Not after what it had done, the carnage it had unleashed. With a lethal snarl, I pinned it down, my muscles screaming in protest as I forced its thrashing body to the ground, my jaws closing around its neck in a vise-like grip. It let out one final, gurgling roar, a sound choked with fear and defeat, before its body went limp, its once-glowing eyes fading to dull, lifeless ash.

A heavy silence settled over the ravaged forest, the tension dissipating like smoke in the wind as I stood there, my chest heaving, the taste of blood thick on my tongue.

What *was* that beast? The sheer size of it, the raw power radiating off of it—it was unlike anything I'd ever encountered here. Sure, the Wonders of Nexara could be dangerous, full of creatures, traps, and mazes, but I've never seen anything like *that* before. The way it moved, the chilling glint in its eyes—it was unnatural, a twisted mockery of the natural order, corruption that whispered of a darker influence.

My gaze shifted to Thalia, and the sight of her lying broken and bleeding amongst the debris—her normally vibrant auburn hair dull and matted—brought me crashing back to reality. The red haze of rage ebbed away, replaced by a deep, aching concern that twisted in my gut. She was alive—but barely. Her breaths were shallow, ragged gasps that caught in her throat. Relief warred with a surging panic within me as I cautiously took a step towards her, my paws treading lightly on the torn earth.

Slowly, hesitantly, I continued to approach, my eyes meeting hers. I could see the raw fear reflected in their gray depths, the disbelief, and something else—a flicker of recognition. Something that made my chest tighten with an emotion I couldn't quite name. I lowered my head, my senses overwhelmed by her scent, now mingled with the coppery tang of blood. Gently, I sniffed her injured arm. The claw marks were deep, ragged tears in her flesh that showed glimpses of bone beneath. A wave of nausea rolled over me at the sight of her pain, the shallow rise and fall of her chest. I wanted to comfort her—to let her know I was there, that I wouldn't let any further harm come to her. I nudged her hand with my nose, a low rumble vibrating in my chest.

She reached out, her fingers trembling as they brushed against my snout, a feather-light touch that sent a jolt through me. I closed my eyes, leaning into her touch, feeling a fragile connection spark between us. It was gentle, reassuring—a beacon of light in the darkness—and it made me want to stay by her side, to protect her, to never leave her vulnerable again. A soft whine escaped my panther, the sound a low, mournful plea, as if begging her to understand. It was as if he recognized something in her—a vulnerability that mirrored my own, a fragility that called to him, demanding he stand guard. The rumble in my chest deepened, a silent promise to keep her safe, a vow I knew, with every fiber of my being, I would keep.

But I couldn't stay—not like this. Not while she lay bleeding, her life fading away with each passing moment. I studied her pale face, the way her eyes fluttered shut, fighting to stay open. *She's losing too much blood.*

A wave of panic crashed over me, threatening to drown me in its intensity. I lowered my head, pressing my ear against her chest, listening to the frantic rhythm of her heart, each beat growing fainter, more fragile. She didn't have much time, and the crushing weight of helplessness was infuriating. My instincts roared, every fiber of my being screaming at me to do something, but I was powerless to heal, powerless to do anything but watch her slip away. What use was my strength, my beast, if I couldn't save her?

I began pacing, the soft earth giving way beneath my heavy paws. My mind raced, desperately searching for a solution—a way out of this nightmare. The beast inside me snarled in frustration. It clawed at the surface, desperate to act again, to take full control and unleash its anger on anything to help ease the pain we were both feeling. But what good was brute force against such a delicate injury? All I could do was watch, the hopelessness consuming me, tearing me apart from the inside. She needed help—real help, not the destructive strength that we could offer. She needed a healer, a touch far gentler than mine.

I let out a low, pained growl, the sound tearing from my throat. My gaze darted back to Thalia. She was barely conscious now, her breaths shallow and ragged, each one a struggle. I couldn't lose her. Not like this. Not after finally finding a connection—a sense of peace—I hadn't known since my grandmother. When I lost my grandmother—when I failed to protect her—my panther started taking full control, shutting me out when I shifted, leaving me lost in the beast's rage. The memory of the village burning, the screams echoing in my ears, was a constant reminder of my failure. I wouldn't let that happen again. I wouldn't fail Thalia. Not when she'd become the new source of my peace, the gentle hand that soothed the beast within.

I took one last look at her, memorizing the curve of her cheek, the delicate slope of her nose, before turning and sprinting into the forest. The undergrowth whipped past me as my paws pounded the earth with a single, desperate purpose. There had to be something—someone—who could help. A healer, a potion, anything. And I would find them, no matter what it took. I would scour every inch of this forest, every corner of this world, if I had to.

But amidst the fear and desperation, a single, unwavering resolve solidified within me. I would always come when she needed me. I would always be here, a silent guardian in the shadows, whether she liked it or not. And this time, unlike the fragmented memories of my past, I would remember every moment of it. Every second of her pain, every flicker of fear in her eyes, would be etched into my memory, a constant reminder of my vow to protect her.

Chapter 17

Thalia's POV

The sound of a voice—unfamiliar, yet gentle, as soft as a warm breeze—brought me back to reality. My eyes blinked open, the world around me blurred and hazy. Slowly, the shapes began to solidify, the colors to deepen, and the first thing I saw was a young man I didn't recognize, his face filled with concern, his brow furrowed with worry. "How do you feel?" he asked, almost tentative, as if he feared the answer.

Suddenly, like a dam bursting within my mind, everything came rushing back. The chilling shriek that echoed through the forest, the horrifying sight of the grotesque creature lunging towards me, the sharp sting of pain as its claws tore through my flesh. And the majestic form of the panther, its powerful body shielding me, its fierce growl echoing in my ears. My heart lurched in my chest, a wave of panic flooding me as I shot upright, my senses on high alert. My eyes darted around, searching frantically for something—someone—anything familiar to anchor me in this swirling vortex of fear and confusion. My heart raced as the adrenaline pushed away the lingering grogginess that still clung to me. My breath came in quick, shallow gasps, as if I'd just run a marathon. And then I saw him.

Nox

He was standing just a few feet away, his eyes wide with a mixture of fear and relief, a look of raw, utter relief washing over his face. He let out a shaky breath, his shoulders relaxing, the tension visibly draining from his body as he rubbed his hands over his face, as if trying to compose himself. I could see the tension slowly fading away from him, replaced by a cautious hope that flickered in his emerald-green eyes.

The unfamiliar guy beside me shifted nervously, his eyes flicking between Nox and me, his gaze darting back and forth like a trapped bird. He looked terrified, his face pale and drawn, his lips trembling slightly as he spoke. "She's good for now," he said, his voice shaky and uncertain, "but you really need to get her to a proper healer. I-I only know so much. I did what I could, but her injuries are beyond my limited skills."

I tried to focus, to ground myself in the present, but everything felt strange—disconnected, like I was only half here, adrift in a hazy fog. Pain throbbed through my arm, a dull, persistent ache that pulsed a constant reminder of the severity of my injuries. The dried blood, a gruesome crimson stain, stuck to my skin, the coppery scent still lingering in the air, thick and metallic. The stranger's words barely registered, lost somewhere in the swirling whirlpool of my disorientation. My eyes locked onto Nox, searching his expression, desperate for an anchor in this bewildering reality. There was something different there—something deeper than just relief. Concern, fear, and something else I couldn't quite place flickered in his emerald depths, a complex tapestry of emotions I couldn't decipher.

"Where am I?" I managed to croak, my voice barely a whisper, raspy and raw from disuse. My throat felt dry and scratchy, each word a painful rasp as it passed my lips. My head spun, a dizzying carousel of fragmented memories and unanswered questions, as I tried to piece together the events that led me here.

The guy shifted again, wringing his hands nervously, looking hesitant before answering, "You're safe for now. At least... as safe as you can be in this place." He swallowed hard, his Adam's apple bobbing nervously. "I-I found you and did what I could to stabilize you, patched you up as best I could, but you really need more help than I can give. Your injuries are... extensive." His gaze flickered back to Nox—a silent plea for reassurance—who nodded curtly, his jaw clenched tight, the tension still obvious in his posture.

Nox took a step forward, closing the distance between us, his eyes softening as they met mine. "Thalia, you're going to be okay," he said, his voice steady and reassuring against the rising wave of panic, though I could hear the underlying strain beneath it, the tight control he was maintaining over his own emotions. He knelt beside me, his hand reaching out to rest gently on my uninjured arm, a light touch that radiated warmth. The warmth of his touch sent a wave of comfort through me, a grounding presence amidst the chaos, a lifeline in the swirling storm. "We're going to get you to someone who can help. You just need to hold on a bit longer. Just stay with me."

I swallowed hard, the pain a searing brand in my throat, making it difficult to think, the world around me blurring in and out of focus like a poorly adjusted lens. My gaze flicked to the unfamiliar guy, who looked out of his depth, clearly trying his best but overwhelmed by the gravity of the situation. He shifted from foot to foot, wringing his hands, his eyes darting between me and Nox.

Nox turned to him, his eyes darkening slightly, a mask of control slipping over his features. "I'll take it from here," he said, his tone firm, a subtle dismissal in his voice.

The guy nodded quickly, relief flashing in his eyes as he stepped back, giving us space. He mumbled something that sounded like, "Of course," before practically sprinting away, eager to escape the unsettling scene. I could feel my body growing weaker, the exhaustion creeping back in, threatening to drag me under once more into the oblivion of unconsciousness. My vision wavered, the edges darkening, the vibrant colors of the world fading into muted shades of gray, but I fought to stay awake, my gaze fixed on Nox as if he were the only thing tethering me to reality.

His hand squeezed mine, a reassuring pressure, grounding me in the present. "Just stay with me, Thalia," he whispered, his voice softer now, almost pleading, a hint of desperation threading through his words. "I promise, I won't let anything happen to you."

I managed a small nod, a flicker of movement against the overwhelming tide of exhaustion. My eyes still locked on his, searching for why he was here—why he was helping me—as my eyelids grew heavier, lead weights dragging them down. I could feel myself slipping away, losing the battle against the darkness pulling me back under into its silent embrace, but this time, I wasn't afraid. I knew I wasn't alone. The warmth of his hand in mine, the sincerity in his voice, was a shield against the fear.

THE NIGHTMARE CAME SWIFTLY, PULLING ME DEEPER into the shadows of my mind

I stood alone in the middle of a dark forest, aged trees looming over me. The air was cold, biting into my skin. An unnatural silence hung in the air. There was no sound—no crickets, no distant animal calls, not even the whisper of wind through the branches. Just silence.

I heard it then—that low, guttural growl that made the hairs on the back of my neck stand on end. My eyes started scanning the shadowy

depths of the forest, but there was nothing there. Just the oppressive darkness and the lingering echo of the growl. Panic clawed at my insides, a cold dread spreading through me, the darkness pressing in on me like a suffocating blanket, making it hard to breathe. I started to run—blindly, desperately—my feet pounding against the cold, unforgiving earth, my lungs burning with each frantic breath.

The growl grew louder, closer, and I could feel it—something was chasing me, something malevolent, something hungry. My legs felt heavy, as if the earth itself was trying to drag me down, roots and vines snaking up from the ground like grasping claws, trying to ensnare my ankles. I stumbled, my hands hitting the ground hard, the impact jarring my bones, dirt and leaves clinging to my skin like desperate pleas. The growl turned into a roar—a terrifying sound that seemed to come from everywhere at once, reverberating through the forest.

I pushed myself up, my hands scraped and bleeding, trying to run again, but the forest seemed endless, a labyrinth of shadows and fear, designed to trap me in its suffocating embrace. The darkness shifted, swirling and mingling, and I saw them—glowing eyes— piercing, evil eyes—staring at me from the shadows, burning with an unholy light. The creature emerged, its twisted horns like jagged blades against the darkness, its dark red fur matted and thick, the stench of decay clinging to it filled my nose. It was the same beast from before. But here, in this twisted version of reality, it seemed even larger, even more menacing—its power amplified by the fear that pulsed through me.

I backed away as it stalked towards me, each step slow—as if it knew there was no escape. My back hit a tree, the rough bark digging into my skin. I could see the hatred in the creatures eyes, the pure hunger, a reflection of the darkness that was here to consume me. It lunged, its massive claws swiping, sharp and deadly, but not at me—at Nox.

Nox appeared out of nowhere, a sudden, unexpected presence, throwing himself between me and the creature, a shield against the impending violence. I screamed—a raw, painful sound that echoed through the empty forest, a desperate cry as I watched the beast's claws tear into him, ripping through flesh and bone. His body crumpled to the ground, lifeless, his eyes dulling, losing their vibrant green, as they met mine for one heartbreaking moment, a silent farewell. The shock of it paralyzed me, my heart shattering into a million pieces, the pain taking over every inch of my body as I watched him fall.

I screamed again, my voice breaking—raw and ragged—my vision blurring with tears as the world around me dissolved into a hazy, distorted mess. The creature turned its eyes back to me, a cruel satisfaction in its gaze, a twisted mockery of my grief, as if it took pleasure in my despair. It moved towards me, its massive form blocking out all light, and I could feel the suffocating helplessness, the chilling inevitability of my fate closing in.

The ground gave way beneath me, I was falling into an endless abyss, watching as the darkness swallowed me whole. My stomach lurched, my body weightless, as I plummeted into nothingness. The creature's roar followed me, echoing in my ears, a final, conquering sound, its glowing eyes the last thing I saw before everything went black, leaving me lost in the embrace of the void.

My eyes snapped open, my body drenched in a clammy sweat. I struggled to control my ragged breathing and focused on steadying my trembling hands. The terror, the panic, clung to me like a second skin. I had watched Nox die—seen him fall, helpless against the creature that had hunted me through the twisting corridors of my nightmare. The vivid image replayed in my mind, a cruel, relentless loop, each time twisting the knife deeper into my chest.

"It was just a dream," I murmured. The room around me slowly swam into focus—a large, unfamiliar room made of dark stone

194

glowing in the flickering light of a crackling fire to my right. Heavy, dark curtains were drawn over a large window, obscuring the world outside. The bed beneath me was massive, the kind that seemed to swallow you whole, with soft, luxurious linens that felt like heaven against my aching body.

I blinked, disoriented, trying to piece together the pieces of my scattered memory. The room was elegant, almost regal, with delicate carvings on the dark wooden furniture. A plush ivory rug, thick and soft, covered the cold stone floor. A tall bookshelf stood against the wall to my left, filled with old, worn books, their spines cracked and faded. A few candles flickered on a nearby table, their soft light illuminating the otherwise dark space, casting dancing shadows that seemed to shift and writhe in the periphery of my vision.

Where was I? The question echoed in my mind, a desperate plea for understanding. The fear from the attack—the lingering chill of the nightmare—still gripped me, its icy fingers tightening around my throat. My body ached with every small movement, a dull throb resonating through my limbs. My arm, grazed during the attack, pulsed with a sharp, insistent pain as I shifted. I had no idea how I ended up here, and the unfamiliarity of the room—the heavy silence—only heightened my anxiety, a knot tightening in my stomach. My gaze darted around the room, searching for any sign of familiarity, any clue to my whereabouts, but there was nothing—no one. I was alone.

My head pounded, and I struggled to calm my breathing, each inhale a shaky gasp. My hands clenched the soft sheets beneath me, the fabric bunching between my fingers as I tried to make sense of everything. The last thing I remembered was Nox, his strong arms around me, his reassuring presence as I slipped into the darkness.

Panic bubbled up in my chest, a suffocating wave, the vivid memory of Nox's lifeless body, pale and still, flashing before my eyes. The image seared itself onto my eyelids, a horrifying reminder of my dream. I had no idea where I was, who had brought me here, or what had happened after I'd lost consciousness. It had to be Nox—right? No one else knew where we were.

I forced myself to calm down. Whoever had brought me here had taken care of me—that much was clear. My wounds were tended to and expertly bandaged. The fire crackled merrily, still alive, suggesting someone had been here recently, stoking the flames to keep the room warm. I was dressed in a clean, oversized t-shirt, soft and comforting against my skin, and it carried a familiar scent of cedarwood and fresh rain that made me pause, my breath catching in my throat—Nox.

The realization sent a shiver down my spine. I was still wearing my pants from the Wonders of Nexara, but my socks and shoes were missing. Despite the care someone had taken with me, the fear lingered, a cold, unshakable shadow clinging to me as I struggled to piece together what was happening, to fill in the blanks of my lost memory.

I swallowed hard, the lump in my throat making it difficult, pushing myself to sit up, wincing as a sharp pain flared through my body, a searing reminder of my injuries. Every movement seemed to take twice the effort it should have, my muscles protesting with each shift. I took another deep breath—a slow inhale and exhale—swinging my legs over the side of the bed. The soft rug on the cool stone floor felt like clouds against my bare feet, a comforting sensation, and I wiggled my toes, enjoying the brief distraction from the fear and confusion that gnawed at me.

Slowly, I rose to my feet. My legs were shaky beneath me, threatening to buckle. I paused, steadying myself against the sturdy bedpost, my gaze flicking around the room once more, searching for any clue—any hint of where I was—before landing on the heavy wooden door. One step at a time, I moved towards the door, my bare feet silent on the soft rug, my fingers brushing against the cool, carved wood of the door frame before wrapping around the smooth metal of the handle. With a deep breath, a silent prayer for answers, I turned it and pulled the door open, stepping out into a hallway.

The hallway beyond was dimly lit, bathed in the soft glow of the moon from the window at the far end. My heart skipped a beat— a sudden flutter in my chest—as I took in the familiar surroundings: the long corridor, the dark, rough stone, the ornate tapestries on the walls. Recognition washed over me as I let out a shaky breath, a mixture of relief and disbelief bubbling up inside me.

The realization made me laugh—a soft, manic sound that escaped my lips before I could stop it. It was the hallway I had run into Zarek in before. I never thought I'd be happy to be here, in the home of the Shadow Brothers.

I leaned against the doorframe for a moment, letting the feeling wash over me, a wave of relief that threatened to knock me off my feet. I straightened, pushing myself away from the door, taking another deep breath, the pain flaring up the more I moved.

I moved cautiously toward the wide, curving staircase, listening for any signs of them, straining my ears against the quiet hum of the house. There was muffled talking coming from somewhere downstairs—voices low and serious—a murmur of words I couldn't quite hear, before a door slammed somewhere in the house, making me jump. I froze as loud footsteps approached the stairs, each one echoing through the hallway like a warning.

Gripping the smooth wood of the banister as I looked down the long, winding staircase, my body tense and unsure, a tremor running through me. My head swam slightly from the effort of standing—a dizzying wave of lightheadedness—but I ignored it, forcing myself to focus on the figure emerging from the shadows below. Nox appeared at the bottom of the stairs, his dark hair falling across his forehead, his eyes narrowing as they locked onto mine. I could see the tension in his broad shoulders, the way his jaw clenched, the subtle shift in his stance that spoke of a readiness to act.

"What the hell are you doing out of bed?" he snapped, his voice sharper than I expected, laced with a raw edge of concern, the worry beneath it barely masked by the irritation. He took the stairs two at a time, his long legs eating up the distance, closing the gap between us faster than I could react.

I swallowed, leaning more heavily against the banister, my body trembling from both exhaustion and the intensity of his gaze. "I... I just needed to see where I was," I whispered, hating how small and vulnerable I sounded, but unable to change it. The nightmare lingered, the memory of *his* death vivid, making my voice waver. The metallic scent of blood still clung to the air, a phantom reminder of the terror I'd experienced.

Nox stopped a few steps below me, his eyes searching my face, the frustration slowly melting into something softer—something that made my chest tighten. He let out a long breath, rubbing a hand over his face, his shoulders slumping. "You shouldn't be out of bed. You're hurt, Thalia. You need to rest."

I attempted a shaky smile. "I'm fine, feeling much better."

Nox stared, his face unreadable, then raised an eyebrow, silently calling me out on my lie. "Fine? Really?" he said, his tone dripping with disbelief. He took a step closer, his eyes locking on mine, their weight piercing through every flimsy excuse. "You're pale as a ghost, shaking just from standing, and you think you're 'fine'?"

I opened my mouth to protest, but the words caught in my throat. I wanted to insist I was okay, that I didn't need coddling, but the exhaustion dragging at my limbs and the fear still clinging to me betrayed me. I looked away, my grip tightening on the banister as I tried to steady myself. The floor seemed to sway beneath my feet.

"Thalia," Nox's voice softened, almost pleading. He reached out, his hand resting gently on my arm—his touch warm and steady—sending a strange shiver through me. "You don't have to pretend with me. I know you're not fine. You went through hell. Just... let me help you."

His words unleashed a torrent of emotions. Memories of a childhood spent fending for myself in Nyvorthia—where trust was a fragile illusion—rose to the surface. I'd learned early that people always left, that I'd always disappointed. Relying on anyone had only ever brought pain; a pain so sharp that it had become the cornerstone of my existence. I hated feeling weak. Hated the vulnerability that now clung to me like a second skin. Hated needing anyone. It went against every carefully constructed wall, every defense mechanism I had built around myself, brick by painful brick. But looking up at him, seeing the genuine concern etched into his features, made something inside me falter.

I let out a shaky breath, nodding slowly. "Okay," I sighed, my voice barely audible. "I'm trying here." I added a touch of defensiveness clinging to the words.

A hint of a smile played at the corners of Nox's lips. He moved closer, his arm wrapping around my waist, supporting me as I leaned into him. "I know you are," he murmured, his voice filled with a surprising warmth.

I stared at him, bewildered by his sudden shift in demeanor. "I don't get you," I sighed, shaking my head as he began guiding me back towards the room, his arm securely around me. One minute he was practically snarling at me, the next he was gentle and caring. My head hurt even more from trying to understand him than from my actual injuries.

He chuckled softly at my words, the sound almost comforting in the dim hallway. Each step was slow and careful, his presence a steadying force against the inner turmoil that still raged within me. "Yeah, I don't get me either sometimes," he replied, a faint hint of amusement in his voice. There was a genuine quality to his confession, an openness that surprised me. His guard was down, and for a fleeting moment, I felt like I was glimpsing the real Nox.

As we reached the doorway, I glanced up at him. There was something in his eyes, something raw and unguarded. It made my chest ache.

"Thank you," I whispered as we reached the bed, my legs giving out beneath me as I sank onto the mattress. He leaned in, adjusting the blankets around my shoulders, his gaze holding mine.

"Get some rest, Thalia," he said, his voice low and calm, the undertone of worry still present. "I'll be here if you need anything."

I nodded, my eyes growing heavy as exhaustion threatened to pull me under yet again. I watched him add more wood to the fire, the flames casting more shadows on the walls, before he turned towards the door, his silhouette framed by the flickering glow.

A wave of fear washed over me at the thought of being alone. The darkness still lingered—the nightmare too recent, too real. "Stay," I mumbled, the word barely audible as sleep tugged at my consciousness.

Nox paused, his hand resting on the doorframe. He hesitated for a moment, as if considering my request. Then he nodded, walking back towards the bed. I felt the mattress shift as he sat on the other side, his back against the headboard, his gaze fixed on the dancing flames.

I let my eyes drift shut, the warmth of the fire and Nox's steady presence lulling me into a sense of security. The last thing I saw was Nox—his features soft in the glow of the fire, his gaze fixed on the flames.

Chapter 18

Thalia's POV

My throat felt like the desert, dry and scratchy, and my head throbbed faintly as I forced my heavy eyelids open. The ache wasn't as bad as before, a dull thrumming rather than a sharp, stabbing pain, and my entire body felt lighter. I blinked against the soft light filtering into the room, my vision blurry and unfocused as I struggled to make sense of what I was seeing.

Legs. Long, muscular legs clad in dark denim.

I squinted, trying to determine if I was still caught in some strange, hazy dream. My mind felt sluggish, like it was wading through thick molasses.

Yep, definitely legs. And really nice ones at that.

It took me a moment—a slow, dawning realization—to understand that I was staring directly at someone's thighs, my gaze fixed on the toned muscles beneath the fabric. I blinked again, my sleepy mind finally beginning to catch up with my senses. A small, confused smile tugged at my lips as I tilted my head back, my gaze traveling slowly upward—taking in the broad shoulders, the strong arms, and finally, the sleeping face of Nox. His dark hair was tousled, falling across his forehead, and his long lashes rested against his cheeks. He looked peaceful, almost serene. Completely different to the usual brooding intensity he carried.

He was still sitting up, his head leaning back against the headboard, an arm resting possessively on my waist, his presence somehow both protective and gentle. The usual tension that radiated off him was gone, a tension I was only now realizing I'd grown accustomed to. He looked so relaxed, so at ease, despite the slight scowl that seemed permanently etched on his features—a scowl that usually spoke of guarded emotions but now seemed softened by sleep. His breaths were steady, his chest rising and falling with a calmness that was almost hypnotic, making me want to relax even more, to burrow into his warmth and let the peace of the moment wash over me.

His dark curls—usually hidden beneath a hood—framed his face, some falling across his forehead in a way that softened his usual sharp demeanor, giving him an almost boyish charm. The morning light peeking through the window highlighted the angles of his face—the strong line of his jaw, the high cheekbones, and the faint stubble that dusted his skin, a testament to the fact that even in sleep, he held an air of rugged masculinity. There was something almost fragile about him like this—the way the shadows danced across his features, accentuating his beauty in a way I hadn't fully appreciated before. A beauty that was usually overshadowed by his intensity.

His lips were slightly parted, and even with the hint of a scowl, held a vulnerability I rarely saw. It made him seem almost approachable. It was like all the walls he constantly kept up had fallen away in sleep, leaving behind only the raw version of himself, the version he protected from the world. The sight made my heart tighten in my chest, a strange mixture of tenderness and

Chapter 18

protectiveness washing over me. I found myself studying the way his lashes rested against his cheeks, long and dark, the delicate curve of his cheekbones. I had never been this close to him before —never had the chance to truly observe him.

I had to bite back a giggle at the insanity of the situation—waking up to find myself practically using him as a pillow, my head nestled against his side, his steady breathing a soothing rhythm in my ear. I was staring at the long lines of his legs like some kind of confused child. But within the amusement, there was also something comforting about it—something that made the fear and pain of the last few days feel a little more distant.

I shifted slightly, trying not to wake him, but his arm tightened around my waist instinctively, pulling me closer. A soft gasp escaped my lips at the sudden movement, but it was quickly swallowed by the quiet of the room. I froze, my gaze flicking back to his face, expecting to see his emerald eyes, but he didn't wake. Instead, his face seemed to relax just a little more, the usual scowl easing as he let out a soft sigh. The tension that always seemed to radiate from him was gone, replaced by something close to peace. It was a side of him I'd never seen, and it made something flutter in my stomach.

A strange mixture of affection moved through me, a touch of something that felt dangerous. I didn't know what any of this meant—why he was here, why he was being so gentle with me after weeks of hostility, or why seeing him like this made my chest feel so tight.

I shouldn't be here with him, resting my head on his lap, watching him sleep. It felt illegal. Forbidden. Like I was trespassing on sacred ground.

Part of me knew that this was a dangerous game I was playing— letting down my guard with someone as unpredictable as Nox.

His moods shifted like the wind, leaving me off-balance. And yet, I found myself unwilling to move, unwilling to break the spell that had settled over us.

I closed my eyes, my thoughts twisting in circles. What did I even mean to Nox? Was this just his sense of duty? Or was it something deeper? My fingers twitched slightly, brushing against the soft fabric of his shirt. I wanted to move—to pull away and put some distance between us before he woke up and the familiar walls slammed back into place—but I couldn't bring myself to do it. His sleeping face held me captive. It was a reminder that maybe he wasn't as heartless as he wanted everyone to believe.

I stayed like that for a while, letting the minutes stretch on, untethered from reality. Studying the gentle rise and fall of his chest, the way his arm cradled me close—it all made the world outside, with its problems and demands, feel far away. It was as if we existed in a bubble, suspended between dreams and reality. I knew I was delaying the inevitable, the moment where the spell would break, and I would have to face everything. Reality would come crashing back, and with it, all the unanswered questions and the inevitable chaos that always seem to follow me.

But then, I felt it—a subtle shift beneath me. The almost slight tightening of his muscles, the way his head turned slightly, his breath catching in his throat. My heart gave a small jump and without thinking, I closed my eyes, pretending to sleep.

There was a moment of stillness, and I could almost feel the confusion radiate from him as he realized the situation we were in —me, with my head in his lap, him holding me close. I listened as he let out a soft breath as his hand moved slightly, like if he was debating whether to pull away or stay where he was.

Slowly, I felt his fingers brush against my hair, the pads of his fingertips against my skin as he tucked a stray strand behind my ear. It was such a gentle gesture, so unexpectedly tender, that it made my chest tighten until it felt like it was going to explode, a rush of warmth flooding through my veins. I had to fight to keep my breathing even, shallow and measured, to keep up the illusion of me still sleeping. Even as every nerve ending in my body was *screaming* to touch him back. He paused for a moment, his fingers lingering near my temple, and I could almost hear the thoughts racing through his mind, a silent whirl of questions.

After a moment, I felt him shift again, the muscles in his arm tensing slightly as he carefully moved it away from me as he tried not to disturb me. He was being so cautious, so careful—as if he didn't want to wake me from a peaceful dream—and it sent a strange mixture of longing and bliss through me.

I heard him let out another breath, this one a little heavier. He shifted his weight, the mattress dipping slightly beneath him, and I felt the bed sway gently as he moved to stand. I kept my eyes closed, my lashes fluttering against my cheeks, listening as he walked quietly across the room, his footsteps soft against the floor. The rustle of fabric as he adjusted his clothes, the faint creak of the door as he pulled it open—it all painted a picture of him leaving, and a pang of something bittersweet settled in my chest, a lingering echo of his presence in the quiet room.

The door clicked shut, and I opened my eyes, staring at the spot where he'd just stood, a ghost of his warmth lingering in the air. I pulled the blanket tighter around me, trying to hold on to the comfort that Nox's presence had brought—the scent of cedar and rain still clinging to the sheets—but it was slipping through my fingers like sand.

I sat up slowly, the plush comforter sliding off my shoulders. I couldn't stay in bed forever, drowning in my emotions. Swinging my legs over the side of the bed, I planted my feet on the soft plush rug and pushed myself to stand. My legs wobbly at first as I made my way to the door.

My hand hovering over the cool metal of the handle for a moment. I didn't know what I would find on the other side—if Nox would still be the same Nox as before, or if things would be different between us.

"No, don't go there," I told myself, shaking my head, pushing those thoughts aside.

Plus, I really needed to get back to my dorm for a much-needed shower. The lingering scent of Nox, while intoxicating, was a constant reminder of the moment we just shared, and I needed to wash everything away and clear my head.

I opened the door slowly, the hinges creaking slightly, and peeked out into the hallway. It was empty. The shock of cold against my bare feet sent a jolt up my spine, waking me up more.

My fingers trailing lightly along the smooth surface of the wall while I made my way down the hallway. I reached the top of the grand staircase and paused, glancing down into the open area below. The sunlight spilled into the space, illuminating the gleaming stone floors and the few pieces of dark, heavy furniture scattered around.

I heard faint voices drifting from somewhere below—the low murmur of conversation that I couldn't quite make out. I hesitated again, my hand gripping the wood of the banister as I debated whether to go down or stay hidden. Part of me wanted to retreat, to go back to the shadowy safety of the room and avoid whatever waited for me downstairs. But I knew there was no running from this.

I started down the stairs, each step echoing softly in the vast, quiet space. The voices grew louder as I got closer, and I recognized one of them—Zarek. His tone was calm, measured, but there was a sharp edge to it, something serious that made me pause at the bottom step.

I couldn't make out the words, but I could feel the underlying tension in his voice. Even without understanding what they were saying, I knew it wasn't good.

I took another small step forward, moving closer to the curved doorway that led to the main room. The flickering light of the fireplace danced on the walls. I peeked further around the corner, my eyes landing on Zarek and Damon. Both were standing near the large fireplace, their faces set in serious, almost grim expressions.

Zarek was speaking, his hands moving in animated gestures as he talked, his brow furrowed in concentration. Damon stood beside him, his arms crossed tightly over his chest, his gaze focused intently on his brother. His jaw was clenched, the muscle ticking beneath his skin. The tension between them was almost suffocating, the kind of tension that made the air feel thick and heavy, difficult to breathe.

They were talking about me. I knew it with a certainty that settled deep in my bones. I took a deep, steadying breath, trying to calm the tremor in my hands, and stepped out from my hiding place— my gaze locking onto Zarek's just as he looked up and saw me.

The conversation stopped abruptly, both brothers turning to face me, their tones shifting dramatically. Zarek's eyes softened, a flicker of relief passing through them. While Damon's eyes darkened, his features hardening at my presence.

"Morning," I said, forcing my voice to be steady and my eyes to hold theirs.

Zarek shot me a small, reassuring smile, the corner of his lips tugging upwards as he nodded. "Good morning, Firefly. Come on in. We were just talking. Right, brother?" He clapped Damon on the shoulder, a gesture that seemed to stiffen him.

Damon's eyes narrowed slightly, his gaze flickering between me and his brother. He didn't say anything, but the silence was heavy. I took another step forward, feeling really out of place.

"How are you feeling?" Zarek asked, as I sat down on one of the plush couches.

"Surprisingly good, just a little sore," I admitted. "But I need to get back to the dorms. I could really use a shower and a change of clothes." My eyes flickered between the brothers, searching for any hint of what they were hiding—what they were talking about. Zarek's signature smirk appeared, a playful glint in his amber eyes, while Damon continued to look at me with that same expression, the one that didn't hide the disgust he felt for me.

"You can use mine," Zarek offered, motioning back towards the grand staircase, his tone light, almost teasing. "It's much better than the ones in the dorms."

"That's okay, I should really get back," I argued, standing up, a sense of unease creeping up my spine. "Just need my shoes," I added, giving an awkward smile, hoping to deflect the offer without causing offense. Zarek has always been kind to me, and I didn't want to impose more than I already had.

Zarek raised a perfectly sculpted eyebrow, his smirk widening as if he found my reluctance amusing. "Thalia, it's just a shower. Trust me, the water pressure here is divine. And I even have fluffy towels."

Damon huffed, rolling his eyes towards the high, vaulted ceiling. "If she wants to go, let her go, Zarek. She's not a prisoner here." His words were clipped, laced with an icy edge that made me bristle. A small, petty part of me wanted to stay a little longer just to irritate him, to push his buttons.

I glanced between the two brothers—Zarek, with his easy charm, teasing smile, and aura of warmth; and Damon, with his cold eyes, defensive posture, and the clear hostility radiating off him in waves. It made me wonder how these two polar opposites could possibly be brothers. I knew they weren't biologically related; the differences in their features and demeanor were too different. But what had brought them together? How did the three of them, including Nox, become the 'Shadow Brothers'?

"I'll be quick," I finally conceded, my voice quiet as I looked at Zarek. There was something in his eyes, something that made me feel seen, and less like an intruder in their bizarre world. It was probably just his natural charm, his ability to put people at ease.

"Lead the way," I added, a genuine smile playing at my lips at Zarek's reaction. I followed back towards the stairs, trying to ignore the way Damon's eyes burned into my back. While Zarek and Nox were warming up to me—in whatever confusing and complicated way it was—Damon was most definitely not. His disapproval was a physical presence, a shadow clinging to me as I ascended the stairs.

MY EYES WIDENED AS I TOOK A FEW HESITANT STEPS into Zarek's room, immediately struck by the oddness of it all. His room was nothing like what I thought it would be. It was light, airy. With soft, calming colors that gave it an almost delicate feel. The walls were a pale, baby blue—like the sky just before sunset—and sunlight poured in through two large windows.

There were plants everywhere—vines cascading from the ceiling like emerald waterfalls, potted flowers blooming in vibrant colors on the windowsill, and even a small, meticulously pruned bonsai tree in the corner. It felt alive, like stepping into a secret garden hidden. The air smelled faintly of wildflowers and fresh earth, and

I could almost feel the magic that seemed to pulse through the room, a gentle hum of energy, a subtle reminder of Zarek's Fae heritage.

The bed was large and inviting, with a white sheer canopy that draped elegantly over it. The bedding was a mix of crisp whites and calming blues, covered with delicate embroidery. Crystals hung by the window, catching the light and casting small rainbows across the room—their subtle glimmer adding a touch of enchantment to the already magical space.

In one corner, a beautifully carved wooden bookshelf stood tall, filled with leather-bound books and small trinkets scattered. Shells, polished stones, and bits of sea glass—that seemed almost out of place, yet somehow they fit perfectly.

The room was filled with intriguing differences—earthy, natural elements mixed with the soft blues of the sky, and hints of something else, almost reminiscent of the sea. It was like stepping into a sanctuary. A perfect blend of Fae lightness and something deeper, as if the space itself was a reflection of Zarek's very soul.

As I stood there, taking it all in, absorbing the unexpected beauty of his personal space, I felt his eyes on me. He was watching me intently, a flicker of amusement dancing in his eyes. But it felt as if he was waiting to see what I thought of this private part of him, this space he had so carefully created. It was as if he was offering me a piece of himself, waiting to see if I would accept it.

I turned to meet his amber eyes, "It's... beautiful," I said, my voice full of awe. "Not what I expected at all, but... it suits you."

Zarek's lips curved into a broader smile, the amusement in his eyes replaced by a quiet satisfaction. He shrugged lightly, as if brushing off the compliment, a gesture that seemed almost shy. "Glad you think so."

He motioned towards a door on the far side of the room. "Bathroom's through there. Take your time," he added.

I nodded, my heart still pounding a strange rhythm, and made my way across the room, the soft rug beneath my bare feet. As I reached the bathroom door, I paused, glancing back at Zarek. He was still watching me, his eyes filled with that same mix of curiosity and something I still couldn't quite understand.

"Thank you," I said, the words hanging between us, filled with more meaning than I could explain. Zarek gave a small nod before I turned away, stepping into the bathroom and closing the door behind me—the click echoing softly in the quiet room.

The moment I was alone, I let out a shaky breath and leaned against the door for a moment, trying to steady myself. There was something about Zarek—something about his room, this place— that made me feel like I was seeing a part of him that no one else got to see, what he hid beneath his playful exterior.

First Nox, and now Zarek. A wave of confusion washed over me. I needed to process what the hell was going on.

I pushed away from the door, my eyes scanning the bathroom, taking in the details. It was just as beautiful as the rest of his room —light, spacious, with soft blue tiles and a large, inviting clawfoot tub that sat beneath a frosted window. The scent of lavender hung in the air, a calming fragrance that eased the tension in my shoulders.

Sinking into the tub, a soft moan escaped my lips as the hot water engulfed my body, soothing my aching muscles and washing away the grime and exhaustion of the past few days. I started to scrub with a soft cloth, surprised to find that most of the dirt and dried blood had already been cleaned off my exposed skin. It was clear someone had tried to clean me while I was unconscious, and the thought made me feel a strange mix of gratitude, irritation, and slight embarrassment. Who had cleaned me? One of the brothers?

The thought sent a shiver down my spine. I reached for the soap, laughing as I looked at what Zarek used—it was shaped like a perfect seashell, intricately carved, and it smelled expensive, with a hint of something fresh and distinctly masculine. Of course, he'd use something like this. It was so... Zarek.

I let myself sink deeper into the water. The events of the past few months replayed in my mind. Everything seemed to be happening so fast—being brought to this strange academy, the brothers' unpredictable behavior, the intense, almost overwhelming moments of connection with Nox. And now, here I was, in Zarek's room, using his tub as if it was the most natural thing in the world. The sound of soft footsteps outside the door made my eyes snap open.

"Thalia? You okay in there?" His tone was light, teasing, but there was a hint of concern that made my stomach flip.

I cleared my throat, trying to steady my voice, to inject a note of normalcy into the situation. "Yeah, I'm good. Just... enjoying the luxury." I smiled, hoping he could hear the humor in my words.

There was a pause, and then I heard him chuckle softly—a warm, comforting sound. "Don't get too used to it. You might never want to leave."

I rolled my eyes, shaking my head even though he couldn't see me. "I'll be out soon. Promise I won't drain all your hot water."

"Take your time," he replied, his voice gentle. "No rush."

I heard his footsteps retreat as I started washing my tangled hair. There was something about Zarek—the way he could effortlessly switch from teasing to sincere—that made me feel something. It was confusing, and I wasn't quite sure how to process it. From the beginning, his teasing had always been lighthearted—the opposite of his brothers. With Zarek, there were no death stares, only looks filled with curiosity and amusement.

Why had he always been so playful and kind, while his brothers acted like they wanted to murder me every chance they got? It didn't make sense.

After a while, I finally forced myself to get out of the tub, the water now lukewarm, my skin pruned and slightly pink. I wrapped one of his soft, *fluffy towels* around myself as I stepped out onto the plush bath mat. I caught a glimpse of myself in the mirror—my hair damp and tangled—my skin flushed from the heat, a little battered and bruised but still me. The girl beneath the dirt, blood, and fear was still there.

I found a robe hanging on the back of the door, a deep, luxurious ivory color that looked far too expensive to belong to me. I hesitated for a moment before slipping it on, the soft fabric sliding against my skin, the scent of Zarek clinging faintly to the fibers. I took a deep breath, inhaling his scene as I stepped back into his room.

Zarek was sitting on the edge of his bed, a book open in his lap, his eyes flicking up to meet mine as I entered. He gave me a small, appreciative smile, his gaze traveling down my body, briefly lingering on the robe before meeting my eyes again, a flicker of desire dancing in their depths.

"Looks good on you," he said, his voice teasing, but his eyes were serious.

I felt my cheeks heat up and I glanced down at the robe, fidgeting with the sleeve, suddenly self-conscious under his gaze. "Thanks. I, uh... didn't want to put my dirty clothes back on."

He nodded and stood up, crossing the room to a small wardrobe tucked away in the corner. "I figured. Here," he said, pulling out a neatly folded set of clothes and handing them to me. "They might be a little big, but at least they're clean."

I took the clothes from him, my fingers brushing against his for a fleeting moment. The brief contact sent a spark through me, a jolt of electricity that made me tingle all the way to my toes. I looked up at him, catching the way his eyes studied on mine, something unreadable flickering there, a silent question hanging in the air.

"Thanks, this is part of the reason I wanted to go back to my dorms," I teased, trying to deflect the intensity of the moment—to ignore the tension that seemed to buzz between us like a live wire.

He shrugged, giving me that easy, disarming smile of his. "Don't mention it. Besides," he added, his tone turning playful as his eyes swept over me again, a hint of mischief in his gaze, "I think these would look better on you."

I laughed, shaking my head, trying to ignore the way his words made my stomach flutter. "I'll look like I'm a kid wearing their dad's clothes."

He laughed with me, his smile bright and real as his hair fell into his eyes. He reached up to push it back, a casual gesture that sent another unexpected wave of heat through me. There was something about the way he looked at me—his gaze holding mine a little longer than necessary—that made my stomach churn with a mixture of nerves and excitement.

Get it together, Thalia, I mentally scolded myself. Falling for him —for Nox—was absolutely not an option.

"Speaking of parents, winter break started a few days ago. They must be freaking out that they haven't heard from you—it is the holidays, after all."

There was a moment of silence between us. I swallowed, the warmth of the moment slipping away slightly.

Of course, he doesn't know you don't have any parents—Wait, what? Winter break has already started?

"What do you mean? How long was I out?" I asked, my voice cracking slightly as panic started to fill my chest.

Zarek's playful demeanor vanished, replaced by a worried frown that tugged at his brow. He stepped closer, his hand gently reaching out to cup my cheek. "Hey, hey, it's okay," he soothed, his thumb brushing a stray tear away. I hadn't even realized I was crying.

Don't cry, Thalia, don't cry, I told myself, hating the way my emotions seemed to be spilling over. I guess I was on the edge of a complete breakdown.

"You were out for a few days—maybe four or five," he continued, his voice a low rumble that vibrated through me. "You needed rest. We didn't want to push you."

My mind spun, trying to grasp the news. The world had continued moving while I was stuck in oblivion, lost in the suffocating darkness. Four or five days lost, gone, vanished into thin air.

"Thalia, breathe," Zarek said softly, his hand tilting my chin up to meet his gaze. "I know it's a lot, but you're okay now. When Nox found you, you were almost..." He trailed off, his eyes clouding with something darker.

Dead. I was basically dead. The word echoed in my mind, sending a shiver down my spine.

I took a shaky breath, nodding, trying to regulate my breathing. "I'm okay, it's fine, I'm fine." The words felt hollow even to my own ears.

He gave me a look that showed he could see right through my bullshit. But he didn't say anything, giving me a moment to process as his fingers traced my skin lightly.

For a moment, we stood there, eyes locked. There was a charged energy that made my skin tingle—a pull towards him that was getting harder and harder to ignore. I cleared my throat, breaking the spell, and gestured to the clothes in my hands, trying to deflect the intensity of the moment—to regain some kind of control. "I should probably get changed."

He stepped back, giving me space, his playful smile returning, as if a switch had been flipped. "Right. I'll just... be over here, pretending not to look."

"Or you could leave," I reply, raising an eyebrow at him, a playful smirk tugging at the corner of my lips.

"I wouldn't want you to hurt yourself," he shoots back, his eyes shining with a challenge, "what if you fall?" There was a teasing pitch to his tone.

"Whatever, turn around, Zarek," I said, shaking my head, and he obliged, turning his back to me with an exaggerated sigh, a dramatic flair that made me smile. He was such a dork, but a charming one.

As I quickly changed into the clothes he'd given me—a soft, comfortable t-shirt and loose-fitting sweatpants—I couldn't help but steal a glance at him over my shoulder. Even with his back turned, there was something about his presence that made me feel alive—a spark of warmth in the cold emptiness that had settled within me when I was a child.

"Okay, done," I said, and he turned back around, his eyes scanning me before nodding in approval, another smile gracing his lips. It was a warm, genuine smile, one that reached his eyes and made my heart flutter.

"See? Told you they'd look good," he said, his grin widening, a hint of desire dancing in his eyes. It was a look that made my cheeks flush.

I rolled my eyes but couldn't stop the smile that spread across my face. "If you say so." My voice was softer now. The playful banter was a much needed distraction.

"Did you need a ride to town or wherever you're going for break? You can use my phone if you need to contact your family," Zarek offered, looking around for his phone, his brow furrowed in concentration as he rifled through drawers and patted his pockets.

"Oh no, that's okay. Are the dorms still open through break?" I asked, walking back to hang his robe up where I found it, my fingers lingering on the soft fabric—trying to appear casual.

"Sort of, but why would you want to go back to the dorms?" He stopped his search, studying my face and body language, his eyebrows scrunching together as if trying to decipher a complex puzzle. He seemed genuinely lost by the idea, as if spending the holidays alone in a dorm room was the most illogical thing in the world.

"I prefer to be alone for the holidays," I lied, forcing a small smile, hoping it would convince him. I didn't have anywhere else to go, no family to return to, but the thought of admitting that made me feel pathetic. "Do you have a brush I could use?" I added quickly, trying to change the subject, to steer the conversation away from my personal life—from the gaping hole where family should have been.

Zarek's eyes narrowed slightly, a flicker of understanding in their depths, as if he saw right through my flimsy excuse. "Oh, Firefly, when will you stop lying to me," he chuckled, shaking his head as he started walking towards me, his gaze fixed, his presence filling the room.

A blush crept up my neck, a wave of heat spreading through my body as Zarek stopped only inches away. He didn't just stop, though. He braced an arm against the shelf behind me, effectively boxing me in. The air crackled with a sudden, charged tension.

His proximity was overwhelming, the warmth radiating from him a physical force. I craned my head back, meeting his gaze—determined not to be intimidated, though my heart hammered against my ribs. A silent challenge, something primal and exciting, sparked between us. My mouth went dry. His amber eyes, intense and searching, held mine captive. He leaned closer, the scent of cedar and sandalwood filling my senses, making my head spin. I could feel his breath ghosting across my skin. He reached up, his arm brushing against mine, sending a shiver down my spine, as he grabbed a brush from the shelf. The movement was slow, deliberate, and somehow predatory. My breath hitched. I was acutely aware of every inch of him—the hard line of his jaw, the way his muscles flexed beneath his shirt.

"Here you go," he murmured, his voice low and husky, laced with something that sounded dangerously like amusement. A slow, satisfied smile played on his lips, as if he'd just won some unspoken battle. His fingers brushed against mine as he handed me the brush—the contact brief but electric.

"Thanks," I managed, my voice barely a whisper. The word felt thick and heavy in the charged silence between us.

For a heartbeat, neither of us moved. The air thrummed with unspoken words. His eyes held mine—a silent dare—as if he could see the turmoil within me, the warring desires. He was so close, I could feel the heat radiating from him, a magnetic pull I struggled to resist. I found myself leaning just slightly towards him, drawn in by an invisible force. My breath hitched again.

"Anytime, Firefly." He winked, a playful glint in his eyes, and finally pulled away—leaving me breathless and disoriented with the brush clutched in my hand and a heart that was threatening to beat its way out of my chest.

I took a shaky breath, trying to steady myself as I turned away, focusing on taming my tangled hair—the bristles of the brush a small, grounding sensation against my scalp. But the image of his face—so close, so intense—lingered in my mind. I couldn't help but wonder what would have happened if I had let myself lean in just a little more, if I had surrendered to the pull I felt towards him. Towards Nox. The thought sent another wave of heat through me, a confusing mixture of desire and a prickle of unease. What was this connection between us? It was exhilarating, terrifying, and I had no idea what to make of it.

Chapter 19

Thalia's POV

Zarek left me alone as I got myself together, trying to wrap my head around the fact that I had been out for days—and the confusing, unfamiliar feelings I was developing for not only Zarek, but Nox as well. It was unsettling, this pull towards them. Was I just that desperate for some kind of belonging?

I'd heard stories about the Gifted—how having multiple partners was said to be a natural extension of their power. But in Nyvorthia, it was seen as nothing short of shameful, even repulsive, a blatant sign of moral decay. They're so quick to judge, so eager to condemn. They spoke of it with open disdain, their noses wrinkled in disgust. They whispered about the Gifted, painting them as immoral and depraved, yet envied them. They feared what they didn't understand, what they couldn't control.

And now, here I was, struggling with emotions I couldn't explain. A confusing pull towards not one, but *two* of these powerful beings. Emotions that, if voiced aloud, would surely make me a target.

Chapter 19

As I reached the bottom step of the staircase, I recognized Nox's voice instantly—deep, commanding, yet laced with a softness I hadn't heard before. It caught me off guard, making me pause. For some reason, I wasn't ready to face him yet, not after the strange intimacy of this morning. The way his presence had felt both comforting and unsettling, a paradox that left me breathless. The memory of his touch, the warmth of his hand against my waist, sent a shiver down my spine.

Instead, I made my way towards what I thought the kitchen would be, hoping to avoid having to face any of them. My stomach growled—a timely reminder that I hadn't eaten in what felt like forever—adding a physical hunger to the emotional chaos churning within me.

I entered the kitchen, the scent of something savory wafting through the air, a welcome distraction from my anxieties. I peeked into a pot simmering on the stove—a thick, fragrant stew filled with chunks of meat, vegetables, and herbs. It looked delicious, and the warmth emanating from it seemed to beckon me closer. I reasoned that they wouldn't mind if I helped myself; after all, I've been here for god knows how long.

I found a bowl in one of the cupboards and ladled some of the stew into it, the warmth of it spreading through my hands, a small comfort in the vastness of the house, a tangible reminder of the simple pleasures in life. I carried it over to the table and sat down, blowing gently on the steaming liquid before taking a cautious sip. The rich flavors filled my mouth—a burst of savory satisfaction—and I closed my eyes for a moment, savoring the taste, letting the warmth spread through me, chasing away the lingering chill.

As I ate, my mind wandered back to the brothers. I still couldn't quite figure them out—their complex dynamic, their undeniable connection to me, and the baffling reason they were helping me. Zarek had been kind, almost protective, his touch lingering in my

221

memory. Damon, on the other hand, seemed to view me with an unnerving suspicion, his words sharp and accusatory, as if he saw me as a threat. And Nox... well, Nox was an enigma all on his own, a silent, watchful presence that both intrigued and intimidated me.

I was halfway through my bowl of stew when I heard the door open. I looked up to see Nox standing in the doorway, his tall frame filling the entrance, making him seem even larger than I remembered. His eyes locked onto mine, a flicker of surprise crossing his face before it hardened to the familiar mask of aloofness.

"You're up," he said, his voice neutral, almost strained, as if he were holding something back.

I swallowed, setting my spoon down, the clatter echoing in the sudden silence. "Yeah. Zarek said I was out for a while." I tried to keep my tone light, casual, but the weight of his gaze made it difficult. There was something about Nox that always put me on edge. He made me feel both seen and exposed, like he could peer into the deepest recesses of my soul.

He walked further into the room, his eyes never leaving mine. "You were. You needed it." He paused, as if considering his next words, his brow furrowed in thought, a crease appearing between those emerald eyes. "How are you feeling?"

There was an unexpected gentleness in his question, a subtle concern that caught me off guard. I hesitated, searching his face for any sign of his usual indifference, but found none, only a flicker of the real Nox that made my heart skip a beat. "I'm... okay. A little overwhelmed, I guess." I shrugged, offering a faint smile, trying to downplay the chaos swirling within me. "Just trying to figure out what's going on, but physically, I'm better." The throbbing headache that had plagued me earlier had subsided, leaving behind a dull ache.

Nox nodded, his features softening slightly, a flicker of relief crossing his face. It was fleeting—gone as quickly as it appeared. He moved to the counter, leaning against it as he crossed his arms over his chest, the casual posture negating the gravity of his gaze. "There's a lot to explain. But for now, just focus on getting your strength back." His eyes flickered over me, assessing, as if he was trying to gauge how much I could handle, how much I already knew.

I glanced down at my bowl, my appetite suddenly gone, the stew now a cold, unappetizing lump. "Why are you helping me?" The question slipped out before I could stop it. I raised my eyes to meet his, hoping to find some clue to the enigma that he represented.

Nox's jaw tightened, and for a moment, I thought he wouldn't answer. His silence stretched making me even more anxious. Then he let out a slow breath, his eyes darkening, a shadow passing over his features, like a cloud obscuring the sun. "Because whether you like it or not, you're part of this now. And that means we protect you." His voice was firm, resolute, leaving no room for argument, a declaration that echoed in the small kitchen.

I frowned, confusion swirling in my mind, his words only deepening the mystery. "Part of what? Why would I need protection?" I pressed, needing more than just cryptic pronouncements. I needed concrete answers, something I could grasp onto. Nox pushed off the counter, his eyes narrowing slightly—a hint of impatience in his movements, as if my questions were wearing on him.

"Can you just trust me on this?" His voice was firm—a warning that the conversation was over, that I wouldn't get any more answers from him. At least, not now. He turned as if to leave, but paused at the doorway, glancing back at me, his gaze softening just a fraction, a flicker of warmth in the otherwise cool depths of his eyes. "Finish your food," he added, his voice a low murmur. And with that, he was gone, leaving me alone in the kitchen once more, the silence amplifying the questions echoing in my mind.

"Finish your food," I mocked under my breath, the words echoing in the empty kitchen. My appetite had disappeared along with Nox, replaced by a growing irritation. I pushed the bowl away, the metallic screech against the countertop a jarring counterpoint to the silence. My thoughts were a tangled mess of questions and half-truths, a chaotic swirl of confusion and suspicion. Part of what? Part of some grand scheme I hadn't been informed of? Why was *I* involved in any of this?

I couldn't stand the non-answers, the constant deflection, the feeling of being deliberately kept in the dark. It was like trying to navigate a catacomb blindfolded, each step a gamble, each turn leading to another dead end. If I was truly part of this—whatever *this* was—I needed to know what was going on. I needed the full picture, the unvarnished truth, not the carefully curated fragments they deemed safe for me to know. Rinsing my bowl in the sink, I made a decision. I would head into the lion's den to confront Nox, Zarek, and even the infuriating Damon, and demand answers.

The main room was bright, the sun pouring in through the tall windows. Zarek and Damon were seated on the couches, close together as they spoke in hushed tones, their voices too low for me to decipher. They both looked up as I entered, their conversation stopping abruptly.

"Don't stop on my account," I said, trying to keep my voice steady, projecting a confidence I didn't quite feel, as I walked over to them.

"How are you feeling after the bath and getting some food in ya?" Zarek asked, his voice warm and welcoming, gesturing for me to sit down, his concern evident in his amber eyes.

I opted for the furthest seat from them, wanting to maintain a certain distance, my eyes flickering between the two brothers, trying to gauge their moods, their intentions. "Much better," I replied, my voice firmer now, the need for answers overriding my initial hesitation. "I need answers. Like can someone please tell me what the hell has been going on?"

Damon let out a small huff, leaning back in his seat—his posture radiating a casual indifference that I knew masked a deeper tension. "We were just discussing that, actually," he said, his tone flat, devoid of any warmth or reassurance.

Zarek shot his brother a look, a silent reprimand, before turning back to me, his eyes softening with a mixture of apology and concern. "You're right. You deserve to know what's going on. But it's... complicated."

"Complicated?" I repeated, frustration bubbling in my chest, the word a dismissive brush-off that only fueled my anger. "I've been dragged into this, whatever this is, and no one's bothered to tell me why. I deserve an explanation."

Zarek nodded, his expression apologetic, acknowledging the validity of my frustration. "I know. And I'm sorry for that. There are things at play here that are dangerous, and we didn't want to overwhelm you while you were still recovering." His words were carefully chosen, a delicate balance between explanation and evasion.

Damon scoffed, his voice accusatory, cutting through the careful diplomacy of Zarek's words. "She's part of it whether she likes it or not, maybe more than we know." His words hung in the air, heavy with insinuation.

A chill ran down my spine at his words, his implication sending a shiver of unease through me. I swallowed, looking between them —the weight of their gazes pressing down on me. "Then explain it to me. All of it," I demanded, my voice trembling slightly.

"Don't act like you are completely oblivious," Damon said, his words sharp, laced with a biting sarcasm, his eyes narrowing as they bore into mine, as if daring me to challenge him. "Or are you rea—"

"Damon, stop," Zarek snapped, his voice edged with irritation, his patience clearly wearing thin with his brother's antagonistic attitude. He cast a warning glance at his brother before turning back to me, his eyes softening. "Alright. But you need to promise that you'll hear us out, and that you won't do anything reckless." His words were a plea for cooperation, a request for me to trust him.

I frowned, a knot of anxiety tightening in my chest. "No promises," I retorted, "Just tell me." I wasn't going to be manipulated or controlled—not by them, not by anyone.

Zarek took a deep breath, his gaze holding mine, a silent acknowledgment of my frustration. "There's a lot you don't know about Nexara, about what's coming," he began, his voice low and serious, the weight of his words hanging heavy in the air.

I stared at him, my mind racing, trying to process the significance of his statement. "Okay," I prompted, my impatience growing, "And what's coming?"

Damon leaned forward, his eyes narrowing with barely concealed hatred, his words dripping with a venomous disdain. "There are forces at work that want to control Nexara, to use it for their own gain. And *you*, Thalia, are their focus. Why is that?" His question hung in the air, a pointed accusation, a challenge to my supposed innocence.

I clenched my jaw, feeling my frustration boil over at his tone, his words cutting into me like a blade. Add getting under my skin to the list of things Damon was good at. He seemed determined to see me as an enemy, and his constant suspicion was wearing me down.

"Oh, good gods, Damon, why do you assume I'm some strong evil force out to get you?" I snapped, the words flowing out before I could stop them. "You treat me like a threat when all I've done is try to survive here. I'm just as confused and lost as you."

His eyes remained cold, unwavering, fixed on me. "Things just don't add up. You show up here with no real explanation, claimed to have no powers, and yet you're somehow part of all this. It's suspicious, to say the least." His words were a carefully constructed argument—designed to undermine my credibility, to paint me as a deceptive intruder.

I could feel my temper rising higher, the shadows starting to flicker at my fingertips, a physical manifestation of my growing anger. I didn't understand what was happening, why I was suddenly capable of manipulating shadows, but I knew it was connected to my emotions, to the rising tide of frustration and fear within me. Damon's constant suspicion, his unwillingness to see me as anything but a threat—it grated on me, and I was done with it.

"Damon, that's enough," Nox's voice cut through the tension, a warning clear in his tone, his sudden appearance adding another layer of complexity to the already charged atmosphere.

Damon huffed, leaning back into the couch, his eyes still locked on mine, a smoldering resentment in their depths. "Just don't pretend like you're *innocent* in all of this," he muttered, his voice dripping with distrust.

I took a deep breath, trying to rein myself in as the shadows danced more violently around my fingers, flickering like dark flames. I clenched my hands into fists, forcing the shadows to recede, trying to maintain control.

Zarek leaned forward, his voice softer as he addressed me. "Look, Thalia, I know this is a lot. But there are people who would use you—use all of us—for their own purposes. We're on the same side here." His words were a reassurance, an attempt to bridge the gap that Damon had so deliberately burned.

"Are we?" I asked, staring directly at Damon, whose jaw clenched so hard it looked like he may break a tooth. I couldn't ignore his blatant hostility towards me. "Why me?" I continued. "Why am I involved in this? I didn't ask for any of it."

Zarek hesitated, glancing at Damon and Nox before turning back to me. "We don't know—not yet, at least. But there's something about you. Something that's attracting it. We're still trying to figure it out ourselves." His words were honest, a frank admission of their own uncertainty.

Damon let out a cruel laugh, his eyes rolling. "She's more than just '*important*.' She's a wildcard, a fucking question mark. And that makes her dangerous."

My patience finally snapped as I glared at him. "You don't know anything about me, Damon. All you see is a threat, but hell, maybe I *am* a threat to your fragile ego."

The room fell into a tense silence, the air thick with animosity. Damon's shadows flickered, and for a moment, I thought he might actually kill me. That his anger would finally boil over into violence. But instead, he just stood, his eyes no longer that deep blue, but now black, bottomless pits of rage and resentment. The transformation was unsettling. A glimpse into a darkness that lived within him, a darkness that seemed to mirror the shadows flickering at my own fingertips.

"Just remember what I said," he muttered, his voice low and menacing, directed at Zarek and Nox, before turning and leaving the room, his footsteps echoing down the hallway. I noticed Nox following him out, his silence adding another layer of unease to the already charged atmosphere.

I looked back at Zarek, who was watching me with a mix of sympathy and admiration, his gaze a comforting presence in the wake of Damon's hostility.

"Thank you," I said quietly, my voice barely audible, grateful for his attempt to mediate, to offer some semblance of understanding. "For at least trying to help me understand."

Zarek shrugged, "We're in this together, Thalia. Whether Damon likes it or not."

"And what about Nox? Is he... uh... okay with this?" I asked, feeling embarrassed at the slight desperation in my voice, the question betraying my growing concern for his opinion of me. Something had shifted between Nox and me since the Wonders of Nexara, a silent understanding, a connection that confused the hell out of me.

Zarek's expression softened, a knowing smile playing on his lips. "Nox is... complicated," he said, pausing as if searching for the right words, his gaze distant for a moment. "But he cares. He might not show it the same way, but he's on board. He knows what's at stake."

It's hard to read Nox—he was guarded, mysterious, his emotions always hidden behind that steely exterior, a wall he had carefully constructed around himself. But there had been moments, fleeting as they were, when I thought I saw something deeper.

Zarek leaned back, studying me for a moment before he spoke again. "You know, Nox isn't used to letting people in. None of us are, really. But you... you've gotten under our skin." He smiled, the corners of his eyes crinkling. "In a good way, I think."

"Well, at least two out of three don't want to murder me anymore," I joked. "I don't think I've gotten under Damon's skin in a good way." I added, though it came out more nervous than I intended.

Zarek's eyes sparkled, and he leaned in slightly, his voice dropping to a conspiratorial whisper. "Give it time. Damon's not as tough as he pretends to be." His gaze held mine for a moment, and I felt a flicker of something made me feel a little less alone, a little less adrift in the swirling chaos.

I gave him a small smile, a silent acknowledgment of the unspoken connection between us. The sound of a familiar rhythm of footsteps echoed through the hallway. I looked up just as Nox entered the room, his eyes narrowing slightly as he took in the scene, his gaze lingering on me for a moment before flicking to Zarek, an edge of something I couldn't quite place lingering in his tone.

"Am I interrupting something?" Nox's voice was low, a quiet rumble that filled the room, his gaze flicking between Zarek and me, a silent question hanging in the air.

I straightened, a slight flutter in my chest, a nervous reaction to his presence. "No, just talking," I said, trying to keep my tone neutral, casual, but the awareness of his presence made it difficult to maintain the facade of composure.

Nox crossed his arms over his chest, his expression unreadable, a mask of indifference, but his eyes remained fixed on me—a silent, watchful presence that made my skin tingle. Before Nox could respond, the tension ratcheted up another notch as Damon stormed back into the room, his entrance as abrupt and disruptive as his exit.

"We need to talk about what happens next," he announced, his voice sharp and commanding, his gaze immediately settling on me —his eyes cold and calculating, as if assessing my worth, my potential threat. "You want answers, Thalia? *Fine.* But that means you're going to have to prove you aren't a *threat.*"

I frowned, a mix of irritation and curiosity bubbling within me. "What do you mean? I don't have to prove shit to you." My defiance flared, fueled by his constant accusations. I wasn't going to jump through hoops for him—not after the way he has treated me.

Damon's lips curled into a smirk, one that didn't reach his eyes, a cruel twist of his lips that betrayed his true intentions. "Training. If you're going to be part of this, you need to be ready. No more being a liability." His words were a deliberate jab, a reminder of my perceived weakness—my dependence on them.

I clenched my jaw, his words cutting me deep. The memory of Nox protecting me in my dream flashed through my mind. "I'm not a liability," I shot back, my voice rising with anger, my cheeks flushing with indignation.

Damon raised an eyebrow, his gaze challenging, daring me to prove him wrong. "Then prove it. Training starts tomorrow morning. Don't be late." He turned on his heel and left the room without another word, his abrupt exit leaving a lingering tension in the air.

Zarek sighed, shaking his head, his expression a mixture of exasperation and amusement. "Don't mind him. Damon's... well, Damon. He'll come around eventually." His words were an attempt to smooth over the rough edges of his brother's abrasive personality.

I wasn't so sure. There was something about Damon—something in the way he looked at me, like I was an unwanted puzzle piece, an anomaly that didn't fit into his carefully constructed world—that made me doubt we'd ever be on the same side. But if this was what it took to get the answers I needed, to understand my place in this strange new reality, then I'd do it. I'd endure his hostility, his suspicion, if it meant getting closer to the truth.

"I should be getting back to my dorm," I said as I started to stand up, my eyes moving to Nox's. His expression made me stop in my tracks, a sudden shift in his demeanor that sent a wave of anxiety through me.

"Absolutely not." His tone was sharp, his brows furrowed down. The firmness in his voice that made it clear this wasn't up for debate. His words were a command, not a suggestion.

I blinked, taken aback by his sudden assertiveness, the force of his words momentarily silencing my own protest. "Why not?" I tried to keep my voice steady, but there was a hint of frustration there. "I've been here long enough, and I think I can—"

Nox shook his head, stepping closer, his eyes turning a dark forest green as they locked onto mine, the proximity of his body radiating a warmth that made my breath catch in my throat. "It's not safe. You're staying here, where we can protect you." His words were a declaration, a promise of safety, but also a subtle reminder of the dangers I was apparently in.

The room seemed to shrink as he closed the distance between us, the weight of his look pressing down on me. I could feel the heat of his presence, the way his eyes bore into mine—searching, questioning.

I opened my mouth to argue, to insist that I could handle myself, that I didn't need their protection—but Zarek stepped in, his voice more gentle than his brother's, a calming presence in the midst of the brewing storm. "Nox is right, Firefly. It's better if you stay here for now. We don't know who might be looking for you. You can't trust everyone at the academy." His words were a gentle reminder of the unseen threats.

I swallowed, my gaze flicking between the two of them, their words echoing in my mind—a chilling reminder of Professor Lorian, of the strange spiritual meeting I had interrupted, his cryptic words playing through my mind like a broken record.

I will make sure she's ready for you.

Despite my desire to be away from them—from Damon—I couldn't deny the logic of their argument. "Fine," I conceded, "but I'm not dealing with Damon's dramatic ass when he finds out I'm staying here."

Nox's expression softened, just a fraction, a subtle shift in his features that hinted at a deeper emotion. "Don't worry about him. Just trust us on this."

I looked away, feeling the weight of his words settle in my chest. *Trust.* It was such a simple word, but it carried so much with it—a weight of expectation, of weakness. Who have I ever *really* trusted? The question echoed in my mind.

Zarek gave me an encouraging smile, "We'll make sure you're comfortable. It's not so bad here, you know. Besides, you don't want to be going back and forth to your dorm after training with the devil." He finished with a wink, his grin playful as always.

I laughed at Zarek's attempt to lighten the mood, "I guess I don't really have a choice." My words were a surrender, but also an acceptance, a willingness to trust them, to let them guide me through this unfamiliar and dangerous territory.

Nox's gaze lingered on me for a moment longer, his eyes searching mine as if he wanted to say more. But instead, he simply turned and left the room, his silence speaking volumes.

Zarek reached out, his fingers lightly brushing my arm—a fleeting touch that sent a shiver of awareness down my spine. "It'll be fun having you here. And hey, it's a bonus for me that you're a beautiful female," he added, a flirtatious charm that eased the lingering tension.

I rolled my eyes, laughing again, his light hearted banter a welcome distraction from the weight of the situation. "I still need my things, you know. Can I at least get them, or am I officially a prisoner here?" I teased, giving him a mock stern look, playing along with his flirtatious banter.

"Yes, yes, on it," Zarek said with a playful grin, his eyes twinkling with amusement. "Anything for my favorite prisoner." He gave me an exaggerated wink before turning and walking out of the room, leaving me alone with my thoughts—with the lingering presence of Nox, with the weight of whatever coming for me.

Chapter 20

Thalia's POV

The academy was a ghost town as Zarek, Nox, and I made our way towards my dorm. An eerie silence stretched endlessly as the cold wind swept through the empty courtyard, carrying the scent of winter and rustling the bare branches of the trees. Without the usual bustling crowds of students, the academy felt strangely exposed—the emptiness unsettling in a way that made every shadow seem deeper.

I pulled Nox's jacket tighter around me, shivering as the chill crept through the fabric. His scent was calming, wrapping around me like a comforting blanket. The air was heavy, almost oppressive, and I couldn't shake the feeling that we were being watched —even though I knew logically that we were alone. It was as if the academy itself had eyes, hidden in the dark corners and shadows.

"Kind of creepy, isn't it?" Zarek said, breaking the silence. He looked over at me with a half-smile, his breath misting in the cold air. "I never thought I'd say this, but I actually miss the noise."

I gave him a small smile in return, glancing around. "Yeah. It's weird without everyone here. Like the place is... haunted or something." My voice echoed slightly off the stone walls, emphasizing just how empty it was. "Plus, you just miss all the attention," I teased with a small laugh.

Zarek gasped dramatically, placing a hand over his heart. "Me? Miss the attention? How could you accuse me of such a thing?" His playful smile cutting through the cold. "But, I suppose having someone to impress makes this whole eerie walk a little more worthwhile."

Nox walked a few paces ahead of us, his eyes scanning the surroundings. He hadn't said much since we left, his focus seemingly elsewhere, but I could feel the tension radiating off him—as if he was prepared for something to jump out at us at any moment. His presence, though silent, was strangely comforting —like an unwavering shield between me and the unseen darkness.

The pathways, usually packed with students, were deserted, the benches empty, the training fields stretching out like barren wastelands. The academy that had once felt alive now seemed utterly lifeless, the vibrancy drained away. The emptiness felt wrong, like the academy itself was holding its breath, waiting for something to happen.

Zarek nudged me gently with his elbow, drawing my attention back to him. "Hey, don't look so spooked," he said, his eyes twinkling with mischief. "You've got us with you. What could possibly go wrong?"

I snorted, rolling my eyes. "Oh, I don't know. Plenty of things, considering my track record," I replied, raising an eyebrow.

He grinned, a welcome warmth against the cold. "Fair point. But still, you're safe with us." He glanced ahead. "Right, Nox?"

Nox glanced back at us, his eyes meeting mine for a heartbeat before flicking to Zarek. "Just stay close," he said, his voice carrying a seriousness that cut through the momentary lightness.

I nodded, falling silent as we continued walking. The leaves crunched beneath our feet, the only sound breaking the silence. There was something about Nox's tone—something that made the hair on the back of my neck stand up. The academy might have been empty, but the sense of danger was still very real.

The women's dorm loomed above us, dark and quiet, the windows like empty eyes staring out into the night. I hesitated for a moment before stepping forward, the sense of unease still clinging to me like a second skin.

"Do you need us to come in with you?" Zarek asked, his voice softer now, the playful edge gone.

I shook my head, offering him a small smile. "I think I'll be okay. It's just grabbing a few things, right?"

Nox stepped closer. "Be quick. And if anything feels off, you call out."

I nodded, the seriousness in his eyes making my heart skip a beat. "Got it. I'll be quick."

With one last glance at the two of them, I turned and made my way inside, the door creaking slightly as I pushed it open. The dimly lit hallway stretched out before me, the shadows seeming to shift and move as I walked. The silence was deafening, each of my footsteps echoing off the walls, and I couldn't shake the feeling that I wasn't entirely alone.

I took a deep breath, trying to steady myself. I just needed to grab my things and get out. The sooner, the better. Walking into my room felt different, like something was off. I noticed things were slightly moved around—books out of place, drawers not quite closed. Maybe Elara had been in here? No—it was locked when I came in.

A chill ran down my spine as unease settled deeper. I grabbed a bag and started stuffing clothes into it, moving as quickly as I could. I grabbed my essentials—clothes, a few books, my journal —anything I thought I'd need while staying at their place. As I turned to leave, I heard a creak from the hallway. My breath caught, and I froze, listening. The silence returned, heavier than before. Slowly, I moved towards the door, my heart pounding in my chest. I peered out into the hallway, my eyes searching the shadows.

"Hello?" I called out softly. No response. The silence pressed in on me, heavy and suffocating. I swallowed, stepping back into my room, my hand gripping the door frame for support. My knuckles turned white as I held on. I needed to leave—now. My instincts were screaming at me to run, to get as far away from this place as possible. A small, hysterical laugh bubbled up, quickly dying in my chest. I really should look into therapy. Maybe a nice padded room would do me some good.

I slung the bag over my shoulder and made my way back down the hallway, my footsteps as quiet as I could manage. As I reached the entrance, I could see Nox and Zarek waiting just outside, their figures visible through the small window in the door. Stepping outside, the cold air hit me like a wave of relief. Both of them looked up, their eyes locking onto mine.

"Everything okay?" Nox asked, his voice low, but the concern was evident.

I nodded, though my heart was still racing. "Yeah. Let's just... get out of here."

Zarek stepped forward, wrapping an arm around my shoulders and pulling me into his side. "Hey, you're alright." he said, his voice was filled with a comforting warmth that seemed to thaw the lingering chill.

Nox didn't say anything, but he moved closer, his presence solid and grounding. I could feel the tension in him—the way his eyes kept scanning our surroundings as if expecting something to come at us from the shadows.

We started walking back, and I kept close between them, the cold night air biting at my skin. The academy loomed behind us, dark and silent, and I couldn't help but feel like we were leaving something unfinished.

Zarek broke the silence after a few moments, his tone light, trying to lift the mood. "So, how about some hot chocolate when we get back? I think we've earned it after that little adventure," Zarek suggested.

I couldn't help but smile, the tension easing just a bit. "Only if you make it," I said, nudging him lightly.

He grinned, his eyes sparkling. "Deal. My hot chocolate is life-changing, just you wait. I'll even add marshmallows, for the *full* experience."

Nox glanced over, his lips twitching slightly as if fighting a smile. "Let's just get back safely first," he muttered, but there was a softness in his voice that made my chest feel a little lighter.

"How did you see the house?" Nox asked after we had been walking in silence. The forest around us was dark, the cloudy sky allowing only the faintest slivers of moonlight to filter through the trees.

"What do you mean? I have eyes," I teased, my voice carrying a hint of playfulness.

Nox glanced at me, the corner of his lips twitching as if he were fighting a smile. "Funny," he said, his tone dry. "I mean, it was hidden—warded."

I blinked, caught off guard. "Warded? So, only certain people can see it?"

He nodded. "It's supposed to be invisible to anyone who doesn't know the right... markers." He paused, his eyes going distant for a moment. "But you saw it as if it were just any other house."

I frowned, my brows knitting together. "I don't know. It just looked... normal to me. Maybe it wasn't as warded as you thought."

Zarek, who had been walking a few steps ahead, turned around, a smirk tugging at his lips. "Or maybe you're just special, Firefly. And here I thought we were the only mysterious ones."

I rolled my eyes, though a small smile tugged at my lips. "Yeah, yeah. Let's not get carried away." I looked over at Nox, who seemed deep in thought. His expression was guarded, but there was a glimmer of curiosity in his eyes.

A shiver ran down my spine, the forest suddenly feeling colder, the shadows around us growing deeper. "Is that a good thing or a bad thing?" I asked, trying to keep my voice steady.

Zarek shrugged, stepping back to walk beside me. "Could be both. I think it just means you're even more interesting than we thought." He nudged me lightly with his elbow.

I gave him a sideways glance, my lips twitching up. "You really know how to make everything sound like an adventure, don't you?"

"That's because it is," he said with a wink. "Danger, mystery, handsome companions... What more could you ask for?"

I couldn't help the laugh that fell from my lips, the sound echoing softly in the quiet forest. "I don't know who has the bigger ego, you or Damon."

Nox cleared his throat, his eyes flicking to Zarek. "Let's stay focused. The wards being visible to her might mean more than we realize." He turned his eyes back to me. "We'll figure it out."

The way he said it—so sure, so steady—made my chest tighten. I nodded, matching his pace as we continued walking through the forest. The cold air nipped at my skin as we continued walking.

"Thalia..." Something whispered softly. I strained my ears, trying to make out the sound, but it was faint, blending with the rustling of the wind through the trees. I glanced up at Nox and Zarek, but they continued walking, their expressions unchanged. They hadn't heard it.

The voice came again, another faint whisper that sent a shiver down my spine, making the hair on the back of my neck stand up.

"Thalia... you can't run..."

I swallowed hard, my eyes scanning the darkness around us. The shadows seemed to shift, almost like they were reaching out towards me. My heart pounded in my chest, and I took an involuntary step closer to Nox, my hand brushing against his arm.

"Did you hear that?" I asked, my voice barely above a whisper.

Nox turned his head slightly, his eyes narrowing. "Hear what?"

Zarek looked down at me, his brows furrowed in confusion. "Thalia, what's wrong?"

I hesitated, glancing between them. The voice had stopped, but the feeling of unease lingered, wrapping around me like a cold, invisible hand. "I thought... I thought I heard something but never mind."

Nox's eyes darkened as he immediately began scanning the trees, his posture tensing. "I didn't hear anything," he said, his voice low, but I could see the concern in his eyes.

Zarek stepped closer, his expression softening. "Hey, it's probably just the wind." He tried to smile, but there was a flicker of worry behind his eyes.

I nodded, though the unease in my chest didn't let up. The voice felt too real, too deliberate. Zarek must have sensed my jitters because he bumped his hip against mine, drawing my attention. "Why don't you tell us something about you before you came to the academy?"

"You're just trying to distract me, aren't you?" I asked, raising an eyebrow at him. A small smile played on my lips, trying to hide the genuine curiosity I felt. His attempts at distraction were endearing, though I wasn't about to let him know that. "It won't work, Zarek. Though, I am curious. What kind of stories are we talking about? Childhood mishaps? Tales of heroic feats? Or perhaps..." I paused, my gaze narrowing playfully, "embarrassing moments you'd rather forget?"

He grinned, unrepentant. "All of it"

Nox glanced back at us, his gaze lingering on me for a moment before he spoke. "We'll need to be careful tonight. If there's something about you that allows you to see through the wards, it could be part of attracting attention we don't want."

I swallowed, the weight of his words settling heavily on me. "Do you think someone's watching?"

Nox's eyes flicked away, his expression unreadable. "It's possible. We need to be cautious."

Zarek sighed dramatically, though his eyes were serious. "Great, more shadowy figures lurking around. Just what we needed."

Despite the tension, I found myself leaning closer to Zarek, grateful for his attempts to lighten the mood. "Maybe they'll be scared off by your charm."

He chuckled, his eyes sparkling. "They should be. I'm terrifyingly charming."

Nox shook his head, but there was the faintest hint of a smile on his lips. "Let's just get back without drawing any more attention."

As we approached the house, the sense of unease only grew. The shadows seemed deeper, darker—alive. They twisted and shifted, reaching for me as if they knew my name. I studied them while walking, my heart pounding in my chest. These shadows were different—more sinister. Mine flickered softly, like they were ready to react. But these... these felt malevolent, as if they had a will of their own, eager to pull me into them. I shivered, feeling their cold presence inching closer, a silent promise of something far worse than I'd imagined.

As we entered the clearing, I looked over my shoulder to see the shadows hanging in the trees, watching. The whisper came again, louder this time, like a scream in my ear.

"Thalia... I'm coming..."

I stumbled, my breath hitching as fear surged through me. Nox's arm was suddenly around me, steadying me. "What is it?" he asked, his voice urgent.

I shook my head, trying to regain control of my racing heart as my eyes scanned the tree line. Zarek's eyes widened, his expression shifting. "We need to get inside. Now."

The three of us hurried towards the house, Nox's arm still protectively around me. The shadows seemed to ripple, almost as if they were laughing at us, mocking our retreat.

We reached the front door, and Zarek ushering me inside. Nox followed, his eyes scanning the treeline one last time before stepping in and shutting the door firmly behind us.

The warmth of the house enveloped me, but the chill of those whispers lingered, echoing in my mind. Zarek turned to me, his eyes scanning my face. "Are you okay?"

I nodded, though my hands were still shaking. Nox's jaw clenched, "I'll go talk to Damon."

Zarek nodded in agreement, his usual playful demeanor replaced by something more serious, but then his signature grin returned, accompanied by a wink. "We'll get some hot chocolate started— extra marshmallows, just for you."

I watched as Nox ascended the stairs, his posture rigid with tension. The shadows seemed to cling to him as if trying to follow, and I couldn't help but feel a pang of worry as he disappeared from sight, heading to find Damon.

Before I could dwell too much on it, Zarek's hand gently tugged at mine, pulling me towards the kitchen. "Come on," he said, his voice softer now, trying to bring some levity back. "Let's get you warmed up with that hot chocolate. I promise, it's going to be the best you've ever had." He gave me a reassuring smile, his eyes searching mine, as if to make sure I was okay.

The warmth of his hand was comforting, and I let myself be led away.

Chapter 21

Thalia's POV

The morning sun filtered weakly through the window, painting soft, pale streaks across the hardwood floor. Dust motes danced in the golden rays, creating a dreamlike atmosphere. I stretched, my muscles aching from the tension of the night before, a dull throb resonating deep in my bones. Nox had been adamant about me staying in his room while he was out, his usual quiet demeanor replaced by a protectiveness that bordered on possessive. I couldn't understand why the sudden shift with him—his possessiveness was unsettling—but I guess it was better than the alternative of him ignoring me altogether. A strange warmth bloomed in my chest at the thought. *What was happening to me?* This strange place, these strange men... they were stirring something within me, something I refused to acknowledge right now.

The faint scent of cedar and rain still clung to the air, a subtle reminder of his presence, and I found myself drawing a deep, steadying breath, trying to absorb the lingering calm.

Today was the day—training with Damon. My stomach twisted into a tight knot as nerves crawled through me, a tangled mess of dread and a strange, fluttering anticipation. Damon didn't exactly hide his disdain for me. His icy glares and cutting remarks were a constant reminder of his disapproval. To him, I was a liability at best, a threat at worst—a fragile girl stumbling through a world she didn't understand. He'd made it crystal clear, in his usual blunt and unforgiving way, that I had to prove myself. Not just to survive here in this dangerous world, but to show that I wasn't some weak link in whatever looming battle was coming. He didn't see me as an equal, not even close, let alone someone worthy of trust. In his eyes, I was just another potential enemy, a burden that could get his brothers killed.

As I dressed, pulling on a simple training outfit from Combat Training, and descended the creaking stairs, the house embraced a hushed stillness—a quiet sanctuary in the early morning light. The silence was broken only by the faint, melodic humming of Zarek from the kitchen, a soft, almost whimsical tune that eased some of the tension coiling in my gut. The comforting aroma of fresh coffee, rich and inviting, greeted me as I lingered in the doorway, hesitant to break the peaceful spell.

Zarek turned, his amber eyes lighting up as he caught sight of me, a warm smile spreading across his face. His dark hair, usually styled with meticulous care, was slightly disheveled, giving him a boyish charm. "Morning, Firefly," he greeted, a knowing smile tugging at his lips. He nodded to the steaming mug on the counter, a swirl of cream disappearing into the dark liquid. "Thought you could use some caffeine before you face the demon."

Despite the tight knot of anxiety still twisting in my stomach, I let out a breathy laugh, the sound a little shaky. "Thanks, I think I'm going to need it." I muttered, grabbing the cup. The warmth of it seeped into my hands, a comforting weight that grounded me just enough to calm the jittery edge of my nerves.

Zarek leaned against the counter, his gaze soft but teasing, a playful glint in his eyes. "You'll be fine. Damon's all bark." He paused, a mischievous flicker crossing his features. "Mostly."

I raised an eyebrow, taking a cautious sip of the hot coffee. The rich flavor spread across my tongue, a welcome distraction from the nagging worry. "You sure about that?" I asked, my voice laced with skepticism.

Zarek's grin widened, his wink more playful than reassuring. "Well... no. But I'll step in if he goes too hard. Wouldn't want him to actually break our little Firefly, now would we?"

I smiled, a small, hesitant curve of my lips, though the nervousness still lingered—a persistent hum beneath the surface. I wasn't sure if I believed him, not entirely, but I appreciated the sentiment nonetheless. We both knew I wasn't banking on any rescue, not really. I had to prove I could handle myself, that I wasn't just a delicate flower waiting to be protected.

After finishing my coffee, savoring the last warming sip, I made my way to the back of the house, stepping out into the crisp morning air. The cool breeze, tinged with the scent of dew-kissed grass and blooming flowers, bit against my skin, a refreshing contrast to the warmth of the house. Damon was already there, his tall, rigid figure cutting an imposing silhouette against the early dawn sky, the rising sun painting the edges of the trees with a soft, golden light. He stood still, staring out at the horizon, his hands clasped behind him, his broad shoulders tense beneath his dark shirt. Even without looking directly at him, I could feel the waves of energy rippling off him—controlled, lethal power that seemed to vibrate in the space between us, a force that made the hairs on the back of my neck stand on end.

As I approached, my footsteps crunching softly on the grass, Damon turned slowly, his dark blue eyes locking onto mine with a cold intensity that sent a shiver down my spine. His expression was unreadable—a carefully constructed mask that hid any hint of emotion, save for the thin, hard line of his mouth. His gaze raked over me, assessing, judging, and I felt the weight of it, like he was calculating my worth—*or lack thereof.* It was a familiar feeling, one that I'd come to expect from him, but it still stung, a small, sharp prick of resentment.

"You're late," he said, his tone clipped, cutting through the silence like a sharpened blade. His voice, deep and resonant, held a hint of something dangerous, a simmering anger that seemed to crackle in the air.

I frowned, glancing at the sky. The sun had barely risen above the trees, its golden rays just beginning to pierce through the morning mist. "It's barely sunrise. I didn't realize we had a set time." My voice, though quiet, held a note of sass. I wouldn't let him intimidate me—not this time.

Damon stepped forward, closing the distance between us, his presence towering over me, suffocating in its sheer force. The smoky, bergamot scent of him intensified, swirling around me, making my head spin slightly. "When I say early, I mean early. You should be ready before I even ask." His voice was hard, uncompromising. "If you want to be part of this, you need to be better than everyone else. No excuses." He paused, his eyes boring into mine, a flicker of something unreadable in their depths. "Especially not from you."

His words stung, not because they were unfair, not entirely—but because they mirrored the doubt already festering inside me. The nagging fear that I wasn't strong enough, that I didn't belong here. I clenched my jaw, refusing to let him see how deeply his judgment cut, how much his words resonated with the insecurities that haunted me. "I am ready," I replied, my voice steady, forcing myself to meet his gaze without flinching.

Damon's lips curled into a slow, cruel smirk, a flash of white teeth against the dark backdrop of his stubble. "We'll see about that."

He took a step back, his eyes never leaving mine, the air between us heavy, a silent battle of wills. "No magic, no abilities—just hand-to-hand combat. Let's see if you can survive without your little tricks."

I swallowed the lump in my throat, my pulse quickening, and nodded, a single, sharp movement. "Fine. Let's get this over with." I tried to sound confident, but my voice trembled slightly, betraying my nerves.

Damon dropped into a fighting stance, his body loose yet coiled, every movement fluid but deliberate—like a predator preparing to strike. His eyes were sharp, focused, watching me like a hawk waiting for its prey to make a mistake. "This isn't just about strength, Thalia," he said, his voice low, almost dangerous, a quiet rumble. "It's about control. Lose control, and you lose everything."

I took a deep breath, the crisp morning air filling my lungs, trying to calm the frantic beating of my heart. There was something in the way he said it—something that felt personal, like he was warning me not just about the fight, but about something deeper, something more profound. My skin prickled under the weight of his gaze, a strange mix of anger and something I couldn't quite name flaring inside me—a confusing cocktail of emotions that made my head spin. It wasn't just fear, not anymore. It was something else, something... electric.

I squared my shoulders, jaw set, trying to push down the flutter of anxiety in my chest. The way his eyes seemed to look right through me—stripping away my defenses—made my heart pound against my ribs like a trapped bird. He was testing me, probing for my weaknesses, trying to find the cracks in my armor, and I was determined not to give him the satisfaction. I wouldn't let him see how much he affected me.

He lunged first, his movements quick and calculated, a blur of motion that was almost too fast to follow. I barely had time to react, stepping to the side, my heart leaping into my throat as his fist sliced through the air where I had just been, the force of it displacing the air around me. I countered with a jab of my own, aiming for his ribs, but he blocked it effortlessly, his smirk growing as he pushed me back—his hand like iron against my arm.

"You're slow," he taunted, his voice laced with disdain, a cruel edge that grated on my nerves. "You'll never survive if you can't even handle *this*."

Frustration boiled inside me, a red-hot surge of anger that made my fists clench, my knuckles turning white. He was baiting me—deliberately trying to make me slip, to lose control—and I hated that it was working. I could feel the heat building in my chest, my emotions rising like a tide, threatening to drown me in their intensity. I swung again, harder this time, putting all my strength behind the blow, but Damon dodged with ease, his movements as fluid as water, as if he were anticipating my every move. He was toying with me, and the realization only fueled my anger.

Before I could react, he grabbed my wrist, his fingers closing around it like a vise, twisting it just enough to throw me off balance. I stumbled, my foot catching on a loose stone, barely catching myself before I fell, and the embarrassment burned hotter than the pain in my arm, a flush creeping up my neck.

"Pathetic," he muttered, releasing me as if I were something disgusting, something beneath his notice. His gaze was cold, disapproving, and I flinched inwardly, hating the way his judgment made my stomach churn.

I took a deep breath, trying to steady myself, to regain my composure. I could feel my cheeks burning, both from exertion and embarrassment. I stood up straighter, my eyes locked onto his, determination surging through me—a wave of defiance washing over the fear. "I'm not done," I stated, my voice shaking slightly, but firm.

Damon's smirk widened, a flicker of something akin to amusement in his eyes, and he nodded slightly, as if acknowledging my resolve. "Good," he said, his voice still laced with that dangerous undercurrent. "Then show me." He moved again, faster this time, and I braced myself, my muscles tense, ready to prove that I wasn't as weak as he seemed to think.

The tension between us crackled in the air, thick and palpable, each movement charged with an underlying challenge—a silent conversation of defiance and dominance. Every strike, every dodge, every near miss, was a test—a battle not just of strength and skill, but of willpower, of sheer, stubborn determination. I could feel the weight of his gaze, the intensity in his eyes as he pushed me to my limits. And despite the anger simmering beneath the surface, there was something else—a spark, something that made my heart pound for reasons beyond just fear. It was a strange, unsettling awareness of him, of his power, of the raw, untamed energy that radiated from him like heat from a fire.

I clenched my teeth, the sting of every blocked hit and every missed step digging at my pride. Damon's eyes bore into mine, filled with a mix of disdain—and something else. Something curious, as if he was trying to understand what made me tick, what drove me to keep fighting even when I was clearly outmatched. He moved with an effortless grace that made me feel clumsy in comparison, my movements awkward and uncoordinated.

"Come on, Thalia," Damon taunted, his voice low and almost mocking, a cruel edge that made my blood boil. "My brothers shouldn't have to risk themselves because you can't hold your own."

His words were like a physical blow, driving me forward with a fresh rush of adrenaline. I surged towards him, my frustration peaking, my vision tunneling with anger. For a moment, his expression shifted—surprise flickered in his eyes, a brief flash of vulnerability—as my fist aimed for his face, connecting with his jaw with a satisfying thud.

I lunged again, aiming my elbow for his ribs, but he anticipated the move—his hand snaking out in a blur of motion. He captured my arm just above the elbow, his fingers like steel bands, and twisted it behind my back. The world seemed to tilt as his other arm moved around my waist. My body was now pressed against his, the hard planes of his chest a solid wall against my back, pinning me in place. The air left my lungs, and panic clawed at the edges of my control. His breath was hot against my ear, the smoky, bergamot scent of him intensifying, filling my senses and making my head spin. A strange tremor ran through me, a shiver that had nothing to do with fear and everything to do with... *I didn't know what.* I pushed the thought away, angry at myself for even acknowledging it.

"Fuck you, Damon! Let me go!" I growled, twisting in his grip. I tried to stomp on his foot, but he shifted his weight effortlessly. *He was toying with me.* The realization sparked a fresh wave of anger. A searing pain shot through my shoulder, making my vision blur. I bit back a cry, refusing to give him the satisfaction.

"You let emotions dictate your actions," he whispered, his tone almost intimate—a low rumble against my ear. "That makes you predictable." I felt his body go stiff as I struggled against him. "Don't," he warned, his voice hardening.

Anger boiled over—hot and blinding—and I used my weight to break free, spinning to face him, my breath ragged, my chest heaving. "Maybe I am emotional," I retorted, eyes narrowed, voice shaking with anger. "But at least I'm not cold and a fucking psychopath."

Something in his gaze flickered—an emotion I couldn't quite place. A fleeting shadow that vanished as quickly as it appeared, before his familiar smirk returned, a mask snapping back into place. "Emotions are a liability, they make you weak," he countered as he stepped back and motioned for me to come at him again, the challenge clear in his eyes. "Show me what else you've got."

I charged, my muscles screaming in protest, focusing all my energy into every movement, every punch and kick, my frustration fueling my determination. Damon met each strike with calculated precision, his movements effortless and controlled, but there was a slight change in his demeanor—he wasn't just testing me anymore. He was engaging, pushing me harder, as if he was starting to see me as more than just a burden, as more than just a fragile human girl.

Our bodies moved in a strange, almost brutal dance, the sounds of our breathing and the dull thud of blows filling the training ground, echoing in the stillness of the early morning. The tension between us felt electric, a charged current that ran between us, each clash of our fists a spark that seemed to ignite something deeper, something raw and primal. The anger that had fueled me at the start began to shift, morphing into something else—something raw and unspoken, a strange mix of frustration, adrenaline, and a burgeoning awareness of him that I couldn't quite explain.

Damon stepped forward, his hand shooting out to grab my wrist, his fingers closing around it with surprising gentleness. He twisted, pulling me off balance, and I stumbled, falling against him, my breath catching in my throat. For a moment, we were chest to chest, our bodies pressed together, his eyes locking onto mine. His stare intense, searching. The world around us seemed to blur, the only thing I could focus on was the heat radiating from him, and the look in his eyes—a smoldering fire that seemed to sear right through me, leaving me breathless. A strange mix of apprehension and something else... something that made my stomach flip, a fluttering sensation that was both exhilarating and terrifying.

"Better," he said, his voice a low rumble against my chest. There was a hint of something new in his tone—something that sounded almost like... approval. "You're learning."

I swallowed, my throat suddenly dry, and shoved at his chest, the hard muscle barely giving way beneath my palms. I stumbled back a step, putting some much-needed distance between us. The smoky scent of him lingered in the air around me, making it hard to focus. My skin tingled where he'd touched me, a lingering warmth that spread through my veins like wildfire.

This was just the beginning, and I was determined to prove—not just to Damon, but to everyone who saw me as fragile, as weak, as a liability. I would show them they were wrong.

I wouldn't let Nox or Zarek put themselves at risk for me. The memory of my dream flashed in my mind—Nox, lying there, pale and still, his emerald eyes glazed over with pain, his lifeblood staining the ground beneath him—and my chest tightened painfully, a sharp pang of fear that made it hard to breathe. The image was too vivid, too real, the phantom sensation of his blood on my hands still lingering.

No more running.

No more fear.

I would not be a damsel in distress.

I wouldn't be a burden.

Chapter 22

Zarek's POV

The sun's early rays barely warmed the crisp morning air, casting long shadows across the training grounds like fingers reaching out from the darkness. The tension between Damon and Thalia was palpable from my vantage point —like a taut wire vibrating with unspoken energy, ready to snap at any moment. This wasn't just combat practice; it was something deeper, more intimate—a silent conversation held in the clash of limbs and the exchange of heated glances. Damon's every move was calculated, deliberate, pushing Thalia physically and mentally, probing her defenses in ways only he could. And Thalia, fierce and unyielding, held her ground with a surprising tenacity. She was stubborn, relentless, refusing to be broken by his relentless assault.

There was something different about Thalia today—a newfound spark in her eyes. Maybe it was the way she refused to back down, the fire in her gray eyes that never wavered, even as Damon tried to push her past her limits. Despite the fact that she was clearly outmatched in terms of raw power and experience, she was standing her ground—refusing to submit, refusing to let Damon have the satisfaction of seeing her fall. Her spirit shined through, an inner resilience that captivated me.

A small, involuntary smile tugged at the corner of my lips. *She's impressive*, I thought, my admiration growing with each passing moment. Thalia wasn't like anyone else at Nexara Academy. She didn't rely on flashy powers or the prestige of her lineage like so many of the other privileged students here. There was a rawness to her, an authenticity that was utterly... captivating. She fought to earn her place—not for recognition or glory, but for survival—and maybe, to prove Damon wrong in his harsh judgments of her.

I'd seen her struggle before, watched her doubt herself more times than she probably realized. She tried to hide it behind those beautiful eyes, that carefully constructed wall of indifference, but I could tell. I could see the flicker of uncertainty beneath the surface. Thalia wasn't like Damon; she wasn't born into this world of shadows and secrets, of inherited power and ancient rivalries. She was thrust into it, unprepared and vulnerable. But still, she fought. And that kind of spirit—that real, untamed determination—was impossible not to admire.

Damon, of course, was relentless as ever. His movements were sharp, precise, almost savage, as though he could read her mind before she even made a move. I could see the frustration building within her—her jaw clenching, her fists tightening just a little too hard, the pulse throbbing at her temple. And yet, every time he knocked her back, every time she stumbled or fell, she rose again, dusted herself off, and returned to the fight, more determined than before. It was as if his attempts to break her only served to strengthen her.

She lunged at him with renewed force, her fiery determination blazing brighter with every strike, every parry, every near miss. And for a brief, fleeting moment, I saw it—a spark of something other than animosity in Damon's eyes. It was gone as quickly as it appeared, but it was there. Whatever it was, it made him push her harder, testing her limits, demanding more from her than he had before. It was a strange, twisted form of encouragement, but I recognized it nonetheless.

Thalia's auburn hair whipped around her face like a fiery halo as she lunged again, her eyes locked on Damon, unwavering in their focus. In the sunlight, her hair looked like living fire—alive, vibrant, dangerous. She missed another hit, Damon dodging with his usual infuriating grace and speed, but I knew it wasn't for lack of effort. She wasn't as polished or technically proficient as some of the other students, not yet, but she had a will, an unrefined drive that made her a formidable opponent. Her cheeks were flushed, her breaths coming in quick, shallow gasps, but the stubborn set of her shoulders, the unwavering fire in her eyes, said she was far from finished. She would keep fighting until she could fight no more.

She swung again—a desperate, all-out attack—and this time, her fist collided with his jaw. The thud echoed through the training grounds, loud enough for me to hear. Damon grabbed her wrist, twisting her around with a swift, controlled movement. Her back pressed against him, and for the briefest of moments, I felt a strange, unexpected pang of possessiveness in my chest. I tightened my grip around my coffee mug, my knuckles turning white. I could almost taste the tension in the air, thick and cloying.

"Fuck you, Damon! Let me go!" She growled, her voice laced with a fire that sent a thrill through me. A slow smile spread across my face. "That's my girl," I murmured to myself, thoroughly enjoying the show.

Damon's voice reached me faintly across the distance, a low murmur about emotions. Thalia's expression hardened, her chest heaving as she yanked herself away from him, breaking the contact with a visible shudder.

"Maybe I am emotional," she snapped, her voice sharp, cutting through the air between them like a shard of glass. "But at least I'm not cold and a fucking psychopath."

There it was again—that fire. That untamed spirit that refused to be extinguished. Those stormy gray eyes, fierce and alive, like the sky before a storm. Damon might be stronger, faster, more controlled, more experienced in the art of combat, but Thalia had something else. Something wild, untamed, something that set her apart. It wasn't just her burgeoning abilities or her relentless determination. It was her essence, it was a power she had yet to fully understand, a source of strength she had yet to tap into.

I could see the exhaustion creeping in—the ragged breaths, the slight tremor in her arms as she struck again, the way her movements were becoming just a fraction slower, less precise. But she didn't stop. She refused to give him the satisfaction of seeing her break. And I, captivated by her display of courage and unwavering spirit, couldn't look away.

From the moment she walked into that cafeteria, radiating an aura of quiet strength and vulnerability, I'd known there was something different about Thalia. She wasn't loud or demanding, didn't clamor for attention like so many others. But her quiet strength—the way she carried herself with a quiet dignity despite the hardships she'd clearly faced—demanded attention. Watching her now, fighting not just against Damon but against her own doubts and insecurities, stirred something deep within me. A protective instinct I hadn't realized I possessed. I smiled to myself —a genuine, heartfelt smile that warmed me from the inside out —though a tightness settled in my chest that I couldn't quite shake.

She was my mate—though she didn't yet know it. This beautiful, fiery, untamed creature was destined to be mine, a part of our strange, unconventional family.

Part of me ached to tell her, to claim her, to offer her the protection and belonging she so clearly craved. But I couldn't risk overwhelming her—not with everything she was already facing, the constant challenges and dangers that seemed to surround her. My brothers were in on the secret; that was why Damon had taken to training her with such ruthless intensity. He was convinced she was aligned with the Phantoms, determined to expose her through his relentless challenges, to force her true allegiance into the light. But I knew the truth about my Firefly. She was nothing like them. She was unique—a force of nature all her own.

Nox didn't say much when he heard the news, when I shared the revelation of Thalia being my mate. But I could see the internal battle raging within him—the conflict in his eyes, the tension etched in his posture, the way his hands clenched and unclenched at his sides. It reminded me of how he reacted when Thalia got hurt during the Wonders of Nexara competition; that moment of feral, unfiltered concern had revealed everything I needed to know. His care for her ran deeper than mere friendship, a silent connection that he hadn't yet found the words to voice.

These thoughts flooded back as I watched Damon and Thalia spar, their bodies moving in a complex dance of aggression and attraction. Following my uncle's death, I had left the secluded life I once knew—the sheltered existence he had carefully constructed for me—to venture into the world, driven by a need to discover my own identity and unravel the truth about my parents, about the heritage I had been denied for so long. But beyond that— deeper than that—I yearned for something I had never truly experienced in my isolation: companionship, a connection that had always eluded me, a sense of belonging that had always seemed just out of reach.

As I wandered through the forest, lost and alone, I came upon Nox and Damon. They were training under the moonlit sky, their movements fierce yet playful, a strange mixture of aggression and camaraderie, a reflection of a bond I had long craved. Their easy connection, the obvious understanding that flowed between them, struck a chord within me. And despite my initial reservations, my ingrained distrust of strangers, I approached them. After cautious introductions, after a period of mutual assessment and silent understanding, we unearthed an unexpected connection, bonding over our shared experiences of loss, the burdensome weight of our powers, and the pervasive loneliness that had silently haunted us all.

It was the beginning of a brotherhood forged through shared hardship, through a mutual understanding of pain and isolation —each of us finding solace in one another's presence, a refuge from the darkness that threatened to consume us. For the first time in my life, I felt a true sense of belonging. We were all damaged, broken in our own unique ways when fate brought us together. But it was that very fate—that shared sense of brokenness—that knit our fractured selves into something whole, something stronger than we could have ever been alone. And now, fate, in its infinite wisdom and capricious nature, has brought us her. A fiery, untamed woman who, I knew with unwavering certainty, would complete our fractured family—binding us together with a love as fierce and untamed as she was.

Chapter 23

Thalia's POV

Nestling deeper into the silky sheets of Nox's bed, I heard the door creak open, the soft sound echoing through the quiet of the room. My heart leapt into a wild gallop as I sat up, the cool fabric of the sheets brushing against my skin. My gaze was fixed on the doorway, where Zarek and Nox stood, their forms silhouetted against the dim light of the hallway.

The sight of them was enough to make my breath hitch. Their toned bodies were barely covered by their boxers, a full display of defined abs and strong arms that seemed almost supernatural in their perfection. It was a sight that bordered on the unfair—the way they could command such raw, primal beauty even in such a casual state. They looked like the gods of old, come to life with every line and curve designed to steal the breath from my lungs.

Zarek's dark hair framed his face, his amber eyes gleaming with an intensity that made my stomach flutter. Nox stood beside him, a quiet strength radiating from him. And then there was the unmistakable evidence of their arousal—their dicks hard and straining against the fabric of their boxers. The outline of their desire made my eyes widen, an involuntary gasp escaping my lips at the size of them. Both men were definitely blessed, not just in character, but in every physical aspect as well.

As I studied them, I felt a warmth spreading through my body, a lust that was as intense as it was unexpected.

As Zarek sauntered over, his smirk was a slash of wickedness across his face, a clear indication of the mischief brewing in his mind. His hands reached out, trailing possessively over my body, leaving a scorching path in their wake. The heat of his skin was a brand against mine, his raw power a tangible force that wrapped around me, making my breath hitch and my pulse race with an intoxicating mix of excitement and fear.

Nox's eyes locked onto mine, burning with an unspoken promise as he approached, his movements reminiscent of a panther—all grace and deadly beauty. When he reached me, he didn't hesitate, tangling a hand in my hair and pulling my head back, exposing my throat to the powerful promise of what was to come. In that moment, I was caught, a willing captive to their desires, suspended in a moment that felt both thrilling and dangerous—a delicate balance that sent shivers cascading down my spine.

Nox's lips crashed against mine in a kiss that was all-consuming, a searing connection that left me breathless and aching for more. His hands gripped my hips firmly, pulling me onto his lap, where I could feel the undeniable evidence of his desire pressing against me. My back was now to his toned chest as he began to grind against me, each deliberate movement stoking the fire that was rapidly spreading through my veins. The sensation of his body against mine, the feel of his hands exploring me—it was as if he was claiming me, branding me as his, and I found myself surrendering to the overwhelming tide of passion that threatened to sweep us both away.

I couldn't tear my gaze away from Zarek, his fingers tracing a tantalizing path along my sides, just below the hem of my top. His bright amber eyes, almost gold in the dim light, locked onto mine as his hands slipped beneath the fabric, his fingertips became instruments of pleasure, drawing invisible, intricate patterns on the sensitive expanse of my skin. With a deftness that left me dizzy, he peeled away the layer of clothing that separated us, baring me to his hungry gaze.

His mouth captured my breast, his lips closing around my nipple with a force that pulled a gasp from deep within me. The sensation of his suckling, coupled with the rough palm of his other hand that claimed my other breast, sent electric jolts coursing through my veins. My body arched into his touch, betraying my need, responding to him in a way that was as instinctual as it was uncontrollable.

My head fell back against Nox's shoulder, his solid presence a steady anchor at my back. His lips moved with slow precision up the column of my neck, each kiss a counterpoint to Zarek's fervent attention. They were a study in contrasts, yet their movements were perfectly synchronized, as if they were attuned to my every whimper and moan.

And those sounds fell from my lips shamelessly. Each touch, each kiss from them was calculated to unravel me, driving me ever closer to the edge of madness. Their hands and lips were relentless, exploring and claiming every inch of my fevered skin until I was submerged in a tide of overwhelming pleasure.

My clothing, once a barrier between us, seemed to dissolve into nothingness, leaving me exposed to them. I could feel the evidence of my own arousal—slick and insistent—as it slid between my thighs, a silent testament to the power they wielded over my body.

I cried out, my voice echoing in the room as Nox entered me with swift and deep thrusts. His arm wrapped firmly around my waist, holding me close, as if afraid I might slip away. "So fucking tight," he murmured, his voice a low growl in my ear that sent shivers down my spine. "That's my girl, taking it like I knew you would." His words were a heady affirmation, stoking the inferno within me.

As he began to thrust harder, faster, I felt my body stretched to its limits, teetering on the edge of delirium. Each powerful drive of his hips seemed to stoke the flames higher, threatening to consume us both. Their sinful touches were everywhere, igniting my skin with trails of fire that pushed me to new heights of ecstasy.

My body was roaring with sensation, every nerve ending singing with a lust so intense it bordered on pain. It was as if I were made of pure need—a vessel for the pleasure they so expertly wrought from me. I felt like I was going to break at any moment, shatter into a thousand pieces, unable to contain the overwhelming flood of ecstasy that coursed through my veins.

I woke up with a gasp, my body still humming with the remnants of pleasure and slick with the evidence of my desire. Sweat coated my skin as I sat upright, the sheets tangled around my legs. What the hell was happening to me? Why was I having such vivid, intensely hot, and detailed sex dreams about *them*?

Each touch, each kiss, each glance burned into my memory as if it were real. The way their hands had roamed over my skin, the heat of their bodies pressed against mine, the sounds of their pleasure echoing in my ears... it was all too much. I squeezed my eyes shut, trying to banish the images, but they only seemed to intensify.

I need to get the hell out of this house, to put some distance between us before I do something incredibly stupid.

I'm obviously losing my fucking mind.

It's been days of constant training with Damon. Every muscle in my body ached, and my mind felt like it was slowly unraveling under the weight of his pressure and that dream proved it. I could feel the exhaustion settling deep into my bones. As much as I wanted to prove I wasn't a liability, I needed a break—desperately.

The air in the house felt thick, almost suffocating, and the walls were closing in with every passing hour. Nox had been gone for days now, off somewhere that neither Damon nor Zarek would talk about. The absence of his presence only seemed to amplify the heaviness in the house.

"I need to get out of here," I muttered, more to myself than to anyone.

Zarek, leaning casually against the doorframe, looked up from where he was fiddling with one of his rings. His amber eyes glinted with a hint of mischief, the ever-present smirk tugging at his lips. "Well, if you're tired of Damon's death-by-training routine, I've got a better idea."

I raised an eyebrow, trying to suppress the small flicker of embarrassment that sparked from seeing him. "Oh?"

"Why don't we go into town?" he suggested, his tone nonchalant, but I could see the interest in his gaze. "You could use a break. We both could."

The thought of leaving the house, of feeling the open air and being anywhere but *here*, was more tempting than I wanted to admit. The idea of some semblance of normalcy—away from shadows and powers—was exactly what I needed. Maybe not with *him*, but it was better than nothing.

"Fine," I agreed with a sigh, rubbing my sore neck. "Let's go."

Zarek's smirk widened, as if he could sense the storm of tension swirling inside me, unraveling it with a single look. Without a word, he pushed off the doorframe and sauntered toward the back of the house, leaving me to follow. His casual demeanor, that effortless confidence, always left me slightly off-balance, as if I couldn't predict his next move. Yet, the thought of getting away with him stirred a quiet excitement in me—one I wasn't ready to admit.

The cool evening breeze brushed against my skin as we stepped outside, offering a welcome reprieve after days spent training under the relentless sky. My muscles still ached, and the exhaustion clung to my bones, but the prospect of escaping—of being anywhere but near Damon—was almost enough to make me forget how drained I was. Zarek's SUV, sleek and black, waited like a shadow in the dimming light, as untamed and magnetic as its owner. He opened the door for me with a casual grace, the gesture somehow more intimate in the fading dusk.

Sliding into the passenger seat, I sank into the soft leather—its comfort a far cry from the hard earth I'd grown accustomed to. Zarek climbed in beside me, his presence filling the small space. Neither of us spoke as we pulled out of the driveway, the towering trees surrounding us giving way to the narrow road. The silence between us wasn't empty—it was charged, every second stretching, magnifying the subtle pull that had been simmering beneath the surface.

"Where exactly are we going?" I asked, unable to stop myself from glancing at him, the curiosity clear in my voice.

He glanced at me, one hand resting lazily on the steering wheel, his amber eyes gleaming in the low light. "Same place you and El went last time," he replied, his voice smooth and teasing. But beneath the usual playfulness, there was something else—a warmth that made his suggestion feel more like an invitation. "Figured it's the one place you're familiar with. Unless," he added, his lips curving into a smirk, "you're up for something more adventurous?"

"How did you know where we went?" I shot back, narrowing my eyes but feeling the faint tug of amusement pulling at my lips. The challenge in my voice mirrored the sudden spark in the air.

Zarek chuckled, a low, rich sound that rippled through the space between us. "I have my ways," he said, the mystery in his tone hanging there like an unspoken dare.

I rolled my eyes, attempting to suppress the smile that was starting to break through. "Stalker. Let's stick to familiar today."

Time seemed to pass differently in his presence, every moment stretching, bending around us. Before I knew it, the town square appeared before us, bathed in the soft glow of holiday lights. Twinkling strings of light draped across the buildings, and a towering Christmas tree stood proudly in the center, its ornaments glittering like tiny stars. The air was crisp and filled with the scent of pine and freshly baked cookies—a world away from the harsh training and constant pressure at the academy.

Zarek parked, and as we stepped out, the festive atmosphere wrapped around me, easing the tension that had gripped my body for days. I took a deep breath, savoring the sense of normalcy that this place offered. For the first time in what felt like forever, I could breathe.

"Coffee?" Zarek asked, his voice quieter now, as if he could feel the shift in the air between us.

I nodded, though my thoughts were more focused on him than the food. "Sure."

He led me toward a small café on the corner, its warm glow spilling out onto the street. The moment we stepped inside, the cozy atmosphere wrapped around us like a blanket. The scent of coffee and fresh pastries mingled with the soft lights, and the waitress greeted us with a smile that lingered on Zarek a little too long. I felt a strange tug in my chest—irritation, maybe—though I tried to brush it off. Zarek, ever the charmer, handled it with an effortless ease.

We took a seat by the window, the space between us humming with unspoken tension. As I glanced around, memories of my last visit with El surfaced, but this time felt different. The weight of Zarek's presence made everything sharper, more intense. He leaned back in his chair, his gaze locked on mine, and the pull between us—subtle, unacknowledged—seemed to grow stronger.

"So," I began, my curiosity breaking through the quiet as the waitress left us. "What's this really about, Zarek? You don't exactly strike me as the 'let's grab a coffee' type."

His amber eyes flickered, and for a moment, his usual smirk faded, replaced by something deeper, something real. "Maybe I wanted to give you a break before Damon completely wore you down," he said, his voice steady, almost too gentle. "Or maybe"—he leaned in slightly, his eyes never leaving mine—"I needed a break from everything, too."

His honesty took me by surprise, and for a moment, I didn't know what to say. The vulnerability in his words—the way his gaze softened, even if only for a moment—made the space between us feel dangerously intimate. My heart stuttered, caught off guard by the weight of the moment.

I shifted in my seat, trying to ease the tension before it swallowed me whole. "Where's Nox been?"

Zarek's expression darkened, his playful edge returning as if to shield him from the seriousness that lingered beneath the surface. "He's handling something," he said, his voice lower now, guarded. His gaze met mine, and for a brief second, the mystery of Nox's absence hung between us. "Don't worry about it," he added, offering me a small, almost reassuring smile. "He'll be back soon enough."

Though his tone was light, the weight of what wasn't being said gnawed at me. But as Zarek's eyes held mine, that magnetic pull between us surged again, silencing any further questions. I wasn't sure where this was headed, but the way he looked at me—like he saw more than I was ready to reveal—left no doubt that something between us was changing.

After we finished at the café, Zarek and I stepped back into the cold, the festive lights illuminating the snow-dusted streets. The town was busy, its energy alive and comforting, and for a moment, I allowed myself to get lost in it. Zarek walked beside me, his hands tucked casually into his pockets, the sharp angles of his face softened by the glow of holiday lights.

I tried to focus on the normalcy of it all—the couples, the children, the laughter—but something about the night felt different, like a shadow had stretched over the town without anyone noticing. It started as a vague discomfort, a knot forming low in my stomach. My steps slowed, and I found myself scanning the crowd, the faces that passed us, the way the air seemed to ripple with an energy I couldn't quite place.

Zarek glanced at me, sensing the shift. "You alright?"

I hesitated, unsure how to explain what I was feeling. "I don't know. Something's... off."

His amber eyes narrowed slightly, and I could see him switching from casual companion to something more protective, more alert. "Off how?"

I opened my mouth to respond but stopped. A cold shiver ran down my spine, and instinctively, my eyes darted to a man standing near the edge of the square. He was watching me. His face was blank, unreadable, but there was something in his gaze—something dark. His presence felt wrong, like he didn't quite belong in this festive scene.

I swallowed, trying to shake the unease, but the feeling only deepened. As I turned away from him, my attention was drawn to another figure—this time a woman standing across the square.

She was dressed like everyone else, bundled in winter clothes, but there was something unnatural about the way she moved, her gaze fixed on me with an intensity that made my skin crawl.

"Zarek," I said, my voice quieter now. "They're watching us."

He followed my gaze, his jaw tightening as he noticed the people I'd been drawn to. "Stay close," he said, his voice low, a protective edge slipping into his tone.

We continued walking, but my unease only grew. Every few steps, I caught glimpses of more figures—each of them subtly watching, none of them blending into the joyful energy of the town. It wasn't just their presence that unsettled me. There was something deeper, something darker. A disturbance, a weight I couldn't name, but that I felt growing heavier with each passing moment.

Then, without warning, the world seemed to shift around me. The colors of the holiday lights blurred, the sounds of laughter and conversation fading to a distant hum. I stopped in my tracks, my breath catching in my throat as the sensation deepened—a strange pull twisting in my chest.

Zarek's hand came to rest lightly on my arm. "Thalia?" His voice was concerned now, sharp.

"I... I don't know what's happening," I whispered, my pulse racing. "It's like... like something's wrong. Like something's... breaking."

Zarek's expression darkened, his gaze scanning the crowd, but the people around us carried on—oblivious to the strange tension thickening in the air. I could feel it—a fracture, something not right with the balance of everything.

"Life and death."

The thought came out of nowhere, an unsettling realization that I couldn't fully grasp.

As I looked back toward the figures watching us, the sense of dread intensified. It was as if I could feel the pull of something beyond life—something unnatural, twisting the very air around them. It was disturbing the natural order, and the more I focused, the clearer the disturbance became.

"What are you feeling?" Zarek asked, his voice pulling me out of the strange fog.

"I don't know," I replied, but the words felt like a lie. I did know—deep down, something inside me was recognizing the disturbance. There was a wrongness here, a fracture that I hadn't been able to sense before, but now it was screaming at me.

"We need to leave," I said quickly, my voice sharper than I intended.

Zarek didn't argue. His hand slid to the small of my back, gently guiding me through the crowd. We moved quickly, my heart pounding in my chest, the figures still watching, still following with their eyes. The further we walked, the more the sensation clawed at me, the imbalance pressing down on my chest like a heavy weight.

I stole another glance behind us, my breath catching as I locked eyes with one of the watchers. His gaze was cold, empty, and for a moment, I felt something flicker—a connection, a darkness that seemed to seep into the very air between us. And then, it was gone.

Zarek must have sensed the urgency growing inside me because he leaned closer, his voice low and serious. "What do you feel, Thalia? Tell me."

"I think..." My voice wavered, the words foreign on my tongue. "I think something's disturbing the balance. Between life and death."

His eyes widened slightly, though he hid his surprise well. "Are you sure?"

I wasn't sure. But the sensation crawling under my skin, pulling at my senses, told me I was right. "Yes."

Zarek kept his hand at the small of my back, guiding me through the crowd, but I couldn't shake the feeling that something was wrong. As we moved, I stole another glance behind us, and that's when I noticed it—the watchers weren't just standing still anymore. They were moving. Slowly, deliberately, as if they were trying not to draw attention, but their eyes remained locked on me, following every step I took.

The man I'd noticed earlier, the one with the blank expression, was now weaving through the crowd, his gaze cold and unwavering. The woman across the square was moving too, her eyes dark and sharp, her pace just a little too smooth, like she was gliding through the people around her. It was unnatural, like they weren't part of this world.

My pulse quickened, the sense of dread growing with every passing second. "Zarek..." I whispered, keeping my voice low as the sensation of being hunted crept under my skin. "They're getting closer."

Zarek tensed beside me, his body instinctively shifting between me and the threat. "Keep moving," he murmured, his voice calm but laced with tension. "We'll lose them."

But even as he said it, I knew it wasn't going to be that simple. The air around us felt thicker now, almost oppressive, as if something was tearing at the very fabric of the world. The festive lights that had once seemed warm and inviting now felt distorted, their glow dimming as the shadows stretched unnaturally long.

"The veil is fracturing."

The thought slammed into me, and I stumbled slightly. It wasn't just a feeling anymore—it was real. I could sense it—the very fabric between life and death tearing, unraveling in the presence of these figures. I didn't understand how I knew, but the knowledge pulsed through me, undeniable.

Zarek's grip on my arm tightened, grounding me. "Thalia," he said firmly, his voice cutting through the fog of fear settling in my mind. "Stay with me."

I nodded, forcing my legs to keep moving, but the watchers were closing in. There were more of them now. I counted at least five—maybe more—dispersed throughout the crowd. Each one moved with that same eerie precision, their eyes never leaving me. And as I watched, something shifted in their expressions. It was subtle, but I could see it. They knew I had sensed them. They knew I was trying to leave.

The man nearest to us suddenly changed direction, quickening his pace, his gaze darkening with intent. The others followed suit, their movements becoming more coordinated, more predatory.

"We need to go," I said, panic edging into my voice. "Now."

Zarek didn't need to be told twice. His hand slipped from my back to my wrist, and he pulled me faster through the crowd. The festive market stalls and holiday lights blurred past us as we moved, but I couldn't shake the growing sense of unease twisting in my chest. The watchers weren't just following anymore—they were closing in.

As they drew closer, the world around them seemed to warp. The air rippled, and it felt as though the space between us was thinning—as if the boundary between life and something darker was beginning to blur.

One of the watchers—a tall, gaunt man with sunken eyes—was only a few steps behind us now. His hand twitched at his side, and the ground beneath my feet seemed to tremble, ever so slightly. I could feel it—whatever dark force was at work, it was getting stronger, closer.

"Arethax."

The name echoed in my mind, foreign but familiar, like something from a distant memory. I didn't know who or what it was, but the weight of it pressed down on me—a suffocating presence that seemed to pulse with the same dark energy radiating from the watchers. My body started to feel sluggish, weighed down by the sheer wrongness of everything around me.

Zarek pulled me out of my daze with a sharp tug, his grip firm but reassuring. "Almost there," he said, his voice low but determined.

We rounded a corner, ducking into a narrow alleyway that led away from the busy square. The noise of the crowd faded behind us, replaced by the eerie silence of the darkened street. My heart pounded in my ears as I glanced back again, but the watchers hadn't stopped. They were still coming, their figures now silhouetted against the soft glow of the holiday lights, their presence an unnatural blight on the festive scene.

"They're not going to stop," I muttered, my breath coming in short bursts.

Zarek's jaw clenched, his eyes scanning the alley ahead of us. "I know."

As we reached the end of the alley, I felt it again—the strange, disorienting pull in my chest, the fracture widening. The veil between life and death was breaking, unraveling in the presence of these dark figures. And as the watchers drew closer, I could sense it deepening, like they were feeding off the disturbance, drawing power from the imbalance.

The gaunt man was the first to step into the alley, his sunken eyes gleaming with malice. "Thalia, you know you can't run from this," he said, his voice low and hollow, like the whisper of dry leaves skittering across a graveyard. A chilling wave washed over me, raising the hairs on my arms and prickling my skin.

"Arethax."

The name whispered again, and this time, I felt its presence closer —watching from somewhere beyond. I couldn't move. My mind raced, the sense of the imbalance, the fracture, pulling me deeper into something I didn't understand.

"Stay behind me," Zarek ordered, his voice cold, protective as he moved with the fluid grace of someone born to command darkness. His body shifted subtly in front of mine as the shadows around him stirred, swirling like tendrils of ink stretching out toward the night. The teasing warmth from earlier had vanished, replaced by an icy, focused resolve. Darkness was his element, and in that moment, he became a part of it—a force of nature blending seamlessly with the night around us.

The gaunt man stepped forward, his hollow gaze flicking between Zarek and me, a sickening smile creeping across his face. "You think you can protect her?" His voice was like a death rattle— hollow and ancient. "You have no idea what's coming."

I could feel it—the fracture, the fabric of our existence straining under the weight of its presence. My instincts screamed at me, the pull inside me demanding I act, that I *do something*. Before I even realized it, the shadows inside me stirred, rising to the surface.

I could feel something else stirring within me—a force that was not just darkness, but a flicker of light, fighting to break through the suffocating tension. My heart raced, the sensation growing stronger, pulling me toward something deeper, something ancient and primal that I didn't yet understand. A strange mix of fear and exhilaration—of raw power—pulsed through me, and before I could stop it, the shadows inside me responded, unraveling and swirling with a shimmer of light at their edges, forming a protective shield that hovered between us and the encroaching danger. It felt instinctive, like breathing.

Zarek's shadows intertwined with mine, his darkness and my light mingling together in a strange, mesmerizing dance of protection. His tendrils of shadow lashed out with lethal precision, wrapping around mine like two forces in perfect sync—a dark ballet of power. But where his darkness was sharp, unyielding, like shards of obsidian, my light softened the edges, casting a translucent glow that shimmered like a delicate veil between us and the unseen watchers in the alley's shadows.

The power inside me surged again, a tidal wave of energy crashing against my bones, and without thinking, I let it out. The shield of light expanded, brighter now, more solid, a tangible force against the encroaching darkness. It shimmered like polished glass, casting a faint glow through the narrow alley, illuminating the dust motes dancing in the air. But the light didn't diminish the darkness—it blended with it, swirling together with Zarek's shadows in a breathtaking display of power, creating a barrier that was both ethereal and terrifying. A chaotic yet harmonious mix of order and chaos, of life and death.

Zarek glanced back at me, his eyes flicking between the glow of my shield and the shadows he controlled. "You're full of surprises," he muttered, though there was a faint smirk tugging at his lips.

Then, out of the darkness, Damon appeared. His form seemed to materialize from the shadows themselves, his striking blue eyes cold and deadly as they fixed on the gaunt man cowering before us. A low growl rumbled in Damon's chest, a sound that vibrated with barely restrained power. Shadows swirled around him—dark and restless—like living extensions of his fury, licking at the edges of the alley like hungry flames.

"Damon," I breathed, a mixture of relief and unease flooding through me.

The gaunt man paused, his sunken eyes narrowing as Damon stepped forward. His figure was no longer languid and predatory but cautious. The other watchers stopped too, their eerie movements faltering under the weight of Damon's dark power. The alley itself seemed to shift, the air thickening as the shadows around Damon coiled and writhed like they were alive, feeding off his anger.

"Leave," Damon said, his voice a low, dangerous growl. The command echoed through the narrow alley, rippling through the thick air like the crack of thunder.

The gaunt man faltered for the first time, his gaze flicking nervously between Damon, Zarek, and the glowing shield that pulsed between us all. His thin lips curled into a slow, sinister smile, and my heart sank as his words slipped through the oppressive silence.

"You can't protect her forever, demon." His voice was quiet—a hollow whisper that seemed to resonate inside my mind. "Her time is running out."

Damon's expression darkened, and the shadows around him thickened, almost becoming solid.

The man's empty eyes flicked to me, his gaze piercing through the shield I had created as if he could see right into my soul. "This is just the beginning," he whispered, his voice carrying a chilling finality. "Arethax is closer than you think, Thalia. You're out of time."

The words hit me like a physical blow, the name *Arethax* reverberating in my mind, cold and ominous. I didn't know what it meant, but I felt the weight of it—felt the darkness that came with the name. My hands trembled, the power I'd released still humming through me, but fear knotted in my stomach.

Zarek's shadows lashed out again, more violently this time, aiming to strike the gaunt man. But before they could connect, the watchers vanished. One by one, they disappeared into thin air, dissolving into the darkness like they had never been there at all.

The oppressive weight in the air lifted, but the fear remained. I couldn't shake the man's words, couldn't ignore the cold certainty in his gaze when he'd said *Arethax* was close.

Damon stepped closer, his dark blue eyes scanning the empty alley. "Cowards," he muttered, his voice sharp.

The silence that followed was deafening. The weight in the air had lifted, but I could still feel the echoes of the disturbance. My light flickered, then slowly began to fade, merging back into the shadows until only the faintest trace of it remained. Zarek's shadows withdrew, though they lingered protectively, as if waiting for the next threat to emerge.

"Who is Arethax?" I finally asked, still trying to process what the hell just happened. A strange pressure settled over my chest, making it hard to breathe. The alley—moments ago filled with an unnatural chill that prickled my skin—now felt strangely empty, as though whatever malevolent presence had lingered there had simply vanished, leaving a void in its wake. I glanced at Damon and Zarek, searching their faces for answers.

Zarek's jaw was tight, his amber eyes narrowed as he scanned the alley. He didn't answer, but his silence spoke volumes. Whatever Arethax was, it wasn't good.

Damon, however, met my gaze head-on, his expression unreadable —a mask of cool indifference that did nothing to ease my growing unease. "It's the reason we're in danger," he said, his voice low and gravelly.

"Danger?" I echoed, the word catching in my throat. I'd known, on some level, that something wasn't right. But hearing Damon say it so bluntly, so matter-of-factly, sent a shiver down my spine.

"It's a... a force of darkness from another realm," Zarek finally said, his voice hesitant, as if he were choosing his words carefully, each syllable measured and deliberate. "An ancient being who wants to... unbalance our world. To tip the scales." His gaze flickered to me.

"Tip the scales?" I repeated, trying to make sense of his words. "What does that even mean?" My mind raced, trying to grasp the implications of his cryptic statement.

Damon let out a harsh laugh, the sound devoid of humor—a bitter, almost cynical edge to it. "It means Arethax wants to destroy everything," he said, his eyes glinting with a cold, hard anger. "It wants to plunge Nexara and all other realms into eternal darkness."

"And what does that have to do with me?" I asked, my voice barely above a whisper. The pressure in my chest intensified, a cold dread settling in my stomach. Why were they telling me this *now*? Why did these watchers—whoever they were—seem to know me? To want me? And what had I done to attract the attention of such a destructive force?

Damon's gaze intensified, his blue eyes boring into mine, as if searching for answers I didn't possess. "We don't know yet," he admitted, "Still can't figure out why you are the center of its attention." He looked away then, his gaze sweeping across the empty alley, as if searching for a clue—a missing piece of the puzzle that would explain this terrifying connection between me and this ancient being.

"Where's Nox?" I asked, my voice sharp as panic creeped into my chest.

"He's on his way to the house," Zarek replied, his tone calm and patient.

Damon turned toward me, his expression unreadable as always. "I'll take her back," he said, his voice steady, but carrying a weight I couldn't quite place.

Damon stepped closer, his presence almost suffocating in its intensity. The weight of his gaze was enough to pull me from the panic bubbling inside, but it didn't ease the tension gripping my chest. Without a word, he extended his hand toward me, his dark blue eyes locking onto mine. The shadows around him stirred like restless tendrils, ready to move the moment I accepted his offer.

I hesitated, my pulse quickening as I glanced at Zarek, who gave me a small nod, his expression softening with reassurance. But there was something about him—his shadows were alive, and I could feel them reaching out to me, pulling me into his orbit.

"We'll be quick," Damon said, his voice low, but there was an undeniable edge to it.

Reluctantly, I placed my hand in his. The moment our skin touched, the world around us shifted. His shadows curled around us like a blanket, cold and weightless, yet somehow suffocating. The light from the town, the distant sounds of holiday music and laughter—it all disappeared, swallowed by the darkness. The alley, the town square—everything vanished as the shadows surged up, pulling us into their embrace.

For a moment, it felt like we were floating through nothingness, weightless and disconnected from the world. The sensation was disorienting, my heart pounding wildly in my chest as I tried to make sense of the space we were in. I couldn't see anything—there was only blackness, a void stretching endlessly in every direction. But Damon's grip on my hand was firm, grounding me even as the shadows closed in around us.

"Relax," Damon's voice came through the darkness, calm and soothing. "My shadows won't harm you."

Easier said than done.

The cold seeped into my skin, the shadows brushing against me like living things, their touch both invasive and strangely comforting. It felt like they were reading me, exploring the edges of my power, testing the light that had risen inside me back in the alley.

We emerged from the shadows into the open air, my feet hitting solid ground again. I stumbled slightly, the sudden transition from the void to reality throwing me off balance. Damon's grip tightened around my hand, steadying me before I could fall.

The house loomed ahead, familiar and ominous, its dark silhouette barely visible against the night sky. The cold air wrapped around me, stark and biting after the suffocating embrace of the shadows.

Damon's gaze lingered on me for a moment longer, his expression still unreadable. "You handled it better than most," he said, his voice softer now, though there was still that edge in it.

I glanced up at him, catching the flicker of something in his eyes —approval, maybe? But before I could respond, the sound of footsteps echoed from the direction of the house. I turned just in time to see Nox approaching, his figure a shadowy blur until he stepped into the light spilling from the house.

Relief flooded through me, but it was quickly tempered by the uncertainty of what had just happened—and what was still to come. Nox's dark eyes locked onto mine, his expression grim as he approached.

"Are you okay?" Nox asked, his voice low, but there was a tension beneath his words, as if he already knew the answer wasn't simple.

I nodded, though I wasn't entirely sure how to explain what I'd just experienced. "Yeah," I said, my voice a little shaky. "I think so."

Damon's shadows shifted beside me, his presence lingering—ever watchful. It almost felt like his shadows had taken a liking to me —more so than Damon himself.

"I'll be back. Nox, stay with her," Damon announced, his voice firm, before he disappeared into the darkness, swallowed by the shadows as effortlessly as he had emerged from them.

Chapter 24

Thalia's POV

A few hours had passed, and the house was eerily quiet, except for the crackling of the fire. The shadows danced along the walls, flickering with each snap of the flames, but even the warmth of the fire did little to settle the chill that had lodged itself deep in my chest. I couldn't sit still anymore. Anxiety gnawed at me, each passing minute feeding the growing sense of dread in my stomach. My mind raced, circling around the events from earlier—the cryptic threats, the strange pull I'd felt in the darkness. Something was wrong, and every nerve in my body screamed that I needed to do something, *anything*, instead of sitting here, waiting.

"Where are they?" I finally asked, my voice sharper than I intended as I paced in front of the fireplace. I could feel my heart pounding, the unease spiraling out of control. The silence was too heavy, the waiting unbearable.

Nox, who had been sitting quietly, looked up, his green eyes briefly widening as if I'd caught him off guard. For a second, he looked like a deer in headlights—an expression so uncharacteristic of him that it only deepened my unease. Seeing Nox, usually so composed, with even a hint of uncertainty made my stomach clench harder. But he quickly masked it, his usual unreadable calm slipping back into place, as if he hadn't just betrayed a flicker of fear.

"They'll be back," he said, though his voice lacked its usual confidence. His eyes flicked nervously toward the window, betraying his own concern as his fingers tightened around the leather of the armrest.

I stopped pacing and turned to face him, crossing my arms over my chest, trying to hold myself together even as I felt myself start to unravel. "And where were *you*, Nox?" I asked, unable to keep the edge out of my voice. The question had been lingering in the back of my mind since he left, but I hadn't wanted to push him before. Now, with hours gone by and no sign of Zarek or Damon, I couldn't help it.

He stiffened slightly, his gaze meeting mine for a brief moment before he quickly glanced away. "I was... handling something," he said, his tone clipped, almost defensive.

I raised an eyebrow, waiting for him to elaborate, but he didn't. The silence between us grew heavier, filled only by the popping of the fire. I could see the tension in his posture, the way he was avoiding eye contact, and it only made me more suspicious. Nox was good at hiding things—too good—but this was different. There was something he wasn't telling me, something more than just concern for his brothers.

I sighed, running a hand through my hair, frustration bubbling up inside me, threatening to spill over. "I was holding it together, you know? I really was. But the fact that they're not back yet..." I trailed off, my voice faltering as the worry clawed at me, each word catching in my throat. "It's starting to eat me alive."

The words hung in the air, my fear laid bare between us. I started pacing again, my footsteps echoing against the stone floor, the fear creeping closer, threatening to drown me. I didn't want to admit it, but I was even worried about Damon—his cold, intense presence, the way he threw himself into the darkness without hesitation. And Zarek... Zarek, with his charm and easy banter. But now they were both out there, and I had no idea what they were facing. No idea if they were okay.

"Yeah," I muttered to myself, shaking my head, trying to fight back the tears that were beginning to sting my eyes. "I'm losing it."

Nox stood and crossed the room, his footsteps almost silent on the stone floor. He stopped just in front of me, his expression softening just a fraction. "You're not losing it, Thalia. They're strong. They know what they're doing—" He hesitated, and for a moment, his eyes searched mine, as if looking for something—some kind of reassurance or maybe a sign that I wasn't about to fall apart. "We'll find them if they don't return soon."

His words should have reassured me, but the growing sense of dread only deepened, wrapping icy tendrils around my heart, squeezing until it ached with a dull, persistent throb. Something wasn't right. And the worst part was the helplessness—the waiting, the uncertainty of it all was like a knife twisting in my gut, each rotation sending fresh waves of nausea churning through me. My hands trembled as I fisted them at my sides, trying to find some semblance of control.

Nox's voice cut through my thoughts. "Are you worried about Damon?" he asked, genuine surprise coloring his tone.

"Well yeah, he may be a complete asshole, but that doesn't mean I want him hurt or dead," I sighed, running a hand through my hair again. "Gods, maybe I *am* losing it if I'm worried about *him*." I let out a short, manic laugh, the sound brittle in the quiet room.

Nox didn't smile, but there was a flicker of understanding in his eyes. "He has that effect," he said quietly.

I let out a shaky breath, my chest tightening again. "I just want them to be okay."

Nox's eyes softened at my admission. He stepped closer, his presence grounding in a way that Damon's intensity or Zarek's teasing charm couldn't be. For a moment, we stood there in the quiet, the fire crackling softly behind me.

"They *will* be," Nox finally said, his voice steady and reassuring, though I could tell even he wasn't entirely sure. "Damon's strong, and Zarek..." He trailed off, a faint, almost imperceptible smirk tugging at his lips. "He'll charm his way out of anything, as usual."

I tried to smile, and though it was weak, it didn't feel entirely forced. There was something in the way Nox looked at me—an openness I hadn't seen before—that made the fear feel just a little more manageable.

"Thank you," I said, my voice quieter now, the words carrying more weight than I intended. It wasn't just for his reassurance. It was for being here—for standing by me when everything felt like it was unraveling.

Nox's gaze held mine, and for a moment, the space between us seemed to narrow, the tension shifting from anxiety to something else—something deeper. His eyes searching mine as if trying to find the right words, the right way to bridge the gap that had always lingered between us.

"I'm not going anywhere, Thalia," he said, his voice low—almost a whisper. There was a promise in those words, a sincerity that made my chest tighten.

Before I could think better of it, I took a step closer, the pull between us growing stronger, undeniable. It was like an invisible thread tugging us together, defying the space that separated us. His eyes flickered, widening slightly, surprise swirling within their emerald depths, but he didn't pull away. Instead, he mirrored my movement. His hand lifted, hesitant at first, then brushed lightly against my arm, sending a shiver down my spine. The contact was electric, igniting a warmth that spread through my veins, chasing away the lingering chill of fear and uncertainty. His touch was gentle and careful, and my heart pounded louder in my ears—a frantic rhythm against the sudden quietness of the world around us. The air crackled with an energy I couldn't name—as if we were two halves of a whole, finally finding our way back to each other. I held my breath, waiting, hoping he wouldn't break the spell, and wouldn't shatter the fragile connection that was forming between us.

I could feel it—the sense that maybe, in this chaos, there was something steady. Something real. Something worth holding onto. Nox leaned in, his face inches from mine, his breath mingling with mine as the tension tightened, thickened—the world narrowing down to just the two of us. The scent of cedar and rain enveloped me, a comforting presence in the midst of the storm raging inside me. I closed my eyes, bracing myself for... a kiss? A touch? I didn't know. But I was ready for whatever he offered.

But just as the distance between us seemed to vanish, the door to the house swung open with a loud creak, and we both jerked back, startled. My heart leapt into my throat as I spun around, my pulse racing for an entirely different reason now—a mixture of guilt and the unwelcome intrusion of reality. Damon and Zarek stood in the doorway, shadowed figures against the dim light spilling from the hall. They both looked utterly exhausted.

The air between Nox and me shifted instantly, the unspoken moment we'd been leaning into shattering as reality came crashing back. The warmth of his nearness vanished as he straightened, his expression slipping back into its usual calm mask, though I could have sworn I saw a flicker of disappointment in his emerald eyes before it disappeared.

Relief surged through me, almost overwhelming, and for a moment, I couldn't speak or even move. Damon's cold blue eyes were the first to find mine, his expression as unreadable as ever, though there was a flicker of something softer—something like relief. Zarek, on the other hand, gave me a tired, lopsided grin, trying to brush off the weight of whatever they had just faced.

Before I knew it, my body moved on instinct, pulling both of them into a hug. I couldn't stop myself; I needed to feel them, solid and real, to know they were truly here, safe. The tension that had been coiling in my stomach since their departure finally began to unravel.

"Awh, were you worried about us?" Zarek teased, his voice light and playful as he wrapped me into a tighter hug, pulling me flush against him. "Maybe she's got Stockholm syndrome if she just hugged *Damon*." He shot Damon a sly grin, which only deepened the faint crease of irritation on Damon's face.

"We need to go," Damon said, his voice cutting through the moment with cold precision, clearly unamused by Zarek's jab. His jaw was tight, the muscle ticking beneath his skin.

Zarek's playful smirk faded, his grip on me loosening as the gravity of Damon's words settled over the room. The teasing atmosphere evaporated instantly, replaced by a palpable tension that crackled in the air like static electricity. Whatever had happened out there, it had changed everything. It had shifted the very air we breathed, replacing the lighthearted banter with a heavy, suffocating dread.

"And where exactly are *we* going?" I asked, confusion knotting my brow. The academy had always been the one place I thought we could count on—a fortress, a sanctuary from whatever was out there. A place of learning and magic, not a launching point for some unknown danger.

Damon's gaze met mine, his expression hardening. His voice was sharp, clipped. "For once can you not be difficult?" The words were laced with an icy undercurrent.

Zarek sighed, his amber eyes, normally sparkling with mischief, now held a shadow of concern. "Damon, stop. Thalia, we're not taking any chances. We need to stay ahead of them." He gave me a look that told me more than his words ever could—a silent plea for understanding.

"Okay, so tell me where we are going?" I asked, my voice steady despite the growing tension. My eyes flicked to Nox, and the memory of our moment by the fire sent an unexpected warmth rushing to my cheeks. The intensity of his emerald gaze, the way his hand had brushed against me... I quickly looked away, trying to regain my composure, but I could feel the pull between us still lingering—a magnetic force that drew my attention back to him again and again.

Damon let out an exasperated sigh, the sound loud in the quiet room. His hands ran roughly over his face, as if trying to wipe away the frustration, but my gaze caught on the dark streaks across his fingers. Dried blood.

"We don't have time for twenty fucking questions right now," Damon snapped, his tone harsher than usual as he stormed up the stairs, frustration radiating off him in waves. "We just need to go." He yelled, the force of his anger slammed against me like a physical blow.

I stood frozen for a moment, watching him disappear, the weight of his words sinking in. Before I could even process the fear coiling in my stomach, Zarek slung a casual arm around my shoulders, pulling me close with his usual easy charm. The warmth of his touch was polar opposite to the icy chill Damon had left behind.

"Don't mind him," Zarek said with a playful grin, though his eyes held a touch of seriousness. "He hates going home."

I blinked, turning to look at him, confused. "Home?" The word felt strange—foreign in this context.

Zarek nodded, his playful tone dropping just slightly, as if the word carried more weight than it should. "Yeah. You'll get to meet who created that demon." His gaze shifted toward where Damon had disappeared upstairs, a flicker of something darker passing over his expression. "Damon never handles it well."

"The dark kingdom awaits, my lady," Zarek added with a playful bow, his lighthearted grin returning despite the weight of everything going on. His ability to keep things casual, even in the face of chaos, was always a bit disarming. It must be a blessing and a curse for him. A way to shield himself from whatever darkness loomed over them all.

I forced a smile, trying to mirror his lightness, though the mention of where we were headed—*the dark kingdom*—sent a chill through me. It sounded like a place of nightmares, a place where shadows held dominion and light dared not tread. "I'm sure it'll be... lovely," I replied, though my voice betrayed the growing unease gnawing at me.

Zarek's grin widened, but there was something almost sad in his eyes, before he brushed it off. "Oh, you'll love it," he teased, his voice laced with a hint of irony that I couldn't quite decipher.

As Nox walked past us, heading upstairs, he patted Zarek on the shoulder in a silent exchange that spoke volumes between brothers. A wordless understanding passed between them, a conversation that excluded me. I watched him disappear up the steps, feeling a pang of guilt. Guilt for the warmth I felt towards him, for the connection that sparked between us. I bit my lip, my thoughts swirling back to the moment by the fire with Nox, to waking up beside him, the pull I'd felt between us still lingering in the air, a silent promise of something more.

"So you and Nox, huh?" Zarek's voice cut through my thoughts, teasing but with a mischievous grin that told me he'd picked up on more than I'd realized.

I blinked, turning to face him, my cheeks warming. "What? No, it's not like that," I stammered, trying to shake off the sudden wave of embarrassment. But Zarek's smirk only deepened.

"Oh, sure," Zarek drawled, clearly amused. "Because that moment in front of the fire didn't look like something at all." He raised an eyebrow, his eyes dancing with amusement.

I could feel my face flush even more as I shot him a glare—though it didn't help that he was still grinning at me like he knew exactly how to push my buttons. Like he knew exactly what I was thinking, what I was feeling.

"I don't mind sharing," Zarek added with a wink, his grin turning downright devilish.

I stared at him, wide-eyed, not entirely sure if he was joking or being serious—though with Zarek, it was always hard to tell. He was a master of flirtation, a walking enigma wrapped in charm and mischief. My brain struggled to come up with a response, but before I could say anything, he flashed me one last smirk and headed upstairs, leaving me standing there, flustered and a little off-balance.

Typical Zarek—always leaving chaos in his wake.

Chapter 25

Thalia's POV

We stepped from the shadows into a kingdom that felt utterly alien. The land before me was like a vision from a fever dream—dark, haunting, and intensely beautiful all at once. The crimson moon hung heavy in the sky, and the air itself was thick with an ancient power—a weight that pressed against my chest and stole my breath.

Before us loomed a towering castle, the structure was both majestic and menacing, a testament to the raw power that resonated through the very ground we stood on. Each tower strained towards the moon as if yearning for its touch, while shadows clung to the ancient stone like spectral guardians. Beneath the shadow of the castle, a sprawling valley unfolded, carved by rivers that mirrored the blood-red sky above.

I took a hesitant step forward, the loose gravel crunching beneath my boots, the sound amplified in the unnerving silence. The ground beneath my feet pulsed with a faint, infernal heat, as though the very earth were alive. Twisted, skeletal trees clung to the cliffs, their branches reaching out like gnarled claws, eager to ensnare any who dared to stray from the path.

This was Damon's homeland—a place as harsh and unforgiving as he was. The raw power, the beauty laced with danger, the ruthless shadows that clung to every corner... It was a land forged from darkness and fire, a reflection of his very essence. The weight of its presence settled on my shoulders, a physical burden that made my heart pound.

Beside me, Damon was an anchor in the swirling chaos. His dark blue eyes, usually guarded and cold, held a flicker of vulnerability. He belonged here, in this realm of shadows and flame, while I was an intruder—a trespasser on sacred ground. And yet, a strange sense of belonging tugged at me, an inexplicable connection to this alien place.

The moon bathed his face in its eerie light, highlighting the sharp angles of his cheekbones and jaw, the intensity of his gaze. A ghost of a smirk touched his lips, as if he sensed the effect this place was having on me.

"Thalia," Damon began, his voice low and strained. "This place... it's not safe. Not for you." His gaze swept across the menacing landscape, taking in the unseen dangers lurking in the shadows. "But right now, it's our only option."

I drew a shaky breath, the heavy air clinging to my lungs like cobwebs. "I understand," I managed, forcing my voice to remain steady despite the tremor in my hands. I met his gaze, determined to show him I wasn't afraid, though the raw power of this realm made my every instinct scream at me to flee. "I'll be careful, Damon."

His jaw tightened, the conflict evident in the clench of his fists. "Stay close," he commanded.

Zarek's usual playful demeanor was gone, replaced by a grim mask of alertness. His amber eyes, normally alight with mischief, were narrowed, scanning the surroundings with a predator's intensity.

"This place can sense weakness. It preys on the vulnerable." Zarek warned, his voice low and serious. Nox stood rigid, his jaw clenched, every muscle in his body coiled tight. He moved with a predator's grace, each step measured and deliberate.

"Don't stray from the path," Nox added, his voice rough but laced with concern. "The shadows here are hungry. They'll swallow you whole if you give them the chance."

I nodded, keeping pace as Damon led the way—his steps deliberate, yet burdened by the gravity of his choice. This was his home, yet bringing me here was a risk.

We descended the path as one, our steps synchronized, our breaths echoing in the silence. The path shimmered with a creepy, internal luminescence, as though lit from within. Every step felt heavy with the weight of centuries, the oppressive darkness pressing in on us from all sides. Yet, despite the menacing atmosphere, there was a haunting beauty to this alien world.

The valley stretched before us, a vast expanse of darkness punctuated by the crimson glow of the moon and the scattered flames of torches and bonfires. Beneath the skeletal trees, clusters of small, purple flowers bloomed, their petals glowing with an airy light. I paused, mesmerized by their delicate beauty. It was a reminder that even in the darkest of places, life—and even beauty—could find a way to thrive.

Damon noticed my pause and glanced back, his eyes softening momentarily at the sight of me marveling at the unexpected blossoms. But the tenderness was fleeting, quickly replaced by his usual wariness.

Ahead, the rivers flowed like veins of fire. The water moved sluggishly, as if burdened by the weight of centuries of secrets. Mist rose from its surface, swirling into the air like ghostly apparitions. Ancient bridges—their stone arches carved with glowing symbols

I couldn't decipher—spanned the fiery waters, beckoning us towards the heart of the castle.

Despite the harsh atmosphere, there was a strange harmony to it all. It was a realm where darkness reigned supreme—but even here, there was a perverse kind of beauty.

The castle grew larger with every step, its silhouette growing more menacing as we approached. Gargoyles perched on its towers, their stone eyes eternally vigilant, while thorny vines snaked up the walls, encircling balconies like protective serpents.

I felt a wave of anxiety wash over me—a suffocating mix of awe and fear. Damon slowed his pace as we reached the final stretch, his eyes fixed on the castle's form. He seemed lost in thought, wrestling with memories he'd rather forget. With a shake of his head, he pushed those memories aside and turned to me, his expression grim.

"Stay close," he repeated, his voice urgent. "Don't let your guard down for a moment."

I nodded, there was a strange sense of belonging, a connection with the darkness that echoed within me. We were about to enter the heart of Damon's world—a realm as dark as it was beautiful—and I was ready.

The iron gates groaned open as we approached, their echoing protest shattering the silence. Nox and Zarek flanked us, their eyes, sharp as honed blades, scanned the shadows, their bodies coiled tight with a readiness that spoke volumes. Even they, these formidable warriors, were on edge—and that alone amplified the gravity of the situation.

A grand hall stretched before us, dark stone dimly lit by flickering torches and the eerie red glow that filtered through stained-glass windows high above. The fractured light cast distorted patterns on the floor, adding to the unsettling atmosphere.

We reached a set of massive double doors at the far end of the hall, the dark wood carved with scenes of battles and mythical creatures. Damon paused before them, his hand hovering over the ornate handle, a deep breath rattling in his chest. "My father," he said, his voice low and steady. "He's unlike anyone you've ever encountered. Choose your words carefully, Thalia."

His words sent a jolt of fear through me, a cold dread that tightened my chest. But I forced myself to meet his gaze. "I can handle it," I assured him, though the truth was, I had no idea what to expect.

The doors swung inward with a groan, revealing a throne room shrouded in darkness that seemed to consume the very light. At the far end, elevated on a dais of obsidian, sat a throne carved from the same dark stone, its sharp edges and large size radiating an aura of power and menace. And upon that throne sat a figure —his form massive and imposing, yet perfectly still, like a statue of some ancient, forgotten god.

Damon's father.

His features were sharp, chiseled from stone, his eyes burning with an unsettling red fire, like embers glowing in the abyss. Long, dark hair—streaked with silver at the temples—framed his face, and a thick, dark robe, its edges embroidered with shimmering symbols, draped over his shoulders. The room pulsed with an evident darkness.

Damon stepped forward, every movement controlled, every muscle taut, as if preparing to face a predator. "Father," he said, his voice formal, devoid of any warmth or affection. "We have returned."

The figure on the throne remained silent, his gaze fixed on me, piercing me with an intensity that made me want to shrink back. It was a look that saw into my very soul, stripping away every defense, every secret. I fought the urge to flinch, meeting his gaze with as much strength I could muster, refusing to cower.

"So," he finally spoke, his voice deep and resonant, echoing through the chamber with an ancient power that made the stone tremble. "This is the *human* you've brought into my realm."

The way he uttered the word "human" dripped with disdain—a mixture of curiosity and contempt. I swallowed hard, feeling the tension radiating from Damon beside me.

"I am," I replied, my voice unwavering despite the tremor of fear that ran through me.

A dark chuckle, devoid of humor, echoed through the room. His gaze shifted to his son, "You've always had a weakness for those beneath you, haven't you?"

Damon's jaw tightened, but he remained silent, his gaze locked with his father's—a silent battle of wills raging between them. The demon king's eyes returned to me, sharper now, assessing me with a renewed intensity.

"We shall see if she's worth the trouble, then," he mused, leaning forward.

The weight of his words settled over me like a challenge, a test I couldn't afford to fail. The raw, ancient energy that emanated from him pressed against me, making my own power stir within, a faint echo in the presence of his overwhelming force. It was like standing before a storm, knowing that a single misstep could unleash its full fury.

"What is it you want from me?" I asked.

His lips curved into a cruel smile, his eyes remaining cold and merciless. "Survival," he answered simply. "If you can survive, you may prove worthy of my son's trust. But do not mistake this for a welcome, Thalia. You are an intruder here—prey for the shadows that hunger for your soul."

The temperature in the room plummeted, a chill that seeped into my bones. But I held my ground, my gaze unwavering. "Can't be as bad as dealing with your son," I retorted.

His smile widened, a flicker of genuine amusement finally reaching his eyes. "Then let the games begin," he said softly, a dark promise underlying his words.

And with that, the world dissolved into a suffocating darkness.

The shadows closed in like icy tendrils, wrapping around me until I felt as if I were suffocating in the void. My body was paralyzed, as if the air itself had turned into a liquid, pressing down on me. There was nothing—no light, no sound—only the pitch-black void that seemed to swallow everything whole. Panic clawed at my throat, a sharp, brutal pain, I tried to fight back, struggling to focus, desperately seeking an anchor in the chaos.

Then, the whispers solidified, morphing into voices, taunting and cruel. I recognized the tone, the sneering laughter of children, sharp and piercing like shards of glass. I was seven years old again —small and alone in a crowded marketplace, the stench of fish and sweat heavy in the air. A group of older children circled me, their faces contorted with mockery. Their fingers, grimy and pointed, jabbed at my patched-up clothes, my unwashed hair.

"Look at the little beggar girl!" one of them sneered, his voice dripping with venom.

"Doesn't she stink?" Another one chimed in, shoving me hard. I stumbled, my hands scraping against the rough cobblestones. Their laughter a chorus of cruelty that echoed through the marketplace, drawing the attention of passersby who stopped to stare, their faces a mixture of amusement and disdain.

My heart pounded against my ribs, a frantic drumbeat against the rising tide of shame and rage. I saw the shadows stir—a dark, protective instinct rising within me, twisting around my small frame, hungry and reckless. But this time, I wasn't just reliving the memory—I was experiencing it with the awareness of my older self, a helpless witness trapped within my own past.

My vision blurred with tears of anger and humiliation, and I saw my younger self lash out, a wild, desperate surge of darkness erupting from me. I lunged at the children, my small hands outstretched, my nails like claws, a primal scream tearing from my throat.

Their laughter turned to screams as they scattered, their eyes wide with terror. But at the last moment, something held me back. The raw, animalistic rage subsided, leaving a hollow ache in its wake. The shadows that had enveloped me retreated, leaving me trembling, my breath ragged, my small body consumed by a wave of shame and self-loathing. The memory faded, but the feeling of shame lingered, a heavy weight that settled in my gut.

The scene shifted, the darkness swirling and reforming. I was older now—a teenager scavenging for scraps in back alleys. The gnawing hunger in my stomach was a constant companion, a dull ache that never subsided. My clothes were threadbare, my body thin and weak from days of surviving on stale bread and stolen fruit. The world was a blur of indifferent faces, people who stepped over me as if I were invisible, their eyes sliding away, their expressions a mixture of pity and disgust. The shame of begging, the desperation that had driven me to steal, the constant fear of being caught—it all washed over me, raw and vivid.

The next memory hit me like a physical blow, a dark wave that crashed over me, leaving me gasping for air. There I was, trapped in a narrow alley, the stench of urine and decay filling my senses. The man's face was a blur, but his hands were all too clear—rough and calloused, gripping my arms with bruising force, pinning me against the damp brick wall.

I struggled, my panic morphing into fury as his hot, alcohol-laced breath assaulted my cheek. My nails raked across his face, my feet lashing out, connecting with whatever they could find. Yet he only laughed at my attempts—a sound that chilled me to the bone. Something within me snapped at that moment. A blinding wave of darkness erupted from me—a raw, uncontrolled force that struck him with deadly precision.

He crumpled to the ground, his body going limp as blood started to pool around him, his eyes staring blankly at the sky. Horror washed over me as I stared at the lifeless form at my feet. My hands trembled, though I couldn't tear my gaze away from the gruesome scene I had created. This was a memory I had deliberately pushed into the recesses of my mind—a dark secret I had buried in the deepest, most inaccessible part of my psyche, locked away behind layers of denial and manufactured normalcy. Yet, there it was, clawing its way to the surface—unbidden and unfiltered—demanding my attention with the relentless persistence of a nightmare that refuses to end.

The guilt and shame were suffocating, a crushing weight that threatened to break me, to splinter my already fractured soul into a million irreparable pieces. I had always known there was something different about me—something dark and dangerous lurking beneath the surface. But I had never imagined, not in my wildest nightmares, that I was capable of taking a life. The realization that I *had* done so—even in self-defense—was a truth I couldn't escape. It was a shadow that would forever taint my soul.

The floodgates of my suppressed memories burst open, unleashing a torrent of agonizing recollections. It wasn't just a passive viewing of the past; it was a visceral reliving, a drowning in the raw sensations of my most traumatic experiences. The sting of the orphanage matron's slap, the bitter taste of stale bread crusts, the gnawing emptiness in my belly, the bone-chilling cold of winter nights spent huddled in doorways, praying for the dawn—each sensation was as vivid, as agonizingly real, as if it were happening in that very moment.

I was trapped in a nightmare of my own making—a horrifying spectacle of my most vulnerable moments. Each memory was a weight, a stone tied to my ankles, dragging me deeper into the abyss of my past. The shadows around me thickened, swirling and forming into monstrous shapes, feeding on my guilt and despair. My body trembled uncontrollably, racked with sobs I couldn't contain. Each gasp for air was a struggle, as if the very atmosphere had turned against me, pressing down on my chest, squeezing the life out of me. My mind teetered on the edge of madness.

This was the demon king's intent—to break me, to shatter my spirit, to leave me a hollow shell. A vacant vessel, drowning in the abyss of my own tormented past. He wanted a puppet, a marionette with severed strings, dancing to his sinister tune. And I was dangerously close to surrendering.

And yet, amidst the chaos of my past, there was a flicker of something else—a stubborn determination that had carried me through the darkest nights. As I sifted through the shattered remnants of my childhood, I found myself clinging to those fragments of strength I had unknowingly gathered along the way. The time I had stood up to a bully twice my size, the nights I had spent staring at the stars, dreaming of a life beyond the confines of my reality, the small, almost insignificant acts of kindness I had shown to others, even when kindness was a luxury I could barely afford. These moments were mine—precious and untarnished—and they were just as much a part of me as the pain. I realized then, with a clarity that startled me, that my past, with all its lurking shadows and deep, jagged scars, had not just molded me into a survivor; it had also laid the groundwork for the person I was destined to become.

The realization was both terrifying and empowering—a dizzying rush of opposing forces. I was a tapestry woven from threads of sorrow and joy, of loss and love—a complex and intricate being shaped. And as I emerged from the murky depths of my memories, blinking in the sudden, almost blinding light, I understood that the darkness within me was not a gaping void to be feared, but a hidden wellspring of power waiting to be harnessed. I was not defined by my past—not anymore—but by the choices I made in the present, by the person I consciously, deliberately chose to become. A surge of raw and untamed force echoed through the very core of my being, igniting a spark that quickly grew into a raging fire.

I would not break.

I would not surrender.

I would rise.

A blinding light erupted from within me, forcing the shadows to recoil. They hissed and writhed, their shadowy tendrils recoiling as if burned by the sudden, intense burst of raw energy. A startled gasp escaped my lips as the light grew stronger—fueled by every painful memory I had confronted, every demon I had faced, every tear I had shed in the lonely silence of my past. It wasn't about erasing the past, about pretending the darkness didn't exist; it was about acknowledging it, accepting it as a part of me, and using it to forge an unbreakable strength within my very core.

With a final, desperate surge of determination, I pushed harder—the light within me blazing like a supernova, expanding outwards until it filled my entire being. It wasn't just light; it was the embodiment of my will, my defiance, my absolute refusal to give up. I felt the oppressive grip of the shadows snap—its hold on me broken, driven back by a force it had clearly never encountered before.

The demon king's expression was no longer one of confident amusement. His eyes were wide with shock and disbelief. A muscle in his jaw twitched, his regal composure cracking under the weight of my unexpected resistance. His voice, when he finally spoke, was low and laced with a fury that rumbled like distant thunder.

"No one has ever resisted my test," the demon king snarled, "No one... except—" His words hung in the air, unfinished, his eyes flickering towards Damon—a silent acknowledgment of his son's past.

I met his gaze, my own eyes blazing with a newfound fury. My body trembled with exhaustion, my legs threatening to buckle beneath me, but my voice rang out, clear and strong, infused with the same light that pulsed through my veins. "Guess I'm not just a *human*, then," I retorted, a smirk twisting my lips despite the exhaustion pulling at me.

The demon king's eyes widened in surprise. The brutal darkness that had threatened to consume me now recoiled, leaving behind a stillness that hummed with raw power—*my* power.

"I have important matters to attend to," he growled. He was annoyed, *thwarted*, and it was glorious. "I will summon you when I am ready." He rose from his throne, his towering figure radiating an aura of power and displeasure, and strode towards a hidden door at the far end of the throne room, dismissing us with a flick of his hand.

I turned, my legs still shaky, my breath coming in ragged, and faced the three brothers. Damon stood closest, his usual mask of stoic control shattered. His dark blue eyes were wide with shock, his lips parted in unspoken questions. It was more than just a surprise; it was a profound awe mingled with a vulnerability I had never seen in him before. For the first time, Damon appeared genuinely at a loss, his carefully constructed walls crumbling.

Zarek, usually so smug and self-assured, stood just behind Damon, his amber eyes alight with raw relief. It was as though a crushing weight had been lifted from his shoulders, his usual arrogance replaced by a genuine admiration. He let out a long, slow whistle, a grin spreading across his face. "I knew you had it in you, Firefly."

But it was Nox's reaction that truly unsettled me. His face was a storm of conflicting emotions, his usual iron control wavering. His emerald eyes blazed with a mixture of rage, fear, and awe. His hands were clenched into fists, his knuckles white, his entire body trembling with barely contained anger.

"You—" Nox began, his finger pointed at me. He seemed to struggle for words, his usual quiet composure shattered. "Do you have any idea..." He trailed off, his hands clenching and unclenching at his sides, the muscles in his arms flexing beneath the fabric of his shirt, "what could have happened? You could have—" He stopped again. He looked like he wanted to shake me, to yell, to do something, anything, to release the torrent of emotions raging within him.

I stepped closer to him, meeting his gaze head-on, the echoes of the demon king's darkness still swirling within me. "I didn't," I said, cutting him off—my voice firm, stronger than I felt, the adrenaline still coursing through my veins. "I made it through, and survived." I wouldn't let him see how close I had come to being consumed by the darkness—how the fear still clung to me like a second skin.

Nox's jaw clenched, the muscles in his cheek twitching. "Barely," he growled. But there was a hint of pride in his gaze, a grudging admiration that warmed me more than I cared to admit. "You're fucking reckless, Thalia. Reckless beyond reason. You could have been lost in there."

I managed a small laugh, the sound shaky but genuine. "I think you mean *impressive*," I countered. "Besides, someone had to put that arrogant demon king in his place."

Zarek snorted from behind me, some of his usual playfulness returning. "Definitely impressive," he agreed with a wink, his eyes flicking towards Damon. "But she's right. She made it through. And in this place, that's not just surviving... it's a statement." He paused, a thoughtful expression crossing his features. "A very loud, very bold statement that I, for one, applaud." He clapped his hands together, the sound echoing slightly in the otherwise silent hallway. "Bravo, Thalia. Encore?"

Damon remained silent, his gaze still fixed on me, a strange intensity burning in its depths. "You surprised him," he murmured, his voice low and husky, "No one does that."

"Except you," I replied, my own gaze searching his, trying to decipher the emotions swirling within. I saw a glimpse of the weight of his past—the burden he carried, the battles he had fought alone in this place of darkness, the battles he still fought within himself, against the demons that clawed at his soul.

"Yes," he admitted, his voice raw with honesty—a vulnerability rarely shown. "Except me." He shifted, the movement subtle but charged with an energy I couldn't quite place. "And that," he added, his eyes locking with mine, "is a problem."

"And why is that a problem, Damon?" I asked, my temper rising. If looks could kill, he would be ash beneath my feet. "Do you seriously think I'm a threat after all of the shit that's happened?"

Damon's mask returned—his assessing, judging mask, the one that made me feel worthless despite everything I've been through. It was infuriating how his view of me affected me, whether I wanted to admit it or not. He didn't trust me, and that distrust—sharp and cold—pricked at my skin like a thousand tiny needles.

He stormed past me, the smoky, bergamot scent of him clinging to the air like a phantom touch. He didn't so much as brush against me, but I could feel his energy, a silent warning, a dark promise that vibrated between us. With a final, dismissive glance over his shoulder—a look that conveyed more disdain than words ever could—he exited the throne room, the heavy doors booming shut behind him, leaving me stewing in the silence.

I clenched my fists, my nails digging into my palms. He really knew how to get under my skin. I was tired of being treated like a threat, a liability. I was more than capable of handling myself. Damon would just have to deal with whatever insecurities he had. It was not my job to coddle him, to soothe his bruised ego. He was a shadow demon, for crying out loud—not a wounded fawn.

"So dramatic," I mumbled—the words escaping before I could stop them, completely forgetting Nox and Zarek were still here.

"Very dramatic, but that's demons for you," Zarek said, a playful smile gracing his lips. He placed a comforting hand on my shoulder, his touch sending a jolt of tingles through me. "I think we're all just tired. Let's go get some rest. We can strategize—and argue with Damon—in the morning."

THE NEXT DAY, AFTER SPENDING THE NIGHT TOGETHER in the same room—an experience that was undeniably awkward, punctuated by Zarek's persistent attempts to convince me to share his bed, his playful nudges and whispered promises of warmth eventually gave way to a pout when I refused. Damon, clearly frustrated by the whole charade, finally snapped, "Just sleep with me, you idiot," before dragging Zarek into his own bed, leaving me blessedly alone. Nox, ever stoic, simply settled into a nearby armchair.

The four of us stepped out into the streets of Damon's homeland. To my surprise, the oppressive darkness I'd anticipated was replaced by something entirely different. The place was alive, vibrant, pulsing with an energy I hadn't felt before. Sunlight, a warm, honeyed gold, filtered through the twisting branches of towering, ancient trees. People moved with purpose and ease, chatting and laughing, their voices weaving a comforting harmony that filled the air. It was almost impossible to believe this was the same place we had entered.

Stalls lined the main streets, overflowing with exotic fruits, gleaming trinkets, and hand woven tapestries. Children darted through the crowds, their carefree laughter echoing against the dark, polished stone facades of the buildings. Even the colors seemed more vivid here. The air hummed with a subtle magic—a gentle caress against my skin.

Damon walked beside me, his expression softer than I'd ever seen it. He moved with a relaxed familiarity, greeting a few passersby with curt nods and a quiet word or two. I could feel his pride in his homeland—a silent, steady thrum emanating from him. Zarek had his usual casual stride, his amber eyes sparkling with mischief as he noticed my open awe. "Not what you were expecting, was it?" he murmured, leaning in just close enough for only me to hear, his warm breath tickling my ear.

"No, not at all," I admitted, my gaze sweeping over a group of performers setting up in a nearby square. It was like the entire kingdom had transformed overnight. I caught sight of Nox a few steps ahead, his eyes scanning the crowds—always on guard. Even amidst the laughter and music, his posture remained tense, his senses attuned to any potential threat. Despite the apparent peacefulness, there was an undercurrent here—a reminder of the power that lay just beneath the surface.

"Don't let the beauty fool you," Damon said, "This place has its dangers. It's not always this... serene." He looked at me then, his blue eyes intense, as if trying to convey something deeper.

I nodded, feeling a mix of emotions swirling within me as we continued walking towards an open park. It was a beautiful space, with lush grass, clusters of wildflowers, and a fountain at its center. There were families scattered across the park—some having picnics, sharing laughter and stories, others watching as children played tag. The air was filled with the sweet scent of blooming jasmine and the gentle melody of a nearby street musician.

For a moment, I allowed myself to let my guard down, the vibrant energy of the park washing over me like a balm—it was a perfect illusion of serenity. I almost wanted to believe that this was all there was to Damon's world—that the shadows and danger were merely figments of my imagination.

"So, what now?" I asked, turning to the three men beside me.

Zarek gave me a grin, his eyes glinting with mischief. "Well, that depends, Firefly. We could show you more of the city, introduce you to some of the... interesting characters that reside here, or maybe take a detour somewhere more... exciting," he purred, his voice laced with a playful suggestiveness.

Nox, who had been quiet until now, shot Zarek a warning look. "We need to be careful, Z. We're not here for sightseeing," he said, his emerald eyes scanning the perimeter of the park. "Remember why we're here. We have a job to do."

Damon nodded in agreement, his gaze drifting over the park, assessing every shadow and every movement. "Nox is right. We can't afford to let our guard down, not even for a second. But..." His expression softened for a moment, his blue eyes meeting mine with a hint of understanding. "There's no harm in taking a moment to breathe."

I smiled, appreciating the sentiment. "A moment, then," I said, letting my gaze wander over the serene scene, trying to burn the image into my memory. "Just one moment to pretend everything's normal—that I'm not caught in some bizarre, otherworldly adventure."

Zarek chuckled, his grin widening. "Normal? I don't think any of us have ever been normal, Thalia. Not even close. But sure, let's pretend." He winked at me, and I couldn't help but laugh, the tension easing just a bit, replaced by a flicker of genuine amusement.

The four of us lingered by the fountain. For a brief time, we allowed ourselves to simply exist—together, without the weight of the unspoken threat hanging over us like a dark cloud.

The hours passed more quickly than I realized. For a brief time, my world felt normal, almost... peaceful. But like a fragile bubble, the peace shattered. It started with a flicker in Damon's expression—a subtle tightening of his jaw that I probably wouldn't have noticed if I hadn't been watching him so closely. Then, as if drawn to his unease, shadows began to slither across the ground toward him, coiling and uncoiling like restless serpents.

"Father's calling," Damon muttered, an almost imperceptible eye roll hinting at his frustration. He glanced back at us, his voice lowering. "Looks like playtime's over. We need to head back."

The shadows—now thicker and darker—coiled around his wrist like a living bracelet, pulsing with a faint, inner light. He sighed, a heavy sound that seemed to carry the weight of the world, mumbling something under his breath that I couldn't make out. With a last, lingering look at the fountain, we turned and made our way back to the castle. The warmth of the afternoon seemed to evaporate with each step we took.

"WHAT IS IT THAT YOU NEED, DAMON?" ASTAROTH, Damon's father, asked, his voice echoing through the grand hall as we entered.

I knew Damon, Nox, and Zarek wanted to keep me out of this discussion. They had tried to dismiss me, saying it wasn't my concern—a matter best left to the Shadow Kingdom's inner workings. But after everything I had endured—after the pain, the violation of my very being—I needed answers, I needed to know the name of the bastard responsible.

"As you know, Arethax is coming. We could use your support, Father," his tone both respectful and commanding. His words were sharp, each syllable carrying a weight that made it clear this was not a casual request. His father studied him for a long moment, his dark eyes like chips of obsidian, before his gaze shifted to me—a flicker of something unreadable in their depths.

"You really should stop playing around, Damon," Astaroth said, his tone almost dismissive, a hint of amusement lacing his words. "It's a waste of time. You know that eventually, when you're strong enough, you'll be next in line to rule this kingdom." The smile that spread across his face—slow and predatory—made my stomach twist. It was a smile that promised power and cruelty in equal measure.

Damon didn't flinch, his expression unwavering—a mask of controlled fury. "You and I both know that *you* will be next. Arethax will come for you. Why not use the resources from Nexara before it's overtaken like the other realms?"

A shiver ran up my spine at his words. Other realms had already fallen? Just how powerful was this Arethax? The weight of the situation really settled over me. The stakes were higher than I had imagined.

Astaroth's eyes narrowed slightly, the amusement fading to be replaced by something colder, harder. "Hm." He turned his gaze back to me, as if evaluating me, weighing me up like a piece of meat in a butcher's shop.

"I will consider it," he finally said, his voice carrying an edge of disdain—a casual dismissal that grated on my nerves. "And when the time comes, you will know my decision."

A bitter laugh escaped me before I could stop it. Damon's head whipped toward me, his eyes flashing with a warning, a silent reprimand. But I couldn't help myself. The sheer arrogance of him—the casual disregard for the impending doom—was too much to bear. "Are you fucking kidding me?" I said, my voice laced with disbelief. "I get that you're supposed to be the devil or whatever, the big, bad ruler of the Shadow Kingdom, but that's so low, even for you."

Astaroth's eyes widened slightly at my outburst, but I didn't care. I had faced worse than his disapproval. I had stared into the abyss and survived.

"When *it* comes for your realm, when your precious Shadow Kingdom crumbles around you, don't expect our help," I snapped, turning on my heel, unable to bear his presence a moment longer. I walked out of the hall, my heart pounding a furious rhythm against my ribs, leaving behind a very pissed-off Damon, a surprised Nox, and a Zarek who was desperately trying to keep a straight face, his lips twitching with suppressed amusement.

The heavy oak doors closed behind me with a resounding thud, a final punctuation mark on my defiance. And then I heard Astaroth's voice echo from within, cold and sharp as shattered ice. "I suggest you get your plaything out of here, now, Damon." His words were loud, meant for me to hear, but I didn't pause. I didn't even flinch. I kept moving, my steps steady and resolute, refusing to let his words sink any deeper than they already had. They bounced off me like pebbles against a stone wall.

The cold air of the hallway met me like a slap. I took a deep breath, trying to steady myself, to calm the storm raging within. I knew I had crossed a line—broken some unspoken rule of courtly etiquette—but I couldn't stand there and let him belittle everything we were trying to do, dismiss the very real threat looming over us. Not when so much was at stake. Not when the fate of entire realms hung in the balance.

Chapter 26

Thalia's POV

"You really couldn't keep your mouth shut," Damon growled, grabbing my arm and pulling me through the shadows with a force that made me stumble. Zarek and Nox followed close behind, their expressions mirroring my own surprise at Damon's sudden action. The world blurred around me —a dizzying swirl of dark energy—until we abruptly stopped, the familiar sight of their home coming into view.

"Nope," I said, popping the 'p' for dramatics, trying to regain some semblance of control after being manhandled through the shadows. "And for the record, it makes perfect sense you are the way that you are. Considering who spawned you, I'm only surprised you're not worse. Actually, no. I take that back. You know, I didn't think I could meet someone more revolting than you," I snapped, the words tumbling out before I could stop them. A slight pang of regret echoed in my chest at my own harshness, but I quickly pushed it down.

"Fuck, Thalia, you have no idea what you just did," Damon's words were sharp, like shards of glass, as he released my arm. It was almost as if he needed the physical contact to anchor himself, to control the storm brewing within him. I opened my mouth to retort, to fire back another sarcastic remark—but the look in his eyes silenced me. It wasn't just anger; there was something deeper, something raw and vulnerable that looked almost like fear.

"You put yourself in danger back there," Damon finally said. "Astaroth... he doesn't take disrespect lightly. Especially not from someone like you—someone he sees as beneath him, insignificant."

I crossed my arms, trying to mask the sudden unease his words brought. "Well, someone had to say it. If someone like *me* had to say it, then so be it. I'm not just going to stand there and let him act like we're insignificant. We're not."

Zarek, who had been lingering nearby, a silent observer to the escalating tension, stepped forward, his expression a mixture of amusement and concern. "You have guts, Thalia, I'll give you that. Real firecracker. But Damon isn't exaggerating. Astaroth isn't someone you can just mouth off to. He's dangerous, powerful, and holds grudges."

Nox nodded in agreement. "Next time, think before you speak. We're walking a tightrope here, and we can't afford any more risks —especially not ones caused by impulsive outbursts."

I swallowed, the weight of their words settling in my stomach like a lead ball. Maybe I had been reckless, maybe I should have held my tongue, but I couldn't bring myself to regret it. He needed to know that we weren't just pawns in his twisted game. Still, the genuine worry etched on their faces, made my chest tighten—a pang of guilt mixing with the remnants of my outburst.

"Fine," I said, my eyes rolling involuntarily—my usual defensive mechanism kicking in. "I'll try to be more careful. But I won't just sit back and let him—or anyone, for that matter—walk all over me. I've had enough of being treated like shit."

Zarek clapped his hands together, the sound echoing in the sudden quiet, breaking the tension that had settled over us like a thick fog. "Alright, enough of this heavy stuff. It's Friday night, and I think we could all use a drink. Or several. My treat." He winked, that playful glint returning to his amber eyes. He had a knack for lightening the mood, even when I felt like I was drowning in it. "How about we head inside and forget about all of this for a while?" He gestured towards the house.

"THALIA!" A female voice called from the woods, making me jump. A dark shape blurred in front of me—Nox, his emerald eyes scanning the tree line, his body coiled tight as a spring. "THALIA!" It called again, closer now.

"Is that... Elara?" I asked, peering around Nox's broad frame. He stood like a sentinel. He'd been strangely protective, almost hovering, ever since the Wonders of Nexara. I supposed it made sense; he and that student healer had found me practically drained of life. I was honestly surprised that beast hadn't finished me off when it had the chance. There must have been some powerful protection spell woven into the arena during the games—something that even that monstrous creature couldn't break through.

I was right about the voice. Elara and James burst through the thick foliage, both of them skidding to a halt as they took in the sight before them: me standing behind Nox, who looked ready to pounce, while Zarek and Damon flanked us, radiating an almost palpable animosity. Their eyes—narrowed and sharp—were fixed on my friends, their stances tense and guarded.

"Um, Thalia?" Elara's eyes darted between the three of them, her brows drawing together as she crossed her arms over her chest. "Where the hell have you been? We've been looking all over for you! And why do the three of you look like you're about to start a bloodbath in some random field?"

"Elara, hi—sorry—it's a long story," I said, stepping around Nox. He shifted slightly, a low growl rumbling in his chest. As I walked over, I glanced over my shoulder to see all three of them glaring at James and Elara. Their faces all held an underlying possessiveness that made my stomach flip.

"Well, you can explain on our way back to the academy," Elara responded, clearly not pleased with my vague answer.

"That's if she *wants* to go back," Zarek's voice carried, and I could hear the smirk behind his words. Elara's eyebrows shot up, and my cheeks started to warm. James did *not* look amused, his glare fixed on them, his jaw tight.

"Oh, she *wants* to go back," James said, his voice hard, stepping forward slightly, as if to place himself between me and the Shadow Brothers. "Enough with whatever this is, Thalia. You belong at the academy, not... whatever *this* is." He gestured vaguely at the three of them, his disapproval evident.

I hesitated, looking between them, my gaze flickering from James's tight jaw to the brothers' guarded stances. I could feel the tension rising again, a wave of protectiveness and possessiveness emanating from both sides.

"Enough," I finally said, my voice firm, trying to inject a sense of calm into the charged atmosphere. "I'm going back to the academy. It's my choice. You all need to calm down." This ridiculous standoff was getting us nowhere.

James's expression softened slightly, and he gave me a small nod, his shoulders relaxing a fraction. Elara sighed, relief washing over her features. Damon exchanged a glance with Zarek and Nox—a silent communication passing between them—and they stepped back.

"Alright," Zarek said, shrugging casually, his usual playful demeanor returning—though a hint of possessiveness still lingered in his amber eyes. "Lead the way, Firefly."

I rolled my eyes at the nickname, but a small smile tugged at my lips despite myself. As we began to walk back towards the academy, I felt a strange sense of balance between the two worlds I was caught in—one of burgeoning friendship and unwavering loyalty with James and Elara, the other of danger, uncertainty, and an undeniable pull towards the enigmatic Shadow Brothers.

"What the actual fuck, Thalia?" Elara whispered, her voice laced with disbelief, glancing over her shoulder. I followed her gaze; Nox and Zarek were trailing about thirty feet behind us, their presence a constant reminder of the complicated dynamics that surrounded me. "Why are they following you like guard dogs?" she asked, her tone a mix of amusement and genuine curiosity.

"Um, like I said, it's a long story, but I promise I'm good," I said, though I couldn't help but feel a pang of disappointment not seeing Damon. I supposed he had enough of the chaos I had caused for him today, specifically. The thought stung more than I cared to admit.

"Doesn't seem that way," James muttered, irritation evident in his voice. "You disappear after the Wonders of Nexara, we were worried sick. All we heard was that you were safe, and that's it. No explanation, no contact. Classes started a few days ago." He crossed his arms, his brow furrowed in concern.

I sighed, the weight of their concern pressing down on me. I understood why they were upset, but it still felt overwhelming to be questioned like this—especially when I couldn't explain everything. Not yet, anyway. "I know, and I'm sorry," I said softly. "It was complicated, and I couldn't get word to you guys. Trust me, if I could have, I would have. But I swear, I'm okay." Physically, at least. The emotional turmoil was a different story.

Elara studied me for a moment, her fiery eyes searching mine before her gaze softened. "You better be, Thalia. I don't know what kind of mess you've gotten yourself into, but just remember we're here for you." She looped her arm through mine, giving me a reassuring squeeze. "No matter how crazy it gets."

James still looked skeptical, but he gave me a tight smile. "Just... be careful. They—" He pointed back, making it obvious he was talking about Nox and Zarek, "—are dangerous. I know they seem protective, but there's a darkness to them, Thalia. I'm just worried about you."

"I get it, I get it. I'll be careful, but they're not *out* to get me. They've helped me a lot, actually." My tone was harsh, but I felt the need to defend them—a surprising surge of protectiveness rising within me after everything they'd done for me.

We continued walking, the tension easing slightly as Elara and James filled me in on everything I had missed at the academy. It was comforting to hear their voices, to know that despite everything, I still had friends who cared about me. As we approached the gothic structure of the academy, I glanced back at Nox and Zarek. They kept their distance, almost blending into the shadows of the surrounding trees, but I could feel their eyes on me.

"I'm going to talk to them before heading back to my dorm, but I'll see you guys tomorrow?" I asked, smiling at Elara and James as they glanced at Nox and Zarek for a moment before nodding. They both gave me a big hug before leaving me with my *two guard dogs*.

"We aren't guard dogs, I hope you know I could hear everything," Nox muttered, glaring at Elara and James's retreating forms as he approached. "If they weren't your friends, that would've gone differently."

A laugh escaped my lips at the grumpy Nox before me. Zarek joined in with my laughter, his melodic chuckle echoing around us, causing Nox to turn his glare—now softened with a hint of exasperation—towards us. "What's so funny?" he grumbled, crossing his arms over his broad chest.

"I know, you two aren't *really* guard dogs," I chuckled. "But I'm going to head back to my dorm now. I appreciate everything you guys have done for me—truly—but it's probably best I give you all some space. I did just crash into your secluded lives," I added, the words feeling heavy on my tongue. I didn't want to leave the surprising comfort I felt with them, but I'm sure all of them—especially Damon—wanted their space back.

"No way are we leaving you alone," Zarek stated firmly. He glanced at Nox, another silent conversation passing between them. "If *you* want to stay at the academy, then fine. We can stay here, too." He shrugged as if it were the simplest decision in the world.

"Not only do you have Arethax after you," Nox added, "but you royally pissed off Astaroth."

"We have a room at the academy," Zarek continued, casually draping his arm over my shoulder as he started to lead us towards the main buildings. "You can stay there with us, or we can camp outside your room. Up to you, Firefly."

"No way we would fit in my dorm," I responded, shaking my head. I tried to picture the two of them—all six-foot-plus of sculpted muscle and dark, brooding energy—crammed into that tiny space with me. My little twin bed and minuscule desk were hardly enough room for one, let alone three. And the thought of sharing such close quarters with *them*—with Zarek's playful taunts and whatever was going on between Nox and me... My cheeks flushed at the image, but I quickly pushed it aside.

"We can go to your dorms if my *guard dogs* have to be with me," I added, taking a jab at them.

As we approached the men's dorms, I started to feel my anxiety rising. Students passed us, their eyes widening as they took in the sight of Nox and Zarek flanking me. Whispers followed, and I could feel their curious gazes burning into my back. Nox and Zarek seemed completely unfazed by the attention, but I was not used to it.

Reaching the top floor, we entered their dorm. The deep gray walls, accented with soft lighting and polished herringbone floors created a darkly warm ambiance. A chandelier lit the intricate ceiling moldings. An antique mirror reflected the soft light, creating the illusion of more space. At the hallway's end, a plush velvet armchair sat beside a tall, arched window. Its dark curtains were open, revealing a breathtaking view of the academy grounds below.

"This is your dorm? I mean, I shouldn't be surprised, it seems like you three are above normal standards." I said with a laugh, glancing between the two of them. "It's more like a royal suite than a dorm room. Seriously, a chandelier in what, your living room? It's ridiculous." I shook my head, still taking it all in.

Zarek grinned, nudging me lightly. "What did you expect? We're not exactly like everyone else here."

"And why's that?" I asked, genuinely curious.

His amber eyes flickered down to my lips, and back up to my eyes. "Because we don't pretend to be something we're not. Unlike most people here, we know exactly who we are—and what we want. "

I narrowed my eyes, sensing there was more he wasn't saying. "And what exactly are *you*?"

He leaned in a little closer, invading my personal space. "Monsters, Thalia," he stated, his voice low and husky. "We're monsters.

But at least we're honest about it." A smirk played on his lips, challenging me to react.

Nox moved past us, his footsteps silent as he gestured for me to follow him deeper into the *suite*. I trailed behind him, trying not to laugh at Zarek—his dramatics were almost too much to take seriously, despite the underlying truth in his words.

"You can take my room," Zarek offered as we reached a set of double doors. "Or, you know, we could share." He gave me a playful wink, a smirk playing on his lips, earning an eye roll from Nox.

"She's staying where she's comfortable," Nox said firmly, giving Zarek a warning look that clearly told him to drop it. I bit back a smile at the scene before me.

"Thank you. Both of you. I really appreciate it," I said sincerely. This was all so unexpected, and honestly a little overwhelming.

Zarek gave me a mock salute. "Anything for our favorite troublemaker."

"We'll go get some food. Make yourself at home," Nox said, his emerald-green eyes meeting mine for a moment before he pulled Zarek with him back towards the entrance, leaving me alone in the hallway.

As they left, I stepped further into Zarek's room, the door clicking softly behind me. It was the exact opposite of his room back at their house. The high arched window stretched almost from floor to ceiling, framing a breathtaking view of the academy and the mountains beyond. The sky outside was painted in the last colors of dusk, soft blues and greys blending together.

A large bed, draped in black and silver, boasted a gothic headboard carved with twisting vines and mythical creatures. The room echoed Zarek's personality: elegant, darkly beautiful, powerful yet refined. Against one wall, a dark oak desk held neat stacks of books and papers.

Moving to the window seat that was built into the alcove beneath the window, I settled into the seat, the plush cushions sinking beneath my weight. The world beyond seemed peaceful—the complete opposite to everything that had happened in the last couple days. The attack, the revelations about my powers, the growing connection with Nox, Zarek, and Damon—well, not really Damon. But even with his constant hostility, there was a flicker of *something* there. It was all a whirlwind of emotions that I was still trying to process.

It was strange being here. Just a few months ago, I wouldn't have imagined myself sitting in the room of someone like Zarek, feeling this sense of... belonging. My life had changed in ways I was still struggling to understand, but here, I could almost believe that I was exactly where I was meant to be.

A soft knock on the door broke me from my thoughts. Zarek peeked in, his amber eyes catching mine. "Comfortable?"

I nodded, a small smile playing on my lips. "Yeah, it's... really nice here."

He stepped in, leaning against the doorframe. "Glad you think so. It's got a certain charm, right? Dark, mysterious—just like me." He winked.

I laughed, shaking my head. "Cocky much?"

"But you love it," he teased, his grin widening, revealing a flash of white teeth against his tanned skin.

I didn't reply, just rolled my eyes playfully and looked back out the window. He didn't need an answer, and we both knew it. Even though he was teasing, a part of me couldn't deny the truth in his statement. There was an undeniably pull I felt towards him

—his confidence, his playful nature, and the way his eyes seemed to hold a thousand secrets.

"Anyway," Zarek said after a moment, his voice a little more serious. "If you need anything, just let me or Nox know, alright? You're safe here."

I turned back to him, meeting his gaze. The sincerity in his amber eyes made my chest tighten with an unexpected warmth. "You can stay, if you want." The words slipped out before I could process them, surprising even me. "But I thought you were going with Nox?" I added, suddenly feeling self-conscious about the invitation.

He gave me a reassuring nod, his lips softening into something more genuine. "And miss getting some more time with you? Nah, he's fine. Besides," he added with a wink, "he's probably off brooding somewhere anyway."

I leaned back against the window seat, looking out at the darkening sky as Zarek took a seat across from me. The fading light cast long shadows across the room, giving the already gothic architecture an even more mysterious feel.

The silence between us wasn't awkward, but charged with an unspoken understanding that was both exhilarating and a little terrifying. A strange sense of peace settled over me—a feeling I hadn't experienced in a long time. I found myself glancing at Zarek, taking in his relaxed posture and the way his expression softened when he wasn't trying to keep up his charming facade. There was a vulnerability in his eyes that I hadn't noticed before, a quiet strength that drew me in.

"You really mean it, don't you?" I finally said, breaking the silence. "That I'm safe here. With you and Nox."

He nodded slowly, his gaze intense as he looked at me. "Yeah, I do. I know we might not be the easiest to trust, or understand—especially Damon," he added. "But one thing you should know, Thalia, is that we take care of our own. And you're one of us now."

An unexpected swell of emotion rose in my chest, making me swallow hard. It was a feeling of belonging, a sense of connection that I craved but never thought I'd find. I looked away, my gaze returning to the window. "And why am I one of you now?" I asked, my voice barely above a whisper.

Zarek smiled, a genuine one this time, free of his usual mischief. "Because whether you like it or not, you're stuck with us."

I let out a laugh, shaking my head. "You'll get sick of me eventually," I teased, but a part of me hoped he wouldn't.

He leaned back, crossing his arms behind his head. "You say that now. Wait until Nox starts training with you. He's relentless." He paused, a mischievous grin spreading across his face. "You'll get sick of us before we do you."

I groaned, rolling my eyes. "Please tell me you're exaggerating. Damon's bad enough."

Zarek laughed, the sound echoing softly in the quiet room. "You'll see. But hey," he winked, "I'll be right there with you, making it all a bit more bearable. Besides, someone needs to make sure they don't work you too hard."

"Come in!" Zarek called as we heard a knock at the door. The wood creaked open revealing Nox.

"The food's here. For the love of the gods, Zarek, can you give the girl some space?" Nox sighed, his emerald eyes meeting mine briefly before returning to Zarek.

"She invited me here, so no," Zarek retorted, standing up and offering me a hand. "Come on, Firefly, let's eat. I'm starving."

AFTER DINNER, I DECIDED A QUICK SHOWER WAS IN order, wanting to wash away the lingering stress of the last few days. I rummaged through Zarek's drawers and found one of his shirts and a pair of boxers, deciding they would do for the night. The shirt was oversized, the soft fabric falling comfortably around my thighs. I couldn't help but smile at the faint, familiar scent of Zarek clinging to the material.

I started to brush through my tangled, rat's nest of hair, wincing at the knots, when I heard a soft knock at the door, followed by a moment of expectant silence.

"You can come in," I called out, turning my head towards the sound, the brush still in my hand.

The door opened slowly, revealing Nox framed in the doorway. He looked different in the dimness—less intimidating, the sharp edges of his usual demeanor softened, replaced by a hint of vulnerability. His gaze flicked to the shirt I was wearing, and for a split second, I thought I saw the ghost of a smile play on his lips before his expression returned to its usual form.

"Hey," I said softly, offering him a small smile. "Everything okay?"

He seemed to hesitate, shuffling his feet slightly, before stepping further into the room with a nod, closing the door gently behind him. "I just wanted to check on you. Make sure you're comfortable," he murmured, his voice lower than usual.

I set the brush down on the dresser, turning fully to face him. "I'm good, really. Thank you for everything today. I know I made things... complicated," I admitted, thinking back to the confrontation with Astaroth and the strange new power that had surged through me.

Nox shrugged, his gaze softening slightly, the tension seeming to ease from his shoulders. "Complicated is kind of our thing, isn't it?" he replied with a hint of dry humor. "Besides, you handled yourself well. Astaroth is... difficult. But you stood your ground."

A small, self-deprecating laugh escaped me. "Yeah, well, I don't think he liked that very much. He didn't seem too pleased with me—nor did Damon."

Nox's lips twitched, the hint of a smile returning. "No, probably not. But you showed him you're not afraid. That's important."

There was a moment of comfortable silence, and I found myself studying him—the way his shoulders seemed a little less tense, the way his eyes held something other than their usual guarded look. There was a warmth in his gaze that I hadn't noticed before, a subtle shift in his demeanor that made my heart beat a little faster.

"You know," I began, my voice softer, almost hesitant, "you don't have to keep looking out for me like this. I mean, I appreciate it— more than you know, but..." I trailed off, unsure how to finish the sentence.

Nox shook his head, cutting me off gently. "I want to. We look out for each other. That's what we do. And besides," he added with a hint of teasing, "you're not as much trouble as Zarek is."

I laughed, the sound light and genuine, the tension easing from my chest. "Well, that's a relief. I was starting to worry about my reputation."

"Get some rest. Tomorrow will be another long day. And if you need anything... we're right here." He said, his eyes locking with mine.

I nodded, "Thanks, Nox. For everything."

He gave me one last nod, his eyes lingering on me for a moment longer before turning and heading towards the door. Just before he left, he glanced back at me, his expression softening—a genuine smile finally gracing his lips. "And, Thalia?"

"Yeah?" I replied, my voice barely a whisper.

"That shirt suits you," he said, his voice low and husky.

With that, he slipped out of the room, closing the door quietly behind him, leaving me with a lingering smile on my face. I climbed into Zarek's bed, pulling the covers around me, and let myself relax, the tension finally draining from my body.

Sleep took over fast, but my dreams were far from peaceful. They were chaotic, swirling with dark images and unsettling whispers. Astaroth didn't let up after I fought off his darkness— no, he retaliated instantly. His shadowy presence invaded my subconscious, twisting everything familiar into a grotesque mockery.

The nightmare began in a twisted version of the room I had just fallen asleep in. Shadows crept along the walls, taking on monstrous shapes, their claws scraping against the stone. The sconces flickered erratically, as if struggling against an unseen force. I stood there, alone, with an overwhelming sense of dread pressing down on me—suffocating me. The walls started to close in, the familiar carvings distorting, turning into faces, each one whispering my name—a chorus of chilling whispers that echoed in my mind.

I turned, desperately trying to find an escape, my heart pounding against my ribs, when I saw him—Astaroth. His eyes burned with an unnatural light, a cold fire that seemed to sear into my soul, and a cruel smile played across his lips. He moved towards me, his form dark and imposing, tendrils of shadow swirling around him like hungry serpents. I tried to call for help, but my voice wouldn't come. My throat felt tight, constricted by an invisible force, and fear wrapped around me like a vice, squeezing the air from my lungs.

The door burst open, splintering wood flying through the air, and Zarek appeared—his face a mask of fury. He charged at Astaroth, a warrior facing a demon, but the shadows lashed out sending him crashing into the wall with a sickening thud. I screamed, my voice finally breaking free—a desperate cry of terror. Shadows wrapped around my body, tightening, holding me in place, their icy touch searing my skin. Nox and Damon appeared next, both of them fighting their way through the oppressive darkness, their movements a blur of motion, their eyes filled with a primal rage as they fought to reach me—to break the hold of the shadows. But Astaroth only laughed, a sound that echoed through the room, a sound that chilled me to the bone.

He raised his hand, his fingers long and skeletal, and the shadows wrapped around Nox and Damon, lifting them off the ground like puppets on invisible strings. They struggled, their faces contorted in pain, their muscles straining against the suffocating grip as Astaroth's hold tightened. I felt helpless as I watched them fight, unable to do anything but witness their torment.

"You think you can defy me, little girl?" Astaroth's voice was cold, mocking, dripping with contempt. "*You* are nothing. *They* are nothing." His words were like poisoned daggers, piercing my heart.

I tried to fight back, tried to summon any power, but it was like trying to grasp smoke. My hands felt empty, my body weak, drained of all energy. The shadows tightened around me, pulling me towards Astaroth, his smile growing wider, more predatory.

"You will never be safe," he whispered, his voice echoing in my mind—a chilling promise that burrowed deep into my soul.

I awoke with a gasp, my heart pounding, my body covered in a cold sweat. The room was dark, the only sound was the soft rustle of the curtains as a breeze drifted in from the open window. I sat up, my hands trembling as I ran them through my hair, trying to shake off the chilling echo of Astaroth's voice.

The door creaked open, and Zarek rushed in, his eyes wide with worry, his face etched with concern. "Thalia? Are you okay? I thought I heard you scream."

I looked at him, my eyes still wide with the remnants of the night-mare, my breath coming in ragged gasps. "It... I'm fine," I whispered, my voice barely audible.

Zarek crossed the room in an instant, sitting down on the edge of the bed. He reached out, his hand warm and comforting on my shoulder. "It was just a dream," he said, his voice gentle, soothing, his eyes searching for mine, trying to reassure me.

I nodded, trying to steady my breathing. "It felt so real," I admitted, my voice breaking. Zarek pulled me into a hug, his arms wrapping around me tightly.

The door opened again, and Nox and Damon appeared, their faces mirroring Zarek's concern. Nox's eyes softened as he took in the scene, his usual quiet demeanor replaced with a gentle worry, while Damon stepped closer, his expression guarded but his eyes betraying a flicker of worry. "Nightmare?" Damon asked, his voice quiet, unusually soft.

I nodded, pulling away from Zarek slightly, though his arm remained around my waist. Nox stepped forward like he wanted to comfort me, but stopped—hesitant—his hands clenching and unclenching at his sides.

Damon's jaw clenched as he forced out, "It was just a dream."

I took a deep breath, "Sorry to freak you guys out," I apologized, my voice still shaky. "This is why I should've just gone to my dorm. I'm fine, I promise."

Damon nodded curtly, his gaze intense. "Get some rest."

Nox and Damon turned to leave, but Zarek stayed, his arm still around me. "Do you want me to stay? Just until you fall asleep?" he asked softly, his voice a gentle caress.

I hesitated for a moment, weighing the comfort of his presence against the fear of burdening him, before nodding—unable to deny the solace his presence offered. "Yeah... I think I'd like that."

Zarek smiled—a small, reassuring smile that chased away some of the lingering shadows, as he moved to the other side of the bed, pulling me back against him. I closed my eyes, focusing on the steady rhythm of his breathing, the warmth of his arms around me, the solid reality of his presence anchoring me to the present. Slowly, the tension began to ease, the fear began to recede, and I allowed myself to drift back into sleep.

Chapter 27

Thalia's POV

The sun filtered through the window, waking me up. Zarek was still sound asleep beside me, his arm wrapped around me in a tight, possessive hold. I was nestled against his side, feeling small in comparison to him. He looked so peaceful—his lips parted slightly, his dark hair tousled into a charmingly messy bedhead. I found my gaze drifting to the tattoos that covered his chest—a mesmerizing web of designs that started just below his collarbone, flowing down and across his pecs and shoulders. The black ink moved fluidly across his skin, some spiraling down his muscled arms, wrapping around his biceps like dark vines, and trailing down to his forearms, disappearing beneath the edge of the sheets. The tattoos seemed to tell a story, a silent narrative etched across his body. I couldn't resist the urge to gently trace my fingers along the lines, captivated by the artistry and the way the ink seemed to suit him so perfectly.

Zarek stirred, his eyes fluttering open as a lazy smile formed. "As nice as this feels—and as much as I don't want you to stop—you better be careful before this escalates," he teased, his voice a low rumble against my fingertips.

I felt my cheeks flush instantly, realizing he was turned on, my fingers freezing mid-trace. "Oh, uh—sorry," I stammered, trying to pull away, but Zarek's hold only tightened.

"No need to apologize, Firefly," he said, his thumb gently stroking my back, sending a wave of tingles through me. "I just didn't expect to wake up like this. Not that I'm complaining."

I rolled my eyes, trying to hide my embarrassment, but the heat in my cheeks betrayed me. Zarek's grin widened, and he gave a dramatic sigh, his bare chest rising and falling beneath my hand. "We should just stay like this all day." His tone, laced with playful suggestion, made my blush deepen.

I pushed against his chest, attempting to put some space between us, but Zarek held me firmly in place, his expression softening. The playful glint in his amber eyes faded, replaced by something softer, more sincere. "Hey," he said gently, his eyes locking onto mine, all traces of teasing gone. "You doing okay? After last night?"

I hesitated, then nodded. "Yeah, I think so. It was just... intense. I just have a lot to process."

His smile softened, and he brushed a strand of hair away from my face. "Good. I'm here if you need me to scare away nightmares or just... be a pillow." He chuckled.

His thumb brushed against my cheek as his eyes studied my lips. I could feel my heartbeat quicken—his touch gentle but firm, sending a tingling sensation through my skin. Those mesmerizing amber eyes locked into mine, like he was searching for... permission, maybe?

My body moved on its own, drawn in by an irresistible force. I closed the distance between us, pressing my lips to his. A spark ignited the moment our lips met, a wildfire of heat spreading through me, consuming me. His arms tightened around my waist, pulling me closer as he deepened the kiss. It began as a soft explo-ration—tender and hesitant—but quickly escalated, fueled by a hunger neither of us could deny. The way his lips moved against mine—soft yet firm—melting me against him. His fingers tight-ened on my waist, eliciting a moan from deep within me. The kiss grew more demanding, more urgent—each touch, each move-ment a testament to the growing need between us.

His hand slid down my back, dipping lower, cupping my ass, pulling me flush against the undeniable evidence of his arousal. A gasp escaped my lips, a jolt of pure electricity shooting through me at the feeling of him against me. He groaned, his lips trailing down my neck. His scent—that intoxicating mix of ocean and cedar—filled my senses, making it hard to think, hard to breathe.

"Zarek," I breathed, my voice barely a whisper, my fingers tangling in his dark hair, holding on as if he were my lifeline.

He hummed against my skin, his hand moving between my legs, his fingers finding my center through the thin fabric of my boxers. A light moan escaped my lips, my body already thrumming with anticipation, craving more. He slowly started to tease me, circling my clit with his thumb, the heat radiating from his touch almost unbearable.

"Tell me what you want, Firefly," he murmured, his voice husky, sending a wave of goosebumps across my skin. The words were a challenge, an invitation—but I couldn't think straight, the words caught in my throat, trapped by the rising tide of pleasure. A strangled whimper escaped instead, a desperate plea. The pleasure was a sharp, sweet ache, coiling low in my belly, tightening with each passing second, each tantalizing touch. I felt him chuckle against my neck, the vibration a delicious torment as he continued to tease me, the friction building the fire within me, higher and higher.

A gasp left my lips as Zarek flipped us, him now hovering over me, his amber eyes burning into mine—filled with a mixture of desire and amusement. His hand moved back to my center, his fingers sliding inside the waistband of my boxers, his touch sending a fresh jolt of electricity through me. His head dipped back down to kiss my neck, his lips trailing fire as they moved lower, nipping at the sensitive skin just above my collarbone. Another whimper left my lips—his touch consuming, all-encompassing, blotting out everything but the feeling of him.

"You like that, Firefly?" he whispered, his voice rough, edged with desire.

I nodded slightly, unable to speak—lost in the sensation of his touch, the world narrowing to just the two of us: the feel of his hand, the sound of his voice, a symphony of sensation. He chuckled, his fingers working their magic, building the pressure, the pleasure, bringing me closer and closer to the edge, to the point of no return.

"Use your words and maybe I'll let you come," he whispered in my ear, nipping at it, sending a fresh wave of heat through me—a jolt that shattered my last bit of control.

"Y... Yes," I managed out in a moan, my mind spinning, my body arching into his touch as I felt myself getting closer, the edge drawing near—a precipice I was about to tumble over, willingly, eagerly.

"Good girl," he said, his voice a low growl as he twisted his fingers up, his thumb pressing my clit again. A wave of pure bliss washed over me, my body tightening around his fingers. My breath hitched in my throat, a strangled cry escaping my lips as the pleasure intensified, spreading through me like wildfire, consuming me entirely.

His thumb continued to stroke my clit, drawing out the last tremors of my orgasm, milking every last drop of pleasure from me. My breathing came in ragged gasps, my body still tingling with the aftershocks, the echoes of pure bliss. Zarek leaned down, his lips brushing against mine, soft and tender.

After what felt like an eternity, the world slowly started to filter back in, the fog of pleasure receding, leaving me flushed and breathless.

"We should probably get up before Nox or Damon come barging in. You know how they are," he whispered, his voice husky, a hint of amusement in his tone.

I blinked a few times, the reality of what just happened between Zarek and me slowly sinking in. A blush crept up my neck, staining my cheeks as I nodded, suddenly shy.

Zarek chuckled as he moved off of me, sitting up with his signature smirk. For a moment, everything felt almost normal—almost peaceful. As if the dangers lurking beyond these walls, the threat and the unsettling mystery surrounding my own past, were just distant worries. It was a welcome release I didn't know I needed, a brief respite from the constant tension that had become my new normal.

"Come on," Zarek said, standing up and offering me his hand, his amber eyes sparkling with warmth. "Let's get some breakfast before class."

WALKING INTO FUNDAMENTALS OF MAGICAL THEORY, my steps faltered slightly under the weight of countless eyes on me. The air felt thick, heavy with judgment, the whispers loud enough to prickle my skin. Rumors, some subtle and others not-so-subtle. I took a deep breath, scanning the room, hoping to spot the familiar comfort of Nox's presence—but he wasn't there. My heart sank a little, a knot of anxiety tightening in my stomach. I moved to find an empty seat, when Mira—surrounded by her usual entourage of puppets—deliberately blocked my path.

"Well, if it isn't the infamous Thalia," Mira sneered, her voice dripping with condescension. "Thought you were dead? God, I was hoping you were. Would've made things so much easier."

A ripple of laughter spread through the small group surrounding her, a few students snickering nervously while others stared with open disgust. "I heard she only got into the academy because she's been spreading her legs for the right people," another student called out, his voice loud enough to carry across the lecture hall. "Pathetic, isn't it? Sleeping her way in."

My heart pounded in my chest, anger and humiliation clashing in a violent wave. I forced myself to stand my ground, keeping my expression carefully neutral despite the heat rising to my face—the sting of their words like a hit to the chest. "Move aside," I said evenly, refusing to give Mira the satisfaction of seeing me falter.

Mira's eyes flashed dangerously, a predatory gleam in their depths, and the circle tightened around me—a pack of wolves closing in on their prey. "Why don't you show us what makes you so special, huh?" She stepped closer, invading my personal space, her eyes narrowing into slits. "Or maybe you need someone to remind you of your place, slut." Her voice dripped with malice, a tangible threat hanging in the air.

I clenched my fists, my nails digging into my palms, the urge to lash out—to unleash the raw power I've discovered simmering beneath my skin—was almost overwhelming. But Damon's face flashed before my eyes, his stern voice echoing in my ears—*Control, Thalia, always have control over your emotions, even when provoked.*

The taunts grew louder, more bold, fueled by Mira's lead. Other students, eager to join the spectacle and curry favor with her, chimed in. Their laughter echoing around me like a pack of hyenas.

"Maybe she's hoping to get through the whole Shadow Brothers lineup," one sneered.

"Is that how you got the Shadow Brothers to take you in as their pet?" another added, the words dripping with envy and resentment.

"You'll never be good enough for them, bitch," another voice spat, raw and venomous. Mira looked like she was ready to snap, her patience wearing thin, her fingers twitching. Just as she reached out—her hand extended as if to grab me, to inflict some physical mark of her dominance—a voice, cold and sharp as shattered ice, cut through the tension, silencing the room in an instant.

"Back off. Now." Nox, his voice low and laced with a deadly calm.

His presence was like a thunderstorm breaking over the scene. His emerald-green eyes had darkened to a dark forest green, blazing with anger. Every head snapped toward him, and the crowd instinctively parted as he strode forward. There was a raw power in his movements, each step a warning.

Mira hesitated for a moment, her bravado wavering under Nox's piercing gaze. "We were just—"

"I don't care what the fuck you were doing," Nox interrupted coldly, stepping directly between Mira and me. "If I see anyone trying to mess with her again, I will personally handle them." He locked eyes with each of the students. "Is that clear?"

Silence fell over the group, the tension suddenly replaced by an uneasy fear. Mira's expression shifted from anger to reluctant submission, the irritation evident as she mumbled something unintelligible before she and the others slowly dispersed.

Once the crowd cleared, Nox turned to me, his anger softening. "You alright?"

I nodded, "I can handle them."

He gave a slight nod, but the storm in his eyes hadn't completely faded. "I know you can. But I won't allow this bullshit anymore. Come on—sit up there with me." Nox nodded towards his usual seat.

All eyes were on us as we made our way across the room, the whispers not entirely silenced but much more subdued. I sat beside Nox, and he surveyed the room, his glare scanning the students as if trying to remember their faces. His hood was pulled up, and those curls fell across his forehead, casting shadows over his intense gaze.

Butterflies filled my stomach for whatever dumb reason his action brought on, but also guilt. I had crossed a line with Zarek this morning, a line I hadn't intended to cross, and I wasn't sure what that meant for us. Would he hate me? Would he think I was leading him on? The heat from Zarek's touch still lingered on my skin, a stark contrast to the icy dread that now crept through my veins. I wasn't sure what that meant for Zarek and me—or for Nox and me. Or even Damon, who I was sure would use this against me.

I was snapped out of my thoughts as class started, the professor clearly annoyed by my change of location as he went on and on about the lecture. I tried to focus on the his words, but it was difficult to ignore the way Nox's presence seemed to command the space around me.

As the class drew to a close, the professor's voice broke through my thoughts, sharper than before. "Thalia, a word after class, please."

I exchanged a quick glance with Nox, his jaw tightening. He gave me a slight nod, a silent assurance that he wasn't far. As the other students filtered out, casting glances in my direction, I rose from my seat and made my way to the front of the room.

Professor Walkins, watched me with an expression I couldn't quite read—somewhere between impatience and curiosity. He waited until the room was empty before speaking.

"Miss Thalia," he began, his tone clipped. "You seem to be attracting quite a bit of attention. Not all of it positive."

I swallowed, standing straighter. "I'm aware, sir."

He studied me for a moment, his eyes narrowing slightly. "I hope you understand the importance of your position here. Nexara Academy does not tolerate disruptions, nor do we make exceptions for those who cannot prove themselves worthy." He paused, letting the weight of his words settle over me. "I suggest you tread carefully, Miss Thalia. There are many who would be all too happy to see you fail."

The implication hung heavy in the air, and I nodded, forcing my voice to remain steady. "Understood, Professor."

He gave a curt nod, dismissing me with a wave of his hand. "See that you do. You're dismissed."

I turned to leave, my heart pounding in my chest. As I stepped out of the classroom, Nox was waiting just outside, leaning against the wall, his eyes searching mine.

"What did he say?" Nox asked, his voice low.

I shook my head, trying to push down the mixture of fear and frustration. "Just a warning. To watch my step."

"Fucking prick," he muttered under his breath.

AFTER EACH CLASS, EITHER ZAREK OR NOX WAS waiting for me, their presence a silent but noticeable shield against the barrage of stares and whispers that followed me everywhere. It was overwhelming, this sudden shift in the social dynamics. I supposed it was shocking news. The human was now being escorted by the gifted, the elite who ruled Nexara Academy. Of course, nobody knew I had any gifts of my own; that secret was between the four of us. It was a fragile truce, a delicate balance— and I wasn't sure how long it would last.

As lunch approached, Zarek and Nox walked with me. Zarek's arm was draped over my shoulder, a lazy smile playing on his lips. Meanwhile, Nox glared at the students who stopped to stare, his eyes flashing with a silent warning that made them quickly avert their gaze.

The cafeteria went silent as we walked in. Conversations died down, replaced by hushed whispers and curious stares. Elara and James's eyes widened as we passed their table, Zarek motioning for them to follow us. Elara hesitated, her eyes flicking between me and the brothers. She grabbed her tray and trailed behind us. James, however, rolled his eyes, muttering something under his breath before turning and leaving altogether. A pang of guilt twisted in my chest at his obvious displeasure, but there was also a sense of safety—of belonging—in Zarek and Nox's presence that I couldn't ignore.

We made our way to their usual table, Damon was already there, his expression as impassive as ever. I could sense the annoyance simmering beneath his stoic facade in the tightness of his jaw, the way his gaze swept across the cafeteria, lingering on the whispering groups and curious stares as if irritated by the sudden, dramatic shift in the room's atmosphere. He looked like a predator, momentarily disturbed from its lair.

El took a seat across from me, her eyes searching mine for answers I didn't have. A nervous flutter erupted in my stomach under her stare. Zarek and Nox settled in on either side of me. Damon sat beside Nox, his presence a silent but formidable force. He still hadn't acknowledged me directly, his gaze fixed on some distant point beyond the cafeteria windows. The atmosphere at the table was heavy—the unspoken tension a reminder of how much had changed in just a few short days.

El leaned forward, her voice barely above a whisper. "Thalia, what's going on? Why are they..." She glanced at the brothers, a small crease appeared between her brows.

How could I even begin to explain? Aethrax, the strange pull I felt towards the brothers, the danger that seemed to linger everywhere I went. It was a tangled mess of emotions and instincts I couldn't unravel—let alone explain. Zarek's fingers drummed lightly on the table, a rhythmic tapping that drew my attention back to him. He gave me a small, reassuring smile, as if sensing my inner turmoil.

"It's complicated," I finally said.

Elara's eyes narrowed slightly, her skepticism clear. "Really? Complicated? That's the best you can come up with?"

I opened my mouth to answer, but Damon's voice cut in, low and annoyed. "If you two want to gossip, do it when I'm not around." His attention was still fixed on the window.

Elara's gaze snapped to Damon, "Well, if you guys would give her some breathing room, I could talk and gossip with *my* best friend."

Zarek's arm tightened slightly around my shoulders, his tone playful as he spoke. "Don't worry, El. We're not as scary as we look. Though... " he added with a dramatic pause, "I can't speak for Damon."

"We can partner up in Combat Training *and* gossip, El," I laughed, wanting to ease the tension.

Combat Training had a different energy today. The sun was shining, the field buzzing with activity as everyone gathered to warm up. I glanced over my shoulder to see Nox, Zarek, and Damon standing a bit away, talking amongst themselves. It felt strange— almost vulnerable—without them hovering near me, but also liberating. They were giving me some space.

I turned my attention back to El and James. El was stretching beside me, her eyes darting towards me every few moments, filled with curiosity she couldn't hide. James was nearby, his easygoing smile masking his watchful gaze.

"Okay, spill," El said, her voice low but insistent. She leaned closer, her eyes narrowing. "Why are the Shadow Brothers suddenly glued to your side like they're lost puppies? And don't give me the 'it's complicated' line again."

I sighed, rolling my shoulders as I tried to come up with something that wouldn't sound insane. "It's not as simple as you think. There are things happening... things that I can't explain. Not yet. But they're helping me."

El raised an eyebrow, her expression torn between concern and skepticism. "Helping you? Thalia, these guys don't help anyone unless there's something in it for them. So, what's their angle?"

James, who had been silently listening, finally spoke up, his tone lighter but probing. "Yeah, Thalia, you gotta admit—those three don't do anything without a reason."

I hesitated, my gaze dropping to the grass. I didn't entirely understand it myself. There was a connection—a pull—but how could

I explain that without sounding like I had lost my mind? I looked back up at El, her eyes searching mine, and I forced a small smile.

"Can you guys just trust me when I say I need them? And they... they need me too?"

El's expression softened a little, her lips pressing into a thin line. She sighed, shaking her head. "You always manage to get yourself into the strangest situations, Thalia." Her eyes flicked over to the brothers, lingering on Damon for a moment before she met my gaze again. "But if they step out of line, I'll roast them."

I couldn't help but laugh, "I'll hold you to that."

James smirked, shaking his head. "I can already see it—a fire witch taking on the Shadow Brothers. That'd be one hell of a show."

El grinned, the fire in her eyes unmistakable. "Oh, they wouldn't know what hit them."

As we continued to stretch, the banter helped ease some of the weight I'd been carrying. The brothers—though distant today— were still a presence I couldn't quite shake. My gaze drifted to where they stood, their eyes meeting mine across the field.

Whatever this was, whatever strange bond had formed between us, it made me feel whole. Maybe I should try to explain to them what I was feeling—but I also wanted to understand it better before risking embarrassment. Was it just my loneliness seeking comfort?

"So, are they taking you to the academy formal then?" El asked as we all stood up, her voice light but curious.

"Um, no, I haven't heard anything about it," I responded, glancing back to see Mira approaching the brothers. I felt my blood start to boil. El and James kept talking, but the pounding in my ears drowned them out.

Mira moved with her usual confidence, her gaze flicking to me briefly before focusing on the brothers. Her smile was all too sweet, and I could see her leaning in, trying to get their attention. The sight of her standing so close to them made something twist inside me—anger, jealousy, things I didn't want to acknowledge.

Watching Mira try to insert herself into their circle felt like a violation. Like she was trying to steal something precious. Something that was *mine*, even though I knew it wasn't. It was irrational— crazy even—but I couldn't help the way it made me feel. It wasn't like I had any claim on them.

El nudged me, her brow furrowed as she caught my distracted expression. "Thalia, you okay? You look like you're about to set something on fire."

I forced myself to take a deep breath, tearing my gaze away from Mira. "Yeah, I'm fine. Just... annoyed, I guess."

El raised an eyebrow, a knowing smirk playing on her lips. "Annoyed, huh? Or maybe a little jealous?"

I shot her a glare, but the heat rising to my cheeks betrayed me. "No," I muttered, feeling like a child.

I rolled my eyes, "Can we not make this more complicated than it already is?"

Elara raised an eyebrow, clearly amused. "Complicated? Please, you're making it complicated by pretending like you don't care. It's written all over your face, Thalia."

I sighed, rubbing my temples. "I kissed Zarek, alright? Happy now?" The words slipped out before I could stop them.

"I KNEW IT!" She yelled, her grin widening, practically splitting her face in two. "James owes me lunch." I shot her a warning look, hoping she'd keep her voice down, but it was too late. Several heads turned our way, curious whispers already starting. This was exactly what I didn't want.

I groaned inwardly. Glancing back at the brothers, I prayed to whatever gods existed that they hadn't heard El's outburst. Damon had his arms crossed, a familiar scowl etched on his face, his gaze fixed on Mira with a look of barely concealed annoyance. He looked like he'd rather be anywhere else but here, which, honestly, was probably true. Zarek was smirking, clearly amused by whatever gossip Mira was spewing. And Nox.. Nox's eyes were locked on me, his expression unreadable but intense.

Great, just fucking great. Nox definitely heard.

"Come on," El said, grabbing my hand and pulling me towards the training area. "Let's see if we can blow off some steam."

We made our way to the training mats, James following close behind. El kept throwing me questioning glances, but she didn't press further, and I was grateful for that.

As El and I started sparring, the tension slowly began to fade, replaced by the physical exertion of the movement. James watched from the side, occasionally calling out pointers or teasing us when one of us made a mistake.

El paused after a while, her breathing heavy, and gave me a knowing look. "You know, Thalia, whatever happens, you've got us. Don't forget that."

I nodded with a smile, "I know, El."

She grinned, "Now, come on. Let's see if you can actually land a hit this time."

I laughed as I readied myself for another round. Whatever was waiting for me—whether it was Mira, the brothers, or the secrets I still had to uncover—I knew I wouldn't have to face it alone.

After class, Nox was waiting for me outside the women's locker room, leaning against the wall with his arms crossed in a casual but attentive posture. El gave me a knowing look, before giving Nox a mock-warning glare—a silent promise to burn him alive if he hurt me—then left the two of us alone.

"Are you—uh—interested in the formal?" Nox asked, his voice a little hesitant, glancing over at me as we walked. Was he.. nervous?

I raised an eyebrow, a small smile forming on my lips. "Were you eavesdropping again, Nox?" I teased, nudging him playfully with my elbow.

Nox let out a low chuckle, his lips curving into a hint of a smile. "You didn't answer."

I looked at him, there was something vulnerable in his eyes—a rare softness that made my own defenses falter. It was a glimpse behind the quiet, observant facade he usually presented. "Maybe," I admitted.

"Maybe, huh?" He took a step in front of me, stopping me in my tracks, his nearness both exhilarating and slightly intimidating. "If you are... I'd like to take you."

I was speechless. The guarded Nox was suddenly standing before me, his vulnerability laid bare, and it made my chest ache in the best way. "You'd want to take me?" I asked, still slightly disbelieving.

Nox nodded, his eyes never leaving mine. "Yeah, Thalia. I would." His sincerity was undeniable, radiating from him like a warm embrace.

A smile broke across my face, genuine and unrestrained. "Then I guess I *might* be interested," I replied, my voice light and teasing.

His lips curved into a full smile this time, one that softened his entire face—transforming his features from broodingly handsome to almost boyishly charming. "Good," he said, his voice a little rough, as if the words were caught in his throat. "I'll make it worth it, but you know Zarek will want to come with us." He added the last part with a slight roll of his eyes, a hint of playful exasperation in his tone.

I raised an eyebrow, a playful glint in my eyes. "Oh, is that so? Are you sure you can handle both of us at once?" I challenged, enjoying the unexpected turn our conversation had taken.

Nox let out a low, teasing laugh, his eyes filled with amusement. "I think it's you who should be worried about handling us."

I tried to keep my face straight, but the grin slipped through. "Confident, aren't we?"

He shot me another wide smile that made my heart stop. This was a whole new side of Nox—one I was starting to adore. The playful banter, the unguarded smiles, the intensity in his eyes—it was all so intoxicating. It was strange, how something so simple as an invitation could make me feel so light, so hopeful.

"So, what color are you wearing?" he asked, the nervousness from earlier completely gone.

"I haven't even thought about it." The formal felt like a distant dream, yet the thought of attending it with Nox sent a pleasant thrill through me.

"Let me know," Nox said, "I'll make sure we match. Let's not tell Zarek though." His voice dropping to a conspiratorial whisper.

The way he said it, with such ease and sincerity, made my cheeks flush again. I nodded, biting my lip to keep the smile from spreading too wide. "Okay."

He nudged me gently with his elbow, "And if you can't decide, I could always help you pick. I'm sure we'd come up with something... memorable."

I rolled my eyes, and couldn't help but laugh. "Yeah, I'm sure your fashion sense is impeccable," I retorted.

Nox smirked, his eyes twinkling. "Hey, I know how to match, at least. Besides, anything looks good when you're the one wearing it." The playful edge to his voice was still there, but beneath it, there was something deeper, something that made my pulse race.

He winked at me as he stepped back, giving me a little space as we approached their dorm—well, apartment really. Was Nox actually *flirting* with me?

I could hear the low murmur of voices coming from the living room as we entered. Zarek and Damon were already there, sprawled on the plush couches, engrossed in some animated discussion. Their attention shifted to us the moment we walked in, their expressions changing subtly.

Zarek's eyes lit up, a smirk spreading across his face as he took in the sight of me and Nox together. "Well, well, look who decided to show up," he drawled, his tone teasing, a hint of knowing amusement in his voice. "Did you two get lost on the way here?"

Damon glanced at us, his gaze sharp but curious. He raised an eyebrow, his lips twitching slightly. "Or maybe they were just... preoccupied." His tone was more measured than Zarek's, but the underlying amusement was still there.

"Ha-ha. Very funny," I said, crossing my arms as I stepped further into the room. "Not all of us have the luxury of lounging around all day." I directed my comment at Damon, though my gaze flickered to Nox, who was watching me with an amused expression.

Zarek chuckled, sitting up straighter. "Ouch, someone's feisty today." His eyes flicked to Nox, and his smirk widened. "What did you do to her, brother?"

Nox shrugged, his expression remaining calm—though I could see the hint of a smile tugging at his lips. "Nothing she didn't enjoy," he replied, his voice smooth. I shot him a look, my mouth falling open at this playful side of Nox. He winked, clearly enjoying my flustered reaction.

Damon watched the exchange, his gaze thoughtful before he finally spoke. "You two seem... closer."

There was something in his voice—an undercurrent I couldn't quite place. It wasn't disapproval, but it wasn't entirely joy either. It was more like cautious observation, as if he was trying to decipher the meaning behind our newfound ease with each other. I glanced at Nox, who met his brother's eyes with a steady look.

"We're figuring things out," Nox said simply, his tone carrying a weight of meaning that made my heart skip a beat. It was a simple statement, but it held a promise of something more.

Damon nodded slowly, his eyes shifting back to me. The air seemed to shift, the tension easing as Zarek let out a dramatic sigh. "We should play a game." He clapped his hands together, effectively breaking the spell of Damon's scrutiny.

Nox glanced at me, "What do you say, Thalia? You up for it?"

"Why not?" I sighed, dropping onto their plush, oversized couch, sinking into its comfortable embrace. Zarek grinned, already on his feet and heading towards the kitchen. "That's the spirit. I'll get the snacks." He disappeared down the hallway, his cheerful voice echoing back to us.

As the evening unfolded, I found myself relaxing, enjoying the easy banter between the brothers. Even Damon seemed to loosen up a bit, his usual guarded demeanor cracking to reveal glimpses of a dry wit and a surprisingly competitive spirit. The shadows that had once seemed so menacing now danced playfully around us. It felt like a stolen moment, a secret world tucked away from the prying eyes.

Chapter 28

Thalia's POV

The day of the formal had finally arrived, and with it, a swarm of butterflies took flight in my stomach. My nerves were on edge as Elara worked with the precision and care of a seasoned artist, her fingers easily applying my makeup. We'd done this before—the night of the party—but today felt different, more significant. Like tonight would change everything.

She evened my skin tone with a lightweight foundation, letting my freckles peek through, giving me a natural, sun-kissed glow. A soft peach blush highlighted the sharp angles of my cheekbones, adding a touch of warmth to my pale complexion. For my eyes, she used a palette of warm, earthy tones that brought out the stormy gray, adding soft pink and deeper mauve to the crease to make them look bigger and brighter. A perfect winged liner gave them an elegant lift, and a coat of mascara made my lashes long and fluttery. She finished with a muted rose lipstick that made my lips look fuller and more defined.

I barely recognized myself in the mirror. The makeup wasn't heavy or overdone, but it artfully highlighted everything I secretly loved about my features—the stormy gray of my eyes, the sprinkling of freckles across my nose, the natural curves of my lips.

Elara stepped back, a satisfied grin on her face as she surveyed her work. "You look incredible, Thalia," she said, her eyes meeting mine in the mirror. "They are not going to know what hit them."

I smiled, a blush creeping onto my cheeks that had nothing to do with the makeup. "Thanks, El. I just hope..."

El rolled her eyes dramatically, playfully swatting my shoulder. "Oh please. You could show up in a potato sack and those boys would still be tripping over themselves for you."

I laughed, shaking my head. The thought was both flattering and slightly terrifying. "I guess we'll see."

El grinned, her eyes twinkling with excitement. "Alright, now let's get dressed. We've got a formal to conquer." She pulled me away from the mirror and toward the closet.

As I unzipped the dress that had been left for me, a gasp escaped my lips. It was breathtaking—far more extravagant than anything I'd ever worn. Zarek, when he found out about us all going to the formal, had assured me not to worry. He simply winked and told me to trust him. And he was right.

An emerald-green dress, sparkling with tiny sequins that shimmered like captured starlight, hugged my curves in all the right places. Sheer, embroidered sleeves—delicate as a spider's web—added an elegant touch, while the sweetheart neckline and daring high slit gave it a touch of playful sensuality. It was bold yet refined, a perfect balance of innocence and allure, and it fit like a glove—as if it had been made specifically for me.

My auburn hair cascaded down my back in soft, flowing waves. El had worked her magic, adding a few loose braids woven into the sides and pinned at the back, giving my hair an almost fae-like look.

El's eyes widened, her jaw dropping slightly. "Damn, Thalia! You look sexy as hell!"

I couldn't help the shy smile that spread across my face, a blush warming my cheeks. "You really think so?" I asked, still not quite believing it myself.

"Are you kidding? If Nox, Zarek, and even Damon aren't on their knees when they see you, they're bigger idiots than I thought." El grinned, her excitement contagious. "Girl, you're going to steal the show tonight. Just try not to cause any incidents, okay?" She winked.

"El, you look amazing," I said. She was wearing a deep red dress that hugged her figure perfectly, with delicate lace details on the corset that added a romantic touch. Her chestnut hair was pinned back in an updo, a few strands framing her face, and her smokey eye makeup made her tinted red eyes look even more intense. It was a look that screamed confidence and power—and I knew she would command attention the moment she stepped into the hall.

She grinned, twirling slightly so the dress flowed around her legs. "I figured if you're going to steal the show, we might as well do it together." She laughed.

We walked into the living room, the air catching in my lungs as I took in the sight before me. Damon, Nox, and Zarek stood near the door. It was like they had stepped out of a dream.

Zarek had opted for a more casual look. His black shirt was slightly unbuttoned, revealing a hint of his bare chest beneath, where I could see the edges of his tattoos peeking out. His messy dark hair fell into his amber eyes, partially obscuring the intensity that always simmered within them. A playful smirk tugged at the corner of his lips as his eyes raked over me, making my cheeks flush slightly. He looked effortlessly handsome, with that dangerous edge that seemed to follow him everywhere.

Damon, on the other hand, was impeccably put together. He wore an all-black suit with a crisp black tie, his dark hair perfectly styled—except for that same damn rebellious strand that always seemed to fall across his forehead. His deep blue eyes held an intensity that made it hard to look away—he looked like a fallen angel. Which, considering his demonic nature, was ironic.

And lastly, Nox. He wore an all-black suit as well, but instead of a tie, he had chosen a deep green bow tie that matched my dress perfectly. His dark curls were styled just enough to look polished but still natural, and those piercing green eyes of his seemed even brighter against the dark color of his suit. A shy smile played on his lips, and he shifted his weight from one foot to the other. He looked breathtaking. Seeing them all like this—standing together—made something inside me flutter.

As their eyes landed on me, I felt both powerful and self-conscious at the same time, their gazes roaming over me, making me acutely aware of every detail of my appearance. Zarek let out a low whistle, his eyes glinting with open admiration, a playful smirk tugging at the corner of his lips. "Thalia, you look... stunning," he said, his voice softening as his gaze swept over me again, lingering for a moment on the curve of my neck.

Nox took a step forward, his gaze locked on mine, a shy smile tugging at the corner of his lips. "You look beautiful," he said. He fidgeted slightly, his hands clasped in front of him, as if he wanted to reach out but wasn't quite sure how.

Damon's lips curved into a hint of a smile—a rare and unexpected sight—but he didn't speak a word. A flicker of something unreadable crossed his features as his eyes met mine. I couldn't help but wonder what he was thinking.

I smiled—a genuine smile that reached my eyes, the crinkling the corners kind of smile. "Thanks," I said, my voice a little breathless as I tried to regain my composure, my cheeks flushing slightly under their combined attention. "You all clean up pretty well yourselves," I added, my gaze sweeping over each of them, appreciating their handsome appearances—from Zarek's playful charm to Nox's quiet intensity and Damon's brooding elegance.

Nox extended his arm to me. "Shall we?"

I took his arm, a thrill shooting through me. El stepped up to my other side, looping her arm through mine. "Alright, boys, let's go make an entrance worthy of legends."

We met James outside the grand doors of Evermore Hall, and I couldn't help but smile at how dashing he looked. His grey suit fit him perfectly, accentuating his broad shoulders, and his blonde hair was styled back, revealing his kind eyes. They found mine, and he gave me a small, reassuring smile before El moved to link her arm with his.

"You girls look absolutely breathtaking," James said, his voice warm and sincere.

Elara gave him a bright, playful smile as she looped her arm through his. "You ready to be my arm candy for the night, handsome?"

James grinned, nodding. "It'd be my absolute pleasure, Elara."

Zarek stepped in beside me, a familiar cedar-and-ocean scent swirling around him, as Damon moved on the other side of Zarek. The distant thrum of music and chatter grew louder with every step we took toward the hall. El and James walked a little ahead, their laughter echoing back toward us—a light, carefree sound that eased some of my nerves—while I moved alongside the brothers.

Zarek gave me a sideways glance, his lips tugging into a teasing smile. "Nervous, Firefly?"

I let out a breathy laugh, trying to appear more confident than I felt. "A little. But I think it's the good kind of nervous, ya know?"

Nox squeezed my arm gently as we approached a set of side doors to Eldrin Hall. The massive entrance hall was filled with the warm glow of crystal chandeliers. The room seemed to shimmer and sparkle—from the elaborate, gold-framed paintings adorning the walls to the polished marble floor that stretched beneath us like a shimmering lake. A grand, sweeping staircase led up to a second level, where more guests were mingling, leaning on the carved railing or laughing softly among themselves.

Rich, deep tapestries—woven with threads of gold and silver— hung between gilded columns, depicting scenes of ancient battles and mythical heroes. The scent of expensive perfume mingled with the aroma of freshly polished wood and exotic flowers, lingered in the air, creating an intoxicating blend. People dressed in elegant gowns of silk and satin, and sharp tuxedos, moved gracefully through the hall, their laughter and conversation blending with the faint strains of classical music that floated through the air.

Elara and James turned back to us, their eyes wide with shared excitement, reflecting the glittering lights of the chandeliers. "It looks absolutely magical," El said, her gaze sweeping across the room. I nodded in agreement, completely awestruck by it all.

James chuckled, giving me a warm, encouraging smile. "Well, let's make it a night to remember, shall we? One for the storybooks."

"Absolutely," I replied, a sense of anticipation bubbling inside me.

The music transitioned to a louder, more upbeat tempo, and the dance floor began to fill with couples moving gracefully in sync with the rhythm. Nox and Zarek remained close to my sides— their presence like a protective shield that made me feel safe, yet completely free to enjoy myself. Damon had slipped away into the crowd, and I couldn't help but wonder where he went, and what he was thinking. But I decided to let it go—tonight was about celebrating, about having fun and letting loose, even if just for a little while.

We made our way to the bar—a long, polished mahogany surface lined with gleaming crystal glasses—Nox and Zarek each keeping a hand on me, almost as if they were afraid I'd be swept away by the crowd. When we reached the bar, Nox leaned in, his breath brushing against my ear, sending a wave of heat through me. "What are you having?"

I laughed softly, my eyes meeting his, a spark of playful challenge passing between us. "Surprise me, Nox. I trust your judgment."

Zarek smirked beside me, his amber eyes twinkling with amusement. "Careful, Thalia. You know he's going to take that as a challenge."

I shrugged, feeling light and daring, the atmosphere of the ball emboldening me. Nox's eyes sparkled as he signaled the bartender, ordering a round of iridescent shots for us. It all felt surreal—like I was stepping into a dream, a world I never imagined I could belong to. And yet, here I was.

"Shots already? Trying to get a head start on the festivities, are we?" James teased, grabbing one of the shimmering shots and raising it in a mock toast.

Elara linked her arm with mine, "Let's make a toast. To a night we'll never forget, to new beginnings, and to the magic that brought us all together."

We all raised our glasses, clinking them together with a cheerful chime before downing the shots in unison. The alcohol burned pleasantly on the way down, a warm sensation that spread through my limbs. The music pulsed through me, the beat synchronizing with the steady thrum of my heart. I felt incredible—like every worry, every fear, every doubt had momentarily vanished, leaving behind only a sense of pure, unadulterated joy.

After a couple more drinks, the music and laughter swirling around us like an intoxicating elixir, Zarek nudged me playfully. "So, Firefly? Are you going to grace us with your presence on the dance floor? Or are you going to make us wait all night?"

I laughed, shaking my head at his teasing. "Alright, alright. Let's dance. Lead the way, Zarek."

Nox took my hand, his fingers intertwining with mine, sending a jolt of electricity through me. "We won't let you out of our sight," he said, his voice carrying a hint of seriousness beneath the playful tone. His emerald-green eyes held a possessive glint that made my heart flutter. Their protectiveness felt like a warm cocoon around me, a comforting embrace that shut out the rest of the world, and I realized it wasn't stifling—it was empowering.

As we moved to the center of the dance floor, Elara and James right beside us, laughing and twirling with carefree spirits, I let the music take over. The rhythm flowing through my veins, guiding my movements. The energy around us was electric—everyone dancing, laughing, lost in the moment. Nox twirled me around, his laughter echoing in my ears, and I couldn't help the joyful giggle that bubbled out of me. Zarek moved in rhythm beside us, his smile genuine and easy, his eyes never straying too far from me.

Nox and Zarek passed me between them, a playful exchange that made my head spin with delight, and with each turn, a giggle slipped past my lips. The lights flashed in vibrant colors, illuminating the joy on their faces. I felt a lightness inside me—a happiness that made me want to stay on that dance floor forever, lost in the music and the laughter, surrounded by the people who made me feel like I finally belonged. For so long, I had been carrying the weight of uncertainty, of fear, of not knowing where I fit in—wondering if I truly belonged anywhere. But here, I finally felt seen, valued, and for the first time in what felt like forever, I was simply, undeniably happy.

The music shifted then, transitioning into something slower, a romantic melody that filled the air. Nox's arm slipped around my waist, drawing me closer, his touch sending a wave of warmth through me. Zarek stepped back slightly, giving us space, his eyes soft as he watched us, a gentle smile playing on his lips. I rested my head against Nox's chest, feeling the steady rise and fall of his breath. His other hand moved to my back, his fingers tracing gentle patterns.

The world around us seemed to blur as I focused on the feeling of Nox's arms around me, the comforting presence of Zarek nearby, the laughter of my friends echoing in the distance. It was a perfect, self-contained world—a bubble of happiness and acceptance that I never wanted to leave. Nox moved to whisper in my ear, his voice low.

"You terrify me, Thalia," he murmured, his breath warm against my skin, sending shivers down my spine.

I lifted my head from his chest, my brows knitting together in confusion, his words catching me off guard. "Why?" I asked.

His gaze searched mine, a depth of emotion swirling in his emerald-green eyes, before he let out a soft breath. His fingers brushing against my cheek—a feather-light touch that sent a jolt of electricity through me. "Because I care about you more than I ever thought I could. More than I ever thought possible. And that scares me, Thalia. It scares me because I don't want to lose you... and you could get hurt."

His words made my heart skip a beat, a warmth spreading through my chest that was almost overwhelming. I swallowed, my throat tight with emotion as I looked up at him, my heart aching with a mixture of love and fear. The vulnerability in his eyes, the raw honesty in his words—it was everything I hadn't realized I needed to hear. A validation of the feelings that had been growing between us, unspoken yet undeniable.

I reached up, my fingers brushing against his cheek, my thumb tracing the line of his jaw. "You wouldn't hurt me, Nox," I whispered, my voice barely audible over the music, but filled with a conviction that surprised even myself. "I know you wouldn't."

Nox closed his eyes for a moment, as if letting my words sink in, absorbing their meaning, his long, dark lashes resting on his cheeks. He leaned down, pressing his forehead against mine, his breath mingling with mine—our bodies close enough to feel the beating of each other's hearts. "You have no idea what you do to me, Thalia," he whispered, his voice rough with emotion, his words a confession of the power I held over him, a power I hadn't even realized I possessed.

A smile tugged at my lips, "Maybe I do," I replied, my voice filled with a newfound confidence.

Nox's lips curved into a smile—a slow, tender expression that made my heart melt. He leaned in, his lips brushing against mine in a soft tender kiss. It was slow, deliberate, filled with every unspoken word, every shared glance, every stolen moment between us. It was a kiss that spoke of vulnerability, of trust, of a connection that ran deeper than either of us could have imagined. I let myself get lost in him, a wave of pleasure surging through me like a tidal wave, washing away all my doubts and fears.

He pulled away slightly, his arms tightening around me as if he never wanted to let go, and I knew in that moment that this—this connection, this feeling, this burgeoning love—was something worth fighting for, something worth holding onto, even if I wasn't entirely sure what I was doing, or where this path would lead.

"We need to leave, *now*," Damon growled, startling us. There was a raw urgency in his tone that made the hair on the back of my neck stand on end. Zarek immediately moved behind me, a protective presence at my back, while Nox pushed me behind him, his hand never leaving mine as he pulled me forward. Damon was already leading the way through the crowd. The ground began to tremble —a sudden, violent jolt that sent ripples of panic through the revelers. The joyous laughter and upbeat music were abruptly replaced by gasps and screams, the festive atmosphere dissolving into a chaotic scramble. My heart pounded against my ribs as people rushed around us, bumping and shoving. Zarek wrapped his arm around my shoulders, pulling me tightly against him as the crowd surged, shielding me from the frantic, desperate bodies.

We moved as quickly as we could, Damon clearing a path, his eyes sharp and alert as he scanned our surroundings. We pushed our way towards the nearest exit, and as we rushed through the doors, we found ourselves in a part of the academy I'd never seen before. Lanterns lined the winding paths stretching far into the distance, and delicate fairy lights twinkled, wrapped around the branches of ancient trees. I looked up to see the sky above us twisting and churning, the clouds swirling in an unnatural, menacing pattern. Dark purples and blacks blended together, illuminated by flashes of violet lightning that crackled through the air. It was as if the heavens themselves were tearing apart.

"Arethax," Damon said, his voice grim, confirming my unspoken fear. His eyes were locked on the turbulent sky, his jaw clenched tight. There was no doubt in my mind—this was an attack. Nox's grip on my hand tightened, his eyes narrowing as he looked up at the brewing storm. "We need to get her somewhere safe," he said, his voice surprisingly steady even with all the chaos erupting around us.

Damon's shadows began to swirl around him, restless and eager to escape. But Elara and James were still inside. I couldn't just abandon them—not when they were completely unaware of who was coming, of what they were up against. Hell, *I* wasn't even entirely sure.

"No," I said, my voice firm. "We can't just leave them." Damon's gaze shifted to me, his eyes narrowing, a flicker of annoyance crossing his features.

"Thalia, we *need* to leave. *You* cannot be here," Nox said, turning to me, his eyes pleading, a mixture of fear and concern etched on his face.

"No, I'm not running," I snapped, my voice laced with frustration. "You guys can either help me or just leave." I pulled away from them, turning towards the door—determined to go back—but Damon moved with lightning speed, a blur of darkness, blocking my path.

"Now is not the time, Thalia. Stop being a fucking brat," he growled, crossing his arms.

A screeching scream echoed through the air, shattering the tense standoff. Emerging from the shadows were twisted, grotesque monstrosities that seemed to be woven out of death itself. They were truly horrifying. Eight of them moved in unsettling unison, their long, jagged limbs carrying them with an unnatural, almost gliding grace. Their skeletal bodies were thin and wiry, bones protruding through their taut skin. Their eyes—multiple, glowing red eyes—were fixed on me, burning with a chilling hunger and malice. Their mouths were filled with rows of long, serrated fangs, dripping with a viscous mixture of saliva and foam. All of them seemed laser-focused on me, as if I was the only thing they could see, the only thing that mattered.

Zarek stepped in front of me without hesitation, his shoulders squared, his entire posture rigid. Damon moved into position beside him, the two of them forming a wall between me and the immediate threat.

Nox, however, took off towards the creatures. His body twisting and contorting as he moved. I watched in stunned shock as his bones cracked and shifted, his form expanding, muscles rippling and bulging beneath his skin. His clothes tore away, and in their place, sleek, midnight-black fur erupted, covering his growing frame. A massive panther emerged from the remnants of Nox's human form. Its long, sharp claws scraped against the stone path, sending sparks flying. The panther's eyes—*Nox's* eyes—were a vivid, piercing green, glowing intensely against the encroaching darkness.

His growl was deep, resonant—shaking the very ground beneath us. I felt my entire body vibrate with the force of it, and the shocking realization struck me like a lightning bolt. *Nox was the panther*—the one from the night after the party, the one that had chased me into their home, the one that had saved me during the Wonders of Nexara. It was him, all along. Everything clicked into place, making perfect sense now. Nox had been there, silently guarding me, even when I didn't know who or what he was.

That was Nox. The *real* Nox. The Nox who went to get help and pretended he'd just found me.

I was still reeling from this revelation when Damon's sharp voice snapped me out of my thoughts. "Thalia! Stay focused!"

I nodded, swallowing hard as I took a step back, forcing myself to get into position—to prepare for what was coming. The creatures were closing in fast, their limbs clicking against the ground with an unnerving rhythm, their multiple eyes unblinking as they closed the distance between us. The open area that had seemed so enchanting just moments before was now about to become a battlefield—and I was at the center of it.

The creatures lunged, their screeches piercing the night air, and the brothers sprang into action with a practiced synchronicity. Damon's shadows surged forward, wrapping around the legs of one of the creatures, pulling it to the ground with a sickening thud. Zarek was a blur of motion, his agility unmatched as he darted between the creatures, striking them with quick, powerful blows. The creatures fought back with a ferociousness that made my blood run cold, their serrated claws swiping through the air, aiming for any exposed flesh.

Nox, in his panther form, moved with a lethal grace I found both terrifying and beautiful. He leaped at one of the creatures, his powerful jaws clamping down on it with a sickening crunch. I could see the raw strength in every movement he made—the effortless power with which he tore into the creature, ripping it apart with an ease.

I stood there, my hands trembling, the energy of the storm above buzzing in my ears, the weight of the situation pressing down on me. I could see the brothers fighting with everything they had, their movements fluid and powerful, each of them a force to be reckoned with.

One of the creatures made it past them—coming straight for me. I froze, fear momentarily paralyzing me, but I forced myself to move, stumbling backward, my heart racing in my chest.

"Thalia!" Zarek shouted, his voice filled with panic.

The creature was just a few feet away now. My body reacted before my mind could catch up, a burst of shadows exploding from within me, striking the creature and sending it sprawling backward with a surprised screech.

The sudden release of power left me breathless, my entire body trembling from the effort. The energy I had unleashed felt like it had ripped through every cell of my being—leaving me hollow and in agony. I gasped for breath, each inhale burning my lungs. The creature let out another screech, struggling to its feet—its multiple eyes now narrowed with rage.

"Stay back," Zarek shouted, his voice carrying over the chaos as he moved toward me.

I nodded, still catching my breath, trying to regain some semblance of control. I looked at the creatures, at the chaos that surrounded us, the sheer brutality of the fight. This was my fight, too. I wasn't going to stand by and watch them protect me. I was going to fight—*with* them.

A dozen more creatures were running towards us, their grotesque forms moving with a terrifying speed. Nox was already in motion, his massive paws swiping with lethal precision, while Zarek was now attacking the creatures with his own shadows, which lashed out like whips. Damon's shadows, coiled around the enemy, ripping them apart, pieces of limbs flying through the air.

I pushed my own shadows outwards, creating a protective shield around the brothers, trying to shield them from any blindsided attacks. My heart was pounding in my ears, my focus entirely on protecting them, on keeping them safe.

A searing pain shot through my shoulder, a claw tearing into my flesh. The screech of a creature behind me made my ears ring, the world around me becoming a blur as I was pushed forward, my knees hitting the ground.

A heavy force pinned me down, the weight stealing my breath. Agonizing pain—sharp and searing—radiated through my other shoulder, mirroring the first. It felt as if razors were ripping through skin and muscle, tearing me apart. A guttural growl vibrated above me, hot breath ghosting against my neck. A scream tore from my throat—raw and ragged. My vision blurred with tears as my body began to tremble.

The taste of fear and metal started to fill my mouth. I struggled beneath them, trying to push them off, trying to fight, but they were too strong. Their claws dug into my back, their fangs tearing deeper. I could feel myself slipping, the edges of my vision darkening.

Through the haze of pain, I saw a flash of black—a blur of movement. Nox's deafening roar filled my ears. I felt the weight lift, my body trembling as I tried to push myself up.

Zarek rushed to my side, kneeling beside me, his eyes wide with fear and anger. "Thalia, stay with me," he said urgently, his voice laced with concern. I nodded, though my vision was still blurry, the pain making it hard to focus.

Nox stood protectively in front of us, his body curved and tense, a low, threatening growl rumbling in his chest as he faced the remaining creature. His eyes met mine for a brief moment, filled with a raw fear and desperation that mirrored my own.

Damon's shadows wrapped around the last creature, pulling it away from us with a force that made the ground shake. The creature let out a final, ear-splitting screech before Damon's shadows tore it apart, the pieces disintegrating into nothingness as he approached us.

Everything fell silent for a moment. The only sound was my ragged breathing and the distant rumble of thunder above. Zarek's arm was still around me, holding me up as I swayed on my feet. Blood was already pooling beneath me, staining the ground a dark, crimson red.

Another screech rang out, this one different—deeper, filled with an agonizing pain that seemed to resonate in my very bones. Taller than the previous creatures, with elongated limbs and hollow, sunken eyes that glowed a dull, eerie red. Their bodies were gaunt, their skin a sickly pale color, and they moved with jerky motions. My heart pounded as they advanced towards us, their movements purposeful and menacing. They carried knives—crude, jagged blades that glinted ominously in the dim light.

Nox's fur bristled as he lowered himself into a defensive stance, his eyes locked on the approaching creatures. Damon and Zarek moved into position beside him, their faces grim, their shadows writhing around them in readiness.

"These are different," Damon muttered, his voice tense. "Stronger."

The creatures let out another low, guttural screech as they lunged, their movements swift and erratic, difficult to predict. Nox sprang forward, his massive form colliding with three of the creatures, his claws raking across, leaving deep gashes in their sickly pale flesh. Damon's shadows surged forward, wrapping around five, but they fought against the shadows, pushing forward slowly with surprising strength.

I pushed my shadows out again, willing them to solidify—to form a barrier between us and the relentless onslaught of creatures—but they remained wispy, like vapor, too weak to offer any real defense. A wave of dizziness washed over me, the world tilting dangerously as the last of my strength ebbed away. I stumbled, my vision blurring, and just as one of the creatures lunged, a powerful arm wrapped around my waist, pulling me back. Its blade slicing across my chest, sending a fresh wave of agony through me.

We were outnumbered, and they would just keep coming—wave after wave of grotesque, terrifying forms. I felt the fear building inside me, a cold, suffocating dread. I couldn't lose them. They couldn't get hurt because of me.

I screamed—a primal sound born of pure terror and desperation —as my body began to shake uncontrollably, a burst of power burning through me, hotter and more intense than anything I had ever felt before. Pain ripped through every nerve, the force of it making it feel as if I was being torn apart from the inside out. My vision blurred, the grotesque figures in front of me twisting into monstrous, distorted shapes. The ground beneath my feet seemed to tremble, the very air vibrating with the raw power surging through me. I didn't understand what was happening, but I knew —with a terrifying certainty—that something inside me had irrevocably changed.

Everything blurred, the world spinning, as I felt the cold, unforgiving ground beneath me. The ringing in my ears muffled the chaos around me—Damon's enraged roar, Zarek's frantic shouts, Nox's pained growl—all fading into a dull hum. I tried to fight it, to cling to consciousness, but the darkness was a relentless tide, pulling me under, swallowing me whole. The last thing I registered was a chilling wave of cold seeping into my very being, before unconsciousness claimed me in its embrace.

Chapter 29

Damon's POV

The chaos around me was overwhelming—creatures shrieked, shadows twisted, and the air was thick with the stench of blood and decay. Every nerve ending screamed, every muscle coiled tight, ready to spring. And then, cutting through chaos, I heard it—Thalia's scream. The sound ripped through me, turning my blood to ice.

My head snapped up, frantically scanning the carnage. *Where is she?* The question was a frantic echo in the roaring chaos. *What the hell is happening?* Panic, raw and unfamiliar, clawed at my throat, choking me. A blinding flash erupted from where Thalia stood, momentarily obliterating the gruesome scene in a searing white light.

The force of it slammed into me, knocking me off my feet. The power was so intense, it vibrated through my bones, resonating deep within my core. A wave of pure energy surged outwards— and yet, inexplicably, it parted around us—around me, Zarek, and Nox. An invisible shield, a pocket of calm in the raging storm, protected us from the blast. I shielded my face, squinting against the brightness. It felt like the entire world was being consumed by this incandescent power.

The light slowly began to fade, the blinding white receding like a tide. My vision swam with spots, struggling to adjust to the sudden return of the darkness. Slowly, the scene came back into focus. The creatures—every single one of them—lay scattered across the ground, lifeless, like discarded toys. Their grotesque forms were still, their snarls forever silenced.

I blinked, trying to comprehend the sheer devastation. What in the hells had just happened? What kind of power could obliterate an entire army like this? Scanning the area, my eyes found her. Thalia. She stood amidst the carnage, a fragile silhouette against the fading light. Blood stained her torn and tattered dress—the once vibrant emerald-green now a horrifying canvas of crimson and black. She swayed for a moment, a broken flower in a field of destruction, before collapsing to the ground with a thud that made my stomach twist.

"Thalia!" I roared, my voice raw with a terror I hadn't felt since I was a child, sprinting towards her. Nox and Zarek were already by her side, their faces mirroring the same fear that clawed at my insides.

She was motionless, eyes closed, her skin an unnatural, deathly pale. I dropped to my knees beside her, my hands shaking as I reached for her neck, desperately searching for the faintest flutter of a pulse. Nothing. No heartbeat. No breath. Just a chilling, terrifying stillness.

"No, no, no," I choked out, the words catching in my throat, a strangled sob escaping my lips. This couldn't be happening. Not Thalia. Not her. My vision blurred, tears stinging my eyes as I fumbled to her chest, pressing down, desperately trying to force her heart to beat again. "Come on, come on. Don't do this! Fuck!"

My hands kept pumping, a desperate rhythm against her still chest. *She can't be dead. I won't let her be dead.* But beneath my trembling fingers, her skin remained cold—lifeless. A wave of nausea washed over me, a bitter taste rising in my throat. It was my fault. All my fault.

A memory, sharp and unwelcome, sliced through the panic. The training grounds. Thalia—small and vulnerable—facing me with a defiance that both intrigued and irritated me.

"You're wasting your time," I sneered, my voice dripping with contempt. "You're nothing. You have no real power."

Her chin tilted up, her gray eyes flashing with an anger that surprised me. "Maybe not," she spat back, "but I'm not afraid of you."

I scoffed. "Brave words for someone who can barely hold a shield." I lunged, my shadow tendrils lashing out, wrapping around her wrists, pinning her arms to her sides. "Let's see how long that lasts."

I pushed her, tested her, relished in her frustration, her struggles. It was a twisted game, a way to deflect my own anxieties, my own fears. *Arethax. My father. Losing my brothers.* Thalia was a distraction, a convenient target for my anger, my resentment. Nox and Zarek, blinded by some misguided sense of protectiveness, had forced my hand—making me her reluctant mentor. So I took advantage, letting everything out on her, using her as a punching bag for my pent-up rage. She was a convenient scapegoat, a lightning rod for the storm brewing inside me.

She never backed down. No matter how hard I pushed, how cruel I became, how viciously I attacked—she always met my gaze head-on, her spirit unbroken, her gray eyes blazing with defiance. It was infuriating. It was... unsettling. There was something about her resilience, her unwavering determination, that chipped away at the carefully constructed walls—walls I had built to protect myself from the very emotions I was now experiencing.

Another memory surfaced. The forest—the night she wandered into our territory, trespassing without a clue of the danger she was in. I watched her from the shadows, a predator observing its prey, my own darkness drawn to her like a moth to a flame. She was lost, vulnerable, a lamb wandering into a den of wolves—yet there was a strange peace about her, a calmness that I both envied and resented.

I had hoped that Nox's panther—usually so bloodthirsty and territorial—would go feral, teaching her to stay away from us. I didn't want her here, didn't want her anywhere near Nox or Zarek, poisoning their minds with her innocent eyes and quiet strength. Their fascination with her, their inexplicable protectiveness, was a baffling weakness I couldn't comprehend. It made no sense. She was nothing but a liability—a fragile human girl in a world far too dangerous for her kind. It was a crack in the armor of the Shadow Brothers, a vulnerability I hadn't anticipated and certainly didn't welcome. We were supposed to be untouchable, a force to be reckoned with, not simpering fools pining after a stray.

And now she's gone. The thought pierced me like a shard of ice, the reality of the situation crashing down with the force of a tidal wave. *Because of me.*

Nox was beside me, his usual stoicism shattered, his eyes wide with disbelief and dawning horror. Zarek leaned over her, gently brushing a stray strand of auburn hair away from her face, his jaw clenched so tightly I thought it might break. We were united in our desperation, our terror a evident force in the unsettling silence.

She wasn't breathing. Her chest remained still beneath my hands, her lips turning a ghastly blue. I pressed harder, praying to any gods that might be listening for a miracle. Any god at all.

"We failed her. We failed her, and she still saved us," Zarek whispered, his voice hoarse with grief, barely able to contain the raw anguish that filled his words. He didn't need to say it; we all knew. *I* knew. Thalia—the girl I'd treated with such disdain, the girl who'd irritated me with her very existence—had sacrificed herself for us. For *me*. My shadows writhed around me, mirroring my inner turmoil—a chaotic dance of darkness and despair. She wasn't supposed to be important. She was supposed to be a fleeting annoyance, another obstacle in our path.

This couldn't be real. It couldn't be happening. Why did she do this? Why did she have to be so fucking stubborn, so reckless? So selfless?

"Damn it!" I roared, the sound tearing from my throat, a primal scream of denial and rage and unbearable loss.

I could hear Nox whispering her name, a series of pleas lost in the wind, a desperate prayer to a silent goddess. The cold was seeping into her, the shadows claiming her light, her warmth, her life.

She's so cold.

Thalia, please. Don't leave us. Not like this. I clung to the fading hope—the echo of her laughter, the memory of her wild spirit. She couldn't be gone. Not now. Not when my brothers needed her.

Fuck, *I* needed her.

The guilt gnawed at me—a vicious beast tearing at my insides. The way I'd treated her, the accusations I'd hurled at her, the way I'd pushed her away. I was just beginning to understand what this was—what she meant to me. I was finally ready to admit that she was more than just an annoyance, more than just a distraction. More than just the woman that pulled at my shadows.

She was... *everything*.

The world seemed to close in on me, the battlefield shrinking to the small circle around her lifeless form. All around us lay the grotesque remains of the creatures she had saved us from—a testament to her power, her sacrifice. Yet all I could focus on was her—fragile, lifeless, slipping away from us like sand through my fingers.

Zarek's hand shook as he cradled her head, his lips moving silently, as if he were trying to speak but couldn't find the words to express the enormity of his grief. Nox's hands hovered over hers, as if he was afraid to touch her, afraid to truly accept the reality of what had happened.

"Please, Thalia," I whispered, my voice breaking. My hands continued their desperate rhythm, but my heart was shattering with each moment that passed without a sign of life. "Come back. Please."

I thought of all the moments we'd shared—the arguments, the biting banter, the fleeting moments of connection that I had dismissed, too stubborn and afraid to admit what they truly meant. I had been so blind, so foolish. And now it felt like I was losing the chance to make it right. To tell her that she mattered more to me than I had ever allowed myself to believe. More than I had ever dared to hope.

Zarek's voice broke through, barely a whisper. "We can't lose her," he said, his eyes locked on her face, his expression twisted with grief. "We can't."

Nox's hand finally settled on hers, his fingers wrapping around her cold ones. "Thalia," he said, his voice cracking, the quiet strength he usually possessed completely gone. "Please. You have to come back to us."

I pressed harder, my own breath coming in ragged gasps, my vision blurred with tears I refused to let fall. "You're not allowed to leave us," I said, my voice trembling with the force of my emotions. "You hear me, Thalia? You're not allowed."

Time seemed to stretch on, each second an eternity—the weight of our desperation pulling us deeper into the darkness. I could feel my strength waning, the exhaustion of battle and the crushing fear of losing her draining me. But I couldn't stop. I wouldn't stop. Not until she opened her eyes, not until I saw the light return to them, the spark of life rekindled.

The shadows around me trembled, mirroring the storm within me, as if they could sense the crushing weight of her absence— their edges sharp and restless, like a caged beast desperate for release.

"Please, *Little Shadow*, don't leave us," I whispered. The words were raw, torn from the depths of my soul—filled with everything I had never said. With everything I feared I would never get the chance to say. With all the love I had foolishly tried to deny.

She was our light.

Our *Firefly* in the darkness.

And without her, everything felt meaningless.

Acknowledgments

To my readers,

This book exists because of you. Whether you stumbled upon *The Fractured Veil* by chance or have been awaiting its release, thank you for taking a chance on a new author. This journey has had its share of ups and downs, but knowing this story would one day be in your hands kept me going.

If you've laughed, cried, or escaped into this world—even for a little while—then I've achieved something truly special. Your support means more than words can express.

To my editor,

Thank you for your endless patience and for helping shape this draft into something I'm deeply proud of.

To my family,

Thank you for standing by me—especially on the days I wanted to give up and destroy this book. And for enduring every long-winded rant about my beloved Shadow Brothers. I couldn't have done this without your love and encouragement. The Shadow Brothers live because you listened.

I'm endlessly grateful for all of you.

About the Author

B.R. Vazquez is an emerging author that enjoys spending time immersed in a fantasy or dark-romance novel when she's not writing about the Shadow Brothers. She hopes you enjoyed *The Fractured Veil* as much as she loved writing it, and that you'll join her for the next installment of the *Nexara Academy Series*!

To get updates on the next release, join her on socials @authorbr!

www.ingramcontent.com/pod-product-compliance
Lightning Source LLC
Chambersburg PA
CBHW070807030726
47504CB00003B/730